SOUNDS FROM A CAVERN INVADED ERDE'S UNWILLING SILENCE....

She stilled to listen. She had not imagined it. Something big was moving slowly through the shallow water, shuffling and snuffling, as a bear might do if it had been stirred from early hibernation by the smoke of her fire.

Erde felt no surge of terror. She had already used up her supply. Her sudden calm astonished and confused her, but one thing she was sure of was that she didn't want to kill anything, or even try. She'd had enough of death and killing, and if the proper punishment for her crime was to be eaten alive, then let one of God's creatures be His avenging angel.

The snuffling neared the entrance to her cave and stopped. Its presence was more than sound. Erde could *feel* it out there, its questing like a touch on her skin, the anticipation of it an invisible hand pressing on her brain. It tried the entrance, with the unmistakable scrape of claws on stone. It seemed to struggle, as if it couldn't easily fit through. Briefly, Erde was relieved. Then she realized what this meant about its size. If it was a bear, it must be out of all natural proportion, not God's bear at all but some terrible demon sent by the Devil to drag her to Hell for her crimes.

Mere stone would not keep a demon out, and sure enough, in it came. The sound as it squeezed through the opening was the metallic hiss of a sword being drawn. A smell like a snake pit invaded the cavern as the demon dragged itself across the floor. Erde rolled herself into a knot beneath her cloak, and waited for fangs and claws and oblivion....

THE BOOK OF
EARTH

Volume One of
The Dragon Quartet

MARJORIE B. KELLOGG

DAW BOOKS, INC.

DONALD A. WOLLHEIM, FOUNDER

375 Hudson Street, New York, NY 10014

ELIZABETH R. WOLLHEIM
SHEILA E. GILBERT
PUBLISHERS

First Printing, February 1995
1 2 3 4 5 6 7 8 9

DAW TRADEMARK REGISTERED
U.S. PAT. OFF. AND FOREIGN COUNTRIES
—MARCA REGISTRADA.
HECHO EN U.S.A.

PRINTED IN THE U.S.A.

TO SEATHRÚN ÓCORRÁIN

poet, sibling, old soul—but not necessarily in that order.

In addition, a very special helping of gratitude and appreciation to my editor, **Sheila Gilbert**, for her great faith, bright ideas, and patience well beyond the call of duty.

Burnt offerings also on the altars of other friendly deities of perseverance and good advice: Lynne Kemen and Bill Rossow, Barbara Newman and Stephen Morris, Antonia Bryan, Vicki Davis. Thanks to you all.

"Mythology is psychology misread as biography."

—Joseph Campbell

PROLOGUE

EARTH

The Creation

IN THE BEGINNING:

In the Beginning, four mighty dragons raised of elemental energies were put to work creating the World. They were called Earth, Water, Fire and Air. No one of them had power greater than another, and no one of them was mighty alone.

When the work was completed and the World set in motion, the four went to ground, expecting to sleep out this World's particular history and not rise again until World's End.

The first to awaken was Earth.

PART ONE

EARTH

The Summoning of the Hero

Chapter One

Balanced on the sill, she watched the distant jagged crest of rock where the road climbed up out of the forest. Finally the riders appeared. Banners at first, ghostly white and limp in the dank mountain air. Horses next, also white, cloud horses etched pale against the distant gray of the upper peaks, puffing vapor that rose like departing spirits past the night-black firs.

Erde shivered. She dreaded this priest's coming, this stranger with his entourage and his dire prophecies, even though it meant ceremonies and feasting and the chance for news from outside her father's isolated mountain domain. The news would be bad, she knew it would. It was always bad these days. But fresh faces would be a welcome relief. At the ripe old age of nearly fourteen, Erde already believed it was true that a young person could die of boredom.

A cry caught at her ear, thrown up from the cobbled yard below. The apple-cheeked crone who watched the chickens with her one good eye and pressed card readings on anyone who'd listen, stared up from her perch on the stone wellhead. The gray light turned her rheumy gaze to silver. Erde hated the chicken-crone. The old woman always seemed to be expecting something of her and would never say what. Erde looked away and pulled the casement tight.

"My lady?"

Forehead tight to the rippled glass, Erde let the cold seep into her furrowed brow, and contemplated the novelty of an unfamiliar face—how gratefully you noticed the peculiar arch of an eyebrow, the odd shape of a lip, how the color of an eye surprised you because maybe no one you'd known yet had eyes exactly that color. She had seen her own eyes in a shard of polished steel that her grandmother kept in a robing trunk. They were very dark, almost black. Her mother's, she was always told, though Erde could not remember. She cracked open the window for another stare across the battlements.

"My lady?"

Far off along the stony path, the cloud horses resolved into living horses, material banners and corporeal men in white robes, a greater number of them than had been expected. Erde could see no pack animals. This priest was very sure of his welcome, to arrive without provisions in such a time of hardship.

"My lady!"

Erde started. "Pardon?"

"Come down from that drafty old window!" Her chamberwoman poured water from a kettle into a stoneware bowl. The steam rose into the chill room like the mist come in off the mountain. "You'll lose your balance and fall!"

"No, I won't." Erde searched the distant blur of bodies, hoping to make out a face, any face, in that line of faceless riders.

The kettle clanged to the floor. "Then you'll catch your death, you with only a shift on! I met three ravens in the stable yard this morning and I've been fearing the worst ever since! Such tales you hear! My grand-auntie Hildy vows she's never known a time so full of ill omens!"

Erde had seen those ravens, all puffed up in the cold and looking grim. She had wondered about them. "Oh, Fricca! I'm in my shift because I'm supposed to be getting dressed!"

"Well, indeed you are, miss, so come down this minute and wash yourself clean!"

"Why should I? Nobody else will. It's too cold to be clean!"

"It's not for you to be caring what everyone else might do."

Her chamber-woman was what Erde had heard referred to as "comely": golden-haired, fair-skinned, and plump, all the things that Erde wasn't. Sometimes she suspected that "comely" really meant kind and silly, for Fricca was both. Like now—venturing no farther than the limit of heat from the fireplace, the chamber-woman pressed her palms to her cheeks until her mouth was a soft red rose of anxiety. "Just think of it, my lady! The baron your father's first Occasion as Tor Alte's lord! Oooh, he'll be so displeased if you're not ready and at his side when the holy brother arrives!"

" 'Sooo displeased . . .' " Erde mocked. "My father's displeased whenever he sees me."

"Not so! Your father loves you. Surely, he's very busy just now, becoming baron, but you're all he has in the world and it wouldn't hurt you to humor him a bit."

"Why do you pretend it matters what I do?" Erde pivoted on the high stone sill and jumped down, her bare feet slapping against the planking. She knew a proper lady would step first to the window seat, toes pointed, then float daintily to the floor. But even if she could manage such a performance, Erde would never allow Fricca the satisfaction of witnessing it. "As if my father's humor was ever as mild as displeasure."

Fricca made clucking noises as she sponged Erde's face and arms. "Oh, yes indeed, and aren't you just your father's own child!"

"No!" The thought horrified her. "I am my mother's!"

"That's as may be, God rest her soul, sweet sweet lady."

Erde's chin lifted. "And my grandmother's granddaughter."

"And rest hers also." Fricca touched the corner of her apron to her eye. "So recently departed."

"It feels like forever!" Erde moaned.

But it had only been three days. Three impossibly long days. Erde fought another turn of the nausea that had plagued her all morning. How sad and empty those three days had been, without her best friend, her boon companion. Perhaps she so dreaded the priest because he came to lay her dear grandmama in the holy ground, putting thereby to rest her own mad hope that the old woman might yet rise off the cold stone bier in the chapel where only a single tallow candle kept her company. If she could have faced her father, she would have complained. How dare he claim he couldn't afford the beeswax to light his own mother's road to eternity?

"Now don't you be going all stiff on me! It's only water!" Fricca tossed the wash-felt into the basin with dispatch. Her solemnity, like a fair-weather cloud, quickly passed. "There! It's time to make ourselves beautiful!"

Erde hunched her shoulders. Why did the whole world not mourn this death as she did? "I'm not beautiful."

"Nonsense. Look at the magnificent long hair on you!"

Fricca caught up the heavy shining darkness that flowed down Erde's back and let it slide through her hands like water. "Who about here has glory hair like this?"

Erde shook her head irritably. People always talked about your hair when they couldn't think of anything more important to say about you. "I don't care if I'm beautiful."

"Of course you do! Every girl wants to be beautiful! You're just gloomy with the baroness' passing, but life goes on, you know." Fricca bustled to the bed, where a white velvet ceremonial gown lay in state under the canopy, on a length of sun-bleached muslin.

Like Grandmama in the chapel, Erde mused, cold white on white. The gown had been her mother's, packed away for twelve years. Suddenly her father had insisted it was a waste to let it molder in the chest. The seamstress had hardly needed to alter it at all.

"Draw tight the bed curtains," she intoned grimly. "Let the dead rest in peace!"

Fricca waved her hands as if shooing hens. "Such things you say!"

"Grandmama would never make me wear that."

"Rest a piece, yourself, and come off with that dull rag, now." Fricca held up a new silk shift trimmed with delicate gold. She dangled it this way and that, letting it catch the firelight. "Oooh, what a wonder! Fit for a young virgin bride, which, God willing, soon you'll be! Come, lucky girl, slip it on."

The slick cool silk was like eelskin in water, like icy hands touching her all over. Erde plucked at it fitfully. "It hardly covers me at all! And it clings so!"

"Doesn't it though!" Fricca eyed it with sly envy. "And will come off as smartly as it went on."

Erde reddened. "I'll wear my old one."

"Oh, don't be prudish! If you think a bed's just for sleeping, it's time you learned better! Lots of girls your age are married by now." Fricca tugged the shift down and smoothed it across Erde's thin back. "Look at the great height of you, and you not even bleeding yet! Sometimes I think you're keeping it back on purpose!"

Erde wished Fricca did not feel that, due to the sudden demise of her lady's only female relative, it had fallen to her to supply a proper education of the bedchamber. But this

suggestion was certainly more interesting than most of
Fricca's notions. "Could I do such a thing?"

Fricca's mouth formed a small plump "o" of distress.
"Of course not! That's black witches' business and none of
yours! We may be all sorry sinners, but I am a good Christian woman and there'll be no talk of witchery in this
house!"

"It'll be awfully quiet down in the kitchens, then."

"Oh, aren't we the big ears! Well, people will talk when
there's news to be shared, but that's just talk and harmless,
too."

"But you said I . . ."

"I only meant that when I brought my auntie's special lady's tonic, you poured it out!"

Erde's blush deepened. "I don't want to get married yet!"

"Tch! With such a temper, who'd have you anyway?
Come on, now." Fricca shook her apron at her. "You must
wear your father's gifts. Just think of the cost!"

Erde hardly could without shame, for despite the "official" word about court, she knew the countryside was in dire
circumstances. Her father insisted that the people needed to
see their lords well fed and in proper array to prove that all
was still well with the world. But all was not well with the
world, and Erde knew she could feed an entire village for
the price of that silk shift. She imagined bartering all the
hated garments in her robing chest for dried meat and potatoes to fill the farmers' empty larders. But who could be
found these days with surplus enough to barter? "I wish he'd
give me a pair of leather riding breeches instead!"

"And I suppose you'd wear such a thing, right out in public?"

"Everyone knows the only sensible way to sit a horse is
astride."

Fricca's eyes rolled skyward. "Holy angels, don't hear a
word she says!"

Erde hid a vengeful smile. She'd hit upon something truly
shocking at last. She liked Fricca well enough and the
woman did show a talent almost equal to her grandmother's
for deflecting the baron's sudden bouts of wrath. But she
couldn't help tweaking Fricca for her cotton-wool thinking.
In addition to missing the comfort of the baroness' company,
Erde missed the reassuring clarity of her mind. She felt cast
adrift, and angry that lesser mortals lived on while her

grandmother had left her, so terribly alone. She tried actually picturing herself in men's breeches. Perhaps her father would have loved her better if she'd been born a boy.

A sharp rap on the door sent Fricca scurrying to snatch up the shining gown from the bed as if rescuing a sleeping child. "Oh, dear, that'll be Rainer—poor lad, how my lord does order him about these days! There, see? He's come to fetch you and you not half ready!"

But Erde knew Rainer's knock and she knew her father's. She could only wish it was Rainer. "It's my father."

"Never it is!" Fricca frantically readied laces and sleeves. "My lady will be out in a minute!"

The heavy door swung on silent hinges and thudded against the stone. "And where is the Beauteous Flower of Castle von Alte?"

Fricca spread the gown and her substantial self screenlike in front of Erde. "Please, my lord! My lady has not finished dressing!"

"What! Not yet? His horses are already at the Dragon Gate! Shall we let a mere priest catch us napping?"

Erde watched her father carefully as he strode past her to the window. Unable to suffer both her own grief and his constant dissatisfaction, she had mostly avoided him since the baroness' death. But she knew well enough that he did not think of this priest, whom rumor preceded like distant thunder, as a mere anything. Yet here he was doing his hearty act, so perhaps he was both sober and in a reasonable mood.

Seeing her father, Erde was always astonished. How could she be related to this giant? He was tall and deeply barrel-chested, with a waist that tucked in beneath his ribs as neat as a woman's, barely widening at the hips. Almost top-heavy, she decided. He had a big head and affected a clean-shaven style peculiar for a man well into middle age but, since his accession, spreading rapidly to the rest of the court. The castle barbers were uncharacteristically busy. The baron's strong, naked chin and his penchant for dark shades of rich velvet offered—when properly brushed and aired—a flattering contrast to his thick, prematurely silver hair. Today he was freshly barbered and wore burgundy finely stitched with that same silver. It occurred to Erde that her father was a little vain.

He flung the casement wide. "Wind's come up again."

In the tall stone hearth, flames dipped and roared as the high-vaulted room inhaled the draft. The tapestries billowed on the damp-streaked walls. The baron sucked air noisily and licked his lips as if tasting something unpleasant. "Might get snow tonight. Perhaps this priest's prophecies are true."

Snow, Erde marveled. People of the upland domains were by long tradition held to be particularly skeptical, but snow in August? In *early* August. No wonder the countryside was so rife with black rumors.

"Please, my lord! My lady will catch her death!"

"Please, my lord," the baron mimicked, and Erde felt a pang of guilt, for it was her father's own habit of mockery that she had inherited. When he turned from the window, she noted how bright and hard his blue eyes were, above his practiced amiable smile. Like a frozen bit of sky. Sometimes the brightness meant he'd been drinking but not enough to really show. Right now, she wasn't sure what it meant. He folded his big velvet-shrouded arms. "Now let's see."

Fricca plumped the white gown awkwardly, still holding it to Erde's chest.

"Not the dress, woman, the girl!"

"Oh!" Fricca bobbed her head and Erde saw her grin foolishly as she gathered the gown to her own chest and stepped aside.

"Well," murmured the baron, "How does our little flower grow? Are our dainty rosebuds swelling yet?"

Fricca giggled. "Oh, just a little, my lord!"

Erde studied the floor, her big toe tracing the cracks between the worn planks. Her father often looked her over as if she was one of his prize warhorses, but since her grandmother's death, something new lurked in his appraising stare. She saw her narrow shape reflected in his eyes: dark hair long to her waist, long face, long slim body more proper for a boy than a young girl. The firelight flickered behind her, as if she was aflame. *I look like a witch at the stake,* Erde thought. She wondered what her father saw.

"Well," he said again, and walked around to observe her sidelong. Then he did something he had never done before. He moved close and rested a finger on her shoulder, then drew it lingeringly down her naked arm. Erde caught her breath. She must not flinch from his touch, and anger him. He had never struck her, though he had often threatened, but before, there had always been the baroness to answer to. "Skin like butter and olives," he mused. "Like your mother's."

Abruptly he dropped his hand and his glance, and turned away with a sharp gesture to Fricca. "Too thin, though, don't you think? What are you feeding her?"

Fricca held up the gown for Erde to step into. "She's a fine eater, my lord, I promise you." She dared to smile at him over one shoulder as she fastened laces. "Surely it's our long walks out on the mountain in this devil's weather that's wearing her out."

Wearing *you* out, more likely, thought Erde irritably.

The baron let the ends of his mouth curl a little. "How is it these walks don't leave you scrawny, woman?"

Fricca rounded her shoulders until her cleavage deepened, and giggled. Erde suddenly felt invisible and ignored. "Ha! You'd never catch Fricca out there in the forest getting her shoes dirty!"

Her chamber-woman shot her a warning glance, but too late. The baron frowned. "Forest? You walk in the forest?"

Fricca shrugged helplessly. "My lord! As if I could keep up with her, racing all through the trees like a boy-child!"

"*Alone* in the forest? This is no boy-child! Where does she go?" He spun on Erde. "Where do you go?"

She almost could not answer. "Nowhere special. I just . . ."

His eyes went dark as winter oceans. "Who do you meet out there? Some boy from the villages?"

"Boy?" The notion astonished her. "Of course not! Everyone knows about my walks!" Her careless spite had stumbled her into trouble. She could never tell her father the real reason she ventured alone into the forest, where the great trees swayed far above her head, and the amber-coated deer ate from her hand. So many of the herd were falling to the Baron's Hunt as it ranged ever deeper into the forest in search of meat for her father's table. Erde studied the huntsmen's routes and led the deer away from them. Of course Fricca could not come. Fricca would betray her, and the deer. "I need the exercise. The guardsmen watch me from the gate tower!"

Miraculously, this seemed to soothe him. He blinked and gruffly waved a dismissive hand. "Brigands and bears! It's too dangerous! I can't allow it." Fricca knelt with her back to him to arrange the lustrous folds of the gown, and the baron took in the round shape of her and her trim waist. A small distracted smile touched his lips. "Well, that's it, then. No more hiking about."

"But, Papa . . . !"

"Would you have the whole court whispering that my daughter is not a lady? Walk the battlements, if you must exercise. Stroll the yards."

"But that's so boring!"

The baron set his jaw. "Your grandmother indulged you." His velvet robe sighed about him as he made for the door. "Fricca! I'll see you outside for a moment!"

The look he threw from the open doorway left Erde fearful and confused. Why should a few mountain walks make him glare so fiercely? *It can only be,* she decided, *that my father hates me.*

Chapter Two

Erde forced herself erect in the huge high-backed chair. It was carved and dark, with its own little vaulted roof to shadow her head. It had been, for the short while she lived, her mother's ceremonial seat. Erde felt strange sitting in it, dressed in her mother's own gown. The chair had sat empty in the great-hall for most of her life.

But this was her first High Ritual at her father's side. She supposed she was now, in title at least, the female head of household, though she wasn't quite sure what that meant. Her grandmama's final illness had swooped in so suddenly, like a hunting hawk. The old woman hadn't had time to instruct her in practical matters.

To her right and a step higher, Erde's father sat rigid in his own larger chair, with its taller, more elaborate canopy. He stared off into the clerestory of the great-hall, his impatience beginning to show. Erde thought it served him right. While her grandmother held the baronial throne, she stood by the entrance herself to greet most humble or most high. A woman ruling a baronage, she told Erde, must take pains to prove she is no mere figurehead. She must meet head-on the day-to-day challenges to her authority. Meanwhile, handy by the door, the Baroness would usher her visitors right on in, and there was none of this endless preening out in the hallway or jockeying for the best moment to make an Entrance.

But the new baron preferred to rule from a distance. His tastes ran to pomp and formality, to the ritual show of power. By your public image are you judged, he insisted, by both your enemies and your friends.

Erde did not care about power, though her grandmother had labored long and hard to pique her interest, brazenly including her in discussions of policy from a very early age.

The court thought it eccentric at the very least; at worst, un-wise. "Putting ideas in the child's head," some muttered, as if the hiatus in patriarchy represented by their current liege was too anomalous to be considered a serious precedent. Erde listened because it annoyed the mutterers, and because her beloved grandmother wished it, but she often com-plained to the baroness that power seemed to be about lim-iting life rather than encouraging it.

"I only hope you learn to appreciate power before you have need of it," the baroness would reply.

"But I have no need of power," Erde would insist. "Papa will marry me off to some other baron's son, and he will protect me."

"Do you think life is so predictable? What if Josef dies before you marry, like my father did? You are a von Alte and his only heir. Have some thought to your responsibility."

Erde could hear the melodious raspy voice inside her ear as if the baroness stood right beside her, instead of lying so still in the chapel. She gripped the velvet folds of her moth-er's gown and willed the dead to get up and walk. Down along the wall to her right, a small door carved with linen-fold paneling led from the hall to the chapel. Staring at it, Erde could almost see it move.

"Erde? Hsst! Daughter!" Baron Josef leaned over the high arm of his throne, reaching past carved reliefs of heroic von Alte ancestors to jog her shoulder roughly. "Remember: he will be humble before you, but you must treat him as you would the highest lord."

"Yes, Papa."

"He is the Church's representative among us."

"Yes, Papa." Her grandmother's honest piety had been broad enough to include the notion that the Church was a power to be feared on Earth as well as loved in Heaven, but Erde had thought her father feared nothing. As of today, she was not so sure.

She pushed herself upright again and tried to sit like a lady. Like her mother would have, despite chronic boredom and the dank chill of the hall. The fine silk velvet of her gown was slippery on the polished wooden seat, and Fricca had pinned the pearled headpiece too tightly in her elabo-rately braided hair. Erde wanted to rip it all out and run off to the comfort of the stable. *Oh, Mother,* she mourned, *I fear I am unruly.*

Gazing about the hall always inspired her, so she tried that out for a while. The great-hall of Tor Alte was a grand and elegant edifice. Like the long, rhyming verses of the von Altes' history-saga, it spoke of a grand and glorious past that Erde wished she had been a part of, for it had surely had battles and dragons in it and must have been more interesting than her life was now. The hall was high and gracefully narrow, and filled with gray light from the clerestory windows. Beneath the tall side galleries, two vast roaring fireplaces surmounted with the von Alte crest faced each other across the width, insufficient to warm so large a hall but cheering in their aspect. The walls were of light-colored stones from the south, of matching size and smoothly dressed. The stout beams and rafters were cut in the shape of branches and polychromed in green and gold. The twenty wooden columns that supported the galleries were trefoil in cross-section and as big around as Erde could reach, like great trees stretching upward to a leafy vault.

Best of all were the column capitals: twenty carved and painted dragons, fierce and magical, each one a masterful expression of the artist's imagination. Now here was power that Erde was interested in. As soon as she could talk, her grandmother had taught her the dragons' names and their long lore-histories and all their aspects. Erde made up stories about them as if they were her dolls. Recalling those idyllic fantasy worlds soothed her now and drew her deeper into the memory. For instance, Glasswind, the third from the right. You wouldn't know it to look at her, but Glasswind had translucent wings that tinkled when she flew, like the glassmaker's chimes, and she was the great Mage-Queen's favorite. In the history-sagas, Erde's ancestors had slain dragons, winning the right to include the figure of a dragon in the family crest. But in Erde's games, the dragons were her staunchest allies. She had flown Glasswind in the service of the Mage-Queen many times.

Erde recalled now that she'd dreamed of dragons the night before, for the first time in ever so long. She tried, but could summon up no detail, only a formless memory of hulking dragon-presence. Another ill omen, like the three ravens? There was talk of dragons in the countryside, fired by the rumors of witchcraft and sorcery, but nobody claimed to have actually seen one. Real dragons. Despite her childhood preoccupation, the possibility alarmed her. She suspected a real dragon would not be as reasonable as Glasswind.

"Don't slump, girl," Baron Josef hissed.

"No, Papa."

Erde pulled herself up once again and tried to mimic her father's haughty, unfocused stare, straight out into space above the heads of the waiting court. But inevitably her eye was drawn downward. Anything was more interesting to look at than the vacant air, even the floor, the vast floor of the great-hall, paved with reddish slates and worn smoothly lustrous by two hundred years of the booted feet of soldiers and courtiers.

Currently, the entire household of von Alte was arrayed across that floor, in two lines with an aisle between, all decked out in the warmest and best clothes they had, from chambermaid to visiting vassal, now beginning to wilt and shift from the fatigue of standing about in the cold, waiting for something to happen. Even the smartly plumed and black-armored honor guard had relaxed from attention. When the baron had first arrived in the hall, with his dark-haired daughter resplendent in her mother's white dress, the priest's horses had just clattered into the castle yard and the opposing lines of courtiers ran straight and clean from the great wooden doors of the grand entry to the foot of the dais at the far end of the hall. One long hour later, the visiting entourage milled about in the courtyard. The court herald came and went from anxious conferences with a huddle of the baron's advisers, and still the priest did not make his entrance. Erde was losing patience with decorum. She wished her father would charge down off his throne and drag the man bodily into the hall.

"Papa," she whispered. "What *is* he doing?"

The baron rearranged his wine-colored robes over his knees. "Playing with me, girl. What else?"

"Oh."

His frank reply was a measure of his irritation. The next obvious question was why, but Erde sensed that the answer had something to do with an unequal balance of power, and might make him angry. She returned to the safety of studying the waiting crowd. Even the chicken-crone was there, staring at her still.

Then she spotted Alla, the only face she really wanted to see, her old nursemaid and her father's before her. Alla was

watching, too, just so that she could wink and make a face
when their eyes met, to test Erde's powers of concentration,
for sitting in her mother's chair she must never giggle or
grin. Alla was the castle midwife and Erde's only remaining
confidante since the death of her grandmother. With a
straight back and a forthright manner, Alla was sneaking
into her eighth decade with every intent of living through it.
Even so, Erde was glad someone'd had the respect to find
her a stool. *Alla will know,* she told herself, *what it means to
dream about dragons.*

At last, there was a stir near the grand entry. The courtiers
neatened their lines abruptly. The elderly court herald dipped
back into the hall with a relieved nod, straightened his green
and black tabard, and gestured to the guardsmen. It took two
strong men to swing each tall wooden door wide on growling iron hinges. Erde heard the herald cough and clear his
rheumy throat, and worried for him. Fricca had told her he
was in bad health. She'd also said that the baron thought it
was time to replace him with a younger man more in keeping with the style of the new court.

The herald faced the outer hall. "Gentlemen of the Cloth!
To the court of Josef Heinz-Friedrich, fifteenth Baron von
Alte, be welcome!" He turned toward the dais, graceful de-
spite the years crooking his spine. "My lord baron! May I
present the envoy from the Church of Rome, Brother
Guillemo Gotti!"

Trumpets shrilled from the galleries. Necks craned. At
last, a release from boredom and the creeping chill! Through
the august columned doorway marched a pair of white-clad,
hooded men. Four even paces back, another pair. Another
followed, then another. Ten, twenty, thirty tall sturdy men
with dark beards deepening the concealing shadows beneath
their cowls. The hall filled with their bulk and the wet-wool
stench of their robes. Their every step was matched. Their
uncanny alikeness made Erde dizzy, suffocated, as if there
was no room within their sameness for so much as a breath.
On the baron's right, the young guard captain Rainer came
to full alert, shrugged his black ceremonial armor into a less
uncomfortable position on his shoulders and signaled his
men to move in close and be ready. Erde decided not to try
to catch his eye. Not now, while he was working so hard to
appear mature and in command.

When the first pair of robed men reached the foot of the

dais, the entire entourage halted as one, as if at an unheard command, then knelt. Silence fell. The court's attention turned toward the door, awaiting Brother Guillemo's grand entrance. After a long moment, the old herald peered side-long into the courtyard, then caught the baron's attention with a head shake and a subtle shrug.

The baron pursed his lips darkly. He studied the men kneeling before him. "Welcome to Tor Alte, gallant servants of the Church," he said finally. "Bring you word of your master, Brother Guillemo?"

"I do," a deep voice intoned from among the paired ranks.

"Step forward then, good brother, and be delivered of it."

"That I cannot, my lord. For I am he, and no man's master."

The baron flushed and the court murmured, for as yet no individual rose to officially identify himself. The baron rearranged his robes some more and settled himself more comfortably. "Your pardon then, sir. But may I know your face, to better welcome you in person?"

Court talk, thought Erde. She often wondered if her father practiced it in his rooms in secret. Nobody talked like that when they were sitting around at ease with each other.

With a rustle of sandals on stone, the entourage rose, and one of the second pair in line moved forward to stand before the dais, arms spread wide as if in supplication. "You honor me, my lord baron, with your understanding that we mean no discourtesy. I should explain that our vow of humility asks of us a ritual anonymity."

Erde suppressed an instinctive frown. She hated to admit to her father's brand of paranoia, but surely Tor Alte's chaplain would have informed the baron ahead of time of such an unusual Church protocol. Besides, how could this priest speak of anonymity, when the name of Brother Guillemo Gotti was already famous in a world where news traveled fitfully if at all? She peered at him more closely. Is that what a famous man looks like, so indistinguishable from his fellows? She stole a quick glance to her right, but her father gave no indication that he noticed anything amiss.

"The House of von Alte cherishes all dedicated servants of God. Welcome again, noble Brother. If your ritual is now satisfied, may I present to you my beloved daughter Erde?"

If the baron had hoped that chivalry would overwin humility, his gambit failed. The robed man bowed deeply but did not remove his hood. "My lady."

This is not Guillemo Gotti, Erde decided suddenly. *How peculiar. Why doesn't the priest speak for himself?* She was sure her grandmother would have rooted out the real man right away, or coaxed him into revealing himself, but Baron Josef chose to play along, launching immediately into a detailed recitation of arrangements for the funeral and the subsequent festivities. He may not have known how many servants worked for him but he knew all the proper protocols.

Meanwhile, Erde surveyed the other twenty-nine white robes and made her own choice. Four pairs from the back, within a few quick strides of the open door, one man seemed slightly shorter, slightly broader than the others. She had first picked him out by the quick gleam that his eyes made, catching the silvery light from the clerestory as they flicked about the hall. Mapping out the exits, or counting the guardsmen? Taking the measure of their young captain so prominently displayed by the baron's side? The other brothers kept their eyes fixed forward. Erde pondered this mystery. Brother Guillemo might willingly ask shelter and board of Josef von Alte, but perhaps he did not trust him. Was it because he came from so far away in Rome, and therefore did not trust any stranger?

She studied her candidate further, taking care not to be noticed. He was older, too, than the others, with pockmarked skin only partly hidden by his thick black beard and anonymous cowl. She could make out a narrow ferrety nose and full red lips. The priests Erde had known from the churches in the villages were mostly pale, dry creatures with bovine dispositions. The castle chaplain was reserved and precise. But this man's face was worldly and manipulative. He reminded her of some of her father's vassal lords, the sort who'd drink with him late into the night and the next day, scheme against him behind his back. She knew they did so. Her chamber-woman had told her all about it. Sometimes Fricca's gossipy nature had its uses.

"And so, my lord baron," the false-Guillemo was saying, "with your noble permission, we poor mendicants will retire to rest after our long journey and pray, in order to properly prepare for this solemn occasion and to be received into such high-born company."

The baron nodded. "My permission, good Brother, and gladly."

The priest bowed and melted back into the ranks of his fellows. When the entourage had proceeded grandly and irritatingly slowly into the courtyard, Baron Josef rose, signaling his guard captain to follow, and strode from the hall. The court relaxed into a hubbub of debate and discussion. Suddenly invisible, Erde slipped from her ceremonial chair and darted through the crowd.

"Alla! Alla!" She caught up with the nurse-midwife as the old woman struggled up the circular stair toward her chamber off the gallery. "Alla! Such a thing I have to tell you!"

"Hello, moonface. Don't be tearing that fine dress, now." Beneath her midwife's white head cloth, Alla's hair was thinning, but her eyes were bright and her round fine-seamed face demanded the same frank honesty that it offered. "Really knows how to lard it on, that one, doesn't he?"

"Listen to me, Alla, listen!" Erde squeezed past on the narrow stair and faced her, mounting the steps backward with the velvet gown hiked up past her shins. "You know what? It's not really him! I mean, that's not him, the one who spoke!"

"Slow down, lightning, so a poor ancient can understand."

Erde gained the top step and took a breath. Seeing Alla always reduced her self-image to that of an eight-year-old, until she caught herself and remembered she was nearly fourteen. "The monk who spoke to Papa is not really Brother Guillemo!"

"And no monk, either, I suppose," the old woman muttered. She scaled the final stairs with a soft groan for each rise, frail but erect, then limped determinedly along the gallery.

Erde dogged her heels. "But I'm sure, Alla, I'm really sure! Why would he do that? Maybe he's not even there! Oh, maybe something has happened to him, and they don't want anyone to know!"

"Hush, bluejay, before your tongue and your wild imagination race you neck and neck to nowhere!" Alla gripped Erde's arm and drew her off the tapestry-hung open gallery into the side hall that led to her room. "Now listen: do you want the whole mountain to hear how its liege lord allowed himself to be drawn into Fra Guill's silly game?"

"But couldn't they see?"

"Perhaps they were not looking. This man bears the imprimatur of Rome itself."

"But, Papa . . ."

"Perhaps he was looking *too* hard."

This last remark Erde did not understand, but Alla's brisk manner made one thing very clear: that this priest came disguised might prove he feared or mistrusted her father, but it also meant that the baron had cause to fear or mistrust the priest.

"And surely he does fear him," said Alla later, when they were safely behind closed doors. "This is no parish priest come begging for Christmas alms. We've not seen his like for a while hereabout." She set herself to brewing rose-mint tea at the tiny hearth that was barely enough to heat her draft-ridden room. Erde thought her father should provide his old wet nurse with better rooms, but Alla claimed she never felt the cold because she came from a much colder place far to the east, called the Russias. "Though he'd never show his fear, not my Iron Joe. He'll be pacing his study now, snapping the ears off our poor Rainer lad for not divining Fra Guill's trick ahead of time. You know how your father hates surprises."

"Why do you call him Fra Guill?" Erde hoped her father wouldn't yell at Rainer too much. She thought it odd to raise a fine young man like Rainer to a position of responsibility, then bully him all the time. The baroness would not have allowed it.

"That's Fra for *fratello*," Alla explained. "It's Italian for 'brother.' But don't you be picking that one up, pipsqueak. It's what they call him in the villages, those that don't favor his doomsday preaching. Mark my words, this one's too dangerous for the likes of us to show him anything but the most obvious respect."

"Is that why Papa was polite, even when the priest was rude?"

"All part of the game, chipmunk. Josef's been looking to turn this visitation to his advantage since he first heard of it. Now he'll be plotting to return the challenge, or figuring out some way to make Fra Guill beholden to him. I only hope he truly comprehends what kind of swamp he's playing in."

Erde sipped at her tea pensively, inhaling scents of spring leaves and wood smoke. She loved Alla's room, with its spare furnishings and the wooden drying racks tied with flowers and herbs. She felt safe there, and welcome. She hitched her stool closer to the little fire. "Alla, is it true Fra . . . er, Brother Guillemo prophesies the coming of dragons?"

"Oh, well, yes, dragons," Alla agreed darkly. "Among other things. It's the other things we should be worrying about. The suspicion he encourages, the fires of doubt he fans in the hearts of the villages."

"I dreamed about dragons."

Alla nodded approvingly. "A good dream, I hope."

"I can't remember. Isn't it a bad omen to dream about dragons?"

"Nonsense, moss-nose! A von Alte has every right to dream about dragons."

"Does it mean they will come?"

"Here?" Alla cackled uproariously. "Just think of it! What self-respecting dragon would hang around here, with no livestock in the fields but some starved milch cow to steal for his dinner?"

Erde grinned at her old nurse over the glazed rim of her tea bowl. "Well, couldn't he just eat people?"

"Of course not!" Alla set her own bowl down. "Where'd you get that idea, calfbrain? Dragons don't eat people."

Erde nodded. Just what the Mage-Queen would have said. "Brother Guillemo says they do, least that's what Fricca told me."

Alla's smirk dismissed both Fricca and Brother Guillemo. "This priest talks about a lot of things he knows nothing about. But don't you go telling *anyone* I said so. Now be off, starling, and ready yourself for the baronessa's final ritual."

Erde's grin fell away like a leaf in the wind. For a moment, safe in Alla's little room, she had almost forgotten that her grandmama was dead.

Cold rain fell as the funeral procession wound down among the jutting rock ledges toward the alpine meadow where ten generations of von Altes slept the long sleep beneath rough-hewn granite slabs.

The rain became sleet as the wind picked up. In the lead, the baron quickened his pace, though the broken scree was icy and treacherous underfoot and his gait was not particularly steady. The court lagged behind, but the thirty robed brothers tightened their cowls about their dark faces and urged the pallbearers onward, though their white-shrouded burden swayed precipitously atop its heavy wooden bier.

Erde left off her searching for the real Guillemo among the hoods and robes and concentrated on keeping her balance. The guard captain Rainer paced beside her, his hand ready at her elbow.

Rainer was from Duchen, a town far to the south. He'd come to Tor Alte as a motherless boy of seven, traveling with his father who was a courtier on the king's business. Erde's only memory of the man was a toddler's misty vision of a tall figure dressed in red, for the same illness that claimed her mother took Rainer's father soon after he arrived. Because the orphaned boy was mannerly and intelligent, the baroness took him into her service, but soon became fond of him, and raised him more like a younger son than a servant. Erde had grown up with Rainer, fighting and playing and sharing secrets as if he were the older brother she very much lacked.

He had grown tall like his father, slim but strong and adept with his sword, and was now working too hard at the business of being an adult to have much time for a younger sister. Though he made sure to pause when they met, to tease her a little and exchange a few words of gossip, Erde missed their giggling and chasing, and lately she sensed a new formality in him, an unacknowledged distance that puzzled and dismayed her. She suspected it was because she was just a girl and Rainer was newly made guard captain, upon her father's succession. Just turned nineteen was a young age to have risen so high, so perhaps he had become overly full of himself.

But not today. Glancing sidelong at his pale, solemn face, Erde was sure that the baroness' death had grieved Rainer as much as it had her. She brushed sleet from her eyes. "If only it would go ahead and snow. Grandmama always loved a fresh fall of snow."

Rainer nodded wordlessly. He slipped off his heavy woolen cloak and draped it about her shoulders without asking, like the solicitous brother he'd once been. Erde's own cloak was warm enough but she knew Rainer worried about people taking ill in the cold, never thinking to worry the same about himself. He was too thin, she decided, too taut across the cheekbones, as if the anxiety she often read in his eyes were absorbing his flesh from the inside. How is my father treating you, she wanted to ask, but now was not the time for conversation, nor this place, so grim and chill, the proper place.

The grass was brown in the meadow, as shriveled as if summer had never happened. The granite marker waited to one side, the size and shape of a stable door, and as gray as the leaden sky. The grave was shallow, a mere depression in the mountain rock scraped bare with pick and hand. But the baroness had been tall and thin, as Erde would be also.

"There will be room enough," she murmured sadly.

Beside her, Rainer shifted, cleared his throat, and said nothing. She wished they could hold hands like they used to in church, keeping each other awake on cold mornings during the sermon. She wanted to weep and lean into him, as she would do with her great horse Micha, exchanging her grief for his warmth and solidity. But she knew if she slipped her hand into his, Rainer would stiffen and ease his hand away. Besides, her father would be angry if he spied her disgracing him with childish tears and displays of emotion. Erde sighed deeply and kept her eyes dry.

The white-robes ranged themselves before the grave like a military escort, at rigid attention in two rows of fifteen, waiting for the stragglers to arrive. To Erde it felt as if she was their prisoner, instead of them being guests of the castle. When the court had finally assembled, one white-robe stepped forward as Brother Guillemo would be expected to do. He signaled the pallbearers to set down the bier. Four of the baroness' most favored retainers, the old herald among them, took up the damp embroidered edges of the linen to lift the slight still weight and lower it into the shallow pit. The fifteenth Baron von Alte stood at the head of the grave and gazed down at his mother's shrouded remains, frowning.

The white-robe who had come forward began the ritual of burial. He kept his head down and his voice low and reverent until the section of the rite where the priest addresses the congregation. Then he let both rise, and augmented his performance with gestures. His cowl slid back a bit as he warmed to a lecture on the wages of sin, warning of a nearby day of reckoning. Erde waited for him to mention dragons but he only decried the wickedness of the worldly in a more general sort of way, exhorting all present to stand beside him in the coming battle against the evils abroad in the land, to take responsibility and clean out the "sinkholes of depravity" in their own back gardens.

Erde was disappointed. She thought his harangue a standard one and over-rehearsed. Tor Alte's own chaplain was also dull but at least he'd known the baroness, and would have done better by being able to say something personal. What did catch her interest was noting that the haranguer was not the same man who'd passed as Brother Guillemo a few hours earlier. Covertly, she located her own candidate in the back rank, but this time she forgot herself and stared too long. His eyes, darting about, met hers and held piercingly until she could gather her wits enough to glance away.

Her heart thudded. She felt short of breath. Throughout the rest of the long, sleet-sodden ceremony, Erde pressed as close to Rainer as he would allow, and did not look up again.

Chapter Three

At the funeral feast that evening, a third false-Guillemo took the place of honor at the baron's right.

Candles flared at the high table and the hearths burned bright. Precious oil smoked in every lamp on the three great wagon-wheel chandeliers. Three days had passed since word had come of Brother Guillemo's offer to reroute his pilgrimage in order to bury the baroness in the full authority of the Church of Rome. The baron's chamberlain had been frantically gathering food and arranging the precise protocols of seating and serving. Household and guests crowded the long horseshoe of stout wooden trestles, grateful for the ceremonial excuse to eat all they could get their hands on.

Tray after tray of roasted meats and sauced vegetables paraded past the high table for inspection. Meanwhile, the new false-Guillemo engaged Baron Josef in a peculiarly one-way conversation. Seated to her father's left, Erde listened while pretending not to. This man's voice was deep like the other two Guillemos', but more nasal. Her girl-child's enforced experience as a listener told her he spoke German like a native. It was his foreigner's accent that was learned. She stored this detail away to pass on to Alla later.

Erde had no trouble searching out her real-Guillemo, but now she was painfully cautious in her surveillance. She did note that he placed himself well inside the ranks of his brothers, along the right side of the horseshoe, and that while the robed and hooded man to her father's right spoke of the cold summer and bad harvest and made an elaborate show of taking a spartan meal of bread, cheese, and spring water, the platter in front of her chosen Guillemo bore only a nibbled crust and some apple parings. But Erde spied him helping himself covertly from his neighbors' bowls and flagons—and only from those portions they had already tasted. Now and then, she caught him staring in her direction.

She herself could barely eat. She considered the group gluttony of feasting to be the least appealing aspect of ceremonial occasions, and resented the probability that this noisy throng of red-faced, greasy-fingered eaters had struggled through the wet, unseasonable cold not to bid the baroness a loving farewell but to stuff themselves with a good meal.

Tonight, particularly, she felt heavy and stupid from the unaccustomed heat in the hall. The din of forced joviality beat harshly at her ears. She drank some wine to wet her nervous throat, and wished the priest would stop looking at her. She knew that, as a baron's daughter, she would always be stared at and would always have people seeking to use her somehow, but she particularly hated feeling drawn into this man's game. It was like being sucked into a current too strong to swim against.

For relief, she watched Rainer as he wandered the circuit of the tables, restless, a mug of ale in hand for camouflage. She found herself thinking how fine he looked, as if she had never really noticed before, how tall and bronze-blond he was in his black captain's tunic. Fricca had once called Rainer "delicate," and it was true that he was not brawny like most of the baron's Guard, the beefy bearded men whom the chamber-women cooed over. His shoulders were not overbroad and he often had to be reminded to stand up straight. But Erde had watched him spar with his men in the stable yard. He was easily their equal in strength and agility, and his greater height gave him an added advantage. What Fricca thought overanxious and fragile, Erde saw as sensitive and elegant. Certainly he was the only member of the baron's Guard who'd learned how to read. The baroness had seen to that. After all, Rainer's father had served His Majesty the King.

How steadfast he seemed to her now as she watched him pace along the tapestried wall, how concerned and reliable. She considered taking him into her confidence and pointing out the real-Guillemo to him, but what if he didn't believe her? Or worse still, what if Alla was right, that both Rainer and her father had noted the deception long ago, and only she, a foolish little girl, thought it was such a big secret? She wouldn't want to seem foolish to Rainer.

"Your table is a marvel, my lord, in times of such hardship." The false-Guillemo drained his cup and refilled it from a clay pitcher of springwater.

"Hospitality is one of our Lord's commandments, is it not?" returned the baron dryly, gesturing for his own cup to be filled with hearth-warmed wine.

Erde fanned herself covertly. Was her father calling the hooded band's bluff with this merciless indoor heat? She found his forbearance with his lecturing guest to be quite remarkable, even as the man detailed far beyond courtesy the plight of the lands he had traveled most recently, how the fertile river plains were plagued with drought and the uplands so unseasonably cold and wet that the frost-killed crops rotted in the fields before ripening.

"Peasant and lord, they're declaring it a punishment from God, my lord baron, and being God-fearing folk, they wonder what it is they've done to deserve such misfortune. One or two bad seasons they're used to, as good men of the land, but my lord, this year makes it six in a row!"

The baron set down his knife, with which he had just speared a prime chunk of venison and paired it with a small potato. His eyes sparkled with drink, but his voice was neutral. "I have petitioned to the king for relief for the villages."

"The king?" The false-Guillemo let just enough space fall between his words to invite comment. "You will surely pardon a visitor's ignorance, lord baron, but from what we have heard in our travels, you will be lucky indeed if help comes from that quarter."

Erde was shocked. The king had surely had his troubles of late, but in her grandmother's court, such disrespect would not have been allowed, even from a foreigner who could be supposed not to know any better. But Baron Josef merely reclaimed his knife and ate, his glance steady on his guest.

"I mean, of course, from which of your king's empty storehouses is such relief to come?"

The baron chewed thoughtfully. "Ah, yes, from where is relief to come? Nearer at hand, perhaps."

"Perhaps, my lord." Again, the pause. The false-Guillemo's hands were folded tightly on the table in front of him. "But we must not hope for help from an earthly king when the Church is our only salvation. Six bad years. Six, you know, my lord, is the Devil's number."

The baron speared another morsel, nodding.

The false priest leaned closer, the folds of his cowl falling about his face so that his deep voice resonated out of pure darkness. "It is not Heaven who punishes us, my lord, nor chance who visits with these plagues. God has sent his Word to our brethren, and we have received it. The true cause is Nature, the Devil's fancy woman, and her host of beasts and sorcerers, turning our own lands against us. A conspiracy of mages, lord baron, of mages, witches, and women, that God calls us to rise up against and vanquish in His Name! What do you say to that?"

A conspiracy of mages, indeed. Erde found herself wishing she could call up the Mage-Queen herself to spirit this horrible man away, all the way back to Rome with every one of his so-called brothers. She noted her father's faintly arched brow and watched his interest, captured initially by the priest's political innuendo, fade before this onslaught of religious rhetoric.

"Good brother, I await further enlightenment."

The not-priest heard the invitation but not its skepticism. "There are dark forces abroad, my lord! Dark forces that thrive on our weaknesses. We've been too careless of Nature, sir. We've relaxed our guard, let her evade our discipline, let her emissaries invade our lives, our very homes. Our women talk of cycles of the moon instead of gifts from God. Our children run loose in the land like young animals, empowering the very forces that seek domination over us! Nature readies herself, my lord. She calls her creatures to her, and soon . . ."

Through the drone of the false-priest's tirade, Erde became aware of a door opening, a scuffle, of shouts rising above the chatter of the diners, a man crying out Brother Guillemo's name as he was subdued by three guardsmen who'd been handy to the entrance. The candle flames danced on the high table and she heard the soft rasp of Rainer's sword easing from its sheath.

The false-Guillemo broke off his speech and sprang from his seat, arms spread wide. He stood for a moment, poised, letting his cup spill and roll to the floor, its clatter punctuating the sudden silence his gesture created. "Soldiers, I beg you! Let this good man be! He does no harm to call my name!"

The other white-robes rose as one to second his protest.

The three guardsmen looked to their captain. In the breathless hush, the pinioned man worked an arm free and reached toward the false-priest with a desperate cry. "Brother, they have come! Protect us, poor sinners all! Have mercy on us!"

Ladies giggled and whispered as the false-Guillemo pushed back his chair and shouldered his way through the throng of his hooded brothers toward the door. "Who comes, friend? What has you so frightened?"

"The dragons! The dragons come!"

In Erde's breast, hope stirred along with apprehension. Dragons? The white-robes murmured and stirred, flowing like a frothy torrent in the false-priest's wake.

"My lord?" asked Rainer quietly from beside the baron's chair.

"Religion's his bailiwick." The baron sipped his wine. "Let him handle it, if he's so eager."

Rainer raised his sword, letting the blade flare in the lamplight, then sheathed it. The guardsmen let the man go.

"You know this man?" the baron asked Rainer. A hovering servant filled his cup again.

"No, my lord. But I'll ask around later."

The newcomer was middle-aged and pasty, as if his job kept him well out of the sun. He fell to his knees on the slate floor, weeping at the false-priest's feet as the other white-robes converged around them, hiding both from sight. The courtiers waited, tittering among themselves, eager for the excitement.

"What now?" the baron murmured, easing forward in his chair.

"Another switch?" Rainer suggested, and Erde breathed a sigh of relief that she hadn't blurted out her Great Discovery to him. Had the entire court been aware of it? She reminded herself to listen to Alla more. Clearly, not saying anything was just part of the game.

"He'll have to get down to business sooner or later," said the baron. "Now that he knows I'm not going to poison him."

"But can you trust him to tell you what his business is, my lord?"

The baron offered his guardsman an icy profile. "I can trust myself to figure it out, Captain."

Rainer's head dipped. "Of course, my lord."

"Brothers!" A new voice rose from out of the throng around the door. "Give the man room to speak!" The white-robes drew aside. Erde's real-Guillemo now knelt beside the weeping man, his hood thrown back, revealing a bald head and large, commanding eyes. He pressed the man's hand piously to his chest. A guffaw from one of the guardsmen's tables against the far wall was quickly hushed.

"Yesss!" hissed the baron thickly. "Now we'll see what he's about."

"It's really him now!" Erde whispered before she could stop herself.

Rainer grinned and nodded, but Baron Josef turned and stared her into silence. The wine sparkle in his eyes was blurred and watery.

"Holy father, help us!" the weeping man pleaded.

"We are all brothers here, my friend," Guillemo reproved gently. He rose, pulling the man up with him. His hands were small, Erde noticed. Darkly furred and delicate. "Have you your voice back now? Can you tell us what you saw?"

"Ohhh!" Ragged sleeves fell back from the palest flesh as the man waved his arms and tried to cover his head. "A great rush of wings past the wheat field, Brother, and a shadow like blackest night falling over the barnyard! And an awful stench, like a hot wind from the very bowels of hell itself. It's the evil come hunting us, surely, just like you prophesied! See, here, its terrible mark!"

"Where? What?"

The man offered his forearm. "Its awful spittle fell in flaming gouts and burned me."

Guillemo grasped the arm with both hands to display to the crowd like a relic. A few red welts marred the hairless skin. "Lo!" the priest exclaimed. "The mark of Satan!"

In the clamor of derision and dismay that followed, the baron tapped his front teeth with the point of his knife and gestured to his captain to move closer again. "Do you believe in dragons, Rainer?"

"Actual dragons, my lord, or convenient ones in our neighborhood?"

The baron chuckled. "Just so! The man is clever, though."

"Sly. Send him packing."

"Not until I've plumbed his uses."

"I'd say it's you he seeks to use, sir."

"Don't cross me, boy!" the baron snapped. "You think I don't see what he is?"

Rainer straightened abruptly. "Your pardon, my lord!"

Erde dared a glance. Rainer's mouth was tight with shame, and she understood his confusion so well. It was like that with her father. Often he tricked you with invitations to intimacy, when really all he wanted to do was to hear himself talk. Sometimes it seemed the baron preferred his subordinates to be crafty rather than intelligent.

Guillemo sat the raving man down on one of the benches emptied by his entourage. His small hands soothed the man's thin shoulders. "Now, my friend, I have no doubt you believe what you saw, but perhaps you were only napping and woke from a bad dream, burning yourself on the hearth grate . . ."

"Oh, no, Brother, I swear . . ."

"Tch, man! Never swear unless you've a Bible to hand!" The priest cocked his head and offered his audience a worldly glance. "Perhaps, brother, you felt a particularly dark cloud passing over?" His gesture was derisive, and the court laughed with him.

"No, I . . ."

"Do you think we are so important, so special here in Tor Alte that the Devil would choose to single us out?"

The man became confused. "But how," he wailed, "are we to know?"

Brother Guillemo smiled at him then, a smile like embers bursting into flame on a darkened hearth. He smoothed back the man's disordered hair as if he were a child and kissed his pale brow. "Oh, my good brother, hear the Truth. No one is too small to avoid the Devil's attention and . . . you will know because I will tell you."

Guillemo was bulky but agile. Levering off the man's shoulder, he sprang onto the bench and spread his arms. His abrupt move, so like an attack, drew gasps around the horseshoe. Swords clanked among the baron's Guard and nearby, a woman shrieked.

"Listen, oh my people! For what if this man speaks true?" His voice was as deep as his fellows' but more resonant. Erde felt it vibrate within her chest. Beside her, the baron sat forward with renewed interest. Guillemo slewed his riveting glance around the hall and pointed at the most crowded table. "Do you know him?"

"Aye!" shouted someone, but Erde thought it came from among the white-robes.

"Is he a good man?" Guillermo demanded.

"Aye!" several more voices answered.

"A humble man?"

"Aye!"

The priest reached behind him to grab the man's burned arm and exhibit it once again. "Then are we not fortunate for this good and humble man who brings us the first true sign? He did not cower in terror of the Darkness but came straightway to report its approach!" He looked down, over the thick brush of his beard, pacing the length of the bench and scowling. "Be wary, oh my people! Be alert to every sign, to every chance of a sign, to every possibility that the Moment is come!" He let his voice drop, as if speaking in private meditation. The only other sound in the hall was the crack of the hearth fires and the chicken-crone snoring in a corner. "For this evil is everywhere, and the innocent are the most easily corrupted." He looked up, singled out a pretty woman nearby. "A young soldier's wife had a sickly child. Instead of bringing him into God's church for a holy blessing, she buys a talisman from an old hag who lives at the end of the village." He stamped his foot, pointing suddenly at the entrance. "And thus, the Devil has a foot in her door!"

Several people glanced nervously behind them.

Guillemo paced along the bench again, turned, and paced back. "Remember, oh my people! The Devil's only foothold in this world is in our hearts! If we would deny him there, he would never triumph! But we do not deny him! Every day without thinking we let him in! A child talks back to his father! A woman argues with her husband! A young girl buys a love charm and, oh my people, see how we suffer for it! See how the lands dry up and the babies starve! See, see . . ."

Guillemo reached both arms above his head as if grasping for the sky, then clapped his palms to bulging eyes and fell gasping to his knees on the tabletop. "See! Oh, I see, my good people! I see the winged servants of Satan abroad in the land, searing the fields with their foul breath, blackening the waters with their reptile slime, setting them to boil with the acid of their tongues! I see demons marching

THE BOOK OF EARTH   43

against us, led by the secret army of witches and warlocks who hide now among us waiting for the Devil's call! Oh! I see the air aflame with dragons! I see the witch-child and the Devil's Paladin ... oh ... !" His face scarlet and swollen, the priest doubled over on the wide boards of the trestle, moaning, scattering cups and platters. Several of the white-robes rushed to aid him, raising him bodily, settling him back on the bench, brushing at his robe and plying him with water and wine. Erde sat frozen in her chair. She hoped she had only imagined that, the moment before he'd collapsed, this final, real, and terrifying Fra Guill had caught her eye.

When it was plain that the priest's vision had passed, the court relaxed, having finally been granted the spectacle they had sat down to receive in his company. On his bench in the midst of his solicitous brothers, Guillemo contrived to look ordinary once more, nodding and smiling, wiping his brow on his sleeve, blotting the saliva from his beard.

The baron watched him fixedly. He drained his wine cup and signaled for more. "See how well he plays them."

Erde wondered if his envy was as clear to everyone around him as it was to her. She wished Alla was there, but the castle midwife was not invited to formal events, and no-body else was listening. The real Guillemo had enraptured them all.

When the priest recovered himself, he asked for the man who had brought the dragon sign and led him to a seat him-self, boldly setting him down to a meal at the baron's table. Then he made his way to the place his former self had va-cated, bowing deeply before easing into the broad velvet-cushioned chair. "Your pardon, my lord baron, for this untimely disturbance ... I fear God does not warn ahead when he sends his Holy Word to me."

Baron Josef studied him for a moment with pursed lips. Unlike his substitutes, the real Guillemo returned the stare unflinchingly. Finally, the baron nodded, as if some negoti-ation had passed between them. He signaled for wine to be poured for them both, and the priest did not refuse.

"God's Word must not be denied," agreed the baron. "Tell me, does God fear we harbor witches at Tor Alte, Brother Guillemo? Should I be checking my stables for dragon scat?"

Erde could not decipher the priest's cocked eyebrow. Was it the expected disapproval or was it amusement?

"The Devil's minions are everywhere, my lord."

"Indeed they are." The baron eased himself back into the velvet cushion of his chair. "I don't recall hearing before of a Devil's Paladin, Brother. Who might he be, fallen angel or human man?"

"He is in the vision, my lord. I myself do not yet comprehend it."

The baron swirled the wine in his cup. "Sometimes I think my mother was a witch."

"God forbid, Baron, for today she lies in holy ground!"

The baron's laugh was careless. "Well, I mean, how else could a woman hold a throne so long? But you were speaking of the children." He waved an unsteady hand. "Before all this. Pray do continue."

"Was I?" Guillemo smiled guilelessly. He tasted his wine, then drank deeply. "With all the excitement, I've quite forgot."

"The *naughty* children," the baron prodded. "Running loose in the woods."

Guillemo chuckled. "The woods, my lord?"

"Yes, yes, like little animals. Erde, my sweet, are you listening?"

"Of course, Papa." Erde sipped at her wine. Hoodless, Brother Guillemo was ugly, with his ferrety nose and his pockmarked skin. But his transforming innocent smile could make you question whether you'd misjudged him. Then he leveled a predatory eye on her and Erde was sure she had not. A true priest in God's grace should not stare so.

"Not your children, of course, my lord," said Guillemo.

"I've only the one, Brother, was widowed early. A motherless child, you know, can run a bit wild. Yes, I think even my daughter could benefit from some proper schooling."

Erde sipped again, to appear occupied. She wished they wouldn't talk about her as if she weren't sitting right next to them.

Guillemo contrived to look both sympathetic and disapproving. "Surely, my lord, a girl her age already has what schooling befits a woman."

"Ah, yes, but her grandmother had her own ideas. So, needless to say, there's work left to do. Fortunately, she's hardly grown. But growing fast, very fast." He threw Erde the odd look he had earlier, from her chamber door, only this time he smiled, as if at a secret between them.

"She's very dark," the priest remarked. "Unusual."

"Her mother's blood."

"Lovely . . ." the priest murmured.

No, a priest should not stare so. Erde looked down, breathless and sick under their shared regard, wanting to rush from the hall and not stop until she was away from the heat and the smoke and breathing free in the sharp mountain air. The need seized her until she was dizzy with it. She grasped for her wineglass and missed.

The baron saw her color go, and raised his arm with a quick snap of his fingers. "Captain!"

Rainer was ready behind the baron's chair. "My lord?"

"I think the child has had enough feasting for one evening. Please see her to her room."

"Of course, my lord."

Erde summoned enough presence of mind to say her proper good nights at the high table, but she was glad of Rainer's steady arm as she tottered from the hall. In the outer corridor, her vision swam, her knees buckled. Rainer caught her about the waist and picked her up without thinking.

"Shall you carry me, then?" she asked foolishly.

The guardsmen stared straight ahead. "It appears I shall, my lady, you not being much able to walk and all."

"Am I not too heavy?"

Rainer laughed softly. "No. Not too heavy."

"I could walk, you know." But it felt better to rest her head against his chest as he paced down the long side hall, to be with someone who was not always judging her and finding her lacking. The dizziness subsided, though the nausea remained. She wanted only to go to bed.

"I hope you're not picking up the drinking habit, my lady." He paused and readjusted her weight to carry her up the broad central staircase.

Erde snorted rudely. "It's my father who's drinking too much!"

"Ah, but my lord baron can drink most of us under the table."

She marveled that men seemed to find this so admirable a quality in each other. "I think the priest could drink more."

"Yes, you would think that, if you're not watching him carefully. But his cup hardly empties."

Erde frowned. Perhaps she'd been feeling too poorly to be truly alert. "Well, I only had one cup of wine."

"Even one can be too much for some, you know."

"It made me sleepy."

"Are you feeling better?"

"My stomach aches so oddly."

"I'll fetch Fricca for you when we get there."

Erde nestled into the dark fabric of his tunic as if it were her pillow. The rhythm of the stairs was soothing. She could hear his heart beating. "Try my father's rooms."

Rainer nearly missed a step. "What?"

"Oh, you know what I mean. That's where she is most times now. She's more his chamber-woman than she is mine."

"Erde! . . . my lady, I mean . . . ?" He shook his head helplessly.

"I'm not blind, you know."

"Of course not."

"I'm almost fourteen, for heaven's sake!"

"So you are, my lady, so you are."

She heard herself giggle and knew the wine truly had gone to her senses. Her only hope was to lie back and enjoy the ride. "Oh, Rainer, you're so proper!"

"I am not," he replied indignantly.

"You are! You used to call me princess."

He paused again for breath on the top step, gazing down the dim curving corridor that led to the tower stair. "I used to call you a lot of things that aren't right for us anymore."

"Who says?"

"Well, uh . . . you know."

"I want to know who says such things! I hate it when you call me 'my lady.' "

"But that's what you are."

She knew that now was the time to ask him, now that the wine had loosed her tongue. "Rainer, are we not friends anymore?"

He headed down the corridor. "Friends? Sure we are."

This was somehow not a satisfying answer, but his long-legged stride quieted her, made her thoughts drift. Her head ached as she thought about Fricca and her father and what they did together in his rooms. Was it the same as love? She knew she could question Fricca, who would eagerly supply every detail. But Erde couldn't bear the thought of knowing such things about her own father.

However, her curiosity, being suppressed, was the more intense.

"Rainer, have you ever kissed anyone?"

"Hey! Are you *trying* to get me in trouble?"

Well, finally. She had shocked the formality out of him. "We used to talk about that sort of thing all the time."

A pretty serving girl came out of a room ahead of them with an armful of linens. Seeing Rainer, she propped her load against the wall and smiled. He nodded stiffly and strode past. "Okay, sure, yes, I have."

"Who? Friends?"

"That is none of your business."

"Well, would you only kiss someone who's beautiful?"

He glanced down at her quizzically, made a turn, took a breath, and started up the next flight of stairs. "That depends. Why?"

"Would you kiss me even though I'm not beautiful?"

The guardsman caught himself just before he sent them tumbling on the stone. "Shhh! What are you saying! Damn, Erde, you are drunk, after all!"

Erde looked up at him earnestly. "No. It's my new idea. If there's something I'm shy about, I learn it from a friend."

"If there's anything you're shy about, I sure don't know what it is."

"But doesn't it make sense?"

"It'd make more sense to be thinking about what your father would say."

Erde frowned. "My father hates me."

"Of course he doesn't."

"He hates me because I'm alive and my mother isn't."

"He loved her," said Rainer simply.

"I miss her as much as he does!"

"Perhaps. But in a different way."

She relaxed against him. "Please, Rainer . . . would you?"

"What? What?"

"Kiss me."

"Don't be silly."

"Please! Just once, so I know what it's like. I'll never make you do it ever again, I promise."

Rainer made his voice deep and serious. "This is unseemly, my lady."

Erde laughed and wriggled in his arms. She closed her eyes and puckered up her mouth until it was a tiny hill above her chin. "Please, please, pleeeese . . . ?"

Rainer sighed. He slowed at a landing, glanced around, then dipped his head and brushed her lips lightly, the barest feather touch with a dry tense mouth. "There." He raised his head and continued upward resolutely.

Erde opened her eyes to the firm smooth line of his jaw and the bronze glint of his hair as it curled around his earlobe. The sculpture of his lower lip was so finely wrought, so like a statue, that she felt the urge to slide her fingertip, just the very tip, slowly along beneath its shadow. A surge of her father's quicksilver envy seized her, sharp as a knife in her befuddled heart. She couldn't quite keep back the tears. "It's because I'm not beautiful, isn't it?"

"What is?"

"You won't really kiss me because I'm not beautiful, like you are."

"Like . . . ?" Rainer stopped and gazed down at her. "What's going on here?"

Erde was suddenly nervous. She had pushed and pushed at something she didn't quite understand until an unseen boundary had been crossed. "Oh, Rainer, I didn't mean to . . ."

"Yes, you did."

"Well, I mean . . ." She twisted her face into his chest. "I'm so confused."

"Erde . . ."

She glanced up, and he tightened his arms around her, gathering her unsuspecting mouth into his, quickly, hungrily, running his tongue along the inside of her lip before letting go abruptly with a soft groan and a shake of his head, like a man coming up through water. "Who says you're not beautiful? Don't let anyone tell you you're not beautiful!"

Erde stared at him in wonder. "Oh."

He gulped a breath, let it out, then laughed harshly. "Holy God, I've surely lost my mind." He resettled her more formally, as if he could hold her at a distance from him, hurrying along in silence until they had reached the door to her room. "I'm going to put you down now. Can you stand? Can you manage until I find Fricca?"

She nodded, tongue-tied, wanting him to go, wanting to cling to him. He let her slide gently to the floor, supporting her still with one arm. As he reached for the door latch, Erde heard him gasp softly. There was bright blood on his hand.

Erde was mystified. "What happened? Are you all right?"

Rainer stared at his hand a moment more, then at her, craning his neck to look her over. "Oh, Princess," he whispered. "It's yours."

"What? Mine?" Then Erde understood. "Oh no!"

"Fricca!" Rainer shouted, no longer equal to the situation. He shoved open the door. "Fricca! Damn! Where are you, woman?"

Thoroughly awake at last and mortified beyond imagining, Erde slipped out of his encircling arm and pushed him away from the door. "No! I'm, uh, all right! I'm . . . oh, God, just leave me alone!"

She darted behind the door and shut it in his face.

Chapter Four

Erde recalled her chamber-woman finding her in the middle of the floor, but not much else until she was bathed and in bed by firelight with Fricca patting her hand and telling her not to worry, that was how it was being a woman. For all her voluble advice-giving, Fricca had neglected to warn her that when this much awaited time arrived, she would feel so completely awful.

"Oh, that'll pass." Fricca was plainly delighted by the turn of events, though she did cast the occasional troubled glance at the ruined white gown now discarded in the corner. She pressed her giggles back into her mouth. "Poor Rainer! Oh, such a face on him! You'd think these young soldiers would be used to the sight of a bit of blood!"

Erde relaxed into the feather bed and let her breathing slow. Perhaps if she feigned sleep, Fricca would go away and leave her alone with the thousand new thoughts raging in her head. She didn't think of Rainer. She couldn't without squirming. He would never speak to her again, and surely she would never dare speak to him. Yet his face filled her vision when she closed her eyes. She had not expected his lips to be so soft.

In the breaks in Fricca's monologue, Erde could hear the sleet ticking at the window glass. In the forest, the deer would be seeking out their winter shelter, the young ones too slight yet to withstand the early weather. Shouts from the feasting echoed up the stairwell. Brassy music and the distant clash of steel.

"Listen to them still going on!" exclaimed Fricca. "You'd think it was a battle won, not a poor good woman laid in the holy ground."

Erde pictured her father, well into his cups with the slimy

priest. She wondered if Rainer had returned downstairs as well, to drink too much and joke with the rest of the Guard and make fun of the baron's daughter, the silly skinny child who couldn't hold her wine. She knew Rainer was always a moderate drinker, but she wouldn't blame him for wanting to lose himself in drink tonight. She turned over with a groan and curled tighter around the source of her unfamiliar ache. "Is Alla asleep already?"

"Nay, the captain went to fetch her. She'll be making up something special for you, that's all that keeps her." Fricca rose to stir the fire and pile on several unnecessary logs, then came to close the bed curtains. "Go to sleep if you can. I'll sit till she comes."

The warm bed soothed, and the flame-flicker on the sheer linen drapes was mesmerizing. Erde dozed but it could only have been a while, for the firelight was still bright on the curtains when sudden noises woke her, loud voices in the outer hall, her door opening.

"Where is my daughter? Is she well?"

Her father, and fully drunk by the sound of him. Erde did not move.

Fricca sputtered out of her nap by the hearth. "Oh, fast asleep, my lord." She gave a small womanly laugh. "After her ordeal."

"What? What ordeal?"

"Ummm . . ." Fricca faltered. Erde guessed there was someone else in the room.

"Out with it, woman," her father ordered.

"Shhh, shhh, my lord!" There was whispering, and Fricca's maddening giggle.

"What? When?"

"Just now! I found the poor child fainted dead away in the middle of the floor." Fricca sobered. "But I fear your fine gift is ruined, my lord. And my dear lady's gown as well."

"Pfft," said the baron. "Just a dress. Her mother would be delighted. Let's see this trophy!"

"Surely not, my lord, with . . ."

"Bring it!"

Fricca reluctantly retrieved the stained garment. The baron snatched it from her and shook it out. He was silent for a long time. Erde heard him walking about in the staccato way of a drunk determined to appear sober.

"Well, Brother," he declared finally. "What do you think of that? My daughter is a woman at last."

"Cause for joy indeed, my lord."

The priest. In her own bedchamber. Erde thought of the deer again and tried to be as still as they were when hiding from the hunters.

"My only daughter," mused the baron thickly. Then he roused himself. "We must announce it. We must have a celebration!"

But Erde detected no celebration in his voice. She heard the scrape of the priest's sandal, his light-footed careful step, as he moved toward the heat of the fireplace. "Certainly you should, my lord, once the usual rituals have been observed." He lowered his voice, which made him sound threatening. "I assume, my good woman, that you've taken appropriate steps, in order to be able assure his lordship that he's hearing the truth of the matter?"

"Steps?" Fricca replied blankly.

"I mean, woman, have you properly examined the girl?"

"Oh, oh, she's fine, your reverence, I mean, she will be, just tuckered out, you know."

"Don't play with me, woman!" the priest growled.

Fricca made inarticulate noises, then fell silent.

The baron snorted. "She hasn't a clue what you mean, Brother. We are a bit less formal here in the benighted provinces. But rest your mind." The gown rustled as he tossed it to the floor. "Truth is in the evidence."

"But evidence can mislead, my lord."

The baron hardly seemed to hear him. "A celebration, then! Fricca! Let's have some wine here!"

"There's a tray already laid in your chamber, my lord . . ."

"But none here. I see none here! Now, woman! Here and now!"

Fricca rustled away. The baron lowered himself with an explosive sigh into the chair by the hearth. The leather creaked and for a while, Erde heard only the snap of the fire and her father's wine-heavy breathing. Then the priest stirred.

"May I speak, my lord?"

"Aye, speak, Brother. You've shown no reluctance so far. In fact, I've been impressed, yes, even moved by your knowledge and concern for the minor political details of a fiefdom that could hardly be of importance to a great man from Rome." He shifted and the leather groaned again. "What's on your mind?"

"Concern for your own interests, my lord, now that I have come to know you personally. And for God's holy commandments."

The baron chuckled. "Are they all under attack?"

"You may mock, my lord, but the Devil lurks behind every door."

"Enough simpering behind priest's rhetoric, Guillemo! We've done with that, you and I, have we not? Leave it to your army of subordinates. If something's bothering you, spit it out!"

"With your permission then, my lord . . . in cases like this, the ritual examination is no mere formality. It . . ."

"Cases like this?"

The priest was silent a moment, offering a reluctance to continue so obviously a ploy that Erde could barely keep silent. She wanted to shout at her father that if he weren't so drunk, he'd see how this man was manipulating him. At length, Guillemo cleared his throat politely. "My lord baron, I sense something irregular here. Could the servant be protecting the girl?"

"Protecting?"

"Well, for instance, you said she never informed you of the girl's unseemly gamboling in the woods."

"Protecting her for what?"

"For your daughter's reputation," the priest prodded silkily, "and for yours. The woman clearly, well . . . favors you, my lord. It's only natural that she'd . . ."

Erde thought she would stop breathing altogether. She could almost hear suspicion clicking into place in her father's wine-sodden brain, like the gears of a clock readying itself to strike.

"For what *reason,* I mean!"

Guillemo's sandals slapped softly against the stone, back and forth in front of the hearth. "Before my, ah, Calling, lord baron, I had in Rome some training in matters of the law. Those old habits compel me yet to review events until my heart is satisfied that they are as they appear to be, or as they have been presented."

A rattle of cups announced Fricca's return. "Wine, my lord."

"What kept you? Give it here!" The baron poured and drank. "So. What of it, man? Go on."

Guillemo resumed his pacing. "A young girl drinks too much, is escorted from the hall by a handsome captain. A while later, she is found by her chambermaid, sprawled on the floor, her garment a ruin."

"Only stained, my lord," Fricca ventured. "A good soaking might save it. And she wasn't sprawled. She'd fainted, poor lamb."

"Go on, Brother," said the baron tightly.

"Well, my lord, as a protector of God's Laws and as your friend, this is the thing I must ask: what about this boy-soldier of yours? Do you trust him?"

"With my life," the baron growled.

"Ah, well, perhaps. But with your daughter?"

Erde heard Fricca's soft gasp, then nothing but the flames and the sound of her father drinking.

Finally the baron said, "They were raised together. He's like a brother to her."

"Reassuring, I agree, though that could put her more at ease with such men than might be proper for a young girl."

"She's an innocent, Guillemo. She knows nothing of men. She walks alone in the forest without thinking what might happen. She . . ." The baron cut himself short. "She's an innocent."

"Yes," the priest replied and Erde heard in his voice the soft rasp of a dagger being drawn. Why did her father keep listening? Why didn't he tell this awful man to go away and let her sleep? She knew she should leap up and defend herself, or run away down the halls to Alla who could handle both her father and the priest. But it was like hearing someone else's story. She was frozen in horrified fascination, and Guillemo was moving in for the kill. "Innocent, exotically beautiful, ripe on the edge of womanhood . . ."

"The boy's as much an innocent as she is."

"Ah, but a man nonetheless. And what young man doesn't harbor a bit of the Devil in his heart?"

Something, a wine cup, fell to the floor and shattered.

"My lord, don't you listen to him!" Fricca exclaimed. "It's a shame! A man of God, saying such foul things!"

A brisk knock at the door silenced her.

"Ah," said Guillemo. "Your patience for a moment, my lord."

Erde heard him whisk to the door for a murmured conference. She prayed he'd be called away on urgent business.

"My lord," he said finally. "If you'll indulge me, some further evidence has been uncovered."

The baron only grunted. Someone, Fricca perhaps, gathered up the shards of the wine cup.

"Bring her in," called the priest. There was a shifting of booted feet and slippers. "Now, my girl. Don't be afraid. You've done nothing wrong. Just tell my lord baron what you saw."

It was only whimpering at first, but Erde's gifted ear recognized the voice of the third floor laundry maid.

"Speak, girl. The truth serves both your lord on this earth and the One in heaven."

"I'm making up beds, your reverence, and I . . . I seen them coming down the hall."

"Who did you see, child?"

"The captain, and my lady Erde. He was carrying her and they was laughing."

The priest cleared his throat again. "Carrying her . . . as in holding her against himself bodily?"

"Um, well, yes, sir, you could call it that."

"And what else?"

"Oh, nothing else, your reverence. They just passed by like they never seen me at all."

"But there's nothing unusual in that, is there? I mean, in being ignored by your betters?"

The servant girl hesitated. Erde heard some sniffling, so well-orchestrated that she would have laughed, were she not already so horrified. She could not imagine what she'd done to make this girl betray her so readily.

"Would it be unusual?" prompted the priest.

"No sir, I mean . . . well, yes, sir, with the captain, sir . . . I mean, after all he's said, sir . . . well, I mean he could have given me a look, you know? Like he even knew I was there!"

"All he's said? Promises? Has he made promises, in return for . . . ah, favors?"

The sniffles dissolved into loud weeping.

"That'll do," the priest snapped. "Return her to her quarters."

The door thudded shut. In the silence, Erde heard

Guillemo moving about. She could picture him, pacing deliberately, his dark face a mask of righteous concern.

"Well, my lord baron. It appears the boy is not as innocent as you thought."

Wood and leather groaned as the baron heaved his bulk out of the chair. "Wake her up, then!"

Fricca found her tongue. "My lord, how can you listen to such tales? That laundry wench is a famous flirt! She's made eyes at every soldier in the barracks. Let the child sleep, she's feeling so poorly ... !"

"Wake her up! We'll hear it from her."

"Calm, my lord," Guillemo urged, and Erde ground her teeth in rage. As if it were not he who was responsible for the baron's intemperance! "We are only considering the possibility. The word of a servant should not carry much weight, and we have a better option. The truth can be ascertained by a simple examination, to be performed here and now in your presence, and the matter be done with."

"Wake her up," the baron snarled. "Or I will!"

"No!" Fricca wailed. "Leave the poor child alone! With you too drunk to know what truth is!"

There was a sharp crack, Fricca's muffled squeal, and the thud and clatter of her soft weight falling amid the metal fire tongs and the ash bucket. Erde was relieved to hear her weeping. Silence would have been more terrifying. Then the baron ripped aside the bed curtains and stood staring down at her, breathing hard. "Get up, Daughter."

Erde gathered the quilt around her, saw Fricca huddled on the floor in the firelight. Her father's eyes on her were like a hunter's. She fought to keep her voice steady. "Yes, Papa."

"Been listening, hah?"

"Yes, Papa."

"Well?"

A knock at the door, Rainer's knock. Erde could not help it. Her eyes darted toward the sound.

"Get it," the baron barked. Fricca had scrambled up and was already there.

"It's Alla, my lord."

Alla pushed past the half-open door. "What's this, Josef? The girl's not so deathly ill that you've need of a priest! Come, this is women's business. Clear out now, both of you. Let me do my work." She flashed Guillemo an unedited look of dislike and shoved at the door to swing it wide. "Bring that in, lad, and set it by the hearth."

Rainer hesitated in the doorway. He held a steaming crock by thick, oversized handles, and his face was soft with concern. Erde could not have known that the look passing between them would suggest so much to a man of the world like her father.

"Bring it in, lad," he mimicked. "Set it down."

"Oh, Josef," said Alla, beckoning Rainer in. "Too much wine. What would your mother say?"

"My mother, as you may have noticed, is no longer about to tell me what to do."

Alla raised an eyebrow. "So much the worse for you. Go to bed before you embarrass yourself. Where's that crock, lad?"

Rainer eased in, eyes tight to his burden. He set the crock down, shot his lord an empathetic glance intended to be of the sort shared between men in the midst of female matters, and turned to go. He found Brother Guillemo between himself and the door.

"Please stay a while, Captain," said the baron pleasantly.

Rainer came to attention. "My lord."

The baron took him by the shoulder and turned him slowly to face Erde. "Now, Daughter, can you answer the good brother satisfactorily? Have you anything to tell me about what went on earlier this evening?"

"No, Papa. Nothing went on." But her bewilderment was disingenuous. She had overheard too much. "It's not what you think."

Rainer's eyes widened, flew to Erde, and the baron caught the glance before each looked away.

"Not what I think, eh? What was it, then?"

"Nothing, Papa! Nothing! I was sick, you know I was sick, and he was helping me like you asked, that's all." He stared at her as if she was suddenly covered in mud. Erde knew she should weep, but she was afraid, so afraid, and could not manage it.

Alla moved past the baron, bringing Erde a cupful of hot liquid. "What is this nonsense, Josef? What poison has this priest been spilling? Don't you know what's happened here?"

"Do you, Alla? Do you really know what goes on in this house? Or are you in on this, too? Am I a fool? I see the way she looks at him!" The baron glared as if Rainer's very presence enraged him beyond bearing. His grip tightened until the young man winced. "I see it now. You're the one she's been meeting out in the forest!"

"Never, my lord! Erde, tell him!"

The baron shoved him backward and slapped him as he might a dog. "My lady, to you, boy!"

Rainer hunched in shame. "Yes, my lord."

Baron Josef grabbed him again. "How long, hah? How long without my knowing?"

"Papa, listen to me! You never listen!"

"I told you she met no one!" Fricca yelped.

Alla faced the baron calmly, hands on hips. "Stop this right now. Send this priest away, and we'll settle this when you're sober enough to think rationally."

"I marvel, my lord," remarked Guillemo from the fireplace, "that your household treats you with such ill respect. Do you not honor God, woman?"

"Shut up, priest!" The baron's face was flushed as deep as his burgundy velvet. "Get me some help."

Alla laid her small hands on his arm to quiet him and to loose Rainer from his rigid grasp. He brushed her aside. "Go!" he growled over her head.

Guillemo bowed and whispered from the room.

"Now we'll see . . ." He twisted Rainer away from him until the guardsman's sword was within reach. With his free hand, he jerked it from its sheath and set the point to Rainer's throat. "You ungrateful pup! I made you and this is how you thank me? You think I'm so gullible? Like some foolish woman you can fool me with an innocent face? I ought to gut you here and now!"

Rainer found his strangled voice. "But what have I done?"

"He did nothing," said Alla. "Didn't you hear her say he did nothing?"

"She's protecting her lover, old woman! Can a priest see that better than you?"

"Papa! You're drunk!"

Rainer dropped to one knee at the baron's feet. "My lord, on my life, I never . . . how could you even think . . . ?"

"Couldn't content yourself with the serving girls, hah? No, they're not good enough for the son of a King's Knight! It had to be my daughter! My precious daughter! MINE!"

Rainer reached out in protest. The baron recoiled. "So

that's your game! Think you can take the old man in a fight!"

"My lord, no!" But he rose instinctively to defend himself.

Baron Josef threw the sword aside. It nearly sliced Alla's shin, skittering past her. The baron swung an arm back and slammed Rainer sidelong, sending him sprawling on the stone floor. Erde shoved her quilt aside and ran at her father like a lunatic, snatching at his arm, screeching at him to stop. He staggered but knocked her away and lunged after Rainer, hauling him up with one hand. As the young man stared at him in disbelief, the baron hit him full in the face, then rammed a knee into his stomach as he went down.

"No! Oh, no!" Erde scrambled to the fallen guardsman, her bare legs scraping across the splintered boards. She fell on him to cover his head with her own body. Now the blood on her garment was his.

"See?" roared her father, swaying above them drunkenly. "You see how she protects him?"

"You are a madman!" Erde screamed. Rainer coughed and groaned beneath her.

Brother Guillemo returned. Swords and white-robes filled the doorway. "My lord?"

The baron wiped his mouth on his sleeve and pointed. "That one."

"Josef," Alla begged. "Think what you're doing! Stop this while you're still able!"

The baron turned slowly to glare at her. His eyes glittered like small unseeing jewels. "Go to your room, old woman, if you know what's good for you."

Brother Guillemo gestured sharply. Two white-robes dragged Erde away from Rainer and tossed her like a sack of grain onto her bed. When Alla tried to go to her, another hustled the protesting midwife from the room. Two more jerked the protesting young man to his feet. Hanging stunned and bleeding in their grasp, he looked to Erde, who could only shake her head in disbelieving horror. Then he raised his bruised eyes to meet the baron's.

"What did I say about being used, my lord? Look around you. I have never lied to you or abused your trust. You'll never have a more loyal man than me."

The baron spat in his face. "Get him out of here."

Erde saw only a bearded death's head as Brother

Guillemo smiled his self-righteous smile and signaled to his men to take Rainer away. With the room emptying and no antagonist left, the baron seemed to lose focus. He looked for his wine cup, and not finding it, drank from the pitcher. Guillemo offered his own cup from the mantle, then bowed to him deeply. "You should rest, my lord. From the shock."

Baron Josef frowned distractedly, then merely nodded and turned toward the door, the pitcher still clutched firmly in one hand.

Chapter Five

Erde was locked in her bedchamber. No visitors came, no one with food or water or even fuel for the fire. *This will be over soon,* she thought, and then when it was not over, she cried for hours, curled up in her nest of bed linens. When she had wept herself dry, she got up and paced, feeling her own rage stir like acid in the pit of her stomach.

She hated him. She hated this so-called father who could listen to a man he'd known less than a day, over his most trusted bodyguard, over the word of his own and only daughter. How could such a thing be?

The window rattled and the drafts howled in the ceiling vaults. The wind hurled sleet and ice against the shivering panes of glass. Winter crept into the room, and still no one came. Erde imagined her father still raging drunkenly around the castle, and the servants too frightened to come to her aid. She made tasks for herself, to ward off the cold and her sense of drifting unmoored in an alien sea. She rationed the remaining firewood. She tore up the white gown and fed the pieces to the flames. She drank the stale water in the pitcher by her washbasin. She moved her chamber pot to the farthest corner to avoid the stink.

She understood nothing that had happened. Her father was always a dangerous drunk, but his rages had never been this violent before. Still, there was a chance it would all be over when he finally sobered up.

The next evening, someone came at last, an older guardsman she did not recognize. He admitted Fricca with a pail of cold water and orders to make Erde presentable.

"It's cold!" Erde complained, "Doesn't he think I've been punished enough?"

Fricca said nothing. The guard stood by the open door and

watched until Fricca insisted he turn his back. Erde was outraged. Did the man not know his place? She begged for
news, for something to eat.

Fricca shook her head, weeping as she sponged Erde's
shivering arms. "Oh, such goings-on, my lady!" Her pale
murmur was nearly drowned out by the splash of the water
into the pail. "Your father is in a mad drunken fury like I've
never seen! Who knows where we'd be if the Holy Brother'd not been there to soothe him and read Scripture to him
and be responsible until he's himself again."

The notion of Guillemo in charge made Erde shiver all the
more. "My father needs a healer, not a priest. Where's
Alla?"

Fricca laid a finger to her lips. "They'll not let her see
him, for fear she'll enrage him further."

"Then what of Rainer?" Erde whispered. "How's Rainer?"

"Locked away, my lady. Oh, the poor foolish lad!"

"Foolish?" Erde pulled away. "Don't tell me now you believe these lies? You know better than that!"

"Oh, my dearest lady-child, I know what *seems,* but in
black times like these . . . I mean, what can we know about
such things?"

"What things?"

"Well, the holy brother says . . ."

"The holy brother knows nothing!" Erde yelled. But she
could see he did, that he was in fact fiendishly clever, for he
was keeping her father from the very people who might coax
him back to sanity. What she didn't understand was why.

At her yell, the guard snapped around and ordered them to
silence, bidding Fricca to hurry. She wept and wept, but
would not speak another word.

When she was done and had departed, still weeping, the
guard took Erde to the great-hall, where her father sat on the
baronial throne in near-darkness. The assembled court stood
grimly silent. Erde thought they looked frightened, a bit confused. Guillemo's robed entourage lined the walls, where
Rainer's men should have been. Torches flared here and
there, and a few people carried lanterns, but the great twin
hearths were still and cold, and no candles burned. When her
eyes adjusted to the dim light, Erde understood the courtiers'
dismay. The baron, always so concerned with protocol and a
pristine public image, was unshaven, slumped carelessly in

his chair, and still wearing his feast robe, which a day later was badly wrinkled and wine-stained. One hand balanced a goblet on his knee. In the shadows behind the throne stood Brother Guillemo.

Erde awaited the stern, perhaps even slightly raving lecture about her behavior, a humiliation she could probably live through. But her father did not even seem to notice her. The guard pushed her to her knees before him, and the Baron glanced unsteadily aside and raised his goblet. A white-robe hurried to fill it. Erde was hauled up and led to a stool to one side of the dais. Her guard stood near. Erde's eyes sought the carved dragon capitals for comfort.

Two of the white-robes dragged Rainer in. His wounds had not been washed or dressed, and his torn black tunic was gray and slick with mud. When Erde rose to her feet in shocked protest, her guard shoved her back down again. Now the court murmured covertly. She could hear a few of the women praying. Rainer could hardly stand, but he shrugged off his escort to face the throne alone, where the baron had now drawn himself up with a drunken glare of hatred. Rainer did not look Erde's way, and she resolved to avoid even a glance, lest it harm his cause.

Brother Guillemo stepped forward to present the charges. Rainer was not allowed to speak in his own defense. Erde tried several times and was silenced, first by Guillemo's command, finally by the callused palm of her guard. Both were made to sit and listen while Guillemo detailed his own twisted version of the events, to listen while the sniveling laundry-maid described what she'd seen in even more lurid detail, to listen while silly helpless Fricca admitted, yes, she had found the baron's daughter weeping and distraught after the captain had left her. It wasn't until the priest had nearly completed his case that Erde understood that only Rainer was on trial. An actual trial, no mere public scolding or wrist-slapping. Sitting rigid on her stool, Erde felt real fear creep into her heart. She noticed that the von Alte dragon tapestries, which had hung on these walls for a hundred years, had been taken down, exposing the pale cold stone. Surely if her father was sober, he would not let all this go on. She sought again the dragons in the upper shadows, but they could offer only silent comfort.

The only voice raised on Rainer's behalf was Alla's, blunt and indignant, and so very sane. Guillemo heard her out without comment, did not even question her testimony, and Erde wondered why he had let her speak at all. His motive surfaced when Alla had said her piece and limped proudly from the hall. Then the priest shook his head warningly. "Satan's wings have brushed us, oh my people. Clearly what this old witch-woman says can never be taken as truth. My lord, she must be looked into. I fear some deeper plot here."

Not long thereafter, Brother Guillemo asked for a verdict, and Erde heard her father slur even the few words required to condemn Rainer to death by hanging, sentence to be carried out the next morning.

She began to scream and did not stop, even when one of Guillemo's white-robes clamped a fist over her mouth and dragged her from the hall.

Chapter Six

Erde knew now what caused a caged animal to go mad and gnaw at its own flesh. Mere tears were not desperate enough for such a catastrophe.

She stood all night on the high sill of her window. She began in the chill silence of thought. After a while, thought became fantasy, and she called on the Mage-Queen to appear and carry Rainer and herself far away to safety. But the fantasy did not sustain her and the early hours of dawn found her rocking and moaning. She had determined that there was no conceivable way she could free Rainer from his cell, and so she went to work on building up the courage to fling herself onto the cobblestones sixty feet below. Maybe then the baron would set Rainer free out of remorse. In truth, her life experience thus far did not include a world in which, when the time came, her father would actually execute his favorite guardsman.

But what finally kept her frozen to the sill was the sight of the chicken-crone sitting on the well-head in the middle of the storm, grinning up at her toothlessly and beckoning.

Then there was a muffled thump outside her door and the scrape of a key in the lock. Erde stayed where she was. If it was her father or the priest come to make her watch Rainer hang, it would be all the excuse she'd need to throw herself from the windowsill.

But it was Alla who eased open the door, stuck her head in, then ducked back, grunting and breathing hard, hauling on something heavy. Erde ran to help her.

"Alla, Alla, thank God! Oh, Alla, what are we to do?"

"Help me, child! Those white-robes of his are everywhere!" The heavy weight was the guard who'd been posted outside. Together, they dragged him into the room.

"Alla, we have to help Rainer! We have to. . . !"

"No time, I can't . . . I've done what I can," Alla panted. "Now it's up to . . ." Her breath failed her briefly. Two bright spots blazed on her cheeks. Her white hair was loose and tangled. She unslung a leather satchel from her back and pressed it into Erde's hands. "Hide this, quickly! Take the key and lock the door behind me!"

"No!" Erde snatched at her sleeve. "You can't leave me!"

"Have to. They can't know I've been here. Your father is . . ."

"Still drunk? No! Is he still drunk? Alla, what's the matter with him? He's never been this bad before!"

The old woman hugged Erde tightly, kissed her, then held her at arm's length. "I know, child, but he's never met his evil genius before. Now, listen, my dearest girl. It's all out of hand. I can't protect you any more. That vicious priest . . . he's after my skin. It's gone way beyond just plying your father with drink and flattery. He and Josef . . . they encourage each other's madness. You should have seen the two of them, hauling the tapestries from the great-hall onto the fire."

"Burned? The von Alte tapestries?" Erde felt a hole grow in her heart.

Alla stroked her cheek. "Yes, kidling. As evil totems of dragon worship. Can you believe the folly of it? Built a raging pyre in the upper courtyard and tossed them in, all the time laughing like boys, while the foolish court all stood about like scared dumb sheep! There's no telling what . . . the priest's talking now about taking you 'in hand' . . . exactly what I fear he means to do, the lecherous bastard, even as he pours evil into Josef's ear about you and the lad. You must get away. You must! Hide yourself in the villages until the priest is gone, or go to the king. No time to send word, just go!"

Shouts from the courtyard blew up the stairwell with the icy drafts. Alla patted her pockets, glanced swiftly around. "Fare ye well, light of my heart."

"But what about Rainer?"

"Don't think of him, child."

"How can I not think of him?" Erde wailed.

"You're best to never think of him again." Alla held their four hands together in a knot. "Be brave, hawkling! Your dragon awaits you!"

"My . . . what dragon?"

Alla ducked away. The clamor from below spread to the upper corridor, men running, boots and swords clanging against the stone. Erde swung the heavy door closed and locked it, then remembered the guard lying near the hearth and worried that he might wake up. Bending closer, she discovered he was not just unconscious. His jaw gaped, his eyes stared. A small stiletto puncture bled at his neck. Erde recoiled with a squeal, then hushed herself, feeling her world turn over. How serious some games became, and how suddenly. *Your father's evil genius,* Alla had said. No one had understood how unstable his balance was until the coming of the priest had tipped it. By dawn, Rainer would be as dead as this poor man, because of her childishness, because she had insisted on an innocent stupid kiss.

Erde cried out as guilt and grief and rage surged over her, spilling strength into her limbs. She grabbed the corpse by the heels and dragged it under her bed, then ran to stash the leather satchel behind her stinking chamber pot. Out in the hall, armor clanked. More men raced past. Someone tried her latch, then pounded on her door. Erde sat down by the dim hearth, easing her breath and her heart so that she could remain calm when the key arrived to let her father into the room.

The baron stared at her from the doorway, weaving a bit, taking in her strange stillness. His hair was matted as if he'd just awakened, yet he was as richly dressed as he would be for a ceremony. He was pale and exhausted, with shadowed fragile eyes, as if his mad rage had held him unwilling prisoner and he was unsure of where it had left him, or when it might seize him again.

"The priest insisted he ought to examine you himself, but I wouldn't allow it. I have to let him have his way with lesser matters, or . . ." He trailed off. His narrowed glance seemed to demand thanks or congratulations. He moved toward her unsteadily and reached to stroke her hair just once, and smooth his finger across her cheek and down along the line of her jaw, like a worm crawling so slowly that Erde thought she would scream with revulsion. His voice was scratchy and weak, but his gaze fixed her intently. "I don't care, you know, that he . . . it doesn't matter, it's nothing. He's nothing, a boy. Not worthy of my little girl anyway, my soon-to-be young woman. A few hours, it will be over, we can forget him and move on. Everything will be as it was, no, it will be better. Matters are changing hereabouts. Tor Alte is not the end of the earth, or won't be for long. Wealth and power lies before us . . . and so much more." His hand was on her hair again, stroking. "But how could you understand such things? When the priest has proved his worth, you'll see. You'll see it was all for your own good."

He leaned over, hesitating for what seemed to Erde an eternity, poised above her, his breath sour with wine. Then he bent and kissed her roughly, his stiff tongue prying open her mouth.

Erde jerked away, shuddering, and hid her face in her hands.

"I know, I know, but you'll see how it will be. I have so much to teach you." He leaned his body against the curve of her back and was about to say something more when an urgent shout down the hall distracted him. He glanced vaguely around the empty room and turned away, closing the door, oh, so very gently as if Erde were still asleep.

Soon Fricca brought a tray with breakfast, and fresh water for the kettle on the hearth. When she spotted the bucket, Erde raced over to splash her face, rubbing her lips over and over until Fricca stared.

A yard servant appeared with an armload of firewood. Bundled in her bed quilt, Erde watched silently, listening for the grim roll of drums in the courtyard. As the room warmed up again, she wondered if the dead soldier underneath her bed would begin to smell, thus giving Alla's mortal deed away.

"Oh, I haven't ceased crying a minute since your grandmother's funeral!" Fricca's hands shook as she filled the kettle. "Who'd have thought we'd have harbored such witchery, right here in our very own nest! No wonder we have summer snow and ravens."

"Who is it, the chicken-crone?"

"What? Lord, no, that's a pure Christian woman. No, I'm not to mention the name, on peril of my immortal soul. But it's that eastern blood of hers, surely, that gives her the power. Isn't the holy Brother right about keeping ourselves ever vigilant? Came along just in time, when we sorely needed the strong right arm of Heaven to protect us!"

Has the whole world gone insane, Erde wondered. Fricca

swung the kettle over the fire and came to sit beside her on the bed. "And you, too, poor lamb! Such a time of it! It's no good way to start out your life as a woman, but there's plenty of men will have you for your other qualities, so you must try to put it behind you. It was none of the poor lad's fault but his own weakness, and we're all best just to move on, now he's gone."

Erde knew her heart had stopped. "Gone?"

Fricca sniffed, wiped her eyes. "Oh, yes, dear. Didn't they tell you? Some of the men were trying to tend to his wounds, but he'd found himself a little knife somewhere and laid right into them. He was killed trying to escape."

Killed?

What was that awful stillness? Had all the air been sucked out of the room? Erde tried to cry out Rainer's name, but the sounds stalled in her throat. Surely she would choke on them.

Fricca mistook her wide-eyed struggle to breathe, to speak. "Yes, and very nearly made it, so the men say. Saved himself from the disgrace of the scaffold and died like the brave lad he was. Oh, you'd be proud! There's blood all over the stable yard." Fricca daubed at her cheeks with her apron. "But there's to be no funeral allowed. The baron's in such a rage—taking it very hard, 'cause he trusted the boy so—wouldn't let anyone near but his own Guard. Ordered the poor broken body hauled up the mountain and left for the wolves!"

Killed? Erde stumbled to the washbasin and emptied herself of all the fresh bread and fruit she had just eaten.

Thinking he was going to die had been the worst pain Erde could have imagined. Hearing he was dead left her without any feeling at all.

Frightened, Fricca brought the baron. "She won't eat, my lord. Won't say a word. Just sits there like a stone."

The baron approached her bedside. Erde noticed he was actually steady on his feet again, brushed and clean but wan, like a man recovering from an illness. He leaned over to look her in the face but did not come too close. "Daughter?"

She let her eyes focus somewhere twenty miles beyond him.

"This won't do any good, you know."

She was on Glasswind, with Rainer beside her, flying in the service of the Mage-Queen.

"I'll not indulge this behavior! What's done is done, and the boy's dead for his treason. It's fit punishment, better than he deserved, and sulking won't bring him back again."

Sulking? Did he think it so minor as a sulk?

Fricca fluttered about, keeping a fearful distance. "Let the holy brother come to her, my lord, to ease her soul with prayer."

"No!" The baron snapped upright. "None but you or I sets a foot in this room, do you hear?" He took a breath, as if shaken by his own vehemence. "A father can deal with his own child."

"Yes, my lord, but she won't talk, I promise you." Fricca wrung her hands. "I've been asking myself, what if she *can't?* You know what they say about the Devil stealing your tongue!" She forgot herself and came near to grab the baron's velvet sleeve. "Oh, my lord, with all else that's gone on, what if Alla has witched her, too, like she did our poor dead Rainer?"

And thus Erde heard the new gospel according to Brother Guillemo, how the unwitting guardsman took the baron's daughter while under the vile influence of a witch's spell, which made the girl forget the whole encounter, though the cries of her unwholesome pleasure had been overheard by the laundry-maid. Later, the witch made a glowing bloody sword appear in the prisoner's hand, and sent demons to unman his guards. This time, the blessed faith of the priest and his brothers weakened the witch's power. The escape failed, but Tor Alte was under dread attack by the forces of Satan. Their souls were in peril. The witch must be discovered and routed out. Invoking the authority of the Church, Guillemo interrogated Alla and declared her to be the very witch in question. He advised her immediate arrest, ordering his brothers to lock her in a cell and guard her closely.

These lies were more than Erde could stand, and she fixed her father with her dark eyes and meant to tell him so, but nothing came out. Her mouth worked soundlessly. Fricca whimpered and cringed.

The baron stepped back stiff-legged, like a dog with its hackles raised. "God's holy angels! Fricca! Not a word of this to anyone! He'll want to burn her, too!"

"My lord, I beg you! Consider the holy brother's offer!

He's our only salvation in this time of peril!" She slipped her hands around his arm and clung to him. "My dear, good lord! Give her into his keeping like he says, for her own sweet soul's sake!"

The baron's face twisted. He gazed at Erde as if it were his own soul in torment. "No. Not with Guillemo, woman, I could never . . ."

"Your pardon, lord baron . . ."

The baron spun on the man in the open doorway, who clearly did not relish being the bearer of one more piece of bad news.

"Well, man? Out with it!"

"It's the witch, my lord . . ."

"What? . . . escaped? More spells and visions?"

"Well, no, sir. Dead in her cell. Hanged herself, my lord."

The baron's shoulders sagged. "Oh, brave woman," he muttered.

Erde stared straight ahead, rocking silently, and felt nothing.

Soon she was alone again, and forced to think about what was happening to her.

She pondered the question of being unable to speak. Perhaps she *was* cursed. Perhaps by the chicken-crone, to her thinking the most obvious candidate for witchery. Certainly not by Alla.

Alla.

Rainer dead. Now Alla dead as well. How strange it felt to form those words in her mind. Erde knew she should feel grief but could not remember how to do it. She remembered feeling grief for her grandmother. Was it a skill one could forget? She discovered quickly that she could still grow bored of sitting still, and so considered her narrowing choices. She could lose herself in her fantasies, fly again with the Mage-Queen and her dragons, or . . . or she could do something. She stirred herself suddenly, raced across the room and pulled Alla's satchel out from behind her chamber pot. She spread its contents on the floor.

Several candles wrapped in a boy's linen shirt. A sleeveless leather tunic, worn but serviceable. Loose woolen breeches and low, cuffed leather boots. A gray knitted prentice cap. A small tinderbox. A thin sharp dagger with leather sheath and belt. A loaf of bread, four apples, and a hunk of hard cheese wrapped in oilcloth. A dark carved box. The objects were real, material, comforting.

Erde opened the box. Inside were a rolled strip of parchment covered with script in a language she could not read, and a large brooch such as one might use to fasten a cloak: a worn rust-colored stone set in silver. Cut into the stone was a tiny figure of a dragon. Erde turned it in the firelight, remembering. She'd often seen her grandmother wear this brooch. Here, then, was the dragon that Alla had said awaited her. She pressed it gently to her lips, surprised at how live and warm the red stone felt in the chill room. She replaced it carefully in the box. She devoured one of the apples, repacked everything into the satchel, and returned it to its malodorous hiding place. Alla had indeed meant her to leave Tor Alte, and had provided the means of escape.

Erde sat down to think.

Chapter Seven

The dagger's keen edge sliced through it easily. Erde gathered up the shorn dark mass of her hair and threw it on the dying embers. The sudden flare seared her eyes, and her nose wrinkled at the odor. The new lightness of her head, with the hair just short of her earlobes, made every motion feel unhinged.

Well past midnight, and outside, the wind still howled. In the cooling room, she stripped to her shift by dim firelight, tucked the hem into the woolen men's leggings. Rainer had let her try on his leggings once, when they were much younger, and Erde had never forgotten the sense of freedom and power such clothing provided. She was grateful that this first time of her bleeding had been short. She needed no womanly inconveniences now.

The linen shirt, worn soft and patched at the elbows, went over her shift and hung past her knees. Erde cinched it up with the dagger belt and sheathed the knife. After all, any boy might wear his older brother's cast-off shirt.

She laced up the leather tunic, then slid on the boots and walked around in them a bit, amazed that Alla could have fit her so well simply by guesswork. She emptied Fricca's latest hopeful offering of bread, cheese, and apples into the satchel, then added her own thick cloak. It made the pack uncomfortably bulky, but strapping it to her back the way Alla had always done on their herb-gathering forays made the burden manageable.

She thought of the nighttime forest, and felt only relief. She pulled the gray prentice cap over her shorn hair, settled the dagger more comfortably on her hip and stood gazing about the darkening room, at the old tapestries billowing in the draft, with their tales of dragons woven in faded hues, the minor cousins of those her father and the priest had burned. She'd no doubt these would be next. She peered into the shadows beneath her costly bed dressings, at the firelit marble mantle carved in the shapes of two trees meeting in an arch, into the recesses of the vaulting above her head where bats sometimes slept off the daylight hours.

There was nothing here that she would miss. No one left that she cared about or did not fear.

Erde took a quick breath and went to drag the dead guard out from under the bed. She was glad for darkness and tried to look at him as little as possible. He was beginning to smell a bit, and she hoped he would forgive her for postponing his last rites for so long. She prayed the poor man wouldn't burn in hell as long as she probably would.

She heard metal scrape as she yanked him by his boot heels, and saw a faint glimmer in the shadows beneath the bed. Reluctantly, she took a closer look. His jerkin was snagged with the blade of a sword.

Rainer's sword! The one her father had tossed away in the heat of his madness. Erde pounced on it, hugging it to her chest as if it were Rainer himself. If she'd had any tears left, she would have shed them then. Instead, she floated in numbness. Something inside her, some gear or mainspring, had broken. She could not feel, she could only act. But action at least offered some sense of forward motion, of being still alive. So she grasped the sword by its hilt and tried to level the blade in front of her. The strain of its weight pulled on her untrained wrist. She could not carry it, but she could not leave it behind. She tore one of her sheets into strips, bound up the sword to blunt its razor edge, and tied it to her own body with more of the sheeting, so that it nestled against her back like a steel spine.

She laid the guard out in the middle of the room, where he would be most visible from the doorway. She drew the bed curtains shut, opened the high casement window and knotted the torn sheet around the handle, draping it artfully over the sill. She took the pitcher, the washbasin, the kettle, anything that would break or make noise. She had planned to scream and tried, but could not. She prayed there was only the one man guarding her chamber so late at night. She stationed herself against the wall just to the side of the door and began flinging things to the floor.

The door cracked open. The young duty-guard peered in

cautiously, not wishing to follow his captain's fate with regard to the baron's daughter. He saw a large body sprawled in the darkened room, then the open casement with the sheet ruffled by the draft. Shouting, he shoved the door wide and sprang in.

When he had bent over the corpse and his back was to her, Erde ducked silently around the doorjamb and ran for her life.

She used all the old back stairs, the narrowest unlit corridors learned in her childhood, where the wind whistled through the chinks in the stone and the people who worked the longest days slept the hardest. The sword at her back set her posture unnaturally straight, the way Fricca had always nagged her to stand. With no clear idea of where she was heading other than somewhere down the mountain toward the villages, she slipped through the dark warmth of the kitchens, past the yawning bakers already beginning their day. The herbal talisman that always hung over the bread ovens to bless the rising had been replaced by a large wooden crucifix. Erde let herself out the scullery entrance. The wind and damp cold hit her full in the face.

How can it really be August, she wondered, wrapping her arms about her against the chill. *Surely I have slept, and in my daze, it has become November.*

The thin dogs sleeping in the lee of the wood yard raised their heads with interest as she approached, but Erde spoke to them in the language of hands and put their minds at rest. She unpacked her cloak and wrapped it shawllike about her head and shoulders, as she'd seen the prentice boys do, then struck out boldly across the cobbled rear court toward the inner gate.

The guards there were throwing dice and arguing. A mere passing prentice was hardly worth their notice when a month's salary hung on the toss. Erde descended into the mud and ruts of the armory yard, head bent, her walk purposeful. Escape was beginning to seem ridiculously easy, when she rounded the corner of the forge and came face-to-face with the chicken-crone, hauling her basket of corn to the bird pen. The ragged ancient peered at her and waved her irritably out of the path. Erde drew her cloak closer and stepped aside to pass. Suddenly the crone snatched at the cloak, spilling corn into the icy mud and raising a piercing squawk as if wolves were in the hen coop.

"Witch! Witch! Witch!" Her mad shriek echoed off the armory walls like a call to battle.

Erde jerked herself free and ran, doubling back toward the stables. She still had a few moments of grace before anyone thought to take the cries of the chicken-crone seriously. She let herself into the long wooden shed nestled against the middle ring wall. Most times, she knew, the horse gate leading from the stables into the outer ring was left unguarded, the animals themselves being touchy enough to give alarm. But the great shadowy forms flared their velvet nostrils and let Erde pass. She found her own horse Micha, bade him farewell, and hurried on.

Now there were the beginnings of commotion in the inner yard, and one gate left to pass, the massive Dragon Gate with its iron portcullis that was lowered every day at dusk. The wheel crank that raised it was inside the guardhouse, windowless but for an arrow slit that looked out on the gate. Its low entrance was barred by a door of rough planks. Erde put her eye to a crack.

Three men on duty: two fast asleep, the third huddled by the smoking firepit, drinking and staring into the coals. Erde knew this one—Georg, a lank and flat-faced fellow who was often on duty when she took an early walk. He'd stall the morning raising of the portcullis in order to hold her in conversation, going on about the long night and his sad lot and the abuses of his superiors. He smiled at Erde a lot, though this did not tell her whether he was her friend.

Back in the inner court, the dogs were barking. Soon the search would be on. Erde had no choice but to try and bluff it out. She gathered the cloak around her head, leaving as much of her boy's clothing showing as seemed reasonable, then rapped manfully on the planks and stood back waiting by the gate.

Inside, Georg fumbled about, rose, and looked out the door. Erde gestured to him casually to open up. He nodded grumpily and turned back inside. The crank rope groaned as the gate inched up. Past the folds of her hood, Erde could see George squinting at her through the arrow slit. A foot off the ground, the iron grille stopped.

"Hey, boy, where you headed in this devil's weather?"

Erde was unsure whether it was better or worse that she could not answer him. She waved.

He left the crank and came out toward her. "You might have a civil reply for your elder!"

Erde shrugged, trying to look shy, even when he reached and grabbed a fold of her cloak. He frowned, rubbing the soft fabric between his fingers. "Who'd you steal this from, eh?" He snatched her hood back, stared a moment, then recognition came. "Well, well. If it ain't the captain's high-born whore. You don't look so good without your hair."

He might as well have slapped her. Erde blinked back tears and set her jaw. She inclined her head proudly at the gate.

Georg snorted. "You want out, your little ladyship? Little late for a walk, isn't it? What is it, a lovers' tryst? The captain ain't dead half a day and you're lifting your skirts for another? Got used to getting a little, did you? My, I like a girl with spirit."

Erde scowled at him indignantly and put her finger to her lips.

"Ssh, ssh, I know, don't wake the castle!" He grinned, then seemed to get an idea, and moved closer. "Tell you what, missy. I'm happy to accommodate you if you do the same for me."

Erde made the mistake of letting hope show in her eyes.

"Oh, that priest may say you're hell-bait, but I ain't afraid. I've always thought it'd be just fine to have a hot little witch-girl to snuggle up into when I come home. What d'ya say? You just give me some of what you gave the captain, and I'll let you go wherever you want." Georg folded his arms and smiled. "What d'ya say? It's cold out here, so cold, and I got a joint needs warming."

Erde finally understood. She shrank back instinctively and tried to bolt. Georg lunged and pinned her against the iron gate. His heavy wine-breath reminded Erde sickeningly of her father. The alarm raised in the inner yard had moved on to the stables. Horses neighed and stomped, and guardsmen shouted orders. But Georg was too intent on pressing his hips into her and working his hands through the layers of her clothing. Erde had no voice to reason with him. She tried to shove him away.

"Oh, like it rough, do you?" He grunted nastily, sucking

at her neck and tearing at her breeches. "Is this how the captain gave it to you? Did he give it to you hard?"

As his fingers groped for parts of her body that no man had ever touched, Erde knew another game had turned deadly serious. She hadn't a chance of fighting him off. His weight pushing at her outlined the chill of Rainer's sword against her back, and the shape of Alla's dagger against her side. The reminder of Alla and what Alla had done to save her calmed Erde and told her what to do.

She forced herself to relax against Georg's body, to let his rough hands find her skin and thrust themselves impatiently between her legs. While he sighed and groaned and fumbled to loose his own ties, she eased the dagger out of its sheath, slid her arms up as if to embrace him, and rammed the slim blade into him as hard as she could.

She felt the blood spurt, hot and reeking, and was glad it was too dark to see his face as he reeled back from her, clutching his neck, his thick hose sagging around his naked thighs. She held tight to the dagger until his spasms jerked it free, then shrugged her own clothes up around her and dropped to the ground to wedge herself into the cold mud until she could roll through the narrow space beneath the gate.

Free of the mud and iron spikes, she stood shaking, fighting nausea but determined not to give up an ounce of precious nourishment. She could not flee to the villages now. She had just murdered one of their own.

The wind tore up the mountain to stiffen her sodden clothing and hurl razor-edged sleet in her face. But to Erde, stumbling up the rocky path toward the uncertain shelter of the forest, it seemed only fitting that her body should be as numb as her heart.

PART TWO

The Journey into Peril

Chapter Eight

She ran until she was well out of the dim light cast by the gateway lanterns, ran until she could blend with the trees. Her feet found their way by memory. She knew every pothole and rock ledge between the castle walls and the forest. But the mud was deep and treacherous, and the windblown sleet like a barrage of tiny needles. Her boots were full of icy water by the time she reached the first dark firs.

She halted there, gasping more from fear than lack of breath, and resettled her pack to ride her back more securely. A disorderly pursuit was forming in the stable yard. She heard men shouting and dogs barking, eager for the chase. The horses neighed and stomped, fearful of the wind and the dark. She had to think; she had to decide, and she had to do it quickly. Tor Alte's half-dozen dependent villages were scattered among the alpine meadows a little way down the mountain. The biggest had its own parish church, and briefly she considered seeking sanctuary there. But she feared the long reach of Fra Guill. To take refuge in a church would be like walking right into his arms. She could not risk the villages now.

Then where could she go? She had food and warm clothing, but she was wet through with rain and the guardsman's blood. Her feet were already numb. Without shelter, she would freeze before morning. Time enough to worry about the long term when she'd found a place where she could light a fire without being discovered. Rainer's sword was a weight on her back but a goad as well, and Erde would not abandon it on the mountainside the way his poor body had been.

The baying and shouting in the castle yard grew louder and more organized. Numb as she was, Erde felt panic stir beneath her skin, like a torrent swirling below a fragile layer of ice. Only Alla's instructions, murmured over and over in a soothing litany, kept her from bolting headlong into the night probably to brain herself on a low-hanging branch or fall off the nearest cliff. She guessed the riders would go first to the villages, so she headed upward into the trees, away from the path, away from the settled valleys, toward the caves above the tree line. Winter bears sometimes went to ground there but right then, she'd rather negotiate with a sleepy bear than with her father or Fra Guill.

She recalled a cave she'd found with Rainer when they were children. Or perhaps the baroness had showed it to them, on one of the long hikes she'd favored in their company. It lay deep in a barren jumble of rock. Its narrow crack of an entrance seemed to lead nowhere, but actually it camouflaged a descent into a system of tunnels and caverns that burrowed much deeper into the mountain rock than they'd had the courage to explore. Erde struck out bravely in that direction. When the sounds of pursuit passed below her on the road and receded downward, she slowed a bit and began gathering bits of deadwood as she climbed, as much as she had strength to carry, bundling it under her sodden cloak in the hope it would be dry enough to burn by the time she reached her hiding place.

It was near dawn when she got there, the thin gray light coming as sullen and cold as a morning in mid-December. It was oddly still, as if even the weather disdained this bare, unlovely height. The wind had died, and snow as fine as frost dusted the air. The cave was there as she remembered it, a jagged fissure like a sideways smile in a wind-smoothed rock that turned its back on Tor Alte and faced east. *Toward the Russias,* Erde thought, *the home poor Alla will never see again.* Suddenly her exhaustion seemed a weight too great to bear. She staggered through the slitted cave mouth and leaned against the rock wall to catch her breath. So easy to drop the load of wood that cramped her arms and bent her back, so easy to collapse right there in the entrance, cold and wet and shivering, where any pursuer could find her. But while Rainer's sword lay cool and rigid along her spine, she could not even sit. Moving like a sleepwalker, she dug out one of Alla's candles, then crept farther into the cave to take a look around.

She passed through shallow chambers musty with old

leaves and animal dung. She listened for the whisper of bats. Her small candle wavered fitfully, but without it throwing shadows all about, she would not have found the second narrow cleft hidden by an edge of rock. Pitch-black, with a cool stony draft that stirred her short-cropped hair and raised goose bumps on her skin. Her candle flickered, and she put up a hand to shield it. Her only refuge lay in that unexplored dark. Erde eased through the crack.

The tunnel led downward, sharply at first and slippery with rubble. Erde followed it haltingly, hand to the rough wall, and felt rather than saw it level out, just before the wall beside her ended and the flickering circle of her candle flame vanished into darkness. She knew she had come into some sort of cavern. The long dying echo of her step told her the cavern was enormous. Raising the candle like a beacon as high as she could did not reveal a ceiling. But it tossed long shadows across treelike pillars of rock that reminded her of the great-hall of Tor Alte. Ahead in the darkness, something glimmered, like the flash of light off a living eye. Erde froze, then let herself breathe again. A still pool spread over the cavern floor. She had spied the reflection of her candle dancing across the dark water like a sprite. She would have stumbled right into its depths, had she not stopped short, fearing the approach of some one-eyed cave demon. When her heart ceased racing, she bent to touch the glassy surface. The water was numbingly cold and tasted earthy, like the fresh dirt of her grandmother's grave. But she palmed it up eagerly, then walked around its shore and lit her fire in a dry high-vaulted side-chamber, where a tiny shard of gray daylight showed far above when she extinguished her candle.

She unslung her pack and laid out her cloak. The dark stains of the guardsman's blood drew a mottled map of her crime across the fine wool. It was cold in the cave, but Erde kicked the cloak away, unable to wear his death a moment longer. She unstrapped the sword and sank to the ground at last, holding it in her lap. She wasn't ready to think about how deep in the earth she was now, how alone and how completely without a plan. She did allow herself to wonder if she'd been rash to run away, if the known evil was, finally, preferable to the unknown. But Alla had wanted her to go, had said she *must* go, to the king, yes, why not? As good a destination as any. But the king was in Erfurt, two hundred miles to the west, down in the lowlands.

The thought of walking two hundred miles made Erde's head ache. She let it loll back against the cavern wall and closed her eyes, her chill hands still cradling Rainer's sword. She found herself imagining that the hilt was warm to her touch, as if someone else had been holding it. Warm enough to ease her shivering. She told herself it was Rainer himself, watching over her in spirit. She knew if she thought about it long enough, she could convince herself that he was actually there in the cave, and this was too eerie even for her, so she pushed the notion from her mind and accepted the uncanny warmth as an omen of his approval that his sword was with her. She built up the fire and steamed most of the damp from her shirt and leggings, but could get no more than halfway through a single apple before exhaustion finally claimed her.

She woke suddenly, as if from a tap on her shoulder, out of a restless sleep colored by vivid nightmares. She was stiff and sore and could not understand why her bed felt so sharp and hard. Then she remembered where she was, and why.

Her small fire had burned out. The cavern was cold and no comforting sliver of daylight from above penetrated the hovering darkness. It was night, then, outside. She had slept through the entire day. Shivering, Erde felt for her cloak and wrapped it around herself, grateful just to be awake.

Her father had raged through her dreams, touching her where a father shouldn't and calling her by her mother's name. Alla had died in flames again and again, and Erde saw Rainer bloodily cut down by the guardsmen's blades, all the while staring at her with stunned, accusing eyes. Fra Guill had stalked her dreams as well, and the man she had murdered.

Murdered. She let the realization settle in. She'd traded a man's life for her own. She held herself very still, feeling the bloodied cloak close around her like a shroud, bringing her no warmth. She'd been better off before she'd slept, while numbness still dulled her conscience. It was always possible she hadn't killed him, she told herself, but she knew she had. A man could not bleed such torrents and survive. She felt her stomach turn. This wasn't right. Too many people were dying for her sake.

Erde threw her head back to moan, and produced only

raspy breath. Her voice. She'd forgotten. She pushed her breath up against her throat in frustrated gasps. If only she could howl her anguish, like the lunatic boy who lived in the stable yard, she'd never ask to speak human words again.

As she struggled vainly to be heard, sounds from the outer cavern invaded her unwilling silence. Guilt and grief fled as Erde stilled to listen. She had not imagined it: soft steady splashes, and breathing. Something big was moving slowly through the shallow water, shuffling and snuffling, as a bear might do if it had been stirred from early hibernation by the smoke of her fire.

Erde felt no surge of terror. She had already used up her supply. She gripped Alla's little dagger, then left it in its sheath. It was sufficient to kill a man, as she knew too well, but small defense against an angry bear. She thought of Rainer's sword, but couldn't bear to bloody its pure shining blade. Her sudden calm astonished and confused her, but one thing she was sure of was that she didn't want to kill anything, or even try. She'd had enough death and killing, and if the proper punishment for her crime was to be eaten alive, then let one of God's creatures be His avenging angel.

The snuffling neared the entrance to her cave and stopped.

Its presence was more than sound. Erde could *feel* it out there, its questing like a touch on her skin, the anticipation of it an invisible hand pressing on her brain. The bear, or whatever it was, tried the entrance, with the unmistakable scrape of claws on stone. It seemed to struggle, as if it couldn't easily fit through. Briefly, Erde was relieved. Then she realized what this meant about the size of the bear. The passage into her cave was tall and not particularly narrow. This must be a bear out of all natural proportion, not God's bear at all but some terrible demon sent by the Devil to drag her to Hell for her crimes.

A demon. Mere stone would not keep a demon out, and sure enough, in it came. The sound as it squeezed through the opening was the metallic hiss of a sword being drawn. A smell like a snake pit invaded the cavern as the demon dragged itself across the floor.

Some vague terror began to penetrate. Erde clutched the sword to her, rolled herself into a knot beneath her cloak, and waited for fangs and claws and oblivion. The acrid snake smell enveloped her. She sensed the demon hovering above her, heard the creak of bones and scales and a vast hollow rasp of breathing as it lowered its head.

The demon nudged her. Its snout was hard and felt as big as her entire body. It pushed at her gently, snuffled a little, then eased its great weight down beside her, sighed, and began to snore.

Erde didn't move a muscle. The demon had decided to rest, and was saving her for breakfast. Somewhere inside, a voice screamed at her to get up and run while she had the chance. She knew she should. But she was so cold, and this demon was so pleasantly warm. The deep rhythm of its breathing soothed her. After a long while of listening to it snore, Erde decided that either it had put a spell on her or she was still dreaming. She gave up waiting to die and drifted off to sleep.

She dreamed of her father again, and poor dead Rainer, fighting. Cruelly they slashed at each other with shining swords much bigger than the one she'd carried away into exile. Their dueling ground was not the familiar battlements or castle yard of Tor Alte. It was flat, a perfect horizon-stretching flatness such as she had never seen, having grown up in a mountain kingdom. It was as flat as she imagined the ocean to be, with no visible end to it. The surface of this plain was unnaturally dark, like earth seared by fire, and so hard that the men's boots rang against it as if it were hollow, a plain of stone. In the distance behind rose a tall line of towers, shrouded in smoke. A cold wind stung the back of her throat, leaving behind the taste of metal. After a long while watching the terrible battle, unable to turn away, Erde became aware that someone beside her was speaking her name.

She woke again, the dream call still whispering in her ear. She stirred and looked up into a pair of round windows, side by side, glowing amber with the rising sun.

Erde blinked and reconsidered. She was inside a cave. These could not be windows but ... She remembered the demon. Eyes. The demon's eyes! Eyes as big as windows, and lit with their own inner fire. She could not scream, but her body convulsed into a protective ball beneath the folds of her cloak. Breathing shallowly, she waited, but the demon made no move. After a while, she found herself wondering why it didn't just eat her and be done with it.

With a careful finger, Erde drew away a corner of fabric from her eyes. The glowing windows were gone. Dawn had returned to the mountain and the faint light filtering down from above outlined a great horned head set on a long muscular neck, powerful forearms and chest tapering past strong short haunches to a stubby tail that lay curled partly around her. It looked like . . . Erde decided the demon meant to trick her, looking like that, so like a . . .

A dragon?

She suppressed her sudden thrill of joy. Of course it could not be a dragon, not here in this tiny dark cave. And joy in her situation was not logical. A murderess about to be eaten should not feel joyful. It was the dream still possessing her, or the demon's spell. But the trouble with dreams and spells was, even if you knew you were in one, it was hard to know how to get yourself out. The joy within her demanded recognition, even if it was a demon's illusion. Besides, why couldn't it be a dragon?

Erde considered further. If it was a dragon, it might be just as hungry as a demon. Perhaps Alla had been wrong about dragons not eating people. Perhaps a dragon and a demon were the same, like Fra Guill said, and she'd be no better off than if it was a demon pretending to be a dragon.

The demon opened his eyes again and blinked at her slowly. Its transparent lids glided crossways like shimmering curtains of rain. Erde sighed. Their beauty took her breath away.

Could she really be dreaming? Would she, raised in the rich legacy of her grandmother's dragon-tales, have ever dreamed a dragon with no wings? And if it was demon-sent, wouldn't it be a bit more terrifying? This creature seemed big enough when crammed into a hole in the ground with you, but looking it over, she saw it was no match at all for the fantasy dragons of her childhood. Glasswind's back alone had been the size of her whole bedchamber. This dragon, if it was one, was closer to the size of her bed.

And what would a dream-dragon, or even a demon, expect of her, for the oddest thing about this creature was that it seemed to want something of her rather immediately. It only stared and blinked, very slowly, but Erde could *feel* its expectation. Strangely, she felt no threat, though beyond the expectation was hunger, hunger like a longing, like the sharp attention of the dogs in the wood yard when she passed them on her way for a walk: demanding looks, as if it was her responsibility to take them with her and tell them what to do.

Erde stirred in her nest of damp wool and clothing. One could not sit forever, waiting to be eaten. The stiffness in her limbs and a desperate need to relieve herself made it seem very likely that she was not dreaming this dragon after all. She needed to see it more clearly. Perhaps then she would know. She sat up slowly and felt for her satchel, found a candle, flint and tinder, and struck a spark. The dragon drew back in surprise, then lowered its big head again to regard the candle flame with something resembling professional interest.

Erde rose, stretching carefully. The luminous eyes followed her. Logic told her this scaly creature might snap her up at any moment, yet she felt inexplicably calm. She faced it bravely, holding the candle high to study it. It definitely looked like a dragon, or at least a sort of dragon. Staring into its eyes was like standing at the top of a tower, windblown and vertiginous, with voices calling you from a distance.

She was seized by a need to touch it. Amazed by her own boldness, she laid her palm on the bony ridge of the dragon's snout. It felt hard and very rough, like worn granite, but suddenly the joy inside her swelled, as if something warm and needy were pouring into her from outside. The surge abated as soon as she jerked her hand away.

My goodness. Erde sat down again to think.

In her fantasies, she had never bothered about how one communicated with a dragon. She had simply endowed them with human speech. But nose-to-nose with this creature, even an ardent fantast such as herself could not imagine its blunt crocodilian jaw producing comprehensible German. Even if it did by some magic find its tongue, she would not now be able to answer it.

But Erde knew well enough that men's words are not the only medium of communication. A dragon was, after all, an animal of sorts, and she'd never had any trouble talking with animals. She knew to put her hands on them—dogs liked their heads held and horses preferred an arm slung about their shoulders—while thinking about whatever it was she wanted them to know. Somehow, the messages got through.

But dogs had relatively simple agendas and were familiar to her. A dragon was another matter entirely.

As she contemplated it, the dragon began to shift its bulk from one forearm to the other and back again. *It's getting impatient,* Erde concluded. *If I can't figure out what it wants, perhaps it will eat me after all, no matter what Alla said.*

She decided to test whether it would allow her freedom of movement. Holding her candle high, she stepped over the thick scaled curve of its tail and marched slowly across the cavern. It made no move to stop her. But as she neared the entrance, she was nearly brought to her knees by a piercing sense of loss welling up inside, as if from the depths of her soul. Erde cringed in pain and hugged herself, spilling hot wax on her jerkin. The dragon wrenched its bulk around in the narrow space and came trailing after her, making soft mewling noises like a puppy. When it reached her and she did not back away, it quieted. The sharp pang in her heart receded and she could stand up straight again. She stared at it, breathing hard. It stared back, beseechingly.

Erde knew then that this creature was not going to eat her, that in fact it was going to attach itself to her and did not want her to leave without it. Cautiously, she let herself feel a little of that joy inside. After all her years of dreaming and fantasizing, here was an actual living dragon, and it had chosen her. However remarkable that might be, Erde felt there was nothing in her life so far that she was as well prepared for. She put her hand on the dragon's nose and bade it follow, and it did.

She retraced her path around the edge of the underground pool with no destination in mind, wandering for the sheer delight of watching the dragon trudge after her like a worried and faithful hound. It waded through the pool, sending huge dark ripples coursing across the cavern to reflect the candle flame in bright, ever widening circles. It followed her willingly enough through connecting tunnels and caves up toward the surface, but Erde felt its anxiety build with the steady increase of gray light seeping down from the entrance. Where the tunnel began its final ascent, the dragon stopped.

Erde blew out her candle and stowed it in her jerkin. The light from above was just bright enough to see by. She decided to make a quick search for more firewood, and started up the crumbled slope. The dragon swayed uneasily from side to side and broadcast its alarm until Erde put her hands to her ears and begged it to stop. She turned and looked back at it, its head down between its claws like the Devil's hunting dog, a dog of living rock, all gray and dusty in the dim light.

I will be back, she thought at it carefully, in simple words, as if speaking to a small child. It lay there listlessly, with a dog's tragic gaze, and she was sure it had not understood.

But it was not just firewood she needed. She needed to be up top under open sky, for a moment at least. The more she thought about it, the more urgent the need became. She headed upward again, her boots skittering across the brittle surface. Small cascades of broken rock rattled down behind her. She knew she was not being careful, but caution came too late. She did not hear the bear entering from above, or see him until he had already seen her, blocking the passage to his winter den.

It was a large bear, and very touchy. His eyes squinted. He could not see well, but smelled her out instantly. He snarled, and one huge paw slashed out warningly. Erde slid backward down the slope and shrank against the wall, but mere retreat did not satisfy the bear. His roar echoed through the tunnel like thunder as he launched himself down the slope. She fumbled uselessly for her dagger, caught in the folds of her shirt, then lost her footing and fell sliding backward.

Dragon! she thought blindly as she plummeted downward in a hail of gravel and angry brown bear. She hit bottom and rolled into a ball, awaiting the crush of rough fur and the terrible rake of claws. Her last tumble brought her face up, in time to see the dragon snatch up the bear, the whole head in its mouth as if that great hairy bulk weighed nothing. While Erde scrambled up, backing against the cavern wall, the dragon shook the big bear once, very hard. It held the limp corpse dangling in its jaws for a moment, then shambled over to lay it down with delicate formality at Erde's feet.

The baron's daughter had found a new champion.

Chapter Nine

Your dragon awaits you.

And indeed the dragon was waiting, with an expectant look in its eyes, glancing from the pile of dead bear to Erde and back again. The bear was beginning to leak blood from its mouth. Sickened, Erde backed away. When the dragon snatched it up once more and dragged it off into a corner, she understood it was only waiting for a sign, for her permission. Turning away while the dragon noisily devoured its meal, Erde recalled Alla's words again, and wondered how the old woman had known.

Perhaps Alla had been a witch after all. Erde knew that she'd put no spell on Rainer, but she'd had many unusual skills and knew many mysterious things. If being a witch meant being like Alla, Erde didn't see why people thought it was such a bad thing.

She risked a glance over her shoulder. Each time she looked at the dragon, she felt that same surge of wonder and joy. But this time she was glad for the faintness of the light, as faint as her heart became at such a sight. The loud crunching and rending was bad enough. This dragon was not a tidy eater and it was ravenous, as one might expect a newly awakened dragon to be if one knew one's dragon-lore, and Erde considered herself a bit of a lay expert.

She was glad to learn that the dragon had spared her not because it was sated or an herbivore or even particularly mild-mannered. It was hungry and possessed a proper dragonlike appetite, yet it had left her alone. Whatever torturous pathways of thought she followed, she reached the same conclusion in the end: her sense of connection with this implausible creature was a true one.

Your dragon awaits you. She wished Alla had given her

just the smallest clue as to what it awaited her for. Dragons, like all magical beings, had a distinct reason for being. You didn't just acquire one out of simple good fortune.

The Mage-Queen was dragon-bound, but the Mage-Queen, a benevolent power, had been Erde's own fantasy, even if she did sometimes wish she was real, or sometimes forget that she wasn't. In the true dragon-lore, such connections with dragons were spell-wrought. They were generally sought by evil mage-lords, who sacrificed their firstborn or sold their soul to the Devil for the privilege. Erde was fairly sure that killing a man in self-defense, though surely an awful crime, was not quite the equivalent in black magic terms, so this small bit of knowledge left her no more enlightened than before.

The dragon finished bolting its meal. Erde sensed this by the expectant silence that settled in behind her and she knew, just *knew,* that the dragon was waiting for more. Her fleeting concern that once its appetite was whetted, it might move on to her was dispelled by the supplicant quality of its waiting, like a giant nestling, mouth slightly agape, helpless but demanding to be fed. The demanding part she could accept. All dragons expect service from humankind. But helpless?

It thinks I brought it the bear, she realized. *And it wants another.* Erde shook her head. Service was all very well and good, but she was going to have to disabuse this creature of the notion that a fourteen-year-old girl, a fugitive at that, could provide it with a steady supply of dragon-sized dinners. She was just coming to grips with the problem of hiding out alone in a cold cave and feeding herself. The little bits of food she'd brought with her wouldn't last more than a day. Feeding a dragon would require entire barnyards. Why couldn't it feed itself?

Overwhelmed, Erde sank to the cave floor in despair and put her head in her hands.

Oh, Alla, what have I done? What can I do now?

Alla had said, hide out until the priest leaves or go to the king. But Alla had not expected her high-born nursling to effect her escape in blood. Erde could not ask even temporary shelter of the villagers now, or for their help in getting to the king. The man she'd murdered had three children, one of whom was sickly. She would have to remain in the caves, sneaking out only at night to steal whatever food she could find, until life returned to normal at Tor Alte. She was sure her father would be less bothered about her having killed a common soldier in defense of her honor. But then, it seemed her father did not believe she had any honor left. Womanly honor, at least. She wasn't sure he valued any other kind, since he'd shown himself so spendthrift with Rainer's.

Ah, Rainer. In the distraction of the dragon, she'd all but forgotten. How could she? No, she'd never forget. Erde called once more to mind the surprise of his kiss and wrapped the memory deep inside where it would always be safe.

The dragon shifted about in its heavy-limbed dance of impatience. Erde lifted her head and sighed in its direction. It had left the bear's head and claws uneaten. She would have to clean up the mess before it began to smell and attract other dangerous wildlife. The dragon moved a step closer and resettled itself doglike on its haunches. It could not lick its chops—its tongue was not flat and so easily manipulated. It was more like a lizard's tongue, thick and oval, tapering to a blunt point. But Erde had noticed that it often let the slender tip hang out of the side of its mouth, where a space was left between its big canines and its double rows of bicuspids. However endearing, this habit was not dignified, and Erde had always believed dragons to be deeply concerned with their dignity. Apparently not this dragon.

As she sat there staring at her new companion, she found herself thinking of sheep, seeing them rather, fat sheep on a soft green hill, like a daydream, only clearer. Very real in her mind's eye. Oddly, these particular sheep were large and brown and very shaggy, not at all like the thin, gray ewes kept by local herdsmen. Yet they were there in her head and she knew they were sheep. Odder still, the landscape surrounding these strange sheep wasn't familiar either. The hills were much too low and gently rolling, the meadows far too green. There was too much sky. Yet this image in her head was as clear and present as one of her own memories.

Erde peered at the dragon speculatively. Was it the source of these alien visions? Could it conjure and send them at will? Even better, could it receive?

Erde cast about for a way to test her hypothesis, and her eye fell on the grisly bear's head. It was easier to look at, now that it had given her an idea. She watched the dragon closely and called to mind, as quickly and forcefully as she could, her last sight of the bear before she had covered her eyes, all fangs and claws hurtling down on top of her. The dragon's head jerked toward the upward tunnel. A fleshy crest that Erde had not noticed before raised up along the curve of its head and neck like the hackles on a dog. When no bear appeared, the dragon looked back to find itself being studied and seemed to understand that Erde had been testing it. It lowered its crest, shook its great head and let its tongue-tip loll out the side as if ready and willing to play this new game. But the only thing that came to Erde's mind were more images of sheep.

Erde's shoulders sagged. The dragon was either stubborn or stupid, or her theory was incorrect. Or perhaps it was so obsessed with its hunger, it could not think of anything else. She wondered how long it had lain asleep deep inside this mountain, working up an appetite.

Despair overwhelmed her again. But Alla had always said that action was the antidote to despair, so Erde decided to follow her original upward urge. She did need more firewood, and maybe some dry grass for bedding. She sent the dragon an image of herself returning to the cave with her arms laden, though she was careful not to promise it food. She didn't wish to face a dragon's disappointment. She laid a reassuring hand on its snout, still full of wonder that she was actually touching a real dragon, then headed for the surface.

She listened at the cave mouth for a long time, but heard nothing stirring, not even an early hawk or raven. The mountain was shrouded in dense fog. Except for its clinging chill, Erde was grateful for the cover it provided. A wind during the night had swept the rock ledges clear of snow, though it had gathered in the nooks and crannies to remind her once again of the unnatural state of the weather, snow in August. For several hours, she clambered back and forth from her cave to the tree line, gathering up every loose branch or fallen sapling that she could carry.

By midmorning, the fog was clearing. Erde stowed a final armload of twigs inside the cave, then climbed to the top of an old rock slide. From there, hiding behind a large boulder, she could see safely down the other side of the mountain.

A half mile away, the towers of Tor Alte crouched on their own lesser summit, like a lost city rising out of the gray mist that filled the valley in between. It did not look at all like home to her. The massive walls were faceless and bleak under the lowering sky. Erde gazed at it for a long time, searching for a sign of life other than the black and green flag of the von Altes, wind-whipped on the highest tower. She sensed she was waiting for an omen of some sort or a feeling from inside, just the faintest homesickness or longing, enough to tell her she should give up her mad flight and throw herself back on her father's mercy. Nothing came. Only the submerged razor edge of the pain she was running from. Only the memory of Rainer's breathless grin as he glanced up at her from the practice yard. She couldn't think of it. She wouldn't. If a memory was too painful to bear, she would put it aside. That dark pile of stone was someone else's childhood home. Every thing that Erde von Alte longed for there was dead. Now she was glad for the numbness, which had returned as soon as she'd set her eyes on those grim towers and grim walls.

So she could not go home, since she had no home to go to. Besides, to return would imply acceptance of Alla's death and Rainer's murder. But knowing she could not go home did not tell her where to go instead, or whether she should leave the dragon where it had found her. Sneaking away without it would surely improve her own chances of escaping undetected, but the notion came and went as if it did not even bear considering. Just when she'd lost everything, the dragon had appeared. This was certainly the sign she was looking for.

Yet she waited, staring down at the fog-wreathed fortress, so still that the arm she leaned on went to sleep. She woke with a tingle when movement below caught her eye and she jerked upright.

A party of several dozen riders appeared outside the Dragon Gate, milling and dodging, no standard raised to identify them. The hounds were no more than a crowd of tiny dancing blurs, but their excited baying carried easily through the mountain quiet. Erde knew the hungry cry of the Baron's Hunt.

Erde flattened herself against the boulder, then scrambled back down the rock slide. Her panic didn't loose its grip until she was well inside the cave, far from searching eye of daylight, where finally she let reason take hold. She laid her cloak out on the floor, piled on as much of the firewood as it would hold and dragged it down the inner tunnel toward her hideout and the dragon. *Her* dragon.

Chapter Ten

She scrubbed the blood from her cloak as best she could, and steamed it dry. She tended the fire. She spent an hour retrimming her shorn hair. She tried to keep too busy to eat, but by nightfall she had finished all her food. It had seemed like so much more when it was heavy in her pack. Now it barely filled her, and the dragon too was hungry, so hungry it could not keep still. It paced in the outer caverns like a caged lion, and she wondered why it didn't go forage for itself the way dragons were supposed to do. Of course, its not having any wings might make that difficult. Dragons were supposed to be able to drop out of the air and scoop up their unsuspecting victims. She'd also assumed all dragons were created fully formed, but perhaps this one was young and still developing its wings. Meanwhile, it would have to sneak up on its prey and drag it away like any other large carnivore.

Listening to it pace and snuffle in the outer darkness, Erde knew that the dragon would drive her back into the open even before her own hunger and growing claustrophobia got the better of her. Up there it could surely feed itself—she hoped then it would cease its steady barrage of sheep images, crowding up her brain when she was desperate for a clear head to make her plans.

Two things she was sure of: she was not going back to Tor Alte now—maybe not ever—and she had to get the dragon out of the caves. She had seen it move fast when it felt motivated, but could it move fast enough to elude the Baron's Hunt, which would surely track them down before long? She had to get it away, down the mountain into the lowlands, where her face wasn't known, where the farmers were sure to have fatter sheep in their meadows and where she wasn't on a first-name basis with practically every deer in the forest. And better to do it sooner than later, while they were both still strong, or before the half-starved dragon devoured her in desperation. Perhaps just down and away was enough of a destination for the time being. If she knew she was heading in the general direction of Erfurt and the king's court, she could learn the way as she went along.

At last the time came when drinking the cold earthy water of the underground pool no longer slaked her hunger pangs. Erde brushed rock dust from her shirtfront, put on all her clothes, and packed up her meager possessions. She made a sling for Rainer's sword from strips of the sheeting that had bound its blade. Now it rested at an angle across her back, with the hilt by her right ear. She settled it comfortably and shouldered her satchel. She sent a *follow-me* image to the dragon and led it to the surface.

The snow and mists had cleared. The temperature was chilly but a little more like a normal mountain night in August. Erde was sure the Hunt had been at the cave mouth at some time during the day. The bits of bare ground seemed more scuffed than she remembered and she smelled horse dung. The Hunt never ranged this high because neither did the deer, which confirmed her assumption that the baron had sent his huntsman after his daughter. She wondered if it was dragon-scent that had kept the hounds outside the cave.

A clear half-moon lit their way, scudding through broken clouds, but the journey down was slow and perilous, slippery with leaves that were already beginning to fall from the trees. Erde knew every trail and the dragon appeared to have remarkable night vision, but she had never traveled these steep-sided woods with a pack and a man's sword strapped to her back. Plus the dragon was curious about everything and a little clumsy. Its horns, matched arcs of shining ivory, caught in overhanging branches. Its claws slid on the rock. It had a pronounced tendency to go crashing through the noisiest brush or to send cascades of loose stones rattling down the mountainside. It was like fleeing through the forest with a very large, dusty child. Erde was forced constantly to impress on it the need for silence, while urging it ever onward.

She rested as often as she dared. She had thought her mountain walks fairly strenuous until now, when she could no longer go home to food and a warm fire after a few hours. But fear kept her moving past her first exhaustion, and later she found new strength for the dragon's sake.

She stayed well away from the mountain villages so that the dragon would have no cause to become interested in them. She wanted it to forage on its own, but in the forests. Mysteriously missing livestock so close to Tor Alte would alert the Hunt. The countryside was aroused enough already, and she didn't want *her* dragon made a target for Fra Guill's dragon hatred. Yet the dragon didn't show much inclination to hunt, despite its hunger. It did halt once, on a hill above an isolated farmstead, at the sound of a dog barking. It raised its huge nostrils to the wind and would not be lured forward. The image invading Erde's mind was finally a new one, a kind of aggressive blank that shoved aside all her own thoughts, rather like blundering into a blinding snowstorm inside your head. Erde suffered a few astonished moments of panic before she could assure herself she wasn't going mad and her brain hadn't broken. She noticed that her face was pressed into a questioning frown, and decided that the blankness was the dragon's way of demanding information.

She conjured the sleeping farmstead in her mind, its muddy rutted yard, its stubby slate-roofed cottage, every detail but its barns and herd stock. She did add in the dog for verisimilitude, but made it a small thin mongrel not worthy of a dragon's attention, too irritating to be bothered with. Finally, the dragon moved on, and Erde learned that its pride was vulnerable and could be played upon to advantage. But she was not cheered by the fact that she had barely yet learned to communicate with the creature and she was lying to it already.

Just before dawn, it began to rain lightly, blown into a chill mist by gusty breezes more reminiscent of October than August. Erde's route, half-knowing, half-random, took them above the village of Tubin, where the richest of the local merchants lived. Erde had visited it many times with her father. One of the merchants there sold the baron all his silks and velvets. Taking shelter in a pine grove where she could look down at Tubin's dark, once fertile valley, she recalled that merchant's elaborately paneled shop, with its crackling hearth fire, and the small supper he laid out for his best customers. She nearly wept. She had never been so cold and hungry in her life.

Tubin was practically a town. It had several main streets and a stout gated wall protecting its market district. Inside the wall, the cobbled church square was lined with the merchants' two-storied stone houses. But most of the town lived outside the wall, among the fields and farmyards. Erde resolved to find dinner here for her dragon and later, for herself, before her strength failed her completely.

She searched out a forest gorge where the dragon could hide, on a dry ledge overhung by tall dark pines clinging to the vertical rock. She rested briefly, then left the sword and her pack in his care. The rain had stopped but not the biting wind. Erde hugged her cloak closely and shivered. She thought it odd, as she trudged through the dark sodden meadows outlying the farmsteads, to hear the bell in the church tower tolling before any sign of daylight, not the quick peals of celebration or the hard-edged clang of alarm but slow and steady like the drumbeat of a marching army.

She heard dogs barking from the cottages closest to the road. Keeping tightly to the deeper shadow of hedges and fence lines, Erde spotted lanterns moving along the road, a group of farm folk murmuring among themselves as they walked into town. She smeared mud on her cheeks and, reluctantly, on her cloak whose fine wool had already once betrayed her identity. She shrugged it high around her shoulders, leaving the prentice cap showing. Nervous about going in among people again but driven by the fever of her hunger, she fell in behind the group on the road, then realized there were others behind them, and more behind them. She saw she was caught up in a moving throng, and nearly bolted. But away from the dim flare of the lanterns, it was dark enough and no one took any special notice of her. She struggled to walk steadily, not to show her abnormal exhaustion in any obvious way. The road was muddy and slick. Cold rainwater lay deep in the wheel ruts and soaked into her boots. But Erde was relieved to be among people again, especially people who weren't chasing her. And she was curious to know what would make the entire countryside head into town in the small hours before dawn. She quickened her pace to catch up with the two men directly in front of her, to eavesdrop on their subdued conversation.

". . . rode into my yard and walked right into the smokehouse," muttered the tall one on the right. "Started cutting down hams. Said the baron ordered it."

"That priest is eating well enough," his companion growled.

"Better than we are."

"Wasn't no surprise though, when he pointed that one out," the stouter man declared. "And she standing right there in the crowd like she'd lived in the village all her life, same as the rest of us."

Erde could not hear the tall man's reply, muttered beneath the woolen blanket he'd wrapped around him for warmth. But the stout man seemed to feel the need to prove his great foresight further. "Sure, remember Podi's cow, after she visited his wife that time? And the smith's cousin, who lost her gold ring in the well? She'd had some dealings with her."

The tall man muttered again. Erde strained and still could not hear him. The stout man's voice only got louder.

"She was *your* neighbor, Deit. You'd better be keeping a closer eye out. What about all this god-forsaken rain and cold? Business so bad all around and you don't wonder why?"

"Don't talk to me!" The tall man's chin finally emerged from its cocoon. "We lived side by side for years with little more than a how-de-do. It was you always tagging after the woman, so even your wife could notice."

The stout man glanced around fearfully, in case someone might have overheard. "Well, hell, a young widow woman usually likes a little company. If I'd have known then . . ."

"You didn't know nothing till she turned you down. Now, my wife was friendly to her. Said she had a healer's gift. Saved my boy from the agues that time. I had nothing against her. Just looks to me like she turned down one man too many."

"Here, now, what're you saying?"

"Nothing, nothing."

"Your trouble is, Deit, you're always saying something."

"I said, I ain't saying nothing."

"Well, I wouldn't, if I were you, not out loud where the holy brothers can hear you or you'll end up in one his visions. You're lucky we're such old friends."

Erde nearly turned and fled. But hunger spoke more eloquently than panic. If there was a crowd in town, there might be food sellers, and if the crowd got excited, it might be easier to lift a loaf or a pie during a distraction. She promised herself that if she spotted so much as the sleeve of a white-robe, she'd be gone in a flash. She let the crowd carry her through the town gates and toward the main square, following the ceaseless grim summons of the church bell.

It was warmer inside the gates, out of the cold ceaseless wind. The streets were narrow, walled in by tall stone houses and shops, overhung with wooden signs that dripped rainwater into Erde's face. The traffic thickened as they neared the square, and she avoided anyone carrying a lighted lantern. She had been in this town before as her father's daughter. Someone might recognize her.

People poured in from the side streets, men and women, old people hobbling along on canes, sleepy-eyed children in their parents' arms. Among adults again, Erde was once more a child, yet she knew her childhood was over, however prematurely. She felt her first tinge of homesickness, of nostalgia for the security of having adults to care for her and tell her what to do. Though their parents' faces were reserved and serious as they moved through the dark wet streets, the young boys darted wildly in and out of the crowd, splashing through puddles, snatching at each other's tunics and hooting as if it were a feast-day celebration. Erde envied their ruthless innocence. Those boys suffered no shame over the sweet-cake they stole from the neighbor's kitchen window, or the dead mouse on their sister's pillow. But then, they had no cause for *real* shame, not like she did.

The memory of Georg flailing backward seized her, filling her nostrils with the sweet-sour smell of his blood. Erde stumbled, her empty stomach turning, and nearly fell. She wrapped her arms around her chest and grasped herself hard for a moment, leaning weakly against the rough wall of a boot-maker's shop, gasping and fighting for balance while the throng flowed past unawares.

Except the hand that caught her elbow. "All right there, lad?"

She was alert in an instant, sure she'd been discovered. She nodded without looking up.

"Sure, are you? You look a bit peaked." The voice was gruff and matter-of-fact. "Look like you slept in a mud puddle."

Erde ventured an upward glance. The man's face was solid, seamy and blessedly unfamiliar. He was quite tall but carried himself with a diffident stoop, in the way of tall people who do not favor always relating downward to the rest of the world. Or, she thought next, in the way of people who wish not to be noticed. His damp, close-cropped hair and beard were silvery gray, but the arm supporting her was strong, his grip on her elbow secure. His cheeks were weather-hardened but somewhat puffy. Erde thought she recognized the signs. But if this man was a drinker, he was certainly sober now. The most striking thing about him was his leather jerkin, worn and sturdy but dyed a deep red. Erde couldn't imagine choosing to wear the color of blood. Still, something about the garment seemed oddly familiar, though she was sure she had never seen this man before.

"Well, can you walk?"

She tried a quick smile and a nod. If he was from town, he would know that she wasn't. She did not want him getting too friendly or inquisitive.

"Speak up, lad. Are your parents about?"

A stranger. She was safe for a while, then. Erde shrugged, shook her head and, inspired at last, put her fingers to her throat in the time-honored explanatory gesture of mutes.

"Oh. That's how it is. I see."

She nodded again, trying now to slip invisibly out of his grasp.

"Well, I'm sorry for that, boy." The man frowned, not without pity but as if the very idea stood in for all the world's other evils as well. "Let me guess . . . when was the last time you ate something?"

Her eyes flicked at him and away so fast that he chuckled out loud. "No need to be ashamed. We're all a little short these days." He dug into the wide studded belt that banded his peculiar red jerkin, and brought out a coin. He flipped it to her, and Erde, untrained in such maneuvers, fumbled it and nearly dropped it on the cobbles before managing a firm grip. She shot him a look of gratitude, even as she wondered why he should bother to help an unknown prentice lad.

Now the man was studying her speculatively, as if he regretted the coin already. Fearing he might ask for it back or demand some service in return, Erde saluted him quickly with her clenched fist and ducked away. He called after her, but she managed to lose herself in the crowd. It wasn't until she was well away from him that she sneaked a glance at the coin. She nearly dropped it again. It was a silver mark, stamped with the king's portrait on one side and the royal coat-of-arms on the other. It conjured a sudden image of festival market days and her grandmother's long-fingered hands, so like her own, counting out in the king's own currency her careful payment for a bolt of Italian velvet or a bushel of exotic citrus.

Erde could hardly believe her good fortune. She held in her hand money enough to buy food for a month, or maybe, several sheep.

Chapter Eleven

She nearly ran after the man in the red jerkin to thank him properly. But the impulse quickly passed. It was only her upbringing talking, appropriate for a baron's daughter but not for a fugitive murderess. Besides, the man must have some ulterior motive to go about giving silver marks to beggar boys. Either that or he was so very rich that having one mark less would mean little to him.

The excitement of this windfall infused her with new energy. She could actually buy her dinner now, like a normal honest citizen. Clutching the coin in her palm as if it were a religious relic, she fell in with the crowd again, streaming along the main thoroughfare that led to the church square. The many lanterns swinging in people's hands made the chill puddled street seem warm and festive. Most of the single-story shops were still shuttered, but here and there, lamps gleamed behind wrinkled glass as the hungrier shopkeepers prepared to open early. The food sellers would bring their wares along on carts and set up at the big event, wherever the crowd was headed. Erde was greatly cheered by the prospect of a hot meal. She strode along in her most boylike gait, just on the verge of enjoying herself.

The market square was already packed with people, with crowds pouring in from all directions. Erde had never seen it so full, even on market days, especially so early in the morning. She thought back through the church calendar, wondering if in the recent chaos of her life, she'd forgotten some major religious festival.

Her own throng arrived at the far end of the broad windy rectangle, opposite the church. Tubin's church was the largest in the baronage, and Erde thought it a proper model for all churches, even though the two-towered sandstone edifice was as yet uncompleted and she had never known it without scaffolding veiling its tall facade. Standing on tiptoe, she could see the top few tiers of scaffolding over the heads of the crowd, the maze of rain-heavy canvas windshields and the ramps and cross-bracing dripping water. Behind it all, like an unfinished sun, rose the outline of the huge round window that the monsignor claimed to be the latest in church design, which he said would surely convince the Bishop of Ulm to elevate it from church to cathedral, and thus bring visitors and pilgrims from far and wide into Tubin's marketplace. Come dawn, the masons would return to continue mortaring the delicate curved mullions. When completed, the window was to be fitted with the finest colored glass imported all the way from Venezia.

She was distracted from her reverie by the aroma of roasted meat, drowning out even the heavy odors of farmer's boots and unlaundered clothing. Searching frantically above the heads of the milling townspeople, Erde spotted the iron braziers burning on sturdy flatbed wagons parked along one side of the square. Flame shadows danced across the painted signs and multipaned windows of the craft guild halls behind. Prentice boys dodged about, dark shapes bobbing against firelight, tossing on armloads of wood, turning the spit-cranks. The spitted carcasses were thinner and stringier than the fare that had always graced the baron's table. Once she'd have thought them too scrawny to be worth cooking. Now she thought differently. Her mouth watered. She thought of the dragon with its tongue-tip hanging out, and laughed in anticipation, except that what came out of her mouth could hardly be called a laugh, being all breath and no sound. It was the first time she'd even attempted a laugh in the three days since she'd lost her voice. Remembering why drained the breath and joy right out of her, leaving only hunger, now honed to a knife's edge of determination. Her whole body tightened like a fist. She had to restrain herself from pushing through the crowd. She had an inkling now of why a person might kill in order to eat.

The first food seller she approached was a thin, quiet woman who glanced at the coin on Erde's palm and shook her head. "You could buy the whole stock and stall with that coin, dearie, and what would I have left to give you in change? Tell your master you need something smaller next time."

Erde nodded her thanks and moved on. The next man

wouldn't even look at her. He was too busy fawning over a
large party of richly dressed men who seemed intent on devouring the entire scrawny lamb turning on his spit, before
it was even cooked. Erde ducked away, wanting to avoid any
local landowners who might know her father. She passed by
a baker's boy unpacking a small basket of loaves and meat
pies onto a portable tray. The pies smelled delicious, but she
was sure he wouldn't have change for her silver mark. At
the next stall, thin chickens dripped over glowing coals.
Erde showed her coin to the red-faced owner, pointing and
nodding at the biggest hen.

The food seller squinted at the coin. "What's that you've
got, boy?"

Erde held it into the light of his pole-lantern. The man
snatched at it, narrowly missing it. Erde sprang back a step,
but pointed again at the sizzling bird.

The man grinned. "Oh, *that* one? Now *that* one'll cost you
all of it." He held out his hand.

Erde shook her head, amazed that she was even tempted.

"You don't think I know where you got that?" the meat-
seller hissed. He began to wave his arms and shout at her.
"What do you think I am! Get away from me, you little
thief!"

Erde backed away from him, appalled. The prentices had
stopped their fueling and cranking to stare in sullen hope of
an interesting fight. Erde turned and fled into the crowd, re-
considering the value of Red-jerkin's gift. Maybe he'd
meant to get her caught. She might be forced to steal her
meal after all.

There was a stir in the market square. Something was going on in front of the church. The throng was lining up now,
in disorderly rows three and four deep. Small children were
being lifted up to sit on their fathers' shoulders. They
blocked Erde's view of the square, but food was more important to her right then than whatever ceremony was about
to begin. She made her way along the back row toward the
end of the line of food stalls to try her luck again. Suddenly,
the crowd in front of her parted in a wave and regrouped to
open a passage from a side street into the square. A hush fell
over them. Even the children lowered their voices. Necks
craned in the direction of a muffled drumbeat and the creak
of wagon wheels. Erde peered around the plump shoulder of
the woman in front of her, and shrank back immediately.

White-robes!

Marching to solemn cadence in their all-too-familiar double-file formation came Fra Guill's thirty acolytes, heads bowed, deeply cowled. Two of them walked a pace ahead, beating small hand drums. The rest pulled a slat-sided wooden cart, leaning into the ropes as if the burden were greater than any mere mortal could bear. Yet the cart was small and it carried only a solitary woman.

Slim torches burned at the cart's four corners. The woman stood tall, gripping the thigh-high side rails, shivering visibly but staring straight ahead. She wore only a rough muslin shift, wet through from the rain, so that her full, handsome breasts and smooth hips were plain for all to see. Erde found herself blushing for the woman's sake. She had never seen a person in such a state of public undress. How could she hold her head so high? Had she no modesty?

Among the watchers, the wives muttered their fear and disapproval, which only barely hid their envy, for the woman was very beautiful. The men shifted about and hiked up their clothing at the crotch.

Then Erde noticed that the woman's wrists were tightly bound to the rails, and she felt her stomach drop away from her backbone and every hair on her body thrill with horror. Now she understood the conversation she had overheard on the road into town. She had stumbled onto a witch-trial. She was unsure why this complete stranger's predicament should compel her so, except that it reminded her of Alla. And it was confusing to sense a faint stirring of pride that the woman could look so strong and beautiful, even when wet and shivering and obviously terrified. Erde had promised to flee at the very scent of a white-robe, but now she found she could not.

When the grim procession had passed and the last white-robe had put his back to her, she stole a glance after them. In the square, at the bottom of the church steps, prentice boys hauled canvas tarps off of a stack of twigs and branches wrapped with grass into thirteen bundles. The canvas had kept the grass pale and dry. The twigs were dark with a coating of pine tar. Inside each bundle was a stack of logs. Erde's horror increased. This was not a trial at all, it was a burning. The white-robes had found a victim. *Run, run,* urged her voice of reason, but morbid fascination held her rooted to the spot.

Her grandmother, the baroness, had a dislike of witch-burnings which many considered peculiar, so they had not been common around Tor Alte during her reign. She would not allow them on her own lands and discouraged her household from attending them elsewhere. Yet it seemed to Erde that she'd heard almost every woman she knew over child-bearing age accused of being a witch at some point or another, particularly if they did something out of the ordinary. The baroness herself came under suspicion as often as any. Erde had never thought much about it. Not that she didn't believe in witches. She'd heard the stories of witches' spells and curses. Sometimes she'd even seen the results. But she couldn't take such talk seriously about people she knew—except maybe the chicken-crone.

But the chicken-crone was old and impossibly ugly. The woman in the church square was still young and lovely, most likely a mother of young children. She must have done something very awful indeed to deserve the stake at her age. But then, Brother Guillemo had passed over the chicken-crone and tried to burn Alla. Erde knew Alla hadn't deserved burning, whether she was a witch or not.

The cart pulled up at the base of the church steps and the white-robes halted with a resounding slap of sandals against stone. She looked for Guillemo among them, but as usual, their faces were deep in the shadow of their hoods. The drumming stopped, the bell ceased its tolling. The sudden hush was deafening, as if everyone in the square had caught their breath. The torches on the cart danced and snapped, the only sound but for a child crying somewhere in the crowd. Their bright heat spilled across the wet paving stones as if the pyre was lighted already. Erde recalled the reflection of herself afire in her father's cold eyes, and wished she'd fled when she could have done it unnoticed. Only by a supreme exertion of will did she keep herself from rushing in blind panic from the square. The witch-woman's frozen stare was like the eyes of the deer before the huntsman's grace stroke, calm with the understanding that struggle was useless and in the end, degrading.

When the silence had stretched almost to the breaking point, one of the drummers threw back his hood, set down his drum, and mounted the steps. Guillemo. Of course. Playing the crowd as usual. Erde shrank farther back into the press of bodies, fearful of his searching gaze, which had proved so adept at picking her out, perhaps even in so large a throng as this where he could not possibly expect to find her. One of the brothers held out a torch to him. The others began piling the bundled wood and twigs inside the cart, ringing the witch-woman's feet. Guillemo accepted the torch with elaborate humility. At the top of the steps, he crossed the entry porch and swung up the nearest ladder to the masons' scaffold. He climbed briskly, torch in hand, to the second, then the third level, where he set the torch into a workman's brazier and spread his arms for attention.

Which he already had. Every eye in the square had been fixed on him breathlessly from the instant he'd grabbed the torch and started up the scaffold.

"Oh my people! I call you to witness!" The priest's deep voice carried to the back of the crowd, echoing like cannon fire off the stone facades of the merchants' houses and guild halls, like the thunder of avalanches rolling down from the surrounding mountains. "The Time of Plague is upon us! As the dawn brings light today, the Light of God will enter this place as we make a bold stroke against Satan, our mortal enemy. But ridding ourselves of one viper does not clean out the whole deadly hidden nest!"

At his gesture to the brothers below, the drums rolled again. A black-garbed priest of the parish ushered two children from inside to stand on the church steps. They had been dressed in white, in clothes obviously not their own. Bitterly, Erde decided Guillemo had missed his proper calling. He should have been an actor, or a creator of theatricals. At least then his madness would have remained relatively benign.

One of the children was a girl nearly Erde's age. The younger, a boy, tried to break free and run to the woman standing in the cart, but the priest held him firm. Guillemo began his harangue, pacing up and down the scaffold platform just as he had on the bench in the baron's eating hall, as if it were a pulpit.

"See here, oh my people, the corruption of Innocence! See here how the Devil hides himself in alluring disguise . . ."

Erde stopped listening. She felt a sob working its way up from deep in her gut. She could not press her hands to her ears or sing hymns to drown him out, as she'd once seen villagers do to a priest who bored them with his sermon. She eased herself backward, letting heads and shoulders screen her view, then turned away as if to canvas the food stalls. To her horror, there behind the baker's boy was the man in the red jerkin, his glance casually taking in the crowd as if he was looking for someone who might not want to be found. Erde feared it might be her, for Red-jerkin was probably one of Guillemo's civilian searchers, or even a white-robe in disguise! She hunched into her cloak and drew up the hood, as if against the rain, which had stopped a while ago. She was trapped. What a bold and reckless notion it had been to come into town!

Fighting for calm enough to consider her options, Erde decided she had a better chance getting past Red-jerkin than the combined forces in front of the church. She observed him covertly for a while from beneath the fold of her hood, and because she was watching him so carefully, she noticed the change in his attention when Guillemo threw into his rant something about the king, some not-so-veiled insult. The crowd pressed forward, murmuring their approval. A few clenched fists were raised. And Erde saw the anger that flushed Red-jerkin's face, his glare at Guillemo as quick and venomous as a snake-strike and as quickly hidden again behind his former businesslike manner.

Perhaps not the priest's man after all. What sort of man, then, to care so much for the honor of the king? Erde knew she was confused about this issue. Tor Alte was too rugged, too far away and too unimportant to be on the aging monarch's visiting schedule. The king was at most an ideal to her, since her grandmother while she ruled had offered all due fealty and respect to this distant sovereign, insisting that a central absolute authority helped keep civilization together. But her son disagreed, and since her death, Josef von Alte had been increasingly vocal about the king's incompetence and irresponsibility, as well as his presumption in claiming sovereignty over so many far-flung baronetcies, especially when his own family lands weren't much to speak of. Her father even spoke positively of the widening split between the old king and his barons.

So Erde thought it peculiar that an obvious man of the world such as Red-jerkin would take a common complaint so much to heart. She felt that she knew a secret about him, and that she was somehow obscurely privileged, even though she hoped never to lay eyes on him again. She wondered if he served any of her father's vassal barons. At least she could see he had no love in his heart for Guillemo.

She meant to sneak past him while his attention was engaged, but then she heard Tor Alte's name flung against the stone facades to echo around the square. A spontaneous roar rose from the crowd, then died away into a darkening murmur. She saw Guillemo pause, high on the scaffolding, waiting them out, quieting them with little waves of his hands until he could be heard again.

"And lo! You've all heard rumor of the trouble at Tor Alte! Now let me tell you the truth of it! Your own, your very own valiant and pious lord cannot keep the Devil from his door! Consider that, oh my people! If the most high cannot protect themselves, woe be upon the lowly! Woe indeed!

"Your own baron's immortal soul was in deepest peril when I arrived, and he never suspecting it! God help *him,* had I not found him in time to root out the Evil that dwelt in that stronghold, poised as it was to seize control!

"But all glory be to God and all his saints, who protected me from evil and put the strength of righteousness in my hand! The witch of Tor Alte is dead and her spells and demons could not harm me!" Fra Guill's right arm shot up, fist clenched as if it held a flaming sword. The crowd roared again and shook their own raised fists. "She claimed innocence like this one here, and like this one here, she was put to the test by the holy office of the Church. Oh my people, that you'd been there to witness it! The fire of His Righteous Wrath shriveled her into cinders right as she stood there, spewing out her pernicious lies!"

You lie! Erde was grateful she had no voice to betray her now when she'd have been unable to keep from screaming her outrage. *Alla took her own life to keep it from your hands!*

"A sacred day!" the priest howled, "A holy day, oh my people! The witch is dead, and her warlock minion!" Again, another growling roar, and again Guillemo waited for quiet.

"But wait, oh my people, but wait . . ." He dropped his arms as if in defeat and hung his dark head as he paced back and forth in an eloquent posture of shame and torment. Then he turned to face the square, palms spread in entreaty. "It is not all good news I bring you this day. We had one holy victory at Tor Alte, and will have another here today. But, oh my people, here is the sad tiding I bring you: though your good baron was saved by God's Will, working through His most humble servant, I did not come to Tor Alte in time to save the baron's only daughter! The black evil that lodged in her grew desperate at my advance, supported by the strength of my good brothers, God's holy champions. It stole away the innocent child's voice to prevent her from speaking its name in exorcism! It corrupted her sweet obedient womanhood!"

The crowd moaned as one. This time Guillemo did not wait for quiet. He let the horrified murmur swell, then raised his own voice over theirs until the very air shrilled with it. Erde's skin prickled with the eerie power he possessed. "That blackest Evil put the sword of Darkness in her hand and raised up her child's arm against an innocent man so that she slew him and then another and another until no man was left to stand against her and she escaped! Escaped, oh my people! This demon incarnate walks abroad among us!"

Erde felt his eyes sweep the crowd, felt his searching glance, felt despair and terror close around her like a vise. She backed up blindly, bumping the spectators behind her. But they were too inflamed with the priest's rhetoric to notice. What soul would believe her now, in the face of such convincing lies? She almost believed him herself, staring at him up there, seeing him as the crowd saw him: a militant saint or angel, larger than life, with the torch blazing behind him and the new dawn bleaching the shadowed tint of his robe to silver.

"And here is my revelation!" cried the man on the scaffold. "Another piece has been revealed to me of the mysterious dream-omen that stalks me every hour I lay down in sleep, my God-sent holy vision of the witch-child and the Devil's Paladin! This is the child, oh my people! The witch-child is come among us and she is a child you all have known, become an agent of Satan who seeks the destruction of your immortal souls! We must call on our God to protect us! THE DAYS OF PLAGUE ARE AT HAND!"

The priest fell to his knees on the swaying scaffold. In the square below, four of the white-robes grabbed the torches that burned at the corners of the witch-cart and stood with them at the ready. Guillemo tore open his robe, spread his arms wide and bared his naked hairy chest to the heavens. "Rise up in flame against the powers of darkness, o my people! Set the holy and cleansing fire of righteousness! Burn this evil from the land ... and ... from ... our ... SOULS!!!"

The four white-robes flung their torches at the witch-cart. The grass bindings on the bundles caught in a rush, speeding

their eager blaze to the tar-soaked twigs. On the church
steps, the little boy began to wail and beat his fists against
the priest who held him. The girl-child just stared ahead,
seeing nothing. Flame and dark smoke exploded around the
witch-woman faster than a gasp of breath. At first she
coughed and tried to turn her head away. The useless poignant gesture tore at Erde's heart. Then the woman's brave
composure deserted her. She struggled senselessly against
her bindings until her wrists tore and bled. Erde's hands
worked at her own wrists. She feared the poor woman might
tear her arms from their sockets, like a wild animal pinned
in a snare. When at last the fire licked at the hem of her
shift, the crowd sighed and leaned forward. The woman began to scream.

Erde spun away through the press of eager spectators,
blind and nauseous, seeing herself burning, breathing that
black acrid smoke, with those same soul-rending shrieks
tearing the life from her own lungs. This would be her fate,
if Fra Guill ever got his hands on her.

Around her, children sobbed and the women crossed
themselves, weeping and fainting. Erde shoved through the
confusion unheeding. When she broke free of the crowd, she
found herself two steps from the baker's tray, where the boy
had left it to climb up one of the brazier carts for a better
view. There, he danced up and down, his small fists
clenched and his eyes riveted to the spectacle.

Erde learned then that hunger is a strong instinct. Like a
rush of cold water, cunning cleared her head. She dropped
the silver mark into the heel of her boot, then quickly doubled up the flap of her cloak to make a pocket. She darted
a glance up and down the line of food stalls. No one watching. Like the baker's boy, the entire throng was rapt by the
witch-woman's death throes.

Except Red-jerkin. He had spotted her from the far end
near the church. Her movement counter to the crowd had
drawn his attention. Erde froze like a wild animal, and their
eyes met. He raised his arm a bit, as if to signal her covertly,
then started to work his way through the throng in her direction. It seemed that he too was seeking to avoid notice, and
this terrified her all the more. What unknown pursuers lay in
wait for her in addition to the known?

Erde let instinct take hold. She stepped up to the baker's
tray, cleared the entire surface into her cloak with one sweep

of her arm. Then for the second time in three days, she turned and ran for her life.

The streets of Tubin were deserted as the unwelcome dawn lightened the narrow band of sky between the rooftops to the color of pewter. The wet cobbles and stone walls shone dully as if the entire world had turned to metal, slick, cold, and gleaming with malice. Clutching her laden cloak against her breast as if it were her life and not mere bread that she carried, Erde ran with the last of her strength. She ran for the dragon. If she could only reach the dragon, she would be safe. Even when her breath threatened to fail her, she would not stop, could not even think of stopping, sure that the echo of her own footfall in the narrow wet streets was the clack of Red-jerkin's booted heels on the paving behind her.

But she cleared the town gates safely and swerved off the main road into the maze of cottages and yards and kitchen gardens. There, she hid gasping behind a hayrick for long enough to assure herself that there was no pursuit, and long enough to gobble one of the meat pies she had stolen without inhaling the bulk of it into her lungs.

When her breathing had steadied, she chose a more concertedly circuitous retreat through the emptied farmsteads. There was no one about, but she was weak and shaking with exhaustion. She had no more flight in her. But the food did help. In one unguarded cottage yard, she found a small flock of goats penned in a muddy thornbrush corral. Erde halted, considering, while she wolfed down another pie. She spotted a coil of rope abandoned atop a barrel, and this somehow decided her. She dug the silver mark out of her boot, then searched out two especially long curving thorns from the brush fence. At the cottage door, she stuck the thorns crosswise into the soft, worn planking to form a tiny cradle, into which she slid the silver coin. The side stamped with the King's Arms was facing out, and she noticed that a horned and rampant dragon supported the shield. An omen of good favor, she decided, pressing at it to be sure it would rest there safely until discovered.

She ate another meat pie. Then she returned to the corral to collect her dragon's dinner.

Chapter Twelve

Erde's dragon-lore suggested that once well fed, a dragon could go several weeks before eating again. She hoped this proved to be true. She'd had enough cause already to wonder if much of the lore in her grandmother's stories was out of date.

The outlook was promising at the moment, with the dragon sated and drowsy beside her on the ledge and three goats out of ten remaining, currently grazing away with surprising equanimity in the gorge below. One was a sturdy black and white spotted milker, taller and sleeker than the rest, evidently due to sheer force of personality. If there was any food to be found, this ewe would claim it for her own. After all, she had stared the dragon down.

Erde had assumed that the violent devouring of the bear was the dragon's only way of dealing with a meal. She'd anticipated the worst sort of bleating and mayhem when she drove the little flock into the gorge and informed the dragon they were his. But the goats seemed almost not to notice the dragon lumbering among them, except for the big spotted ewe. She stamped at it and presented her horns. The dragon regarded her a moment, then lowered its own great horns in imitation. Erde would have sworn that goat and dragon were bowing to one another. Then the dragon turned away and delicately picked up one of the other goats by the scruff of its neck, like a cat with a kitten. The goat hung there placidly while the dragon carried it off to a hidden corner of the gorge. It returned six times and each time, ewe and dragon matched their unequal horns, and the dragon took another. After the fifth, Erde shook her head in astonishment. *At least I'll have milk to drink,* she told herself and promptly fell asleep.

When she awoke, the dragon was curled up beside her. Erde lay still, grateful to be warm and fed and dry, and glad of the chance to study her remarkable traveling companion, to look it over at leisure and in daylight, if the gray afternoon sinking through the dark pine boughs could be called daylight. She thought about the summer that had never really come, and wondered if she would ever see the sun again.

The dragon was muddy from its travels, and its long sleep inside the mountain had left a coating of earth so hard and caked even the constant rain had not managed to wash it off completely. But in the gray half-light, Erde saw that its dull, dust-colored "scales" were actually a richly tapestried hide of grays and browns, ranging from the warm russet deep in the joints between the big concentrically-textured plates on its back that resembled a flexible tortoiseshell, to the smooth and glowing sienna of its belly or the luminous ivory of its razor-tipped horns and claws. The richness was subtle, and brown was the overall impression, but the details were various and stunning. Erde was relieved. She'd been avoiding the conclusion that her dragon was ugly.

Her dragon. How could she call it hers? She didn't even know its name. But it did seem to need her, or think it did, and this was both novel and flattering. It gave her purpose at a time when she could not have imagined one on her own. But now that the dragon was hopefully no longer so obsessed with its stomach, perhaps it was time to talk to it about something other than food. Erde settled herself squarely opposite its snoozing head and composed her interrogative in her mind.

—*Dragon?*

Very quickly, she saw in her mind's eye a dragon yawning and settling into sleep.

—*Dragon?*

The dragon in her mind stretched, yawned more widely, and turned its back on her. Erde's eyes narrowed in pique.

—*DRAGON!*

The dragon in front of her raised its enormous head with a low growl. Erde swallowed. It heard and understood her at least.

—*Did I not find you a fine dinner, Dragon?*

The dragon resettled its jaws comfortably and blinked.

—*So will you talk to me a while?*

She read assent in its mind but resignation in its eyes.

—*If you please then, Dragon, may I know your name?*

She did not ask if it had one. All dragons had names. Her grandmother had said they were extremely proud of them, and that you must be particularly polite when requesting an introduction. Usually their names were unpronounceable and had to be translated into some poetic but inadequate German equivalent.

The dragon did not answer immediately. Perhaps it did not trust her yet. Erde waited. She sensed a struggle and the beginnings of distress. A great blankness filled her mind. Sadness gripped her throat. Not reluctance at all, but a huge, heaving effort to . . . remember.

—*What? You can't remember your own name?*

She had meant to ask more gently. Her own shock and surprise had gotten the better of her. A dragon that didn't know its name? The poor creature's sigh was like a great sob of shame, and Erde gathered every wit she possessed to try to soothe it.

—*You'll remember. Of course you'll remember. You've been asleep too long, that's all. Try this: when I'm trying to remember something, I concentrate on the very first thought I had when I woke up.*

The dragon's struggle felt like muscles toiling in her mind, like men rolling heavy stones uphill or dragging laden carts through the mud. It remembered waking slowly, being drawn as though to a voice . . . suddenly, the memory dam burst. A torrent of images surged through Erde faster than she could grasp: soft green hills, a buried vein of shining metal, farmer's plow breaking the fresh sod, mountains shuddering with inner fire, bright young shoots pushing up through dark humus. Sand and hills and trees and rock and soil.

Earth.

—*But that's my name.*

The dragon looked at her as if she had foolishly stated the obvious.

—*We have the same name?*

Again, assent.

Erde had never heard of a dragon having the same name as a person, but it did show an unorthodox kind of logic, if it—*he,* she now sensed—if he was to be her dragon.

—*There! You see? I told you you could remember!*

But she sensed continuing distress. He had remembered his name, but not who he was or why he was there. Abruptly, she was deluged with doubt. Nothing seemed certain and nothing made sense. The value of life itself was in question. But Erde knew she was not given to such imponderables. It must be the dragon who was desperate for such answers. She tried again to soothe him.

—*Maybe we don't all need to know our purpose right off.*

Earth flooded her with images of stalwart, all-knowing dragonkind, proper dragons who knew their purpose. It was a terrible disaster that he'd forgotten his.

—*You'll remember. Just give yourself time.*

But the dragon would not be consoled. Feeding upon itself, his distress increased until it filled Erde's entire head and brought tears to her eyes and great racking sobs to her throat.

—*Dragon! Earth! Please!*

Surprise, a grasping at self-control, then a grumbling kind of apology. The dragon rose morosely and moved off down the ledge.

—*Wait! Don't go!*

He sent back an image of goats.

—*Oh. Um. Will you . . . ?*

Cautiously, she pictured a question of him eating the spotted ewe.

Emphatic negative. Offense that she should think such a thing, when the she-goat had not yet given him permission.

Permission? Nonplussed, Erde sent back gratitude, which Earth did not seem to understand until she imaged herself milking the goat and drinking the milk. He responded with agreement, then slid down from the ledge to accept graciously the self-sacrifice of any goat except the spotted ewe.

Watching him lumber away into the gorge, Erde had a stark sense of having failed him. But how could he expect a mere human girl to provide answers to such deep questions? Even if you did think of a possible answer, it only led right into another question. Such as, if Earth, being a dragon, had a specific purpose in life, it followed that she also had a purpose in being with him, and what might that be? She doubted it was anything so simple as feeding him and offering him moral support.

But meanwhile, he did have to eat, and because of what

Alla had said and because her grandmother would surely have wanted her to, Erde accepted feeding the dragon and keeping him safe as her responsibility. This gorge would not shelter them forever. It was nearing September and even if the weather suddenly became seasonable again, one could expect the fall snowstorms relatively soon. Her near disaster in Tubin told Erde she had to move on and quickly, away from the inhospitable weather, away from her father's huntsmen, away from the murderous reach of Brother Guillemo Gotti, far from this perilous neighborhood where everyone knew her face and name and took her for a witch.

Chapter Thirteen

They traveled by nights and slept out the days in whatever deep thicket or rock shelter they could find. Each day, Erde was less tired when she lay down than she'd been the dawn before, and less painfully sore when she awoke. The burden of her pack and Rainer's sword lightened as the long miles passed.

Earth learned to travel more quietly and with less interest in the countryside. Though the food-flock was soon reduced to the she-goat, he showed no interest in eating her. After a while, since the goat was agile, traveled well, and seemed content in their company, Erde did not even bother to tether her. She followed of her own accord.

As they put a safer distance between them and Tor Alte, Erde encouraged the dragon to hunt, especially as the time since his last meal lengthened and he continued to show little inclination to do so on his own. She began to wonder if he knew how. At dawn, their quiet time between travel and sleep, she conjured hunting images for him, graphic and colorful enough to inform an idiot, drawn from the days before she'd refused to ride with her father's hunt. Earth responded with his unflinching golden stare and an aura of eager incomprehension. Eventually, Erde stopped their night's travel early and banished him to the woods, insisting that he stay out there until dawn. For the first few days of this new regime, he slunk off reluctantly, only to return as soon as she'd let him. But one morning he was gone until the day was bright and Erde began to worry. Only a day ago, he'd come hurrying back to report that a hunting farmer had discovered him in the woods and run off shrieking. Earth did not understand the man's terror. Erde thought it had even hurt his feelings. But this time, she sensed his satisfaction even before she heard him rustling back through the underbrush. He'd heard a doe calling, mortally wounded, and she had begged him to end her misery. Erde thought he was more pleased at having eased the doe's pain than for the meal she'd afforded him.

The weather stayed dank and gray and unseasonable, but Erde did not suffer as long as the dragon was near. Earth, it turned out, was no cold-blooded reptile. To sleep pressed against his golden belly was like sleeping inside the hearth. Erde often woke in a sweat, dreaming of hot coals, and was forced to move some distance away from him in order to sleep comfortably.

Each dawn, before giving in to her exhaustion, Erde unwrapped Rainer's sword and laid it out beside her, to shine in the early light. Then later, wrapped in heat and fever, she dreamed of him and her father fighting at Tor Alte. Her memory of Rainer's face was more elusive with each dream. She fought to preserve it, but was always distracted. There were stranger things than that entering her dreams: bleak scorched landscapes she didn't recognize and voices whispering words she couldn't understand but knew were full of grim foreboding. These dreams were always plagued by wildfire and torn by harsh clangings and roars she could not identify. They were thick with the odors that hung over the smithy's forge, metal and smoke and acid. Erde could not recall having dreamed in odors before.

One cold gray noon, she woke up screaming, or thought she'd been screaming. She knew it was impossible, only part of the awful dream, but her throat was raw and the dragon was awake, staring in concern.

—*A dream. Only a dream.*

It took some explaining, but finally Earth seemed to understand, and he allowed as how there were places he also went when he was sleeping. They were not very nice either, but he did not seem to have any choice in the matter. She asked him to show her some. The first image that rose up in her mind told her that she and her dragon were sharing the same dreams, or rather, their dreams were mixing, but increasingly, she was dreaming his.

Like the Summoning. Erde called it that for lack of a better name. Often, as she shared Earth's dreams, came the distinct sensation that someone was calling them. Sometimes she actually heard a voice, but then it was Alla's voice or her grandmother's, and she could never understand what they were saying. Sometimes the summons was as vague as Earth's insistent expectation during their first night in the cave. Earth still looked to her for explanation, but she had nothing to offer him. Certainly she could not admit that each evening, she awoke more certain that there was some duty they were meant to be performing, and were failing at. She wished it *was* Alla's voice she was hearing. Alla would know how to answer a dragon.

This distress and their broken sleep plagued them and slowed their progress, but their biggest problem was always food. Erde presumed, as they journeyed south by two, seven, now ten days, that conditions would improve, that at some point, a decent harvest would appear and fields with fatter, healthier livestock. But the bad news that the fake-Guillemo had brought to her father's banquet table was not exaggerated. Unending rain flooded the fields and the kitchen gardens. Blight and mildew and damp-loving snails claimed a huge portion of the crop wherever they went. Erde became an adept sneak-thief and stole, guiltily, what little she could from outlying hen yards and storehouses. But people do not leave much lying about in times of famine. She could not feed herself by thievery. She survived on the she-goat's milk, and on the dragon's foraging. For all his reluctance to take advantage of any but the most willing hot-blooded meals, he did show real talent for sniffing out a mushroom or berry patch, and seemed to know what was safe to eat and what was deadly. Erde's only problem was to remind him to leave her some.

After Tubin, she'd carefully avoided any village larger than a few houses. But on the eleventh night, approaching the outskirts of a town, Erde decided they must by now have passed out of the sphere of von Alte, into some other baron's domain. It was a very small town on a thinly-traveled road, surrounded by small rocky farms. Erde didn't know where she was or exactly how far they'd traveled, only that each dawn, the sun still rose more or less in the direction they'd come. It was time, come daylight, to risk venturing into town again, for news and information, and the chance of finding real food.

In town, it was market day, a good day for one wanting to eavesdrop in the anonymity of a crowd. A weak and uncer-

tain sun was struggling through the clouds for the first time
in several days, and the muddy town square was busy with
carts and pigs and people. But as Erde wandered about trying to appear purposeful, she could see that though it was
nearly September, well after time for the early harvest, the
wood and canvas stalls were only half-stocked and the produce was bug-eaten and scrawny. The farm wives stood behind their canopied trestles and flat-wagons with their arms
folded, grim and irritable with guilt as they refused over and
over to barter food they might soon have to eat themselves
for a broken crock or an old robe they didn't need and
couldn't resell.

Listening to their restless chatter, Erde learned it wasn't
just the poor harvest that threatened these farmers' liveli-
hoods.

"Had little enough as it was and he took the best," a thin
and drawn woman complained to a nodding neighbor. "The
very best, wouldn't you know! And then the baron came after and took his share!"

"Mine, too." The neighbor was plumper but pale and
tired-looking. She jostled a basket of runty misshapen potatoes for emphasis. "Every one worth a prayer, he said. We
must each serve God in our own way. Then he promised a
mass for a better harvest."

The first woman grunted and looked away, staring past
Erde as she paused a few paces away to lean against a
wagon wheel and fuss with her boot. "Does a man deserve
more food because he wears a priest's robe?" the woman
muttered. "Does he deserve better?"

Her companion clucked warningly and resettled her potato
basket, neatening this and that on her table unnecessarily.
Two men walked by, haggling over the price of a thin don-
key limping after them at the end of a frayed rope. When the
men had passed, the plump woman leaned over to her neighbor and hissed, "We must all remember Tubin!"

The other woman crossed herself and nodded.

"Did you hear Mag's baby died suddenly?" the plump
woman began. "Seems there's reason to believe . . ."

Chilled, Erde moved on to another row of stalls. She did
better than many in the market that day. Pretending to be too
shy to speak, she bartered a capful of berries and the two
dozen mushrooms she had carried in the hood of her cloak
for a loaf of dark bread and a salted fish. No one looked at

her with any more suspicion than a solitary prentice boy
might usually arouse, but everywhere she heard talk of ill
omens and Fra Guill and his doom-ridden prophecies. The
warning of Tubin was on every other tongue, and the farmer
who'd stumbled across Earth in the forest had already become famous for miles around.

"Albrecht wouldn't know a dragon if he fell on one," a
grizzled farmer remarked between hammer blows at the smithy's portable forge.

"A bear, most likely," agreed the smith's customer. "He's
been listening to the priest too hard."

The smith let fall a final stroke, then held up the crooked
rake tine to squint at his repair. "Don't be too hasty. What
those trappers from the high hills came across didn't sound
like bearshit to me."

His scrawny apprentice nodded, eyes wide, all bones and
Adam's apple. "Dragon sign! My da's keeping our cow inside the barn all the time now, 'cept when he leads her out
himself . . ."

Completing the circuit of the market, Erde heard a lot
more dragon talk. Dragons had eaten this man's sheep or
that man's dog. Dragons were gathering among the moun-
taintops, awaiting only the foul signal of their Dark Lord to
launch themselves upon the countryside. There was no talk
that day of raising dragon-hunts, but plenty of witch-rumor
and threats of witch-hunt, and finally Erde overheard a rumor of an army that the Baron of Tor Alte (a distant and
mysterious figure to these lowland farmers) was raising to
vanquish the forces of evil and get his stolen daughter back
so her soul could be saved by the Holy Brother Guillemo
Gotti.

An army? Calmly munching her bread, Erde strolled out
of the village when what she really wanted to do was flee
headlong. This last rumor was just stupid enough to be true.
With a touch of the graveyard humor that was becoming her
defense against fear and loneliness and her increasing sense
that the world had gone mad, she totaled up the evils her father's supposed army would face: a small dream-haunted
dragon, a girl, and a spotted she-goat.

Earth found no willing victim in his hunting that day, but
reported being nearly spotted twice by shepherds foraging
for decent grass for their sheep. He was learning to conceal

himself, but the land was becoming more populated as they left the high mountains behind. In the late afternoon, he and Erde lay down in a thicket to nap and slept through nearly till midnight, when both of them bolted up out of a shared nightmare. They had been pressed into a long, narrow, smelly room full of faceless bodies. They could barely breathe from the closeness and the stench. The noise was ear-splitting, and they seemed to be moving somewhere at breakneck speed. The dream upset Earth so much that he nearly forgot his promise to the she-goat.

Desperate for a way to calm him, Erde offered the thing that would have calmed her. She said what they really needed was a wise person with knowledge of magical things such as dragons and dream-visions, a person like her friend Alla. If there had been one such person, there had to be another. She conjured her childhood favorite, the Mage-Queen, who in her fantasies so resembled her grandmother. Inventing as she went along, she imagined a Mage City for the dragon, with many tall white towers gleaming in the sun. Into the early morning, when they should have been sleeping, she told him all the tales she could remember, until she had almost convinced herself that there was such a power in the world, and that the real purpose of their journey must be to find her. Heartened, Earth himself proposed the idea that it might be the Mage-Queen who was summoning him. Out of compassion and a remaining shred of childish hope, Erde did not discourage him. She agreed that the next day would be the first day of their search. Earth then ceased his pacing and moaning to regard her with those expectant dog eyes. *Now?* he seemed to ask. *Can we go now?*

And so they moved on, traveling for the remaining hours until dawn, then slept through the day in a sweet-smelling pine grove, so that Earth could take the next night to hunt. It was almost dry, deep among the pine boughs, where the cold wind was only a sighing in the upper branches. Erde stuffed her cloak with needles and could not remember the last time she had been so comfortable. Sharing Earth's constant nightmares left her eager for the possibility of a length of sleep without them. She barely stirred when the dragon left for the deeper forest.

But she woke to the crackle of fire anyway, and the smells of smoke and charred flesh burning the darkness. She sat up to shake the nightmare from her head but it was not a dream. The fire was there, right in front of her. A small fire, of twigs and pine cones. On the far side of it sat the man in the red jerkin, grilling a small bird carcass on a stick and watching her placidly.

Erde recoiled into her pine bed with a breathy gasp. Feebly, she felt for Rainer's sword where she had left it beside her.

Red-jerkin reached a hand to one side and lifted the sword out of the shadow. "Is this what you're looking for?"

Erde stared at him like a cornered rabbit.

"Easy, now. I haven't followed you all this way to do you harm." He laid the sword down and patted it gently. "In fact, I had just the opposite in mind. You want to learn how to use this thing?"

He waited for her to say something. Erde's return gaze was unblinking. She no longer believed the promises of men who said they were not going to hurt you. Besides, she could not comprehend how this man had sneaked up on her, lit a fire, and actually started cooking a meal without waking her. She'd have been speechless even if she'd had her voice. He was some baron's footpad, or a thief who preyed on travelers in the forest. Where was the dragon when she needed him?

Red-jerkin mistook her quick glance sideways. "Don't worry, I'm alone. Oh, except for the Mule, that is." He saw he'd piqued her interest, or perhaps her concern. His grin was lopsided and sly. "'Course the Mule eats little children for breakfast, so maybe you should be worried." He leaned back from the fire and called softly over his shoulder. "Come on out, Mule. Introduce yourself."

Erde steeled herself for some exotic ogre of a man, this cool thief's monstrous partner. But it was indeed a mule that stepped up to the fire, a white lop-eared ordinary mule. It stood over her and stretched its neck down to study her with jaded, intelligent eyes. Not quite ordinary. Distracted, Erde smiled at it and stroked its soft gray nose.

"Later he'll eat you," remarked Red-jerkin.

Erde's eyes flicked back to him and her smile faded.

"Does this really need to be a one-way conversation?"

She nodded.

"You mean, you can't . . . or you won't?"

Erde shook her head, obscurely irritated that a common thief should accuse her of guile.

Red-jerkin frowned. "Really? I was sure it was just a ploy
. . . how'd it happen? Right, right, you can't tell me. Well,
let's assume I believe you. So, yes and no answers only for
now. Later maybe we'll manage something more complicated. I don't suppose you can read and write?"

Her prideful instinct betrayed her, sat her up straight in
protest. She didn't think to be surprised by the implication
that he could.

"That so? Well, good for you. I'd assumed otherwise, you
being Iron Joe's daughter and all . . ."

Erde froze. He knew. Now she understood. He was some
baron's man, after all. He had found her out and now he
meant to kidnap her and hold her for ransom. She shrugged
and tried to look blank.

"But then," he continued as if she had agreed with him,
"you are also Meriah's granddaughter." He read the soft
crease of Erde's brow, and smiled. "Will you please believe
I don't mean to harm you? Meriah would see to it I burned
in hell. She's sure to be a favorite with the Recording Angel
already."

Erde felt the first stirrings of doubt. Would a thief have
given up a silver mark? It could be what Red-jerkin himself
had called a ploy, but very few people had called her grandmother by her given name. In the firelight, his eyes were
kind. She narrowed her own eyes in what she hoped was a
steely glare.

Watching her, the man's grin turned rueful. "I see her in
you. She was captivating, you know—in her youth and long,
long after. As you will be, milady, if we can keep you alive
long enough." He lifted the bird out of the fire, tore off one
of the leg joints, and held it out to her. "Hungry?"

Erde felt as if she had come into a conversation that had
been going on for a long time without her. Too confused to
pretend otherwise, she accepted the leg gingerly. If he meant
to hold her for ransom, he'd be unlikely to poison her. And
he didn't look so well fed himself, for all his silver marks.
Though his eyes were bright, his cheeks were gaunt, and the
hand that held the spit was ropy with starved muscle. She
guessed he was as hungry as she was. Meanwhile, the bird
was hot and delicious. Trying not to gobble too noisily, she
waited for Red-jerkin to surprise her some more.

He tore off the other leg and stuck the spit upright in the

ground beside him, then ate nearly half the joint before he spoke again.

"Now, introductions, yes? I know who you are, though you are welcome to continue pretending otherwise. I am, or was, Heinrich Peder von Engle, Knight of the Realm in service to His Majesty the King, and at your service, milady." He bowed deeply over his crossed legs like some prostrating mystic, then sank back into his comfortable slouch with a fleeting mirthless grin. "Now I'm mainly Hal Engle, or Sir Hal, when I need to impress a few villagers who don't know any better. Although these days, a King's Knight gets very little respect ..." He glanced away as if to toss aside his chicken bone, and Erde believed he was what he claimed, seeing that same twist of righteous anger catch his face, then pass him by. He had, she could tell, the rare gift of storytelling, for she was already drawn into his tale. She tried harder not to appear so interested.

"I had once upon a time and not so very long ago," he continued, "land and estates to the north of here, maybe two weeks' hard ride, like Tor Alte about as far as you can get from court and still be His Majesty's subject. And I was very much his subject. My duties as a Knight of the Realm kept me in Erfurt a lot of the time. But I left my lands in the charge of my two grown sons, which proved to be such a workable arrangement that I grew farther and farther away from the everyday workings of the domain. I felt free, in my, ah ... maturity, to pursue in between my court duties a special interest of mine, the collection and study of legend and lore relating to the existence of dragons."

Erde's composure nearly deserted her. A dragon-hunter! She had heard of such men, and this one had caught her unawares as he must have hoped he would, for sure enough, he was studying her much too carefully. For the dragon's sake, she must appear unconcerned.

"Are you interested in dragons, milady?"

Erde shrugged, but it was more a convulsive twitch, and Red-jerkin read her nervousness clearly. But he surprised her again. He leaned forward over the dying fire with a barely restrained eagerness totally at odds with his hard-bitten manner. "Oh, lady," he murmured. "Please tell me you have the knowledge that I seek."

Erde snatched at impassivity and held it tight.

"Ah, well," he said, sitting back. "Such knowledge is not

easily won. I of all men have learned this, a dubious privilege of advancing age. Pray permit me, milady, to continue my tale."

Erde could not help it. She nodded graciously, as a baron's daughter should.

Red-jerkin took a deep breath. "As the seasons passed, so did the times of plenty in our lands to the west. His Majesty's vassal lords grew restless. Traveling as much as I was, either on the king's business negotiating with some malignant baron or other, or when I could, following up some report of dragon-sign ... I was unaware that the worsening condition of my estates exceeded anyone else's. The whole kingdom was suffering, after all, but .... oh, yes, my dear lady, I see that look. *Meriah's* look. You might properly call my distraction negligence—I'll bear that guilt fully. But I was also kept in ignorance by my two wastrel sons, who were covering up a profligacy of habit that had not been so evident while the harvests were rich but as soon as ... well, I'm sure a daughter of Iron Joe can well imagine."

Is my father profligate? Did he mean not all high lords considered feasting and velvet robes a critical expenditure? Erde considered the new and revealing notion that her own instinctive scruples might have been more proper in this matter.

Noting her pensiveness, Red-jerkin nodded. "Indeed, your grandmother and I share the misfortune of our sons. Perhaps it is the price of being dedicated to something other than heir-raising. Perhaps if we'd had them together, as I intended ... well, I suppose that might have been even worse, though I can't conceive of how. But I'm wandering, aren't I? Bear with me, milady. Another privilege of age."

Erde was surprised he spoke so self-consciously of his age. Her impression of him was one of strength and great vitality.

"So one gray fall day, a wandering friar begged the hospitality of the household, and managed to find excuses to keep himself there all winter. Meanwhile, the king's relations with his barons were disintegrating, as you recall ... no, perhaps you were too young to be aware of such matters lo these two long winters ago, but I assure you I was extremely busy trying to maintain the King's Peace ... a futile effort, as it turned out, in that winter of the silent revolt. But once or twice between my frantic comings and goings, I met this so-called priest who'd taken up residence in my home, then the deep snows isolated me at court until the spring. He seemed an inoffensive sort, this cleric, if rather given to hysterical prophecies and an obsession with the supposedly divine dominion of men over women and the natural world."

Their eyes met over the fire, and Red-jerkin smiled sourly. "Ah, yes, you are Meriah's get, bless you indeed . . . you're at the mark before I've even loosed my arrow." He leaned forward so that the flames lit his face eerily. "It was Fra Guill who sent you running from Tor Alte, wasn't it? He turned your father against you somehow."

Erde nodded, transfixed.

"Nay, don't look so amazed. I'm no mind-seer. Any man who's dealt with that hell-fiend of a priest and not been cozened by him would see the truth of it. But not the baron your father, I take it?"

Erde shivered, hung her head.

"And not my sons," he admitted softly. "The priest's lust for power gives him a damnable nose for weakness. He ferrets it out like a truffle hound and moves right in to woo and devour." He stirred up the fire, tossed on a few twigs, then neatly sectioned the remaining bird and passed half over the flames to Erde. She took it gratefully and without pretense. This was her first hot meal in nearly two weeks. Red-jerkin—or Sir Hal, as she was finding enough sympathy to think of him—ate for a while with deep concentration, allowing her to do likewise. They passed a companionable silence together, cleaning every morsel from the scrawny bird bones. Finally the knight unslung a leather wineskin and raised it to his lips, then lowered it just before drinking and held it out across the fire.

"Your pardon, milady, for my lapse of manners. I've gotten so used to solitude, I quite forgot I had company." He jerked his head at the mule, who appeared to have dozed off standing by the fire. "He doesn't drink."

Erde wished she was not so easily charmed by his courtier's ease, however out of practice he might claim to be, but the familiarity of it was reassuring, and his dry humor a relief after the rough conditions she'd been enduring. She took the wineskin and sipped from it delicately. She could not help the face she made.

Hal laughed. "Awful, isn't it?"

His laugh was generous and open. Erde smiled with him

just a little as she passed the offending wine back to him. He took quite a long drink of it for a man who'd just complained of its quality, then dug a rag out of his jerkin to carefully wipe his beard and hands, folded the rag, and put it away.

"But what did you do to become the unwelcome focus of his deranged and self-serving visions?" Hal peered hard at her, then waved a hand. "No matter. We'll get to that later." But he continued a little reluctantly, "So, as you have already guessed, milady, with a wisdom far advanced of your youth, after that winter's undeclared rebellion of the vassal-lords against their king, I returned home at first thaw to find that in the same way that His Majesty had become king in name only, I was no longer master of my own lands. My sons had become willing puppets of the hell-priest, who had used the long winter to good effect, spreading his lies and paranoia throughout the domain, turning family, friends, and sworn vassals against me on the grounds of my 'unholy practices.' My fault, my fault, all of it, the cause of the bad weather and failing harvests. My *practices*, if allowed to persist, would soon bring the final wrath of God down upon them all. And as the tide turned against the king, my neighbors were none too eager to stand up for an avowed royalist."

Erde could not mask her surprise.

"Ah, milady, when I say a *silent* revolt, I do mean that loyal subjects of the king such as your grandmother would not have been included in the secret barons' cabal, or even kept informed. But you can be sure this was one song Fra Guill sang to your father in his siren's voice!"

Hal paused, blew some of his anger away in a long exhalation. "Another task that devil's spawn had dedicated the winter to was gathering around him an elite band of 'followers,' fellow fanatics who were coincidentally well-versed in the martial arts." He sighed, then inclined his head in pained resignation. "You see how, even before he had need of protection from the world, he planned for it and carried it out so smoothly that I'd wager even the brothers themselves aren't aware they were recruited to serve as Fra Guill's personal bodyguard."

Hal looked up from his study of the coals. The rage and loss in his eyes were as fresh as an open wound. "Milady, he drove me from my lands by force, he and his white-robed henchmen. Friends turned me away from their gates with arrows and exorcisms. Word spread to the court, and I could not turn to the king without disgracing him, thereby eroding what little power he had left. The final blow was a rumor, the priest's own invention I've no doubt, that the King's Knights were plotting a coup of their own. All seven of us." His mouth twisted but his rage had run its course. He sighed and spread his hands. "Coup de grace. So here I am. Wanderer. Knight-errant, if you will. Not exactly a public enemy, but certainly suspect to any revolting baron. The perfect candidate, if I may modestly point out, to take up the task of protecting the Lady Erde von Alte, so recently gone errant herself in the eyes of the law, her father, and the hellspawned Fra Guill." Hal raised his eyebrows and gazed at her down the length of his nose. "That is, if milady will have me. . . ."

Erde regarded him uneasily. Even if she could speak, she would not have known what to say to him. He knew who and what she was, and did not call her a witch. His tale, if all true—and he was a convincing teller—touched her heart and made him her natural ally. If they joined forces, she could probably stop worrying about starving. But could she really trust him? What of the dragon? Did he mean it help or harm?

Hal could read her doubt. He shrugged, like the merchant who's been told that the price is too high. "Let an old soldier convince you, lady, that he found you much too easily. You've been very very lucky so far. Luck such as yours cannot be expected to hold out. You need a little guidance."

Erde returned his gaze steadily.

"Oh, my, but Meriah would be proud of you." He grinned at her admiringly. "True, you've no reason to trust me or my story, and yes, you've guessed it. I have an ulterior motive that I see no point in concealing further. Perhaps you are wondering what particular practice the heathen brother found most unholy? Something so unthinkable that he could use it to turn my neighbors against me? Well, please believe it was not gluttony or drunkenness, though I have drunk too much in my time, Lord knows, and probably will again. Nor was it lechery, at which Fra Guill himself could beat any man's record." He paused abruptly, flicked a glance at her, and then looked away. "Your pardon, lady, if I touch on anything you may have painful firsthand knowledge of."

Erde shook her head emphatically, frowning.

He let a breath out through his teeth. "Thank God for that. No, I'm sure none of us has heard the real story. But we'll leave yours for another time, hah? The finale of mine, the grand debacle, is that what Fra Guill seized upon to turn my people against me was, of course, my dragon-study, which I had never been secret about and certainly could not deny. He twisted an honest scientific and scholarly inquiry into a pact with Satan himself." He fixed her with an indignant glare. "Can you imagine? He accused me of attempting to raise dragons out of the Fiery Pit to lay waste to the country-side—further waste than I'd already caused, though why I would do this to my own lands he never did explain satisfac-torily. I told anyone who'd listen, and there were damned few by that time, believe me, that despite my knowing as much as any man alive about dragons, I had never yet laid eyes on one and was not even sure I believed in them any-more."

Hal reached into his jerkin as he talked, digging out two small round objects that glinted in the firelight. He jiggled them pensively in his closed hand. "But I made the profound mistake of declaring to the brother one sunny and innocent day, out of the depths of my enthusiasm and before I was truly aware of his power and my peril, that there was very little in this world I would treasure more than to stand face-to-face with an actual dragon. With that casual remark, he ruined me."

Now he fixed his bright gaze on Erde intently, his voice rough with passion. "Ruined or not, lady, the remark still holds true. Having little else to direct my life toward but sur-vival, my dragon-quest continues. We live in dark times, perhaps the darkest, but you know, milady, dragonkind are the purest of God's creations, the elemental embodiment of the life-force, of anything that has meaning. They could be our salvation. The hell-priest has vowed to destroy dragon-kind. I cannot let that happen."

Erde's breath came a bit more easily. She could see he was a man obsessed. And that she had wrongly assumed that dragon-hunter meant dragon-slayer.

"I have become expert over the years at reading hidden signs." Hal cleared his throat. "That is, at interpreting rumor, at hearing what they are really saying in the countryside and what they are not. I've followed many trails and most of them are cold long before I get there. One is not. The one that intersects with you."

He gave her a moment to react. When she did not, he held up between thumb and forefinger the silver mark, or one like it, twisting it back and forth so that it flashed firelight into Erde's eyes. "You know, there're many won't accept this as legal tender anymore." Suddenly he flipped the coin at her. Once again she fumbled the catch.

Hal chortled, satisfied. "Young girls probably don't throw things at each other as much as young boys. Well, so much for your disguise. I might not have given you a second thought, back there in the town. But then my curiosity was aroused . . . I heard there was a search on. So now, tell me, lady, what need you had for ten goats in the town of Tubin when a mere week later I find you with only one?"

The mule, who had wakened from his nap to nose quietly for grass along the edge of the firelight, raised his head suddenly to stare off into the forest, his nostrils flaring.

"Next, the long-term evidence," Hal continued. "The token of an ageless history I'll wager you have no inkling of. Or do you?" He slipped the mark back into his belt and in its place, held up a ruddy cut-stone brooch. "How much did she tell you?"

Erde gasped voicelessly.

"Your pardon for my inexcusable liberties with your luggage, dearest lady. But you cannot know what this means to me. My whole life I have . . ." He leaned forward. "Lady, I beg you, tell me if you know. Are you the Dragon Guide? If you are, I lay my life and my sword at your feet forever."

Erde felt Earth's return well before the mule, who knew it sooner than Hal. He snorted, wickered a warning, and moved to stand protectively at the knight's back.

Hal rose into a crouch, still watching Erde as if his salvation depended on it. "Who comes? Is it he?" Seeing joy and anxiety bloom simultaneously across her unguarded face, he shivered and slid to his knees. "Oh, lady, what will you tell him?"

Erde's only hope, as the dragon's great horned head loomed up out of the forest darkness behind them, was that Hal would not be too disappointed.

PART THREE

EARTH

The Call to the Quest

Chapter Fourteen

Hal rose and turned toward the dragon. His hand was tight on the hilt of his sword, but his face glowed with a tender expectation that touched Erde in a place normally reserved for younger children and small animals. She sent Earth hope and reassurance and her preference that he not greet this stranger as he had the attacking bear.

But Earth seemed to have sensed an Occasion. He drew himself up at the edge of the firelight, as august as royalty. Bright flickers played across his leathery snout and his sharp-tipped ivory horns. His body vanished behind him into darkness. In the small clearing, he seemed enormous and terrifying, and his huge eyes shone brighter than the fire. Erde saw a new Earth, or at least a side of him that was more *dragon* in its aspect, a creature out of myth such as the dragon-seeker wished to see. The mule, she noticed, had backed off into the shadow in a posture of submission and respect.

Dragon and man stared at each other for a long moment. Then the knight grasped his sword and unsheathed it in a gallant sweeping arc. With shaking hands, he knelt and laid the sword hilt-first at the dragon's feet. Earth watched majestically, his golden eyes unblinking. To Erde's surprise, he raised his right foot and placed it down with great deliberation so that the tip of one massive claw rested on the sword's worn and silvered hilt, which Erde noticed was shaped like a winged dragon wound around a tree, its wings creating the cross-guard. *Like a panel from a story tapestry,* Erde thought, *knight and dragon in some old history of heroes and sorcerers.* Her last doubts about the man's motives and sincerity faded, for he had forgotten her entirely. His head thrown back, his gaze fixed on the great head hovering above him, Heinrich Peder von Engle, late of Winterstrasse, wept unashamed tears of joy.

Earth lifted his claw and eased the knight's sword toward him across the mat of pine needles. Hal leaped to his feet. He swept up the sword with one hand, palming moisture from his cheeks and beard with the other. He stepped back, stood tall, and raised the sword in a courtly salute, then sheathed it smartly.

"My lord," he offered the dragon gravely, "I am ever at your service."

Watching, Erde wondered about the history of men and dragons, of fighting men in particular, of their ancient traditions of faith and enmity. Earth had neither offered nor required such formality of her when they'd met. Of course, she told herself, formality would be fairly silly when the dragon can read your mind. Even in her daydreaming, she'd had a very personal relationship with her dragons. Yet Earth had understood Hal's offer of fealty, and had known exactly how to satisfy a King's Knight that his oath had been officially accepted.

Hal had not forgotten her after all. He turned with a slight bow. "Milady, if you will, ask him what he . . . I must know my duty . . . what he requires of me." He paused, visibly confounded. "But how will you speak for him, Dragon Guide, if you have no voice?"

Erde was flattered by this tone of reverence from a man old enough to be her grandfather, but she had no wish to be taken as a mere mouthpiece for anyone, even a dragon. Her chin lifted, she mimed writing. After all, she had a few questions of her own to ask someone who had spent his life studying dragons. The first one would be: what is a Dragon Guide?

It took a while to work out the mechanics, but a cleared patch in the dirt, a built-up fire and a sturdy pointed stick accomplished wonders. Hal crouched over their earthy slate with the distracted intensity of an expert who has waited a long time to ask his questions and is not quite sure where to start, fearful of losing the chance to ask them all. When not directly engaged, his attention wandered inevitably back to the dragon, who lay in a dark pile under the pine boughs, snoozing after a successful hunt.

"I suppose this will do . . . nothing is ever what you . . . Well, ah, let's see . . . what is he called?"

EARTH, she wrote.

He raised an eyebrow, both wondering and amused. "How appropriate. Was it your grandmother who named you?"

Erde nodded.

"Of course," he mused. "She hoped. Or perhaps she even knew." He smiled, but Erde sensed some disappointment that his brisk manner was meant to cover. "Then you are Dragon Guide indeed. Not that I doubted. How do you speak with him?"

PICTURES.

"Pictures? Where?"

Erde put a fingertip to her forehead, between her eyes.

"Right there? Really?" The knight peered at her as if he hoped to discover a third eye. "No language? No . . . words?"

She shook her head.

"Interesting. I'd always imagined it would be like a voice just inside my ear, sort of a . . . well, it doesn't matter now." He turned on the dragon a more scholarly gaze. "Has he told you why he's come?"

HE DOESN'T KNOW.

Hal frowned at the scratches on the ground, cocking his head to make sure he'd read them right. "Perhaps you've misunderstood," he reproved gently.

Erde's headshake was emphatic.

"How can he not know? He's a . . . a dragon." He hadn't said the word aloud yet and the reality of it clearly gave him pause. For good measure, he whispered it again. "A *dragon*."

Erde added a firm underline beneath her scratchings.

"But, milady, you know of course that dragons are the source of all knowledge. Perhaps he doesn't wish to tell you . . . yet?"

Erde was further encouraged. Other people might have said dragons are evil and eat virgin princesses. She smoothed the dirt and began again. HE TELLS ME HE DOESN'T REMEMBER.

Hal massaged his eyes with one hand.

HE HAS DREAMS. She left out "bad," hoping to ease the knight's distress.

"He tells you his dreams?"

I SHARE THEM.

The envy on the knight's face was poignant. "Milady, may I dare to ask? What does a dragon dream?"

THAT SOMEONE . . . she rubbed out "one" and wrote in "thing" . . . IS CALLING HIM.

Hal brightened. "Right! Of course. That's why he's here. He would only come to a Summoning. But he doesn't know who or why?"

HE KNOWS HE SHOULD. HE CAN'T REMEMBER. Erde cleared more pine needles. She would need real room if this conversation got much more complicated. HE IS UP-SET.

"I'm not surprised," replied Hal dryly, finally seeing the humor in the situation.

I SAID IT MIGHT BE THE MAGE-QUEEN. CALLING HIM.

"The who?"

She shrugged. JUST TO GIVE AN ANSWER.

"Oh. Well." He nodded. "It's as good as any, under the circumstances. I mean, I always assumed . . . but what good are assumptions?"

She knew what he couldn't bring himself to say. She felt the same helplessness. A dragon was supposed to be omniscient, all-powerful, the closest thing to perfect outside of God's angels. A dragon was supposed to be a lot of things that this dragon clearly wasn't.

Hal let the reality sink in a while, gnawing pensively on his lower lip as he watched the slow rise and fall of the dragon's dusty flanks. Finally he sighed, shrugged, and spread his hands. "Then we must help him. That must be why I am here."

Erde nodded eagerly. BUT HOW?

"Well, he's a dragon, therefore he has a Purpose. We must help him discover it. Earth. It's an odd name for a dragon, but the name often tells you . . . well, obviously I lack the proper knowledge, but someone must . . . someone will be able to read the signs." He seemed relieved to have fastened on something he could be sure of again. "There are no arbitrary dragons."

She didn't really understand what he was talking about, but his conviction, even in sentence fragments, was reassuring.

He rose to pace before the fire with renewed energy, one

hand tugging fitfully at his beard. "First find out who or what is doing the summoning. That should be easiest to trace since it will issue from some sort of directional source . . ." He stopped, finding himself even with the dome of the reclining dragon's head. He hesitated, looked to Erde with the suddenly wide eyes of a little boy. "Will he . . . may I touch him?"

Erde nodded. She didn't really know if the dragon would mind.

Hal laid one, then both hands tentatively on the fleshy folds of the dragon's crest, and the dragon opened one giant eye. "Earth," said Hal, a long breathy whisper. He slid his hands forward to the base of the dragon's horns and wrapped his fists gently around them. His fingers and thumbs did not quite meet. "All my life . . ." he murmured. He looked to Erde again, and she smiled. Some things just did not need to be said out loud.

"Without a routine, you get sloppy," remarked Hal later as he banked up the fire and laid out his bedroll. "Routine and discipline will get us through the hard times, when we haven't found food or the search has been unproductive for too long."

Erde sensed the knight's entire recent history packed into that simple declaration.

"So here's what we'll do. You've been right to travel at night, even in this godforsaken weather. We'll keep after that. But we'll know exactly where we're going each day and how far we have to travel. We'll eat if there's food and wash if there's water, even if we're too tired to want to. And at dusk when we wake, we'll take an hour with these." He patted his sword hilt, then nodded at Rainer's blade shimmering where she had reclaimed it beside her. "Practice."

Erde managed to look both dubious and incredulous.

"Why not? Why bring it if you're not going to use it?" He reached around the fire for the sword and hefted it casually. "Maybe a little heavy for you to learn on, but . . . was it your father's?" Her offended look puzzled him. He returned the blade to her side. "Well, anyway, no dead weight. You shouldn't carry what you can't use."

Erde wondered briefly if he'd forgotten she was a girl.

"I taught your grandmother to use a sword, when we were . . . keeping company." Hal smiled at her a little too brightly, as if the memory held more pain than comfort. She was delighted to hear that the baroness had encouraged the courtship of a mere knight. It sounded very romantic and sad, and reminded her of Rainer. But the notion of her grandmother wielding a sword was another thing entirely.

"Really. I did. So you see, we were fated to meet, you and I. There are no coincidences. She was built just like you, and many a man's no taller or stronger. But Meriah didn't practice."

He became very involved in smoothing out the wrinkles in his bedroll for a moment, then settled on it with a sigh. "When I heard she'd . . . passed on, I almost came to the funeral. But that hell-priest would have burned me on the spot, so . . ." He shook his head. "Meriah inherited so young. She didn't have time for 'such frivolities,' as she said. Ha. She didn't have time for me much after that. She made a marriage that was 'good for the domain.' She said I lacked a proper ruler's sense of purpose. I . . ." He laughed bitterly. "Am I boring you?"

Erde had never thought of her grandmother's life before marriage. Couldn't he see she was fascinated?

Hal went on as if compelled by her waiting silence. "Well, I never could make her understand my notion of service, you see. She said the king was all very well and good but shouldn't I be seeing to my own lands as she was to hers?" He shrugged, smiling at Erde crookedly, though his eyes were serious. "Perhaps she was right. She ruled well and gave her people security in her own time. But she didn't teach her son so well, did she? She knew he was weak. I hoped she'd send him to me for training, but . . . well, my guess is, she was pinning her real hopes on you." He turned his gaze again on the dragon. "But your duty is not with lands or stronghold. It lies here before you, and I surely know my part in it, which is to pick up where Meriah left off. Why else would I be here? *You* will practice!"

Erde grasped Rainer's sword and mimed being barely able to lift it.

"Now it's difficult," he agreed. "But that's what practice is about. An hour a day. I hope you're not one of those spoiled high-borns."

His tone suggested that he would know how to deal with her if she was, but Erde smiled at him anyway, liking him. So what if he was a minor lord. She wished her own father had been more like this man, and wondered how close he had really come to being her grandfather.

Hal's eyes were back on the dragon. "He'll be after us, you know, that hell-spawned priest, especially now he's decided you're the witch-child of his prophecies."

WITH MY FATHER'S ARMY? Erde scrawled.

Hal snorted. "I heard that rumor, too. Who could feed an army in these times? No, I doubt an army, but there will be pursuit, and if I am killed, you must be able to protect yourself . . . and him."

A new notion. Erde had thought the dragon was protecting her. Why else return to her fire, now that he'd proven he could hunt successfully on his own? YOU DON'T THINK I'M A WITCH?

"What if I did?"

Her eyes widened.

Hal grinned at her. "Never fear, milady. I've known a few witches in my time."

She stared at him expectantly.

"Well, let's say they're like dragons. Never what you expect them to be."

LIKE ME?

"I think that remains to be seen," he replied cheerfully. "After all, we don't know each other very well yet."

His sudden evasiveness gave Erde a chill. Was he suggesting she *was* a witch? She decided to pursue the subject in another way.

WHAT, she wrote, IS A DRAGON GUIDE?

Hal peered at her thoughtfully. "It really must pass down in the blood, for you to be here with him and yet so unknowing. How did you ever find each other? No, wait, first tell me this." He again produced the dragon brooch out of his jerkin and handed it to her as if he'd rather not let it out of his keeping but knew he must. "Does it warm to your touch?"

Erde frowned at it, then laid it to her lips, recalling how she had done so before. The stone was warm, body temperature, as if it were alive. Superstition chilled her. She nearly threw the brooch down but caught hold of herself and merely nodded. Together they stared at it, lying there on her open palm: deftly wrought silver, finely carved red stone, a tiny dragon rampant.

IT HAS NO WINGS, she scratched in the dust.

Hal nodded, and they both turned to regard the dragon asleep in the shadows. After a while, he sighed and took the brooch from her hand, holding it up to the fire.

"Yes, girl, there is magic in the world." He twisted the carved stone in the ruddy light. "Carnelian, I'd say. The setting, oh, probably a hundred years old at most, from the working of it. The stone, well . . . I always suspected Meriah was . . ."

A witch? Erde glanced at him questioningly. He took her hand and wrapped her fingers around the brooch, then enveloped her fist gently with both his own as if she was something rare and precious. "Listen, dearest child, whatever we may think in the here and now, whatever our questions and confusions, our . . . disappointments or misfortunes, the truth is that longer ago than either of us can imagine, an eternal promise was made. This stone is the sure token of it. You are its fulfillment. Can you understand any of that?"

She shook her head worriedly.

"It will come, with time." Hal squeezed her hand and let it go. "The token was passed down and down and down in secret, most of its bearers as unaware as you of the responsibility carried in their blood. Only through exhaustive study such as mine would you . . ." He turned his head away but it was less a negative than a warding off. Erde could read his ache and his effort to accept the evidence of his ears and eyes. Whatever this Dragon Guide was meant to do, Heinrich von Engle felt he was better suited to it than an ignorant fourteen-year-old girl. But acceptance of meanings deeper than he could perceive was part of his scholar's burden. She understood why he focused so heavily on the random luck of lineage.

"No one could know when the time would come," he was explaining, "for the dragon to wake, for the promise to be called upon. The Dragon Guide must guide the dragon through the world of men while he carries out the purpose he's been awakened for. The very purpose, milady, that we must set our lives to discerning." Hal watched her hopefully, as if waiting for some light of revelation in her eyes. Erde could not offer him any, but the knight did appear to have achieved some pragmatic measure of resignation. He waved an arm unnecessarily. "But look, it's dawn already, and a foolish old man with too much talk has robbed you of your necessary rest. Sleep now. The Mule will stand guard."

Erde nodded her good night and lay down. Her stomach was full and her brain was bursting. She'd need many nights of lying awake to sort out the confusion that the knight's arrival had added to an already muddled and complex picture. But tired as she was, this night would not be one of them.

An eternal promise? What if I cannot fulfill it?

She fell asleep listening to the dragon snore.

Chapter Fifteen

E rde woke from a dream-struggle with a real hand clamped firmly over her mouth. She was sure her father had found her. But it was the stranger knight's voice close to her ear, begging her to lie still. Her first clear thought was to regret that she'd misjudged him after all, then to wonder why the dragon did not come to her rescue.

"Hush, milady, you must be still! You must be still!" Hal's quiet persistence finally got her full attention. She stopped fighting him, and he let her go.

"That's better." He sat back on his heels. "Are you awake?"

Erde looked about. Gray light filtered through the pine boughs, hazed with pale floating ash from the dead fire, which she had kicked up in her troubled sleep. She had no idea what time of day it was.

"You cry out in your sleep, did you know?" Hal whispered hoarsely. "Out loud."

Erde stared at him.

"Truth, milady."

She tried her voice. Perhaps it had come back while she wasn't noticing.

Hal watched her strangled efforts. "Well, there's nothing wrong with your workings, I swear it. But it's a providence you woke me. Listen."

Erde heard, in the distance, the baying of hounds.

"Picked up your scent, damn their well-bred noses. I'd hoped the rain would ... well, no matter. We'll have to move in full light for a few hours. Pack up, now. Time we were leaving. *Quickly.*" He held her attention a moment with a hand on her shoulder. "Was it one of ... *his* dreams that frightened you so?"

Erde shrugged. She remembered nothing but a sense of being unable to breathe.

"Well, try to remember it. Whatever it was, it gave you your voice again for a while."

She had no time to think about dreams. It should have been easier traveling by daylight, even as it began to fade into steely dusk, but now speed was essential and the thick pine needle mat was as slippery as a slope of glass. The low-hung branches whipped at her face as Hal urged them swiftly upward through the forest, searching for drier, rockier terrain where their passage would leave a less obvious trace. He set a punishing pace, flanked easily by the she-goat, who had taken a liking to him as a stray dog might. Though the mule now carried her pack and sword, Erde managed a mere short hour before flagging. The knight did everything but drag her along to keep her going, and finally, it was the dragon who lagged behind, as if he didn't really understand the need for all this urgency.

Hal stopped at the top of a rise when it was almost dark. A black sky whipped with clouds showed through the thinning trees. He seemed hardly winded, and the mule, who had followed behind the dragon as if herding him, was cool and dry.

"They'll have us within the hour if we can't move faster." Hal looked up, sucking at his teeth. A bright full moon was rising past the dark branches. "I did think he would have wings . . ."

Catching her breath, Erde let her head loll back to stare at the clearing sky. She could not recall ever seeing such brilliant stars, as thick as daisies in a meadow. Even the moon did not diminish their sparkle, and the sharp music of the hounds cut through the night air like trumpet alarms. The pack was gaining.

"At least we'll be able to see where we're going," Hal remarked. He pointed ahead down the hillside, where a narrow stony valley split the forest with a sudden gash of moonlight on weathered rock. A rush of water fell away in a twisted course among man-sized boulders. "No cover, but we might lose them in the creekbed."

He led them down the rock-strewn slope toward the surging water, past waist-high stones that gleamed as white as teeth rising from the cold dark ground. At the river's edge, the she-goat knelt for a long drink while Hal called the mule to him.

"He is very surefooted, milady. If you ride, we're more likely to elude the pack." He smiled as if it were a Sunday jaunt. "And you will keep your feet dry."

Erde did not argue. The mule was narrow and bony, but her legs were twisted with cramp and the knight's worn saddle looked very inviting. She had no strength left. Only her fear of capture kept her upright and moving. Hal had been right to say she'd been lucky so far. She let him boost her up. Feeling about for the reins, she realized there weren't any.

Hal rested a hand on the mule's dappled neck. "Oh, we did away with those quite a while ago, he and I. Can you manage without? Believe me, he knows better than we which road to choose." He stroked the mule's nose. "Swift as you can now, Mule."

The mule tossed his head as if he hadn't needed to be told, then moved briskly into the shallow, fast-moving water, picking a delicate sure path among the rocks. The she-goat followed, bounding from stone to stone with weightless precision. Hal waited for the dragon to precede him, but Earth stalled at the edge and would not step into the rushing water. He stretched his neck toward Erde and swayed back and forth in misery and confusion.

"My lord, you must," muttered the knight, with the air of a man who senses his rhetoric to be out of date but has no acceptable substitute.

Clinging to the mule as it tottered precipitously downstream, Erde saw in her mind the dragon's panic, so like a child's—lurid, distorted images of vast horizons, of dark and rolling waves, of falling water, wrenching currents and suffocating undertow, all foreign and terrifying to her own landlocked imagination. She'd seen Earth walk into water before, but then it had been shallow and still and comfortably (for him) confined by cavern walls. She tried to project calm and reassurance, but he would have none of it, perhaps because she was as frightened as he was. She didn't know how to swim. Court ladies were not taught how to swim. In desperation, she imaged the Mage City for him, his new goal, for which all fears must be overcome, and this convinced him at least to follow along the bank as fast as he could, slithering snakelike up and down among the boulders.

Hal waded in behind, a dark silhouette against moonlit stone.

The pack was so close now that Erde could distinguish the voices of individual dogs and hear the occasional spooked scream of a horse being spurred against its better judgment through a strange nighttime forest. Her own fear encouraged the dragon's. Together, their terrors built to a fevered pitch until she felt she was actually drowning in the nightmare ocean of Earth's imaginings. She knew this could not be, yet felt the deep wet chill and the water rushing into her mouth. She welded her body to the mule's saddle and gave up all other awareness in order to picture herself swimming, somehow swimming, holding the dragon's great head above the torrent.

The creek deepened as they moved downstream, gathering in wide fast-moving pools between steepening rapids. The piled boulders lining the banks grew higher and higher until they fused into the broken walls of a gorge that rose straight up from the rushing water. The dragon was forced to climb the cuts and ledges to keep abreast of Erde and the mule. The rising sides threw the streambed into deep moon-shadow and the roiling of the water filled the air with noise. They came to the edge of a pool, a smooth oily surface spanning the width of the gorge. The mule hesitated, then launched himself into the frigid darkness.

The real water was colder and wetter than the imagined ocean. It shocked Erde's awareness back to her own predic-ament. The air was dank and roaring. The mule was a strong swimmer but hidden currents in the pool drew them cross-wise, toward the source of the noise, toward a black misted horizon where the river plunged into a gap between two huge upright stones.

A falls! Erde could only stare ahead as she was drawn to-ward the thundering void. The mule struggled valiantly, and the dragon's anguished call filled her head. This was what he had feared. This was what he had seen, before any of them had been aware of it.

Suddenly, a pale form materialized in the shadows along-side, the she-goat dancing on a flat rock that jutted at a slant into the deep water. Her little hooves beat a staccato on her water-smoothed landing and the mule swerved toward her. Hope strengthened his breathless, groaning strokes. He gained momentum against the current, found footing at last.

The current tore at stirrups and saddle and Erde's numbed legs, but he heaved himself out of the water with a wrenching grunt and scrambled onto the she-goat's rock.

Over the roar of the falls, Erde heard the baying of the hounds.

The goat danced back and away, seeming to vanish unaccountably. The mule plunged after her, into a slanting fault that formed a narrow ramp up the wall, hemmed in by an old rock slide from above, so narrow that Erde's legs scraped the stone. The cut climbed toward the top of the gorge, then doglegged away abruptly in an open ledge. Below, the river plummeted into blackness with a sound like mountains falling.

Erde clung to the mule, shivering in the mist-drenched updraft. Past the crumbling edge of the ledge, she could see nothing but a curve of moonlit hills softening the dark and distant horizon. Around the dogleg, the ledge widened, cutting back into the rock to form a shallow cave. The she-goat backed into the overhang and immediately lay down. The mule glanced about, turned himself around gingerly to face the void, then twisted his head around to nudge Erde's knees.

She slid off the mule without thinking, then sank to her hands and knees to crawl back along the ledge. The racketing of the dragon's terror in her brain left her blind to all but a need to rush to his aid. She felt along the wall to the corner where the cut descended and the rock slide closed around it. Scaling a low boulder, she could see across the falls to the far wall of the gorge. Bright moonlight spilled across, outlining the dark bulk of the dragon trapped on a high dead-end ledge in full view of anyone upstream. In full view and well within range of her father's archers, once they reached the edge of the pool. Now Erde could hear the shouts of the men as well as the baying of the hounds.

Oblivious to all but the dragon's peril, she began to scramble up the rock slide toward him, heedless of the precipitous gap and the thundering falls that separated them. The first of the dogs bounded into sight at the head of the gorge.

"NO!" Hal grabbed her roughly about the waist and hauled her backward off the rock. He was soaked through, as if he had swum the pool. "Stay down! You can't help him now! Where's the Mule?"

Erde pointed up the ledge.

"Don't move!" Hal sidled away, then returned with his longbow and quiver from the mule's saddle.

On the far side of the pool, the dogs swooped downstream in a rush. Discovering an impassable depth, they circled and whined at the edge, and made little dashes up into the surrounding rocks and back again. Clattering and shouting, the huntsmen arrived behind them as if already on the attack, several on foot with their crossbows loaded, the rest still mounted, their horses slipping and stumbling on the water-slick stone.

"Nervous, aren't they?" Hal notched an arrow. "Keep still until we know we're seen."

Erde pressed her forehead to the cold rock. The arrival of the hunt was terrifying when seen through the dragon's eyes, far more so than it was in reality—the awful baying of the dog pack, their evil smell filling his nostrils, the vicious sinewy curve of a bow, the steel tip of an arrow gleaming in the moonlight. She could not push reason to the surface past his panic. Her heart raced. Her breath came in silent gasps. Every muscle strained with Earth's helpless need to flee. She gripped the rock with both hands to stay herself from leaping up again.

In a blink, the horrific visions were gone. Erde saw nothing but the backs of her eyelids, felt nothing but the chill grit of the rock beneath her grasping fingers. It was as if the dragon had winked out of existence, leaving her with only her own eyes and ears, and her own more familiar terrors. She looked up. Earth was there as before, clinging to his narrow ledge.

She heard Hal gasp softly, saw him squint in amazement, staring across the gorge. At the pool's edge, the archers milled about, pointing this way and that, cursing and cuffing the whining, confounded hounds, never noticing the hulking creature perched on a ledge in plain view in front of them.

"This is some magic of his," Hal murmured wonderingly.

Erde frowned at him questioningly. She gestured at Earth's dark profile, so clearly etched against the pale moon-washed stone.

"You see him still?"

She nodded.

"Not I. He was there as clear as day, and now only a chunk of the natural rock."

Erde worried about the knight's eyesight, but up till this moment, it had proven exceptionally sharp for a man his age. And the skilled huntsmen below were not the sort to miss so large a target, even at night. Apparently they couldn't see the dragon either. She stared at Earth, trying to separate her awareness from his until he flickered a bit, then actually did blend with the wall behind him. When she blinked, he was there again. She sent him a view of himself as she'd seen him, an innocent chunk of rock on the wall of a gorge. Once he believed her, they both understood he'd done something to save himself without being aware of it. He could not tell her how it had come about.

There was much arm-waving down in the gorge as the hunt-master summoned his men for a conference.

Hal tugged her sleeve. "Recognize any of them?"

Erde nodded. The leader was a stout braggart named Otto, another of her father's recent appointments. Watching him posture before his men, she realized how the new baron had chosen to surround himself with men weaker than himself. Even Rainer, she noted guiltily, but only because he'd been so young. This man Otto was blustery and stupid. Erde scratched his name in the dust with abrupt strokes.

"Who's the best shot?" asked Hal.

Erde pointed out another man, shorter and grizzled, with a large hound tagging his knee. An old pro, this man, who had served her grandmother long and well. It seemed strange to be hunted by men she'd known all her life, even though she'd considered them the enemy since she'd begun leading the deer away from them.

GRIFF, she wrote.

"Griff. Ah, yes." Hal adjusted the aim of his bow. "I recall that man from my days with Meriah. He's much aged . . . but then, so am I."

Otto's sharp voice carried easily over the roar of the falls. "She must have crossed over way back! If we double back fast, we're sure to catch her."

"I thought witches don't cross over water," returned a voice.

"Gave us the slip in the rocks, then. You can bet she didn't go over the falls."

Griff stood apart, studying the walls of the gorge. The dog beside him did not mill and whine with the others. Erde strained to hear his reply. "You know, a girl alone could hide herself anywhere in a spot like this. Some of us ought to stay behind and wait her out."

"Wait here? Are you kidding?"

"A witch can make herself invisible. She might be standing right next to you!"

Hal grinned. "See how jumpy you've made them?" he whispered. "Hunching about like they expect to be spell-struck? Good thing the dogs can't tell him everything they smell out there on the ground."

A good thing also, thought Erde, *that Otto is too insecure in his position to listen to anyone, even a more experienced man who had been hunt-master when the baroness was alive.* It had not been easy leading the deer away from Griff. But her father had demoted the old huntsman, saying he was not "respectful," and replaced him with a lesser man, who was now turning his sensible advice into an argument.

"You're dog-man now, Griff, remember? You'll do what you're told! We've wasted enough time here already! That damned bitch of yours has lost her nose! I've a mind to do her in right now!"

Griff looked up at Otto, then away. So did the dog lying at his feet. "You would have some explaining to do to his lordship."

"Well, he's a fool and so are you!"

The other men shifted uneasily, but Griff only smiled sourly, then gathered up the rest of the dogs and led them back upstream.

Hal unnotched his arrow. "We're safe for now, I think."

Earth withdrew into himself on the ledge above the pool, and stayed that way long after the baron's men and dogs were gone from the gorge. Hal would not let Erde risk the pool and the falls to go to him.

"Is he still there? What's the matter with him?"

Erde looked away from the dragon long enough to scrawl a reply.

THINKING. WON'T TALK TO ME.

"Thinking?"

HOW HE DID IT.

"How he went invisible?"

Erde nodded, keeping her eyes fixed on Earth.

"Yes, well, that will be interesting to hear. Now, no moving about until I've made sure friend Otto hasn't left an

archer or two behind just to hedge his bet." Hal called the
mule to him. "Keep an eye on milady, a close watch, you
hear?"

He took his longbow and quiver, and slipped away among
the rocks. The mule stationed himself in the path and gave
Erde the same concentrated attention she was giving the
dragon. One glance told Erde there'd be no sneaking past
him. So she put all her energy for mental persuasion into
drawing Earth off his ledge. She felt the loss of him in her
mind as a vague but persistent anxiety, a potential for un-
bearable grief. Shivering in her still-damp clothes, she sent
him pleas of love and encouragement, and very specific
how-to pictures of himself climbing down into the gorge.
The dragon did not respond. He was too busy thinking.

Hal returned before Earth did, with a small deer over his
shoulder. The mule woke Erde from her doze with a gentle
nudge.

"They've camped a mile or so up out of the gorge along
the streambed. With luck, we'll be able to slip past them."
He shrugged the deer carcass onto the mule's withers.
"Don't know about you, I'm starving, but we should move
out of this dead end before it gets light." Hal nodded across
the falls. "Any luck with him?"

Erde shook her head, as much to clear it as to answer him.
Anxiety had dulled her hunger, but she wanted more than
anything to be warm and dry again.

"At least I can see him now."

Erde looked, then eased back against the rock as the dragon's presence returned to her in full flood. Hal's concern
faded to relief tinged with envy as he watched the joy spread
across her face.

"Is he all right? Will he come down now?"

Erde nodded, eagerly clearing space in the dirt.

HE THINKS HE REMEMBERS.

Hal waited.

NOT MAGIC, she wrote. SKILL.

The knight looked dubious.

STILLNESS = INVISIBILITY.

Hal frowned, reading her words several times over. "That
would be a very profound stillness indeed . . ."

DEER IN THICKETS.

"But . . ." Hal rubbed his eyes. "Ah, why should I expect

to understand him anyway. What's important is, can he do it again?"

HE DOESN'T KNOW YET.

Hal nodded wearily. "Well, I hope he'll let us know when he finds out. Brush those letters away, eh?" He turned back to the mule. "We've got to get moving before we freeze."

Earth clambered down from his perch with a modestly self-satisfied air. He awaited them in the gorge, but still would not cross the stream.

"Can't he explain about the water?"

IT'S MOVING, she scratched in a sandy spot.

"There's a clue in that," muttered Hal. "Somewhere." He let the she-goat find a drier path around the pool, and they rejoined the dragon where the stream narrowed. Earth seemed surprised and gratified when Erde threw herself at him and hugged him joyously.

"Well, I've had a thought as well," Hal announced. "I know our next destination. It's a short week's travel from here. Not exactly this whatever Mage-Queen you've promised him, and we may not exactly be welcome, but it's as good a place as any to start unraveling this mystery."

Chapter Sixteen

They sneaked past the Hunt's encampment well down-wind, threading precariously through a high tumble of rocks that had once fallen just short of the gravel beach where the huntsmen slept. Down in the shadow of the boulders, the coals of a hastily built cook fire sputtered amidst a scatter of snoring bodies. No watch had been posted, but Hal pointed out a ring of crude crosses, fastened out of twigs and stuck into the sand around the sleepers.

"They'd do better to fear the living," he murmured in Erde's ear.

As they passed by above, the dogs below stirred and whined but did not raise an alarm.

Hal led his party around the crest of the mountain. By dawn, they had descended into the evergreen forests on the far side and felt safe enough to build a small fire of their own in the lee of a rock shelf, just as the sun glanced pinkly off the tall thin spikes of the firs. Erde envied those trees. She would risk a good deal just to stand quietly out in the open sun.

"Exercises tomorrow," declared Hal. "This morning, we rest. It's an advantage that they still think you're out here alone. They'll underestimate your food supply, the water you can carry, the distance you might travel, everything about us."

He cut venison to cook for Erde and himself, then apologetically offered the rest of the deer to the dragon. Earth sniffed at it curiously, then curled up like a vast scaly dog and went to sleep.

"Too dead for him. Dragons are not scavengers," the knight explained as he skewered chunks of venison with lengths of green sapling. He seemed pleased that at least one bit of his hard-won dragon-lore had proven correct. Erde did not offer to explain Earth's bizarre relationship to his living meals. It seemed far too complicated a subject for the limitations of sand scratchings. "But he's eaten recently, has he not? He'll be all right for a while." Hal offered a filled skewer to Erde, who sat huddled in her cloak against the rock wall. "Come on, girl! Work for your supper!"

She roused herself for the skewer, then settled by the fire with eyes downcast. Their narrow escape from the Hunt had left her drained and feeling newly vulnerable.

"You're looking rather sad and thoughtful just now, milady." Hal lowered his own heavily laden skewer into the flames. "I'd rather you ate that up and got some rest, but if there's a tale you wish to tell, I'll stay awake for it."

If only I could *tell it,* Erde mused. But even if she'd had her voice, the tale she had to tell was of events connected only by chronology, not by any logic or meaning that she could perceive. Not like Alla, or the court bard, whose stories always made sense. Events were not random in their tales as they seemed to have become in hers.

She was beginning to understand that the weight dragging down her feet and her eyelids by the end of each night's travel was not just exhaustion. There was also the pain she hadn't faced yet, the true depths of the grief she'd shoved aside in her struggle to survive. Hal's arrival had eased the struggle. He was a resourceful male adult, and she trusted him. Under his protection, she could be a child again, the child she still was inside. She could feel free to grieve.

She let the skewer drift close to the fire as she brooded, until a log shifted. Sparks flew up around her wrist and the raw meat sizzled. Erde jerked her hand back, aware that her other hand gripped the hilt of Rainer's sword so hard that it had gone numb. She lifted it out of the cloak folds and dragged it into her lap.

"How 'bout you start by telling me about that?" Hal pulled his meat out of the fire and blew on it delicately.

Erde regarded him with big eyes and shook her head. She wished she could, but it was still too painful. Even in her dreams, her mind shied away from it. Besides, she knew she could not tell the story of Rainer's death to anyone, not even the dragon, until she understood what he had meant to her.

"Then let me tell you what a fighting man can tell from this stranger's weapon." He spread his wiping cloth on the

pine needles and laid out his too-hot dinner, then extended
his hand. Reluctantly, she placed the hilt in his palm. Free-
ing it from its linen wrappings, he stood, groaning and complaining of stiffness though he settled into his fighting
stance with the grace of long experience. Erde gathered up
the wrappings possessively, resisting the urge to snatch back
the sword and cover its nakedness. Hal held it level, first
balanced on one palm, then gripped and held out in front of
him. His eyes narrowed in concentration. He swung it a few
times, a long sideways arc, then overhand. Satisfied, he resettled himself in a dappled fall of early sunlight to study the
hilt and shaft in detail.

"A well-made blade but plainly presented. A skilled ar-
morer, a day-to-day purpose. A working blade, not a courtier's, definitely not your father's, I see that now. Iron Joe
would never stoop to such an honest blade." He turned it in
the light like a chirurgeon with an old bone. "A newish
blade, not too heavy but on the long side. A tall man, lightly
built, probably young. A blade not often bloodied but scrupulously maintained. A responsible young man, a little insecure yet but proud enough of his ability to spend several
months' salary on a better than average weapon, and unpre-
tentious enough to avoid needless decoration." Hal lowered
the tip of the sword until it just touched the ground. "I hope
this wasn't the man they say you struck dead with a witch's
spell at the castle gate. I could use the man who carried this
blade. I'd make a fine soldier out of him. Don't go killing
them off, milady—there are few enough around as it is."

He glanced over at her, grinning, and found her face
twisted with grief. He had described Rainer so accurately
that it left her breathless. She could almost see him just beyond the fire, sword in hand, fresh from the practice yard,
his favorite place, smiling in welcome. For a moment, she
hated the elder knight. It should be Rainer sitting across
from her now. Why couldn't he have kept himself alive? At
last, the tears came freely. She could no longer hold them
back.

Hal knelt quickly and set the sword aside. "Ah, child, you
can't mind the self-serving inventions of a power-mad cleric.
I know you have killed no one."

Erde shook her head frantically, then both her hands, then
buried her face in them and wept as she had not been able
to since she'd been told of Rainer's death. Brother or lover,

whatever he was, it didn't matter, she wept for him anyway, and for Alla, her only other friend, and for her grandmother, whose counsel and company and strength she did not feel whole without. And she even wept for Georg, whose life she'd been forced to take, so that her own might continue.

Hal reached across the fire and patted her shoulder once, then let her cry.

She wept long after the knight had banked the fire and gone to sleep. She was unable to stop herself. She crawled over to the dragon's side, curling up next to him for warmth, but could not keep the sobs from coming. Wave after wave until her brain was dulled with it. Only when the afternoon gloom deepened under the thick pines and the dragon stirred and woke, filling her mind with his curiosity, needing her attention, demanding her response, did she get hold of herself and dry her eyes. Her grief remained as sharp as ever but having finally given in to it, she could put it in its place. She had to. She could not be dragging about like a stone, weighed down by painful memory. She had to be fit and alert. She was the Dragon Guide, and she knew where her duty lay.

Chapter Seventeen

Erde had thought it was just the usual man-talk, but Hal really did mean her to learn to use the weapon she had carried into exile. He rushed her through their meager breakfast and, while there was still light enough to see clearly, he found an opening among the tree trunks and began shoving the pine mat aside with the edge of his boot.

He waved Erde into action. "Help me with this! Good footing is crucial!" When he was sure she'd keep at it, he trotted away into the woods and came back with two stout sticks that he'd cut, each the length of one of their swords. She was almost disappointed. Now that the mule was packing Rainer's sword, she missed it, as if the time she spent with it was what kept the memory of him alive in her mind. But the stick that Hal handed her was plenty heavy enough.

The dragon watched Erde swing the stick about for a while, then wandered off to hunt. Hal inspected the circle of cleared ground.

"Good enough. Let's get to work."

As he raised his own stick and took up his stance, Erde felt a sudden panic. What if he attacked? What if he humiliated her? But the knight drew her over beside him, a few paces apart, both facing a shared audience of one very jaded mule and a puzzled she-goat.

"Now. Watch my movements and repeat them exactly. No, I said *exactly!*"

The movements seemed neither difficult nor complicated. Erde's confidence soared with her relief. But Hal made her repeat each one until she had managed ten perfect repetitions in a row with no rest in between, and after the fourth simple ready, step, and swing exercise, she was heated up and breathing hard. Her right arm ached in places she hadn't even known she had a muscle.

As soon as he saw her growing clumsy, Hal stopped the lesson.

"Enough for today." He took her stick and tied both of them to the mule's saddle. "Now. Here's how you stretch that arm out so it won't tighten up on you."

And so it went, for many nights' travel through the unbroken forest. They were spared rain for a while, and the temperature warmed slightly as they descended from rock ledges and tall pines through dense stands of birch and golden-leaved aspen, down into maple and wide-spreading oak touched with a blush of early fall color. For a while, the shared nightmares ceased, perhaps because both Erde and the dragon felt safer in Hal's company, perhaps because they were eating more regularly, or simply because he pushed them hard and they were too tired. They would stop at dawn, exercise, eat, and sleep, then wake at dusk, exercise and move on, night after night.

They kept to the cover of forest, staying clear of the towns, skirting the occasional farmstead cut out of the wilderness, avoiding a woodcutter's cottage or two. Finally, when Hal was confident that he could detect no pursuit, he left Erde to sleep one day while the dragon hunted, and rode the mule into a charcoal burners' camp to trade news for bread and cheese.

He found his news was already stale, but being able to offer an eye-witness account of the Tubin burning gave him his choice of supper tables and a full pack to speed him on his journey.

"Came in from the north, like I was headed from Tubin the long way," he explained to Erde later. "Left to the south and cut back east soon as I could. You know what the latest story is?"

She shook her head, her mouth gloriously full of fresh bread and cheese.

"That the Baron's Hunt cornered you where two rivers crossed, and were just about to bind you when you called up a demon in a blinding flash of light to carry you away to safety." He cocked his head at her. "There's just no end to your powers, milady."

Erde smiled back at him, trying to take the witch tales as casually as he did. But they weighed on her increasingly, because she was sure that someday she was going to be made accountable for them.

During the first nights of travel, Hal talked to her as they walked, about the countryside, the route he was taking, where they might camp for the day. But after the first few, he ceased trying to keep up both ends of this one-way conversation. Soon they were traveling in silence, but it was a companionable silence.

"I've traveled alone for two years now." They were setting up camp by a streambed. "There's many out in the countryside that don't know or understand the details of the king's troubles with his barons. Some'll still show a King's Knight some respect, and there are things I can do to help out here and there, so I get along." Hal brushed bread crumbs from his jerkin. "I still wear the Red as you can see, out of respect for His Majesty—only took it off once or twice sneaking into Erfurt to check up on the situation at court. I'm best off staying unobtrusive, so some baron doesn't get a notion to try me for invented treasons. So I'm used to silence. I talk to the Mule sometimes, but I never let myself talk to myself. That way madness lies. . . ."

Erde was not sure of that. She'd talked to herself quite a bit when she'd had her voice. She'd never thought she was going mad until she could no longer speak her mind out loud. Besides, Alla had talked to herself nonstop, sometimes even when you were there in the room with her, and Alla was the sanest person Erde had ever known. Except for her grandmother, although, to Erde's mind, the baroness' dedication to duty and power did occasionally put her sanity at risk. Suddenly the purpose of this line of reasoning became clear: if she dedicated herself to the dragon as it seemed she had been born to do, what would she become? Would she give up love for the sake of duty, as her grandmother had apparently done? Would she give up her lands for the sake of an obsession, as Hal had done? She brooded over this until she remembered she had neither lands nor lover anymore, so what did it matter?

Even so, she woke the knight out of an after-dinner doze by the fire to discuss the issue.

DID MY GRANDMOTHER LOVE POWER TOO MUCH? She formed the letters very carefully in the soft ash layer, as if to render her question more comprehensible.

Hal blinked, yawning. "Hmmm. Well. Yes. Now that's a hell of a question to come out of a young girl."

Erde frowned at him sharply.

"Yes, yes, just let me think. That was a sound sleep you woke me out of. Let's see ... it depends on who you ask, you know?" He sat up, rubbing at his beard as if it might help him to think more clearly. "If you ask me, which you did, I'd say yes, of course, since she loved power more than she loved me. But ask the crofter whose survival depended on her honesty and diligence in running the estates, and he'd like as not say no. At least your grandmother, unlike your father, was capable of wielding power's responsibilities and thinking of someone other than herself. Does that answer your question?"

Erde nodded pensively. She'd thought of power as a license to take what you needed and push other people around. That was what her father did. But not her grandmother? Power as a responsibility was a new concept, yet it made sense in the pragmatic context Hal had offered. She understood she'd been frivolous all those times she'd vexed her grandmother with airy insistences that she didn't care about power. She was troubled by his suggestion that the baroness had considered her to be Tor Alte's proper heir. Had she failed her grandmother without knowing it? Would events have fallen out differently if she'd been a more diligent student in the baroness' unofficial course of study?

At least her grandmother had never spoken of power with personal relish, the way her father did. Yet in following the priest's lead, the baron had given up power to him. Why give it up so readily, if he loved it so much?

Hal was dozing again. She nudged him with her foot. WHY DID PAPA GIVE OVER TO FRA GUILL?

"What has gotten into you, girl? Was it the fish for supper?" Hal struggled up again, groaning as if the effort were enormous. "I know you won't rest till I answer."

Erde nodded, offering an eager placating smile.

"You want the long or the short version?"

SHORT.

"Good, that's easy, assuming your father to have no greater fear for his immortal soul than the next man. So—what does your father want more than anything else?"

TO BE IMPORTANT.

"And what will make him important?"

POWER?

Hal nodded approvingly. "He to whom power is important is vulnerable to anyone who wields it more cleverly than he does. The hell-priest is damnably rich in power just now. I assume he promised your father a share of it."

Erde's mouth worked in instinctive protest. Nothing came out but a puff of frustrated breath.

"But how could he trade his only daughter for the promised share? Well now, that's either a true measure of his obsession or something a bit more complicated. I suspect it's a bit of both. But that's the long answer."

Erde did not want complications. Her mind was drawing long loops, seeking simple connections. Complications could come later.

WHAT ABOUT THE KING?

"How's that?"

THE BARONS LOVED POWER MORE?

"No, he . . ." Hal paused, sucking his teeth morosely. "Well, maybe so. What the king values most is peace. He had power enough to establish it in good times, but not enough to maintain it through times like these. So for now, he sits in Erfurt at their convenience, ruling in name only."

FOR NOW?

"Of course, for now," he replied indignantly. "You think I wear the Red for sentiment? His Majesty is still king by the grace of God, and what other duty could a King's Knight claim but to see his monarch securely on his throne once again?"

For that, Erde had no answer. She sat back, pulling the folds of her cloak up around her shoulders. She had enough to chew on for one day, and finally she let the knight sleep. She hoped it was not too late to become her grandmother's faithful student.

Meanwhile, the dragon practiced becoming invisible.

Chapter Eighteen

Of course, Earth could only be invisible while he was standing still. This meant he must practice while his companions rested, or be left behind. Or so he thought. The dragon had not yet understood that he was the glue that held this oddling band together.

"Don't ever tell him we'd each die before leaving him behind," Hal warned quietly. "He's slow enough as it is."

How quickly men become impatient, Erde marveled, *even with the things they claim to worship.*

"I hope you'll pardon my presumption, milady, but ... can't you get him to move along a little faster?"

Erde shrugged, shook her head. Being unable to speak did offer relief from having to explain herself—or the dragon. The truth was, she hated hurrying him unless he was in danger. Hal was fairly sure that they'd eluded their pursuers for the time being, and she thought what Earth was learning was too important to rush. He seemed so encouraged by having discovered he had at least one skill. Let him practice at his own pace.

"He's getting the idea, at least," Hal conceded. "And I suppose if you're as old as he is, an hour or two of human time seems like the blink of an eye. What can 'hurry up' possibly mean to a dragon?"

Erde steered him toward a bare patch of ground. She now carried a short pointed stick in her vest to use as a stylus.

HOW OLD?

Hal chuckled. "Oh, old, you can be sure. Older than me, even. Can you belive that?" Then he grew grave and drew himself up out of his stoop as he did whenever he talked of dragon-lore. "There are conflicting opinions as to the exact day and hour of the creation of dragonkind. I myself favor those who place it on the First Day. Others are of the mind that dragons were created first among the creatures of the air, which would make it, of course, the Fifth Day. The hell-priest would place them with the fall of Lucifer and the birth of heresy in the world. Now, this *particular* dragon . . ."

The peevish look he turned on Earth, who was once again struggling to catch up, made Erde laugh. The sound was all breath but so unaccustomed that they stared at each other in surprise. Hal's mouth tightened against a grin. "Well, look at him! Does he look like something you'd expect the Good Lord to come up with on the First and Holiest Day? He's ignorant, he's clumsy, he's . . . ah!" His grin bloomed ingenuously. "Is it a disguise?"

Erde shook her head.

"Well, it was just an idea. It's just hard to accept that he's so . . . so like a child."

Erde nodded emphatically.

"Oh, you think that's good, do you? Surely, it takes one to know one." Hal made a sour face, then slowed, chewing on a thumbnail. She imagined him stalking the aisles of his library in just that posture, that is, when he'd had a library. He scratched his beard thoughtfully. "Now, you know, there are a few truly renegade minds who consider dragons to be creatures of nature that are born, grow old, and die like the rest of us. It's a radical notion, very eccentric, but their idea is that dragons mate and reproduce by the laying of great leathery eggs. Of course, I'd never given this theory much credence but . . ." He glanced back at Earth, but the dragon had again pulled to a halt and vanished. "Confounded beast!"

Erde clapped her hands in breathy voiceless mirth.

"Always happy to provide comic relief," the elder knight growled, but his eyes smiled. "Ah, well. Laughter is a healing thing, milady, and you deserve a little, after all you've been through. Maybe we both do."

A week's nights of travel brought them to the edge of a big lake. Erde had never seen a lake so broad. She ran down to the slim, graveled beach to stare out across the dark water, wondering if this was the ocean that the minstrel tales so often sang of, where great sea monsters devoured ships and all the men on them in a single gulp. The waning moon shimmered on ranks of white-capped wavelets driven toward shore in the brisk chill wind.

The dragon snorted at the nearness of all that deep moving water. He refused to share Erde's wonder. He rocked from side to side and would not follow. He pelted her with water terror until his fear overwhelmed her wonder, and she could not help but draw back nervously into the shelter of the trees with him, even though a moment before she had hoped that Hal meant to take them out on this marvelous ocean to dance with the waves.

Fortunately for the dragon, the lake itself was not Hal's destination. He led them along the shore to the lee-side of a sheltered cove where the trees hung low and close over still water, and the moonlight did not penetrate. He chose a weedy bluff back from the edge and called the mule over to unload.

"We'll rest here until morning," he declared, though they'd accomplished only half their usual distance since sunset. "He'll be awake, for sure, but we're better off not bothering him after dark."

Erde touched his sleeve inquiringly. Did he mean *safer*, she wondered. The knight pointed to a curving shadow of land across the cove. She saw a glow that came and went as the trees swayed in the wind off the lake, like a faint winking eye. The scent of wood smoke tickled her nostrils. Hidden among the trees, the dragon sneezed and sent an inquiry about white sun-tipped towers rising above green hills.

—*Soon,* Erde promised him.

She tugged Hal's sleeve a little harder.

"Answers tomorrow," he said, gathering leaves into a pile and laying out his bedroll. "And no fire tonight. Bad enough we're upwind of his expert nose, but it can't be helped. Get the sticks. Time for practice."

At dawn, the cove was sunk deep in mist. The opposite shore was as invisible in the pale light as it had been in darkness. Hal stirred and went to the edge to splash water on his face.

"Arrgh! Cold!" He stood, beard and eyebrows dripping, and stared across the cove. "Huh. Well, let him get some breakfast into him first."

Whoever "he" was, Erde was convinced she would find

him terrifying, if he made the knight so uneasy. She joined him on the misty beach, mouthing a silent WHO?

Hal considered, then shook his head. "No use my trying to explain. You'll see soon enough. If he'll even talk to us, that is." His stare shifted to the dragon, who had spent the night huddled as far into the trees as he could go without losing sight of Erde. "My hope is, Earth will win him over."

After their own meager breakfast, they packed up and started single-file around the cove. There was no path to follow. The woods were a mossy tangle of low branches and downed trees. Hal's mysterious quarry preferred living inaccessibly. In some places, they were forced into the water, and only because it was still and shallow could Erde convince Earth to follow. The underbrush was dense all the way to the shore and very damp, as the mist rose and left the weight of its moisture behind. Behind the Mule, in front of the she-goat, Erde wrapped her cloak tightly around her, but her boyishly cropped hair was drenched by the time they broke through a final curtain of bramble and saplings into a dim swampy clearing sheltered by a dozen or so tall and spreading firs. A low arm of land projected into the lake, its narrow neck protected by a barrier of thicket. Erde could see pale water past the tree trunks on three sides.

"Tell the dragon to stay back in the brush," said Hal. "Even better if he can be invisible. We'll go on to the cottage alone."

Cottage? Erde could see only a pile of forest rubble, lurking like a shadow amid the darker fir trunks. Rubble, or at most, the lodge of a very large beaver. It wasn't much taller than she, but it was set as if by design in the exact center of the clearing. A delicate wisp of smoke curled up from the top of the pile, so she supposed it was the cottage Hal meant. There was even a thick slab of bark at ground level that might be a door.

"Well, here goes," Hal muttered. He marched resolutely up to the bark slab and knocked on it with courtly restraint. If it was a door, he was going to have to stoop mightily to pass through it.

There was no reply.

Hal knocked louder, and then again, with a big stone he'd picked up from beside the door. He waited, pointing to a mutilated area in the center of the slab. "See that? He makes everybody do this! You'd think a fellow living this far away from the civilized world would want a visitor every now and then!" Hal banged on the slab again, then threw the stone at it in disgust. "Come on, Gerrasch, I know you're in there!"

"QUIET!"

Erde held herself in place by sheer will as the pile spoke, or rather, screeched. The voice was harsh and broken, as if long out of practice.

"Quiet, quiet, quiet, QUIET!"

The door flew open and out stormed the pile's occupant. For a moment, Erde feared this Gerrasch actually was a giant beaver. He was short and round and lumpy, with a great mane of curly hair covering his face. He wore what seemed to be a tunic of dark fur, overlaid with a vest of leaves, and he waddled much as a four-legged creature might if forced to walk upright. Seeing no sign of a beaver's large flat tail, Erde breathed a sigh of relief.

Gerrasch planted his stubby feet and spread his arms to grip either side of the doorway. "QUIET!"

"I hear you, Gerrasch," Hal replied.

The creature lifted his moplike head to stare at Hal with veiled but beady eyes. "Then be it." He turned, vanished into the darkness of his hovel and slammed the door behind him.

The knight sighed profoundly, one arm propped against the rubble pile, slowly shaking his head. Erde relaxed a little. It was not fear that made him wary of this exasperating personage.

Hal threw her a rueful shrug. "You'd never know we've been friends for years." He knocked again, softly. "I've brought you a dragon," he crooned.

After a long moment of wind coughing in the pine trees, the door cracked open. "I knew that," said an invisible Gerrasch.

"You know everything."

"Everything, yes."

Behind his back, Hal's fingers drummed a silent staccato. "If that weren't so close to true, I wouldn't put up with you."

Gerrasch remained in shadow. "A minor dragon, yours."

"Oh, really? Then am I to take it you're not interested?"

"Am, am, am, am, am."

"You've a damn funny way of showing it." Now Hal winked at Erde. "Maybe I won't show him to you after all."

"Where?"

"I thought you knew everything."

The door edged closed.

"He wants to meet you . . ."

The door stilled. Bright eyes peered out of the darkness. ". . . when he's sure that your knowledge is worth his bother."

The bark door swung wide. Beckoning Erde to follow, Hal ducked inside.

The inner gloom was thick with smoke and musty animal odor. The twig and rush ceiling curved so low that Hal could not stand fully upright. A circular hearth burned in the center of a dirt floor which was littered with containers of all shapes and sizes: an astonishing variety of earthenware bowls and jugs and wavy glass jars with ceramic tops, brown clay bottles and metal pails, wooden buckets, reed and wicker and woven grass baskets, even a crudely wrought barrel or two, all jumbled together, precariously stacked and piled, and all full of indeterminate substances. As Erde struggled to take it all in, Gerrasch shut the door behind her, plunging them into further darkness.

"Pull up a keg," Hal advised her comfortably.

Erde waited for her sight to adjust to the dim red glow from the hearth, then settled herself on a low cask near the door that looked the least likely to tip over. At her feet lay a basket of broken eggshells, another of pine cones, another of twigs and dirt, plus a box of assorted turtle shells. The rough-hewn walls of the hut formed an octagon, lined floor to ceiling with shelves, each bowing under the weight of more jars, jugs, bowls, and bottles.

The knight lounged silently on his keg. Erde watched him carefully for an indication of what to do next, while Gerrasch shuffled about among the jars and baskets showing only his round back, as if he had forgotten them entirely.

"So here's this dragon," offered Hal finally. "And . . . he comes with a mystery."

Still puttering with his containers, Gerrasch snorted. "No mystery to me."

"Good. Excellent. Exactly why we came."

Suddenly Gerrasch spun around to stare at Erde as if he had just noticed she was there. "Boy or girl?"

"Hard to tell, if you don't see many of either," replied Hal dryly. He resisted reminding the creature of his claim to know everything. "Gerrasch of Eiderbloom, may I present the Lady Erde von Alte."

Gerrasch lurched across the dark room toward her. Erde cried out voicelessly and recoiled off her cask, backing up against the overflowing shelves. Jars rattled. Dried branches crackled beside her head.

"Easy, girl," the knight murmured.

Gerrasch pursued her. He shoved his nose close to hers, blocking her sight entirely so that she saw only a huge halo of hair backlit by the embers and a faint reflection glimmering in his eyes. She turned her head aside, repulsed by Gerrasch's strong musky odor. She looked to Hal for support. But the knight watched impassively, as if from a great distance, his arms folded across his chest.

Gerrasch placed furry, pawlike hands on Erde's cheeks and turned her to face him. His palms were smooth and oddly cool. He sniffed at her, as a dog might inspect a stranger, then pulled his hands away and snatched up one of hers. He pressed it flat like a gypsy fortuneteller and bent his head over it, though the room was much too dark for reading anything. Erde could feel his warm breath on her skin. He sniffed again, muttering, then licked her palm. The hot wet touch of his tongue frightened her. She tried to pull her hand away, wishing to be out of this close, lightless hovel, and away from this malodorous creature who held her fast, staring as if he could see through her in the gloom. Her anxiety roused the dragon. His concern rushed into her head, his loud complaint at being left outside with only the Mule and the she-goat for company. Erde calmed herself and him, and made him promise to stay hidden in his thicket.

"A dragon. Yes. Will be." Gerrasch gave a satisfied grunt and dropped her hand. He shuffled away from her briskly and settled himself in front of the dying fire, opposite Hal. He stirred the coals, tossing on a few twigs. Hal watched him. Erde realized she had suddenly become irrelevant.

"How much?" Hal asked finally.

"Ten," came the gruff reply.

"One."

"Ha."

"Two."

"Ten."

"Three."

"Ten, ten, ten, ten, ten."

Hal unfolded his arms, dusted his palms together. "Forget it. I'm sorry I bothered." Erde was astonished that the knight thought this creature could know anything worth paying for. And if he was so mercenary, maybe it was dangerous to have come here at all. He would likely sell his knowledge of her whereabouts to the highest bidder, who would of course be her father, or perhaps the priest.

Gerrasch clicked his teeth together. "Eight. Eight, eight."

"Four," said Hal. "Not a mark more."

"Five."

"Done."

Gerrasch stuck out his hand. Tiny new flames licked up from the hearth, and Erde could see that his palm was as smooth as a baby's, fresh and pink, emerging from a dark cocoon of fur and rags. As she watched in disbelief, Hal dug into his belt and counted five silver marks into Gerrasch's soft, pink palm. The creature prodded them gently, crooning like a mother, then closed his fist around them. Shining silver vanished into darkness.

Hal looked to Erde. "He'll take it because the king's silver is still the purest."

"Five questions," the creature announced.

"Someday, Gerrasch, your greed will get the better of you."

"Ask. Time is short."

Hal scoffed. "Out here, you've got nothing but time."

"I, yes. You, no. Ask." His beady gaze shifted, then fixed on Erde. "Maybe she ask better."

"Fine with me," said Hal.

Erde frowned at him. She did not understand the game. Either he was playing with her or with Gerrasch, for surely he did not expect this half-man, half-animal to be able to read. But the knight just smiled back at her expectantly. Erde shook her head.

"The Lady Erde declines," Hal declared, "to speak with one so rude and selfish with his knowledge."

It was Gerrasch's turn to look disgusted. He turned his back on Hal with a wave of his pink-skinned paw, and peered at Erde harder. "Ask!"

His intent stare riveted her, and she felt she must answer him somehow. She patted her throat and shook her head.

Gerrasch snatched her hand away. "Ask! Ask, ask, ask, ask!"

She let out an explosion of breath and effort, and felt tears well up hot in her eyes. Gerrasch cocked his curly head, then pressed his soft palm to her throat. "Ah. Oh. Aww. Humm. Yes." His fingers probed her neck. "Word stuck."

"The lady has lost her voice," offered Hal quietly.

"No. No. Voice there. Word stuck." His touch was surprisingly gentle. "Yes, yes. Feel it right ... there."

Erde knew a word had no substance. It could not be lodged in your throat like some kind of fish bone. But it did feel like that when she tried to speak, and Gerrasch had focused on the exact spot she would have chosen, had she been asked to pinpoint the problem. She even had the sense she'd once known what the word was. She had only to remember it and her voice would be restored. Gerrasch pressed and sniffed and she found herself smiling at him. Suddenly the hovel did not feel so hot and close. She put her fingers on top of his and nodded. She thought he smiled back, but in the dim light she could not be sure, and too quickly he pulled his hand away and stepped back, no longer looking at her.

"One answer. Four more. Next?"

"Now, wait a minute," Hal protested.

"True answer, true. Only, she must find right word."

Hal stood, hunched up under the smoke-stained ceiling. "Come on, Gerrasch. I paid good King's Coin for useful information, not the hocus-pocus you cheat the locals with."

"Not hocus-pocus!"

"Oh? Then why can't you—who knows everything—just tell her what the word is?"

Gerrasch whirled away, shaking his stubby arms and head so violently that his curls battered his eyes. "She. She, she must find it!"

"He doesn't mean a real word, of course. It's a metaphor, for finding your own cure."

Erde put out a staying hand, begging him not to harass the creature further. Gerrasch's explanation was oddly satisfying, however whimsical. It made her feel less damaged and she wanted to believe him, though she had no idea how he could know such things.

Hal backed off. "All right. Besides, the questions we came to ask are about the dragon."

"Dirt."

Hal stared at him, then frowned reprovingly. "Earth."

"Dirt. Stone. Sand. Dirt."

Erde recalled how Earth had used these words in image-form to identify himself.

"I wouldn't call him Dirt when you meet him," replied Hal. "He might decide you look good to eat. You know how dragons feel about their naming."

Erde was sure she saw Gerrasch's hair-veiled eyes dart apprehensively toward the door. She wanted to reassure him that dragons don't eat people, but she wasn't entirely sure he was a person. Did being able to speak make you human, no matter what body you wore?

"Dirt, dirt, dirt," muttered Gerrasch. He lifted his heavy chin, sniffing distractedly. "Can't stay here," he hissed suddenly.

"You don't want to see the dragon?" asked Hal.

"Don't need to see."

"Smell him, then. Close up, in person."

Gerrasch was agitated again. "Can't, can't, can't." He grabbed Erde's hand, pulled her to her feet. "Dragon, you, all must go now."

"Our questions, Gerrasch. You owe us four."

Gerrasch whirled on the knight, an outraged bulk of flying curls. "You ask, then! Quick, quick, quick! You are followed."

Hal stilled. "No."

"Yes!" Gerrasch sniffed again, a long intake of breath with his stubby neck extended. "Yes, yes, yes, yes."

"Damn! I was sure . . . how many? Can you tell?"

"One, one."

Erde heard a dog baying, faint with distance.

"One? One man?"

"One, one. That is all." Gerrasch shuffled away from the hearth to pull a canvas pouch from one of the shelves. He hung it over his shoulders crosswise, then went from shelf to shelf, grabbing a pinch of this, a handful of that, and stuffing it all into the pouch. "Next question. Quick, quick. Three left."

"Damn!" growled Hal again. "All right, fast then. This is important, Gerrasch, or I wouldn't have bothered you, you know that."

"Yes, yes! Hurry!"

"Here are our questions—they're all related. Milady, if

you will alert the Dragon that we are followed, he'll pass it on to the Mule."

No need. The dragon had heard the baying from his hiding place. Erde had to use all her powers of persuasion to keep him from bolting without them.

"Question One," said Hal. "The dragon claims to have forgotten his mission: why has he been called? Two, he dreams of an unnamed Summoner: who has called him? Three, where do we go to find the one who calls?"

As Hal said this, an image of shining white towers rose up in Erde's mind. Where indeed?

"This dragon sleeps still." Gerrasch's entire interest seemed to be in filling his pouch.

"Yes, yes, but how can we wake him?"

"You cannot. He must. He, he, he must Now you go."

Hal scraped stiff fingers through his thinning hair. "Come on, Gerrasch! For five marks, I could have supplied that answer. We need your help!"

"No help, no, no, no! Can't!" Gerrasch dug in his leafy vest and flung three silver coins at the knight's feet. "You go now!"

Erde listened. The baying was still far away, still only one voice. Could Gerrasch's "one" have meant one dog? The dragon was relaying pictures of huge packs, many hundreds of monstrous hounds with gleaming razored teeth, but she knew by now that fear made him exaggerate. Meanwhile she wondered, why only one?

Hal had gathered up the coins. He held them out in his open palm. "You agreed, Gerrasch. One cast, then. We have time for one cast."

Gerrasch's pouch was full. With a sharp glare at Hal, he jerked it around to lie against his back, then scuttled away and bent among the kegs and ceramic jugs, muttering furiously. Returning to the hearth, he cleared twigs and stones and a bowl of mushrooms from a patch of dirt floor with one sweep of his wide, flat foot. He lowered himself in front of it and tossed a fistful of objects on the ground: dark, round pebbles, pearly shells, and tiny pinecones, a bone or two, and some strange seed pods, furry and sickle-shaped. Gerrasch stared at the scattering he'd made.

"Well?" prompted Hal. "Anything?"

"One: the purpose is to fix what's broken."

"Broken," Hal repeated softly. "Does it say what it is?"

176 Marjorie Bradley Kellogg

Gerrasch shook his head. "Two: the Summoner is not here."

"Of course he's not here. If he was, we wouldn't be looking for him!"

"Her."

"He . . . oh. Her." Hal nodded. "Well, that's something. So where is she?"

"Three: don't know. Don't. Not here."

"Obviously!" Hal snapped. "Like I said, if . . ."

"Not *here!*" Gerrasch swept a broad arm through the pebbles and shells, destroying whatever coherence had been apparent to him. "I tell what I see! Go away! Get out now! You want more, go to the women!"

"The women know more than you?" Hal prodded mockingly.

"Sometimes. Yes. Different things. Go there!"

"Fine. I was headed there anyway."

"Good! Ask them about the City!"

Hal laid hands on Gerrasch for the first time, grabbing him by the shoulders and staring him in the eye. "WHAT CITY?"

The City. Erde felt an absurd surge of hope, and the white towers shimmered again in her mind. The City. Just the word itself had a magical ring. She didn't know any cities. She'd only heard the word used to refer to places in the Bible, ancient places, places of miracles. Or to the City of Rome, which was the City of Heaven on Earth and was far enough away to seem ancient and miraculous.

"What city, Gerrasch?"

Erde prayed he meant her city. *Ask him where,* she thought desperately, ask him where we should go.

Gerrasch would not be intimidated further. He shoved Hal's hands away. "Ask them. Them, them, them, them."

Hal looked to Erde. "We've gotten all we're going to. Best be off, like he says. Not right to bring our hell-hounds down on his head."

Erde was torn. She had no desire to stand around waiting for her father's Hunt to arrive bows-at-the-ready in Gerrasch's little clearing, but what if he had the knowledge they needed?

Hal read her hesitation accurately. "We'll get no more here. When he's done, he's done."

So Erde nodded and Gerrasch nodded with her.

"Yes, yes, yes, yes. Must go. Quick, quick, quick." He pulled his shoulder pouch around to the front again and began kneading it frantically. A dry crunching sound and the odor of crushed herbs filled the hut, sharp enough to cover even his own musky scent. "Good. Now, come."

He waddled toward the door, snatching up a small woven-grass basket as he went. He dumped its contents on the floor and shoved it into Erde's hands as she followed behind him. At the door, he stopped short and turned.

"No Dirt," he rasped at her. "No Dirt, no, no."

Erde spread her hands in confusion.

"He doesn't want to see the dragon," Hal translated. "I think he doesn't want any knowledge that could be taken from him by force."

"Force, no fear," Gerrasch grumbled. "Bigger magic."

Hal nodded darkly. "We should respect that. Tell Earth to stay well hidden."

Only when Erde had agreed did Gerrasch open the door. He stepped cautiously into the cool dappled light, blinking as if rushing into sudden sun. The distant baying had stopped. He made Erde hold out her little basket, then filled it with his herb mixture. "For later, yes?" The rest he scattered on the ground, circling his hut in a precise and ever widening spiral.

"Covering our tracks," murmured Hal. "He'll want us to do likewise on the way out."

"Good-bye, good-bye, good-bye," Gerrasch sang hoarsely as he broadcast his herbs like a farmer sowing corn.

Hal took Erde's arm and drew her toward the dragon's thicket. "A pleasure as always, Gerrasch. I hope I haven't spent the good king's silver for nothing."

Much closer than before, the baying began again.

Chapter Nineteen

A watery sun shone through the thinning mist. Hal hustled them to the lakeshore, avoiding the thorny tangle that barriered the land access to Gerrasch's clearing. There was not a breath of wind. The lake stretched southward like a clouded mirror.

"It's shallow. He'll have to dare it," Hal insisted as, with a snort, the dragon pulled up short at the water's edge.

When the hound sounded again, Earth waded in with the rest of them.

"He's getting braver," the knight approved. But Erde knew it was because the water was still. Earth could see the sandy bottom and knew it held no terrors for him. He was like a child in many ways, yet he was waking up, slowly but surely. She recalled Gerrasch's comment and wondered, *what will he be like when he's finally, fully awake?*

Hal set a stiff pace through the shallows, following the curve of the shore until a strip of graveled beach appeared. The gravel was coarse and tightly packed. They could move fast with hardly a sign left behind. He kept to the beach for a half mile or so, then turned abruptly inland where the underbrush thinned between the trees and the land rose away from the beach.

"Remember how Gerrasch tossed that stuff around? Follow me and do the same across our trail. The Mule can show Earth what to do."

Erde didn't need to tell the dragon anything. He was already watching the mule carefully, learning about animal stealth. The two of them slipped into the undergrowth without leaving a sign. The she-goat followed closely, and Erde fell in at the end of the line with her basket of herbs, scattering them carefully behind until she ran out. Hal climbed the rise along the shore and halted in the cover of a stand of branchy young pines perched on the edge of a low sandy cliff. He gestured them to silence and listened.

"Odd, isn't it. Still only the one dog."

Erde nodded. She thought the dog sounded hoarse and tired. Through the dense velvet of the pine boughs, the beach was just visible below. She felt Earth's anticipation in her mind. He was unsure, but his fear was tempered with a new sense of readiness.

"Perfect spot for an ambush," Hal murmured. "Or at least to discover what's following us." He whistled the mule to him, unstrapped his bow and quiver, then his sword. He set them carefully on the pine mat beside him like a carpenter laying out his tools. "The Mule can take you ahead while I reconnoiter."

Erde shook her head.

"I know, girl, but it's better than exhausting ourselves running to keep ahead of them."

She nodded as sagely as she knew how.

"Oh, no, you don't. You're not a fighting man just yet."

She unsheathed Alla's slim but deadly dagger. She had cleaned the blade scrupulously out on the moonless slopes of Tor Alte, and used it many times since as a cutting edge. But now as she looked at it, she was sure some of Georg's blood still stained the shining steel.

Hal saw her face twist and misunderstood. "But you'll be fine with the Mule. The Dragon will take care of you."

Even if she could speak, how could she explain? Tell him that guilt, not fear, weakened her? Fear was simple, men understood fear. Fear only needed to be overcome. But guilt? Most men would be proud to have killed in self-defense. Hal would lose his faith in her spirit, in her grandmother's indomitable, supposedly inheritable spirit, and maybe so would she. Well, it didn't matter whether he understood or not, she refused to be sent ahead into hiding with the dragon. He wouldn't have sent her grandmother into hiding. Erde caught hold of herself, grasped the knife with a firm hand, and struck a menacing pose.

Hal hid a wry smile. "Fine. You're not scared. I still can't allow it. Off with you, quickly!"

Erde planted her feet. It was the first time since the knight had appointed himself her guardian that she'd thought to oppose him. He gazed back at her confounded, as if he'd just realized it wasn't actually his right to order her around.

"Milady, be sensible, please. For the Dragon's sake."

Erde felt Earth shuffle closer and settle down, his new readiness like a wall behind her, though the cry of the hound was nearing rapidly. Suddenly the baying stopped. The she-goat, forgotten in her self-made nest of pine needles, rose up and bounded out of the grove and down the steep slope toward the water. At the bottom, she slowed, then lowered her horned head to graze in slow casual circles along the beach.

"Well!" exclaimed the knight softly. "A full-blown mutiny! What's got into you all?"

Tired of running, Erde would have replied. She was not sure what the dragon had in mind. His nose was to the wind. He imaged one dog to her, and one man.

"Promise you'll sit down and keep still?" Hal went to the mule and quickly stripped off the rest of the packs.

Erde knew he would not debate Earth in serious matters. Complain as he might, the dragon's will was still this knight's command. He even looked pleased as he shrugged and settled himself to wait and watch for movement back the way they'd come. Minutes passed, silent but for the soft lapping of the lake and the drone of insects stirred by the pallid sun. Then, sporadic barking, a confused hound's query.

"He's lost the scent. Probably reached Gerrasch's clearing."

With a yelp of triumph, the baying began again. Unperturbed, the she-goat grazed a beach barren of anything that could have been of real interest to her.

"Here we go." Hal notched an arrow.

A large hound, of the brown and black long-eared breed common to Tor Alte's pack, burst through the trees at the far end of the beach. It flew along, nose to the ground and tail erect, singing its rhythmic song of encouragement to the hunter. Suddenly the breeze brought a distraction. The dog halted, looked about, spotted the she-goat, then cried out happily and charged. The she-goat drew herself into fighting posture and presented her horns. The hound neared, slowed, then ran back and forth before the goat, whining piteously.

Erde nudged Hal with a smile. Tor Alte's hunt pack was trained not to attack domestic animals. And she knew this dog. This dog had been one of her father's favorites, a strong bitch that ran well and produced fine litters. But she was no longer young, and as she paced closer, Erde saw she was exhausted and sweat-slathered, her short coat raked with brambles. Still she would pace and whine, until the Man arrived.

It's wrong to run a dog that hard. Erde started up from her crouch in protest.

Hal jerked her down reflexively, his eye fixed on the beach. "Where's the rest of the pack?"

Finally, a lone man armed with a crossbow detached himself from the trees along the shore, having decided no doubt that it was silly to conceal himself so carefully from someone's stray she-goat. One dog, as Earth had told her, and one man by himself. The dragon was learning that he possessed a remarkable nose. The man disarmed his crossbow and called to the dog, signaling her to circle and pick up the trail again. But the goat had walked her pattern over the trail, and Gerrasch's herbs had done the rest. The dog ran about, barking in frustration until the huntsman yelled at her to lie down and wait. She sank to the ground, panting.

The man approached slowly, and Erde saw it was the huntsman Griff, who'd served her grandmother so long and well.

"We know this one," remarked Hal.

Erde nodded. She did not recall Griff having a limp, but he was surely favoring his left leg, and looked as worn out as the dog. The two of them alone was odd enough, then she remembered that Griff was a fine horseman and always rode, even in deep forest or the worst terrain. She wondered what had become of his horse.

"One man, like Gerrasch said. Perhaps a conference is in order." Hal rose slowly, lowering his bow with the arrow still notched, and made a circling gesture to the mule. Erde caught his sleeve and indicated that she could deal with the hound. "All right, but keep at least ten paces apart from me at all times. Multiple targets." He jerked his chin at the dragon. "He stays hidden."

Erde sent stern visions to Earth, who was happy to stay put, once he'd spotted the huntsman's crossbow. *I guess you can't smell out a man's armaments,* she reasoned. She gripped her dagger and hauled her cloak up around her cheeks. While the mule approached noisily from the other direction, Hal and Erde crept down along the lowering cliff until it rejoined the beach. The huntsman was distracted by

the mule. Before he could decide that there was something
unnatural in this assemblage of farm animals alongside a deserted lake, Hal was within range behind him. Instinct made
the huntsman turn, but Hal put an arrow in the sand between
his feet and reloaded before he could set his crossbow. The
hound growled and charged. Erde whistled, the way Rainer
had taught her, and the dog slowed, whining, then swerved
toward her and was soon dancing at her feet. She sheathed
her dagger and knelt to greet it.

The huntsman, breathing hard, lowered his unarmed bow.
His narrowed eyes flicked from Hal to Erde and back again.

"Are you alone, friend, as you appear to be?" asked Hal
companionably.

"Appearances aren't everything. Who wants to know?"
The man could not turn his attention from the odd behavior
of his dog.

"We can have your army against my army," Hal replied,
"or we can talk, like civilized men."

The huntsman searched the empty beach. The tree line
was too far away for a limping, winded man to reach before
the tall stranger's bow stopped him. Plus there was his dog,
leaning happily against the smaller stranger's knee. "Alone,"
he conceded.

"And a little the worse for wear, I'd say."

The man stiffened proudly, though his breath was still labored. The side of his jaw was bruised and there was a fresh
cut over his right eye. "I'm well enough, and I'll be on my
way if you've no cause to detain me. I've nothing worth
your while."

"I meant no offense. And we're no thieves, either."

The huntsman squinted into the pale sun, which Hal had
put behind him. "What are you, then? What do you want?"

"Your name would be an excellent start."

The huntsman shrugged. He was shorter than Hal, though
they were matched in age, and the knight was armed. "I
travel from Tor Alte, with Baron Josef's Hunt."

"Tor Alte. A fair distance. East, as I recall? Does lack of
game bring you so far? There's little enough to spare here as
it is."

The man shook his head. "Answers for answers."

"Fair enough." Hal circled slowly until his face was no
longer in shadow. "Of late, I come from Erfurt."

"Erfurt." Interest flickered in the huntsman's eyes, and was as quickly hidden.

"A friend to His Majesty."

Now the man's brow shot up. "A brave admission to a stranger in these days."

"Then judge me by it."

Erde absorbed this exchange intently, noting its ritualistic formality and how Hal had leaned on the word "friend," as if it meant more than it appeared to mean. The mention of the king seemed to raise a subtext far beyond the usual male sparring for position, as if Griff now saw this stranger as something more than the steely tip of an arrow pointed at his throat.

"You wear the King's Red," he noted.

"Aye."

Griff wet his lips, then said carefully, "A little the worse for wear, I'd say."

Finally, Hal grinned. "And what King's Knight would not be, in these days?"

"None who serves him truly."

"As did your lady, the Baroness Meriah."

The huntsman cocked his head, as if hearing a far-off bell. "Ah. I do know you, sir," he said slowly, "from long ago."

"Yes, you do." Hal lowered his bow. "Heinrich Engle."

"Griffen Hesse." The huntsman stepped forward to take the hand offered him, then stopped, recalling further. "No, it was . . ." He stepped back, bowing. "Your pardon, sir. Wasn't it *von* Engle? Baron Weisstrasse?"

Erde threw Hal a look. He'd never said he was a *baron*.

"Aye, Griffen Hesse, but who can call himself baron, who's lost his lands and stronghold?" Hal kept his hand outstretched until the huntsman gave in to common courtesy and shook it. Erde recalled her father with this man, how he'd treated him like a stable hand. She admired Hal's more generous nature.

Griff found it admirable as well. The look he gave the knight was nostalgic. "That is the news in the marketplace, my lord, though there's some who'd rather not believe it. Some who'd prefer matters to be otherwise, even at Tor Alte itself."

Hal studied the huntsman speculatively, and Griff, perhaps worrying that he'd said too much, shifted and nodded at Erde. "Your lad there is good with a dog."

Hal barely spared her a glance. "Yes. He is. Have you left Tor Alte's service, then, Griff?"

The huntsman started. "No, my lord, I ..." He faltered, frowning, then lowered his gaze to the sand. "Well, sir, it's possible they may take it that way. I haven't been too careful with my mouth."

"I know how that is." Hal nodded and whistled the mule over. "Have you eaten, Griff? Will you share a meager meal with us?"

Seated on a rotting log at the top of the beach, Hal doled out chunks of bread, then unwrapped their dwindling block of hard cheese. Its pungent odor made Erde's mouth water. She took her share and sat apart, as a proper prentice lad should do, but within listening range.

"No wine, I regret." Hal unstoppered his waterskin and offered it. "Where are you headed now?"

Griff glanced over at the hound, now folded in a pile by Erde's side. "Following the dog. On the trail of Baron Josef's daughter, who's run away."

Hal chuckled. "Eloped, you mean? Who's the lucky man?"

"No, my lord, it's nothing like that. My lady's but a child still, and the new hunt-master was sure we'd lost the scent. But I'd an inclination to follow my instincts. And my old Bet's nose."

"So there was, ah ... ?"

"A parting of the ways, yes, there surely was, my lord." Griff's rueful grin was curtailed by his cuts and bruises. "But the men didn't mix in, so I had the best of it, and off I went."

"You'll have made an enemy there, I fear."

"True enough. But it was that way anyway, my lord. Guess I'm just too old to start taking my orders from a fool whose only skill is telling young Baron Josef what he wants to hear."

Erde couldn't think of her father as young, but she understood how a loyal man like Griff would think anyone an upstart who presumed to succeed Baroness Meriah.

"So the girl just up and ran away?" asked Hal casually.

"Well, they say she was lured away by a witch's spell."

"Witches!"

"There's talk of witches all over east, sir."

"You sound skeptical, Griff."

"Oh, I'm as good a churchgoer as the next man, my lord. It's just that, well ..." Griff fell silent a while, chewing his bread, then seemed to come to a decision. "Well, my lord baron, here's the truth of it, and I hope you'll pardon the mention. Young Josef's in the thrall of that same priest who they say turned you wrongly out of house and home. It's Fra Guill who's stirring up all this terror of witches and burning everyone he can get his hands on, and I just can't believe there's as many lurking about as he'd like us to think. But there's plenty who swear by his every word as if it were gospel. Now we're to be looking out for dragons as well."

"Dragons."

Griff eyed him carefully. "Yes, sir. In fact, I do believe your name's been mentioned in that regard, now that I think about it."

"Yes, that's how he usurped me. I'm suspect because of my innocent scholar's interest."

"It's worse than that now, sir. Dragons have been sighted, so they say. You're in league with Satan himself."

"Am I really? How interesting." Hal brushed dirt off his knees and straightened his jerkin. "The Prince of Darkness should take better care of his minions."

The huntsman laughed, a quick bark that spoke of a deep reservoir of anger. "The problem is, some fools will believe him."

Hal's jaw tightened. "My sword awaits him, priest or no."

"I'd do it myself, if I could get in range. He never goes anywhere without four stout men with him, his so-called brothers with short-swords beneath their robes. Does a true man of God need such protection?" Griff stretched legs and arms, warming to his complaint. "And young Josef—the baron, I mean—sits still for all this witch-talk that the baroness would never have allowed. He gives the priest the run of the castle, and takes him around to the other domains where the priest preaches hellfire to the people, then all the high-born sit up late carousing and plotting."

"Carousing and plotting." Hal sucked his teeth disconsolately. "At least that's nothing new."

"Aye, but usually they're plotting against each other." Having given rein to his tongue, Griff seemed in no mood to stop. "Now it seems there's an army being raised, my lord."

"An army?" Hal contrived to look skeptical, but this

man's information was sure to be more than rumor. "What for?"

"The priest and the young baron call it a crusade of believers, gathering to rescue the kidnapped child from the Legions of Satan. And the countryside is in a terror, with no better explanation for their bad luck and misery. But, my lord . . ." Griff leaned closer and dropped his voice, despite their obvious solitude. "I could easily see how this 'crusade' might be aimed somewhere else. When we lost the girl's scent and the new hunt-master was so ready to turn back, the men thought it was fear of her witch-powers. But I had to wonder if he was under orders not to drift too far from Tor Alte, where the Hunt might be called upon to provision the kind of army whose loyalty depends on how well you feed them."

"To many, a full belly is reason enough to offer one's sword in service these days."

"There are not deer enough in the forests for that kind of army."

Hal leaned in closer, elbows on knees. "Aimed where else, Griff?"

"I think you can guess, my lord."

Hal's fists clenched. "At the king! Of course! Times are bad and the throne is now truly vulnerable. That hell-priest has allied himself with the barons' cabal, or they with him. I wonder who's using who. Where is this army? Who else is involved?"

"So far, the army is only a few hundred men marching about under Baron Josef's command, rousting out sinners and witches, and emptying out the peasants' larders in the process. But word is, others are preparing, may even be on the road already. The cabal, as you say, flocking to the priest's crusade." He cleared stones with a sweep of his hand and sketched a rough map in the sand. "Stürn, Dubek and Zittau in the east, Rathenow and Schoenbeck in the north, and then Köthen, your old neighbor."

Hal started. "Köthen? The old man?"

"The elder lord is dead, sir, just last year."

"Not *young* Köthen? In arms against the king?"

"That's not what they call it, my lord."

"Yes, yes. A 'crusade.' Is there any resistance? I must get to the king. Does no one call them traitors?"

"Who'd dare oppose the word of the Church? A mere

whisper of disapproval and there's a white-robe in your courtyard, sniffing out witch-plots."

"Stürn and Rathenow I'd expect, but Köthen! The king's own nephew, who fostered the crown prince! I can't ... I must ... I've wandered enough!" Hal's outrage forced him upward into motion. He paced the sand in broad, abrupt strides. "Isn't it enough that they hold the real power? Now they want the throne for themselves?"

Griff glanced up and down the beach before nodding once. "And I'll have none of it. But I'm outnumbered at Tor Alte right now, so off I came, after the girl. If she really has been witched, so much the worse for me, but a man's got to have a purpose in life, and the trail's old but not yet dead." He ran a scarred hand through his thinning hair and smiled slyly. "Like ourselves, sir, you know what I mean?"

Hal snorted, then laughed outright, his rage deflected as an idea came to him. "Indeed I do." He sat down again and passed along the last of the bread, together with another thin slice of the cheese. "Suppose I was to suggest to you another purpose?"

Griff studied his food thoughtfully. "I might find myself listening, my lord."

"Go back. Be the king's eye at Tor Alte, or if possible, with Baron Josef's army. You could start by spreading word that the baron's daughter is dead."

The huntsman chewed on a curl of crust. "How do you figure that, my lord?"

"Well, if the witch-child is dead, what further excuse for a crusade?"

"They'll say dragons, or the weather. They'll not back off now. It's gone too far."

"Then let it go farther!" Hal's eyes took fire again. His back straightened. "Force them to show their colors! Call it what it already is, what it's been for the last two years! A full-fledged baron's revolt!"

Griff eyed him with wary respect.

"We're not the only ones getting old, Griff. But His Majesty is not dead yet, and his son's a fool whose only asset is his legitimacy. No, don't look scandalized. You know it's true, and so does the king. He takes his help where he can find it."

The huntsman considered this, taking the time to finish off his bread and savor the last of his cheese. "The people do cry out for a leader, sir. Oh, I mean, not where a peer or a white-robe can hear them, but there's hope and desperation enough out there to stoke the wildest rumors. I've heard a few already."

"I'm sure." Hal shook his head warningly. "But when people look for messiahs, they end up with Fra Guill. We must be our own salvation, I fear."

"Yes, sir. But now, what of the girl? I feel ... well, the baroness' own granddaughter—shouldn't someone be looking for her?"

"The girl is safe."

"Ah." The huntsman nodded slowly.

"She's suffered greatly and needs more than anything else to be free of pursuit."

"Hmmm. Well."

"I cannot tell you where she is or how I know this, but you can take it to be true, upon my honor. So, will you do it? Will you carry the lie back to Tor Alte?"

Griff grinned at him. "I suppose if you were a warlock like the priest is saying, you could just witch me into doing your bidding."

"I'd prefer that the king's name had that power."

"And so it does, my lord. So it does."

By midday, the beach was swept clear of their traces and the huntsman had begun his journey back to Tor Alte to spread Hal's "righteous lie."

TO THE WOMEN NOW? Erde scrawled on the sand as the knight checked the fastenings of the mule's packs.

"To the Women, yes. You listen well."

WHAT WOMEN?

"Oh, some friends of mine."

AND GERRASCH.

Hal cocked an eyebrow. "Yes, his also, and you could learn from the old bast— ... your pardon, my lady. You play the squire so well, I keep forgetting ... the old *gentleman's* example: the less you know, the less you can betray."

I WOULDN'T TELL.

"No, not if you could help it." He tightened a final knot with an unnecessarily abrupt jerk. The mule glanced around in surprise. "If Fra Guill will burn innocent women, don't you think he'd relish getting his hands on someone like Gerrasch? Someone truly unconventional, someone 'unnatural' who roots around in the forest gathering herbs and dabbling in magic? I can feel the heat of the stake already. It wouldn't be pretty."

IS GERRASCH A WITCH?

"Milady, please!" Hal quickly obliterated her words with his foot. "Gerrasch is one of God's Holy Innocents, though I doubt the hell-priest would see it that way. So remember, his safety depends on our discretion."

Erde took his cue and carefully scuffed away the rest of her scribblings. Hal seemed to have a lot of friends who required this special secrecy. Erde knew she must honor that need as long as she continued to accept his protection and advice, which she must until she got where she was going. But she could see she was not always going to agree with him.

For instance, she was not entirely comfortable with the notion of the "righteous" lie. She pondered this during their long hours heading southwest into the hills at the far end of the lake. At first she'd thought it would serve her father right to hear the gruesome tale that Hal and Griff had concocted between them, her tragic death by drowning in an icy torrent, her broken body swept away over the falls. She conjured satisfying visions of a remorseful baron, too grief-stricken to leave his rooms. But picturing Tor Alte as she trudged along yet another rocky and unknown road made her homesick for the castle and the life she'd known. Even though her rational self knew that life was ended forever, the child in her longed for it anyway. She began to feel a bit sorry for her father, to regret that she had allowed such a terrible lie to be sent to him. It seemed the burden of her guilt would never lighten, only increase in this inexorable fashion.

YOU WERE GOOD WITH GRIFF, she wrote during a hasty break for a meal. Though they'd been traveling for several hours already, the huntsman's news had made Hal as impatient as the hound had been. He worried aloud about the king, and cursed himself for not staying in Erfurt, under cover, to be there when his sovereign needed him. He talked of armies and strategies and the various possibilities of alliance as he saw them. He muttered about where one could hide something as big as a dragon. He felt they were rested enough and ought to press onward through the night. She had to jog his elbow to bring his attention to her dusty scrawl.

"Good? You mean I was nice to him?"

CLEVER.

Hal studied the letters in the sand as if they might rearrange themselves to read something different. "You're implying manipulation, aren't you." When she gazed back at him noncommittally, he laughed out loud. "Ha! I do perceive Meriah's steel in you! Of course I manipulated him, but not as in playing with him or using him without his knowledge—I merely turned his head so he could view the situation clearly." Hal swept his arm in a wide arc as if the valley behind them with its gray lake and dark trees were the only kind of view he meant. "So he could see where his interests might intersect with ours. That's called diplomacy."

CRAFT.

"Ha! *States*craft!" he declared. "Well, that's what I'm good at—my gift, you might say. For twenty years I've put it at the service of our king, an itinerant manner of service your grandmother never really understood either, but a crucial one to monarchs nonetheless."

HOW CAN A LIE BE RIGHTEOUS? Erde scrawled stubbornly.

"When it will forward the righteous cause." The knight watched her consider this, then added, "Perhaps expedient is more accurate, the *expedient* lie. Does that rest better with your conscience, my lady?"

Erde shook her head.

"You see no difference between our little lie that might save your life and the great big lie Fra Guill is using to raise up an army against you? An army, child! An *army!*"

F.G. IS NOT RIGHTEOUS.

"And I am? Well, thank you for that, at least. I do consider myself a righteous man, imperfect but at least trying to do what's right."

WHAT IS RIGHT?

"Phew! You need a priest, not an old soldier! I mean, a real priest." Hal looked so confounded that Erde finally had an inkling of how the dragon must feel when she could offer nothing profound enough to answer one of his all-encompassing questions. With a look of apology, she wiped the dirt smooth and rephrased her thought.

I AM NOT RIGHTEOUS.

He smiled. "Why ever not? Did you steal a few too many sweets or mumble your prayers at Sunday mass?"

His gentle condescension provoked her pride and a scowl. Impulsively, she wrote, I KILLED A MAN.

Hal read, then glanced up at her quickly. "You did? When?"

ESCAPING.

"Killed? Not just wounded or . . ."

She underlined 'killed,' and lifted Alla's dagger briefly from its sheath.

"So it's not all tall tales they're spreading."

Erde placed her palm over the offending word. She was surprised what a relief it was to tell him at last, to admit her dreadful crime, the crime that burdened her so that each day she trudged along carrying the weight of two. Three, if she counted Alla. Three deaths? Was it three deaths on her conscience? Erde shook her head to clear a sudden fog of confusion. Why did she think it was three when she could only remember Georg and Alla?

"Would this man you . . . killed have prevented your escape?"

She nodded, still distracted.

"Was escape necessary to your survival?"

Erde made herself focus on him. She could tell where his argument was going and did not want him rationalizing for her. She'd hoped he would scold her, or at least glare at her disapprovingly, this "righteous" man. Then she could feel somewhat punished for her sin. But he was taking it ever so calmly. She tried to imagine what penance Tor Alte's chaplain would have exacted in response to such a confession.

"Would this man you killed have hurt you to prevent your escape?"

Erde shuddered at the memory of what he would have done, his invasive touching and clutching, which brought back vividly the memory of what she *had* done. Hal saw tears well in her eyes. He picked a bit of brush to sweep her confession into blank forgiving dust.

Then he said, "Dear girl, just as there can be a righteous lie, there can be a righteous killing. Not a mere expedient, but the only right choice given the circumstances. Self-defense. What would the Dragon have done if his Guide had died before finding him? These are choices we must make, and there will be many such. Then we live with the burden that righteousness has placed on us for acting for its sake. I wish I could tell you that my own experience has been otherwise. Meanwhile . . ." He reached over and clasped her shoulder warmly. "Congratulations. We'll make a soldier out of you yet!"

And Erde thought, *I should have known he'd take it that way.* Even so, she knew his answer, however practical, was one she would never be entirely comfortable with.

Chapter Twenty

They traveled through the night, a long shallow climb into lightly wooded hills where narrow streams fell back along curving lowland glens toward the lake. Despite all indications that Griff meant what he said and could be trusted, Hal wanted to put as much distance as possible between them and the baron's disaffected huntsman. Once he made them freeze, like deer in torchlight, thinking he'd heard the rattle of harness and armor moving past in a valley below them. Skittish, he skirted the open meadows, where the grass was tall and damp, taking the time to go the long way around within the deeper shadow of the tree line. He was not happy that the she-goat lagged so far behind, catching up on her grazing while there was good grass to be had.

"But I'd sure like a moon tomorrow to see our way by, when the going really gets rough," he remarked as they rested beneath a large oak, the biggest Erde had ever seen. In the darkness, she could only guess at its true size from the great girth of its trunk. Hal laughed as she stretched her arms around it.

"I can tell you're a mountain girl. This tree's a midget compared to some of the oldsters along the river near Erfurt."

Erde was content with just the sighing sound of it. She wandered around trying to reach a lower branch. She thought its leaves must be huge, in scale with the trunk, for it to make so heavy and melancholic a rustling.

The hills got steeper as they went on, and the trees closer together. It also got colder. When they finally made camp at first-light, Hal insisted on their weapons practice, and Erde was willing to give up the last of her strength to it because she stayed warmer when she was moving than when she sat still. Afterward, she was too tired to struggle with the stale bread and dried venison that was all that remained of their food supplies. She fell asleep propped up against the dragon's side, with a cup of goat's milk in her hand. Hal eased the chased silver out of her grip and drained the milk himself, then laid her wool cloak over her and let her sleep.

He retired to his bedroll and sat staring at the little cup, letting the gray morning light swell until he could make out the Weisstrasse coat-of-arms embossed on its side. He traced the emblem with his fingertip, then sighed and tossed the cup back in his pack.

Earth dreamed again that sleep-time, more vividly than he had since Hal had joined them. The dream seemed as real to Erde as her own life, and the Summoning took on a new urgency. Later, she recalled an endless enclosing maze of corridors, and knew it was a city, though unlike any city she had ever imagined. The walls were hard and cold and shining dully like the blade of a knife. Where the passages turned, the corners were as sharp as broken glass. The floor was a grid of metal strips, laid with spaces between, like rows and rows of tiny windows, so that Erde could see through them into the vast and roaring distance below. As always, there was the bitter smell, and the smoke and clang of the forge or something like it, so much more acrid and more deafening than the forge she knew at home.

For the first time, she saw herself and the dragon in the dream together, as if she were watching it from outside, yet still hurrying down the corridors, her lungs aching, the metallic air sharp on her tongue, desperate to get Somewhere, only they didn't know where. The voice of the Summoner rang in their ears like a cry of pain.

Ahead, another razor-edged corner, then the corridor darkened and stretched away for an endless distance, as straight as a stone mason's plumb line. They knew that the Summoner was at the end of that distance, and the dragon began to run, so fast that Erde could not keep up. She snatched at him, caught hold of the end of his stubby tail, and was jerked off her feet to be carried aloft behind him, like a battle pennant.

In the nearer distance, the corridor bloomed with sudden brightness. A man of light on a horse of fire, an armored knight with a shining silvered lance, wreathed in glowing smoke. He wore a golden circlet on his helmet, a crown. His visor was down. She was grateful that she could not see his face, for rays of incandescence leaked through the ventings and she knew his face would blind her. His shield, a perfect circle, bore a strange emblem, rather like a spiraled compass rose, dividing it into four nested arcs like the bowls of spoons lying one against the other. Again, these spaces were like separate window openings. Through one, Erde saw trees and rolling meadows; through another, green water and foam-crested waves. The third arc showed a dark mountain ablaze with a fountain of fire, and beyond the fourth was only air, as blue and empty as the sky.

She urged the dragon onward, to get a closer look. But as they sped toward the unknown knight, he seemed to get farther away, shrinking like a dying flame until he was only a pinpoint, as tiny and brilliant as a star. The bright circle of his crown persisted momentarily, and then he was gone. As his light faded in the darkening corridor, the Summoner shrieked and moaned like a mad thing, and the walls trembled with her grief.

Erde woke to the rending cries of the woman she'd seen burned at the stake. Half in, half out of dream, she realized it was the she-goat, bleating in terror. Across the clearing, Hal swung upright on his bedroll with a shouted oath of surprise. A harsh red dusk was falling. The trees thrashed violently, though there was no wind. Erde thought the big oak would uproot itself. The ground heaved beneath them.

The dragon was still deep in his dreaming. Erde shouted him awake with a barrage of thought. He stirred, lifted his head, and the ground quieted.

Hal continued swearing until he'd gotten hold of himself, then he and Erde stared at each other across the strewn contents of the mule packs, scattered by the rolling of the ground.

"Terra is suddenly not so firma," he remarked at length. "Is it over?" He groaned to his feet, dusting himself off unnecessarily. He looked around, noted the she-goat struggling up on wobbly knees by the base of the big oak. "Earthquake. Must be." He coughed, then shrugged. "I've heard of them happening farther south, but here . . . ? Where's the Mule, I wonder?"

Erde rolled over and hugged the dragon's rough-skinned

foreleg. His golden eyes were as wide as she'd ever seen them, and he was shaking.

—*Earth, you were dreaming again.*

His brain still racked with nightmare, Earth relayed an apology.

—*No, it's all right, only . . . the ground moved.*

Earth agreed that it had.

Erde sat back on her heels, studying him pensively. The obvious, sensible explanation was that the agitation of the ground had sparked the trembling in the dragon's dream. But she'd been sure when she awoke that it was the other way around. She cleared a patch of dirt and tried the idea out on Hal.

"Yeah, he was dreaming . . . And?"

THE GROUND MOVED.

"So?" He looked around, whistling for the mule.

Erde added HE DREAMED at the beginning of the phrase.

Hal licked his lips, looked at the dragon, looked at her. "What are you saying?"

She shrugged, then put a period after HE DREAMED.

"Oh, no. No, no, no. Not possible. The earth does not move to any command but God's, not even for dragons."

NAMED EARTH, Erde scrawled, unable to stop herself. Then to keep from feeling completely crazy, she added a question mark.

"Earth . . . quake. Hmm." Hal grew thoughtful, then with a flick of his eyebrows, dismissed the notion as insane. "What does *he* say?"

HE DOESN'T REMEMBER. HE WAS

Hal stayed her hand. "I know, I know—he was asleep."

Erde nodded.

The knight rolled his eyes and went off in search of his mule.

Earth was skittish that evening. First he wanted to stay in the oak clearing and not move until they'd discussed his dream in lengthy detail. When Hal insisted it was perfectly normal to walk and discuss at the same time, the dragon came along, but he stuck very close to Erde, crowding her sometimes dangerously as they moved into the dense and rocky woodlands of the upper hills.

Erde took extra care to avoid getting stepped on, and did

not scold him. She knew how anxious the dream and its aftermath had made him. It had made her anxious, too. She wondered if the sudden sharp chill in the air, like the first tang of winter, had anything to do with the earthquake. Hal was more than usually pensive as well. He had not been granted the moon he'd wished for, and the climb was getting steeper and rockier, their footing increasingly treacherous, with roots and loose stones hidden beneath a slippery layer of leaves. He let the mule lead the way, and they stumbled upward in near blackness, each wrapped in the separate silences of concentration.

But eventually, Hal could contain himself no longer.

"How could he make the ground move?"

His question was rhetorical, since Erde had no way in the darkness to provide an answer, even if she'd had one to offer. She wondered why this latest surprise bothered him particularly, when he was so ready to believe the dragon capable of all sorts of miracles. In fact, expected him to be. Erde wished the knight would stop focusing on what a dragon *should* do, and concentrate on what this dragon *could* do, especially while Earth was struggling so hard to discover what his skills were. Hal was like a stern parent disapproving of a brilliant child because its gifts were not as orderly or predictable as he'd like them to be.

Erde suspected that magic was neither orderly nor predictable. She thought it peculiar that the knight seemed to divide the miraculous into categories: this is possible, this isn't. But she had to keep in mind Hal's long years studying dragonlore. When a man has devoted himself that passionately to something, he's bound to want to see it proven right. Perhaps he just needed enough time with each new bit of information to fit it into his own scheme of things.

Sure enough, half a mile later, he cleared his throat tentatively. "Well. Let's say it's possible. Maybe it is. If it is, is it something he can control?"

She did not know, and neither did the dragon.

And later, she could hear the ghost of a smile in his voice. "You think he'll be practicing moving the earth over and over again, like he does with becoming invisible?"

Erde did know the answer to that one. The quake had terrified Earth. He had no desire to feel the ground move again just yet, or even to attempt doing it on purpose. Mostly, he wanted to think about it and what it meant and, to Erde's dismay, ask her a million other questions that she couldn't answer.

After a rest and a meal break, their ascent grew so sharp that in places Erde had to haul herself upward with her hands. But the trees thinned and the moon at last made a fitful appearance, slipping in and out of slow-drifting veils of cloud. Their route lay over solid rock now, pale ledges each the size of a castle yard, like a vast staircase aspiring to be a mountain. Small trees huddled in hollows where soil had gathered. Tufts of brush bunched in the seams and cracks, and here and there thin grass softened the weathered granite.

The dragon hated the climbing. His thick-limbed body was not built for hauling its own great weight straight upward for hour after hour. His gleaming ivory claws were not meant for gripping stone. He gave Erde to understand that he was sure there was a better way to travel, if only he could remember what it was. She urged him to try, but he could only picture himself first in one place and then in another, with no idea of how he might actually accomplish getting there. Erde worried that he might be feeling bad about his lack of wings—he'd heard Hal complain about it often enough. It occurred to her as she urged him up a particularly steep ledge that each of them was defective in some vital way: Earth had no wings, she had no voice. It was probably why they had ended up together.

The thought made her sigh, and she was tired of sighing. A sigh was an irritatingly melancholy sound but the only one besides a cough or a sneeze that she could still produce. She decided she would ask the knight to teach her how to whistle, something even her grandmother had not allowed her to do.

"Ladies do not whistle," the baroness had always insisted when Erde expressed envy of the stable boys. They could hear a tune once, then whistle it again whenever they wanted to. Erde understood that it might not be appropriate for ladies to whistle in public, but wouldn't it be a good thing to know how to do, to amuse yourself when you were alone? Not that she'd spent much time alone growing up in Tor Alte. That was another thing ladies did not do. If she wasn't with Alla or the baroness, there was Fricca, or some chambermaid. There was always somebody watching, telling her what to do and what not to do.

She thought about all this as they topped a particularly barren rise. The way they'd come spread out behind them in an endless march of nighttime hills glazed with moonlight. Far off, the ghostly shimmer of the lake—and beyond. . . ? Now that Gerrasch had mentioned a city, she was coming to believe that there might actually be such a gathering place for mages. Idly, she conjured the slim spires of her fantasy, to glow like a mirage on the horizon. She felt the dragon in her mind, imaging it with her, and saw its towers grow more real before her very eyes under the power of his belief in it. The breeze gusting across the ledge was damp and raw with chill, but Erde was conscious of how deeply she could breathe, of the sense of lift and freedom that came from being surrounded by all that open space. She felt hopeful. Like a bird must feel, just before taking wing. There were advantages to leaving home, she realized, beyond the obvious one of her survival. She doubted if Hal would ever say, "Ladies do not whistle." Most ladies did not learn to use a sword, either.

From the crags ahead came a sudden distant yowl. The mule's long ears flicked, and the she-goat glanced up sharply from the bush she was eating. The mirage towers vanished, leaving only a darkly crenelated, threatening horizon.

"Wildcat," noted Hal. "Best stick close from now on. We're not the only hungry creatures out prowling these hills tonight."

Erde shrugged her cloak more tightly about her shoulders. Free or not, she wondered if she would ever be warm again.

The intemperate yowl of the cat seemed to follow them, fading in and out with the rush of the wind as they struggled over ledge and through gorge. The mountain brush was as rough as the rock. Erde's cheeks and lips were chapped from the icy gusts. Her hands stung with scrapes and scratches and the brittle ends of thorns. She had thought she was hardened to travel, but her knees and ankles ached from the constant up and down. Hal had never pushed them this punishingly before. For the dragon's sake as well as for her own, Erde insisted they stop more often than Hal was willing to. Always he would offer a courtly apology for tiring them, then want to be off again the next moment.

"Not much farther," he'd promise, already in motion up the slope. "Not much farther." He was tireless, eager, driven, a man with a real destination finally in mind.

She knew they were descending when the wind stopped screaming in her ears, but it still felt as much up as down, and the going did not get any easier. It clouded up again and they lost the little bit of light the moon had offered. Then it began to sleet, a fine blowing frozen mist that invaded Erde's eyes and nose like needles and melted into the layers of her clothing. Twice she lost her footing in a slide of ice and loose gravel, and went tumbling to the bottom of a slope with Hal shouting after her to grab on to something, anything she could, and the dragon wailing in her brain not to leave him out there alone in the darkness. Each time, after Hal had made his way down to help her up, he reminded her how lucky it was she hadn't slipped beside the edge of a cliff, and she began to have some notion of how infuriating, even heartless a man can be when in the throes of some particular obsession.

The dragon had begun to mutter, at least Erde had come to think of it as muttering, the peculiar grunting sound he made when he was fretting about something. This time it was a scent his clever nose had caught but could not identify. He tried relaying it to Erde in the same way he sent images, and she recalled how vivid the odors always were when she shared the dragon's nightmares. But awake, her mental nose was no more sensitive or sophisticated than her anatomical one, so she was no help to him. Earth kept muttering. Obviously the smell was not going away.

The rain tapered off as the clouds thinned again. Ahead of them rose a rank of tall stones, standing almost upright like a slightly drunken army at attention. The mule disappeared among them and the rest followed. Erde heard Hal cursing under his breath as they threaded almost by feel the narrow alley between towering walls of rock. Then a screech and a bleat behind them stopped him cold.

"It's that cat! It's got the goat!"

He whirled to race back to the aid of the she-goat, but the dragon blocked his path. As the goat's outrage escalated into shrieks of panic, Earth struggled to turn himself around, wrenching his bulk from side to side, his claws grinding uselessly against the rock. The shadowy shape of him bucked and swayed, and for a moment, Erde was convinced she saw him blur and fade, blur and fade, then grow substantial once again. She blinked hard, several times. Perhaps she had stared too long, trying to make him out clearly in the darkness, or perhaps . . .

—*This is no time to go invisible,* she warned him. All she sensed in return was a wall of desperation that also danced in and out of substance, as if Earth's existence itself was wavering.

Then new pandemonium broke out behind him. The cat yowled in fury. A moment later, the she-goat came scrambling over the dragon's back, nearly bowling Erde over as she bolted past and collapsed against Hal's legs. The cat did not follow.

Hal knelt over the goat, feeling for damage. "Bit of a mess here . . . that's quite a gash there. Be all right if the bleeding stops." He tried to get her up on her feet but she kept sinking back against him. "Come on now, girl, I can't be carrying you."

Earth crowded in, his great head wedged between Erde and the rock wall. Hal stood back, offering what little room he could. The dragon nosed at the goat, sniffing and muttering. In the dark, Erde could not quite tell what he was up to. She worried that he might at last be considering a meal, if only to put the wounded goat out of her misery. But listening carefully, Erde realized that he was licking her, his huge rough tongue making great doglike swipes across her back, nearly enveloping her horned head and her stick-thin legs. He did not stop until he had licked her all over at least once, and her fur was damp with his saliva. Then he scooped her up in his jaws and stood there, holding her delicately, waiting for the humans to proceed.

"He exhibits a most generous nature," noted Hal. "Unusual in a dragon to be so sensitive to the needs of lesser creatures."

Erde knew he was alluding to Earth's peculiar hunting habits, which were inconvenient if, like the knight, you wished to keep your dragon well fed. But she thought that if dragons were, as Hal claimed, the most perfect of God's creations on Earth, they very well ought to have generous natures. Unlike Man, or most men anyway, who were— judging from her recent experience—the most imperfect. She did notice that whenever Hal expounded on the nature of a "proper" dragon, even speaking in the arcane language of the dragon-lore, it sounded more like what he'd want a leader of men to be, for instance, the king he served so loyally. High expectations indeed. But a man could not be a dragon, nor a dragon a man. No wonder the knight was so often disappointed in both.

They came down out of the standing stones without further mishap, beyond a few additional scrapes and bruises. The icy rain had stopped. The moon had set, but the sky seemed to be clearing at last. In between the scudding shadows of clouds, a few stars could be seen. They reached level ground, a broad grassy ledge, and Hal whistled to call back the mule. Erde heard water falling over rock somewhere in the darkness.

"We'll stop here for the rest of the night." Hal tossed down his shoulder pack and stretched. "We need to get warm, so we'll risk building a fire, if we can find anything up here to burn."

Earth lumbered about with the goat suspended in his mouth until he found a spot to his liking. Erde heard him scratching up grass and dirt into a sort of nest to lay her in. When he was done, the goat curled up in it immediately and went to sleep as if drugged.

Erde helped Hal search out stray twigs and branches for the fire, then walked carefully to the edge of the ledge, where the rock sheered away sharply as if cut with a knife. Beyond, she could see nothing but the deepest night, but she sensed a large volume of space just past this pale, white-veined border, and was intrigued by the current of distinctly warmer air rising up out of the void.

When Hal had managed a small fire, she went over and cleared her usual pallet-in-the-dirt.

WARM! she wrote, inscribing an arrow in the direction of the edge.

"Yes," Hal agreed. "It's quite remarkable, really." And then, despite every strategy she could muster, all during the parceling out of their meager meal and until she finally gave in to her exhaustion, he refused to elaborate further.

Erde woke in daylight, curled up between the she-goat and the dragon, conscious of the sound of birds and an unusual sense of well-being. Frost lay white in the hollows of the ledge, but the sun on her shoulder was actually warm.

She sat up carefully, to avoid jostling the injured animal. The goat stirred with her and rose easily to her feet. Her eyes were bright and her carriage erect and lively. Her spotted coat gleamed like new-spun wool, with no sign of blood or wounds anywhere. She shook herself like a dog and trotted off toward the sound of falling water.

Erde glanced around for Hal, to bring this new amazement to his attention. Then she caught sight of the view. Scrambling up, she ran to the edge of the ledge to stare in wonder. The dragon roused himself and followed.

A valley spread out beneath them, all green and golden in the softly angled rays of the mid-afternoon sun. Like the valley in her dreams, not the rank nightmares she now shared with the dragon, but from her childhood, her dreams of the "safe place," the holy landscape, what her grandmother always called Arcadia.

The valley was long and narrow, embraced by a high palisade of rugged hills such as she had just endured. From the rolling prairie far below, sheer cliffs rose abruptly on all sides, to a point level with Erde's ledge, as if the entire valley had broken free at once and dropped away into the earth. Thin white cataracts plummeted down the cliff face, then snaked in shining ribbons to meet the river that wound and sparkled between velvety patches of forest dotting the bottom land. Huge flocks of birds rose in arching coordinated flight. Above, a pair of hawks circled. Erde heard their screeching blown on the breeze, but nowhere could she spot a sign of human habitation.

And then there was the warmth, a soft draft like a breath from below, carrying the scents of summer. Earth hunkered down to arch his long neck over the edge. He inhaled deep inquiring breaths. The old image of fat white sheep ghosted into Erde's head and made her laugh, a soundless explosion of spontaneous joy.

—*It isn't the Mage City yet, but it's almost as good.*

Daydreaming succulent sheep, the dragon agreed.

"Ready for a little exercise?" Hal appeared beside them with the practice swords, his hair and beard dripping from a dunk in the waterfall. He waved an arm at the valley, grinning from ear to ear. She had never seen him so pleased. But he still would not tell her where they were or what they'd find, once they'd braved the final precipitous descent.

Erde remembered the goat and dragged him over for a

look. Hal's solicitous inspection grew more amazed and de-
liberate as he discovered no fresh wounds anywhere, only
the occasional pink glow of scar tissue.

"Maybe the cat never actually broke skin. Maybe she was
just wet from all that mud and ice."

But Erde shook her head vehemently. She had seen the
dark blood glimmer the night before and felt it, slick and
hot, turning cold on her hands.

"Well, it was the cat's blood, then," Hal protested. "No
wound heals that fast! Unless she's magic." This thought
made him laugh for some reason, and he put the mystery
aside for the time, sending the goat on her way with a be-
mused slap on her rump. "The Mule's gone on ahead—our
'magic' goat can lead us down this time."

Chapter Twenty-One

Erde shed her thick woolen cloak after the first few switchbacks of the long descent. Though it was still damp from the rain, she stuffed it unceremoniously into her shoulder pack and wished the mule was there to carry it for her. Next she found herself loosening the collar tie of her linen shirt. For the first time since leaving Tor Alte, there were too many layers, her clothes felt too heavy. She was actually hot.

She'd forgotten what it was like to be free of rain and mud and sleet, free of the confining weight of wool and padding. She inhaled the perfumed air and felt as light as a feather floating on it. She flapped her arms experimentally, like a dark-headed stork considering flight. Earth picked up this image from her as he lowered himself step by ponderous step behind her. He sent back panicked entreaties of caution. Erde giggled voicelessly, giddy with heat and her newfound sense of freedom. Then a stone rolled beneath her heel and nearly sent her cascading over the edge into oblivion.

Hal heard the clatter of pebbles and glanced around sharply. "Do not, I repeat, do NOT hurry. The way is treacherous."

The dragon echoed this sentiment.

Yes, it's treacherous, thought Erde, *but so was every place we've come from, and at least this has a path.* She was eager to get down it. It was narrow, slippery and steep, but appeared to be a used thoroughfare. Mostly by animals, perhaps, being too precipitous to be satisfactory to any but the truly surefooted. Still, it gave her hope that they might actually be going somewhere, not just wandering about in the wilderness, as she'd sometimes begun to think. If they were getting somewhere, she reassured the dragon, they might ac-

tually find their Mage City. To please him, she conjured the
familiar cluster of tall towers gleaming at the end of a long
white road. She breathed in the sweet warm scent of the rising air and watched the elegant dance of the hawks wheeling
in the sun. She could feel the sun and sudden warmth working on the dragon as well. He, too, watched the birds, with
wonder and longing. She tried picturing him with wings,
vast gossamer webs like Glasswind's, all the colors of the
rainbow. It wasn't right, somehow. It didn't fit. But she
could imagine him in flight, the two of them together, not
soaring like the hawks, but . . . *traveling.*

"Milady, pay attention!" Hal warned again as she stumbled
into him with her eyes fixed on the sky.

They came down off the cliff through an old fall of boulders that spilled out across the bottomland like a stone archi-
pelago in a sea of waving green, a green so rich it seemed
to vibrate before Erde's eyes. The soft air was pungent with
odors. It went to her head, as if she'd inhaled a sweet young
wine. Ahead, the trail vanished beneath waist-tall grass. The
she-goat stopped immediately to graze. Hal stripped to his
jerkin, tossed his cloak over his shoulder, and struck out
confidently across the plain toward a grove of trees in the
near distance. The swish of the grass against their boots was
like the breathing of large animals. Erde followed dreamily,
dazed with sun and heat and sweetness, and the suddenness
of the change.

The grove was a large circle of oak trees, thick-trunked
and ancient. Their broad outer limbs arched high, then
swooped nearly to the ground, enclosing a leafy cavern
within their shade, paved with moss and rounded stones like
river rock. A peaceful stillness hovered there, a sense of refuge and contentment. Erde was reminded of the great-hall of
Tor Alte, with its treelike columns and branching rafters.
This grove had the same grace but lacked its chill solemnity.
Small creatures busied themselves everywhere, among the
leaf piles and in their burrows between the spreading roots.
In the center of this shadowed whispering space, where the
branches thinned, a shaft of sunlight filtered in onto a small
still pond. On the grassy shore, a cairn of rocks stood guard
over a herd of drinking deer. Nearby lingered one or two
very thick and shaggy brown creatures that Erde decided
must be cattle of some wild variety. As they approached the

cairn, she saw the flat top stone was piled with wildflowers as fresh and bright as if they'd just been picked. The deer lifted their heads, muzzles dripping sparkling beads of water. They seemed merely curious, breathing in man-scent and dragon-scent as if both were simply information, then moving away slowly to graze or lie down in the deeper shade.

Erde sensed Earth's quickening interest and his hunger, and felt both consciously set aside. He raised his own great head, deerlike, testing the air, and promptly vanished.

Hal knelt for a drink at the pond. "He's getting very good at that, but why . . .?"

A voice hailed them, a cheery greeting from the far side of the copse. Out of the shadows trotted the mule. In place of his pack and harness, he bore a smiling woman, sitting astride his bare back, at ease and waving gaily. Erde pulled her prentice cap down over her ears and tried to think herself back into her disguise. As the mule shambled to a halt in front of them, the woman slid off gracefully, planted her sandaled feet, and spread her arms wide.

She was small, a head shorter than Erde, with delicate ankles visible below the shin-length hem of her loose-fitting garment. The soft white fabric was dye-printed in shades of blue, birds in flight. Erde could see that the full skirt was split, like baggy leggings. She was instantly envious. This was exactly the sort of garment she had always wanted. She was equally envious of the woman's brilliant infectious smile and the dark cloud of hair that danced around her shoulders as if it was alive. Erde thought she had never seen anyone so beautiful.

"Hello, Raven," said Hal. Erde watched openmouthed as the knight snatched the woman up in a hearty embrace.

When he'd set her down again, Raven held him at arm's length for serious study. "A sight for sore eyes! You're looking well, Heinrich."

He offered a courtly bow. "And you, my heart's desire, as always. How are you all keeping?"

Raven's fine mouth tightened, a brief shrug in her gaiety. "Oh. Well enough, all things considered." She gripped both his hands, then released him gently. "More of that later. What have you brought us this time?" She turned to smile at Erde. "Forgive us. His visits here are so rare and so welcome."

"Of course. Permit me." Hal looked too happy to be embarrassed. He snatched Erde's cap off her head and fluffed up her cropped hair playfully. "Raven of Deep Moor, may I present the Lady Erde von Alte."

Raven laughed and clapped her hands as if at a feat of magic. "Traveling incognito! How exciting!"

Erde was unsure of Raven's social standing or what ceremony might be appropriate. She certainly did not dress like a lady, or as Erde had been taught a lady should dress, or behave like one either, riding about bareback and flinging herself into men's arms. But Erde wished neither to presume nor condescend with one who called the Baron Weisstrasse by his given name and was so familiar with his person. She bobbed shyly, and looked to Hal for a further hint. Her hesitation was not lost on him.

"Raven," he offered slyly, "is Queen of All She Surveys."

"Oh, my lord, you are too kind!" Raven dropped into a ground-sweeping curtsy, then rose out of it with a giggle and hooked Erde's arm within her own. "Welcome, my dear. Erde, is it? Are you hungry? Thirsty? Has he exhausted you with his mad trekking about? Well, no mind, we'll feed you here and rest you and pamper you like you must be used to!"

A flush of pride made Erde wish she could point out to this woman that if she'd been your usual petted high-born, she'd never have made it this far. She also thought it peculiar that Raven spoke in collective pronouns and went about touching or holding everyone she talked to, even a perfect stranger.

"We could all use a little pampering," remarked Hal.

Raven threw him a dark smiling glance. "Oh, you'll get it. When do you ever not?"

He laughed, and stretched luxuriously. "It is very nice to be here. Do you have any idea what it's like out there?"

Raven sobered. "We hear, and none of the news is good. Tell me, which way did you come? Did you meet Lily and Margit on the road?"

"No, but we weren't ever on the road. Are they coming or going?"

"Coming, we hope. From Erfurt. They've been out quite a while. Too long, actually, and we're worried, since Doritt said they shouldn't go at all. But Rose has heard nothing, so . . ." She shrugged as if all this made sense, then cocked her head. "But wait . . . the Mule said three?"

Erde wondered if she actually meant *said*.

"Three, indeed," replied Hal as if he'd heard nothing unusual. "Four, with the goat. He never counts himself, you know."

The she-goat had wandered into the shadows to graze, but Erde could feel the dragon waiting nearby.

Raven gave her musical laugh. "Then someone is hiding . . ."

Hal dipped his head gravely. "My lady Erde, will you make the introductions?"

Erde tried to smooth the doubt from her forehead. Her own identity was revealed, and now she had to trust Hal's judgment that the dragon would be safe. She asked Earth to make himself visible.

He appeared gradually, like a memory returning. A shaft of sunlight rippled across him in waves as the branches shifted in the breeze. Was it a trick of the light, Erde asked herself, that made his color so newly rich? She thought of him as, well, rather dull and dirt-colored—but now he was vibrant with sienna, ocher, and olive. Had his crest always been the dark blue-green of winter spruce? Suddenly, he almost seemed the hero's vision of a dragon, his great amber eyes shining like beacons out of the mossy shade.

"Oh!" Raven's hands flew to her cheeks. Bright tears started in her eyes. "Oh, Heinrich! Oh, wonderful! You finally found one!"

"My lady Erde found him," Hal corrected, looking Earth over with approving surprise. "I found her."

Raven's awe did not include a moment's fear. Nor did she complain that this was small for a dragon, and wingless. She went straight to him and laid her hands on him, petting and murmuring as if to a lover, telling him how beautiful he was and how welcome. She flirted with him, just as she seemed to with everyone she met, and Earth blossomed in the bright warmth of her praise. He stood up straighter and arched his massive neck, then tried to curl his stubby tail. Erde was caught between jealousy and laughter. She'd never seen him preen before, and she could sense a spark of self-confidence waking in him. But then, she hadn't told him he was beautiful all that often. She hadn't thought he was, until now.

"A living dragon," Raven cooed adoringly. "And just this morning, Rose said she thought something remarkable was about to happen."

"He is called Earth," said Hal. "And he needs your help."

Finally, Erde understood. Raven was not just any woman, she was one of *the* women, of whom Gerrasch had spoken.

"Then he shall have it," she replied. "Of course he shall."

Raven led them out of the oak grove and along a faint track that undulated across the rolling grassland toward a darker line of forest crowning a distant rise. While Hal told their story, Raven strolled next to him, her opposite arm slung over the mule's withers, her loose linen sleeve pushed up past her elbow. The arm was slim and brown, as smoothly muscled as a young boy's. Erde felt herself weak and pallid by comparison. She dropped back a few paces, then several dragon lengths, unsurprised when Hal and Raven didn't notice her absence, too absorbed in news and gossip and each other.

Under the full gaze of the sun, Earth was reduced to more mortal dragonkind, though still no longer "dirt-colored." It was as if one filmy obscuring layer had fallen away but others remained, still cloaking the full beauty waiting underneath. Erde sent him an image of a snake shedding its skin, then a butterfly climbing out of its cocoon.

—*I think you're changing. But it's all right, you know. It's like growing up.*

Earth took the notion away with him into his mind to think about.

That same bold valley sun told Erde that Raven, though beautiful, was no longer a girl. Beyond that, her age was mysterious. She behaved so much like a girl, or perhaps, so unlike a grown woman, at least the grown women that Erde had known. She thought Raven was one of the lucky few who can act however they please *because* they are beautiful. People think anything they do must be beautiful also. If someone ugly puts their hands all over you without asking, you're insulted. If a person is as beautiful as Raven, it's no longer an affront. It becomes flattery.

Erde knew she would never be that beautiful. She had also thought she didn't care, but now—watching the inviting curve of Raven's neck as she inclined toward Hal like a flower to the sun, listening to the low, gay music of her voice—Erde knew that she did care, and the understanding made her inexpressibly sad. It reminded her that someone had once told her she was beautiful, but it must have been a long time ago because she could no longer recall who it was. She worried that her memory was fading. No matter how hard she tried to hold onto them, certain details softened, others remained bright. Alla. Her dear grandmama. She felt the loss of them all over again, sharp enough to bring tears to her eyes.

Earth snorted behind her. She felt a clumsy prodding at her back, as if a vast weight was bumping her ever so gently, which it was, the weight of a dragon snout.

She turned, distracted. He had not shown an awareness of her mood before, being too submerged in his own dilemma. Or was it just that, in the unaccustomed sun and open space, he was finally feeling playful? As she faced him, he stopped and dropped back on his haunches to stare at her with his tongue lolling. Erde had to smile, and laugh her breathy silent laugh. How could she do otherwise, with such a great and silly creature as her devoted companion?

They saw scattered groupings of the ragged long-haired cattle in the fields along the trail and later, a large herd of sheep guarded by a slim black and white dog. The sheep barely noticed them. The dog glanced their way, alert, looked at the dragon and then to Raven as they passed, but did not budge from its post.

Bypassing the sheep was hard for the dragon, whose hunger was beginning to preoccupy him. Erde knew this from the constant thoughts of eating in her own head. She was amazed that all these animals took the reality of a dragon in their midst more or less for granted. They seemed curious but unamazed, even though Erde was sure they couldn't have ever seen a dragon before. Almost as if they'd expected him, or rather, since Raven had shown no evidence of prior knowledge, as if they'd *always been* expecting him.

Erde wasn't sure what she meant by that. She considered Earth's peculiar hunting practices. A notion was forming in the deeper part of her brain, not yet whole or coherent, about the nature of the dragon's presence in the world. That somehow, no matter how terrifying he might look, he knew how to "be" without causing distress or even very much notice. Her image of it was the huge bulk of him crossing a beach of smoothed sand without leaving footprints.

Her own thought process mystified her just as much as

Earth did. Often of late, while trudging through the forest or struggling up some stony hill, she'd found herself in the grip of an idea she couldn't quite make out the logic of. Like holding a knitted garment that's come unraveled, a pile of half-sleeves and tangled yarn and loose ends. You search out this end, then that, and tie together the ones that match, but still the shape or size of the garment is unfathomable. Erde had begun to suspect this was because the garment—or the idea—was much bigger than she was.

The grassy trail led over a low hill and down beside a sand-bottomed creek that curled off around the foot of a bigger hill dotted with trees and thickly wooded at its crest. A flock of small birds danced in the bramble hedge along the bank, arguing over the last of the blackberry crop, though there were plenty left for all, dark and glistening on the vine. Erde could have filled her cap twice over, but even better, there were apples on the trees farther up the hill, and here and there a few late cherries glistened among dark green leaves. And pears! She counted half a dozen trees filled with little brown teardrop fruit. She had never seen a pear tree growing wild, only the scraggly seedlings her grandmother had imported year after year from the South in sympathy with the castle gardener, who each spring would swear he'd found just the right spot to help them thrive. As far as Erde knew, there'd never yet been an edible pear produced at Tor Alte. She ran to catch up with Hal and Raven, pointing out this fruity cornucopia that was making her mouth water for something other than stale bread and dried venison.

"Amazing," Hal observed. "As always."

"It's a fine harvest this year," Raven agreed. Erde wondered how she found the energy to smile so much.

"You've heard how it is out east?" he asked.

"Every time Esther goes to market. It's even worse up north, and the west is hardly better. We've sent what we could to our sisters in the villages, and Esther sells at the lowest price she can without, you know, calling attention."

"Umm. Attention like that you don't need, right now."

Raven nodded. "We've had a few close calls of late."

"It's that scourge of a priest," said Hal. "His ravings encourage others to say and do things they'd go to confession for ordinarily."

"These dark times do likewise. People want an explanation for their misery. He gives it to them."

Hal merely grunted in reply and then, their cheer dampened, they paced along in silence, until Raven slipped her arm through his and hugged him warmly. "But we're so glad you've come. We're way overdue for a serious discussion of strategy. Many of us think it's time to pull our heads out of the sand."

Hal frowned. "Let's not get reckless, now. You're most useful here and safe where you are."

"We've always thought that. Now we're not so sure." Then she let him go and waved. "Look! Here's Doritt come to meet us!"

Ahead of them, the path filled suddenly with black, lop-eared goats. A tall woman dressed in brown urged them forward with the help of another black and white dog.

"I'm not coming to meet you," the woman declared as she drew abreast of them, and the herd flowed around them like black silk. "I'm clearing these damn goats out of the yard. Every baking day they come crowding in, thinking they're going to get some. Ha! Dreamers! Well, there, Hal, how are you?"

Hal grinned. "Well enough, Doritt. And you?"

Doritt grasped the hand he offered. "Did she ask about Lily and Margit?"

"She did. I didn't see them."

Doritt frowned. "Pity. Well, here you are anyway." She peered at Erde with frank curiosity. "This lad belong to you?"

"The lad's a lady, can't you tell?" laughed Raven, leaning comfortably into Doritt's side. "Her name's Erde."

Doritt stuck her hand out again. "So much the better."

Erde did not have much experience with handshakes. She was surprised at the vehemence involved. Doritt's hand was as large as Hal's, long and strong like the rest of her. It engulfed Erde's own strong hand completely and made her feel satisfyingly small. Doritt had a plain oval face and the largest, darkest eyes Erde had ever seen on a human being, deep and liquid with intelligence, like a dog's eyes. Her wavy brown hair was caught in an untidy knot at the back of her neck. She fussed with it, tucking in strands that immediately shook loose again with the abrupt motions of her head as she talked.

"Now the Mule says you've brought me another one!"

Erde had quite forgotten the she-goat, who came trotting up now to mingle with the herd.

"I guess I did," agreed Hal. "And I'd like you to take a good look at her. She was mauled by a cat last night."

"It's Linden should have the look, then."

"No, that's just it, the goat is fine. Just absolutely fine."

Doritt peered at him suspiciously. "You're confusing me."

"Well, I'd just like to know how she got so fine, this soon after a mauling."

"There's a tale needs telling here," remarked Raven.

"It will be mostly *his* tale, I suppose." Doritt nodded at the dragon as if noticing him for the first time. Like Raven, she showed no fear, and even less surprise. "Yours?" she demanded of Erde.

Taken aback, Erde could only nod.

Doritt turned to Hal, arms flailing in the air. "You're not planning on leaving *that* with us as well? He'll eat us out of house and home!"

"Oh, Doritt," reproved Raven. "Think of it! A dragon!"

"Well, yes," said Doritt. "Exactly."

Hal glanced back at Earth. "I don't expect he'll be staying long. He's on a Quest. But he could use a good solid meal, if you could see your way to it."

Doritt sighed. "I knew it. Dropping in out of nowhere as usual, telling me I got to round up the old folks and give 'em the ax."

"I think you'll find he has his own very civilized methods."

Doritt fussed with her rebellious hair. "Does he want to eat now?"

Hal looked to Erde, who nodded without even asking Earth.

"We can't refuse a dragon," declared Raven softly.

Tall Doritt shrugged. "Oh, hell, give him the run of the valley. He's a dragon, after all. He's got to eat."

When Earth had wandered off on his own, with dubious backward glances and requests that Erde accompany him, Doritt sent the goats in another direction with the dog, and fell in alongside. By the time they reached the first signs of habitation, Erde knew the good and bad of every creature in Doritt's care. She wasn't sure if the other woman even noticed that she hadn't said a word.

But for its verdant productivity, which would have been astonishing in any place, in any season, the farm was not impressive at first glance. Erde saw no fortifications, no walls, no defining gates to announce where pasture ended and yard began. They were well inside before she recognized that the brash and unkempt foliage threatening the path for at least the last quarter mile was an endless vegetable garden. Everywhere she looked, she saw something edible. She stopped to inspect a bushy plant as tall as her chest and found a dozen fat green squashes lurking beneath its broad prickly leaves. How unfortunate, she mourned, that farmers who grow this well couldn't find enough time for a proper patchwork of garden plots, with their reassuring squared corners and neat rows. Just past the squash, a fruit tree had been left to grow in the middle of a lettuce patch. Erde couldn't imagine Tor Alte's gardener standing for such disorder.

Even the buildings, good sturdy stone structures, were scattered here and there at odd angles, hidden within a clump of trees or half-buried in the side of the hill, their walls choked by some overgrown sage bush or fruity bramble, and their roofs submerged beneath trailing bean vines, looking in sorry need of maintenance.

And where was the center of this chaos of plenty and disrepair? Erde found it too disorienting. You could stroll through this entire farm and never know it was there. Except, of course, for the animals, who created a chaos all their own.

Erde could not spot a single henhouse or hog pen. Animals wandered loose everywhere: chickens, turkeys, and ducks pecking about underfoot; a brown pig rooting with her seven fat children; gray rabbits rustling in the hedges; a small horse dozing beneath a nut tree; huge lazy cats lounging in the dust of the path; and the occasional elderly dog taking the sun. A flock of black geese spotted Doritt from afar and streaked to meet her with much flapping and honking, pressing around her feet and nibbling at her clothes. She scolded and complained, but gave each one of them a moment of her full attention.

Hal halted in a grassy clearing ringed with big old maples just starting to turn orange. With his arm around Raven's waist, he inhaled deeply. "Ah. Paradise found."

Erde joined him with an experimental sniff. The aroma of fresh bread mixed with barn smells and the perfume of fall roses. She wondered where among all these trees a bakery might reside.

Doritt kept walking, turning back midstride at the edge of the clearing with a belated wave. "See you at dinner!" The black geese followed noisily behind.

When their honking had faded into the trees, Hal cleared his throat. "Well, where is she?" For the first time since entering the valley, he seemed not quite sure of his welcome.

"Working." Raven arched her brows prettily. "Did you expect all of us to drop everything the moment you arrived?"

"Um," said Hal. "Well, no. Of course not."

"She went right in as soon as she'd talked with the Mule. Something's been on her mind all day."

Hal laughed nervously. "Maybe she knew I was coming."

"Oh, yes. Well, naturally that would upset her." Raven glanced up to see if he knew she was teasing, then added seriously, "It's something in addition to that."

"Ah. Well then, will she . . . should I . . . ?"

Having made him truly uneasy, Raven smiled and touched his arm reassuringly. "Of course you should. She's waiting for you."

Hal beckoned Erde to him. Resting a hand on her shoulder, he guided her toward the trees. And there, hidden in the shade of the branches, was a shallow flight of neat stone steps leading to a flagged terrace roofed with thatch. The rafters and cross-beams were slender trees with the bark still on them. Crickets and small birds chirped in the straw. A wide wood-framed doorway set in a rough stone wall led into a low shadowy room. Groups of chairs and tables were scattered about, but in here, the disorder was human and comfortable. The furniture was tightly made and the smooth-planked floor was worn to a satiny luster. At one end towered a darkened fieldstone fireplace. At the other, a row of tall windows had been set very close together to let cool light into the room through a break in the trees.

In front of the windows, a woman sat at a spinning wheel easily as tall as she was, surrounded by piles of carded wool. The light filtering in behind touched her pale hair, her white garment, and the soft white wool with the same hazy gleam. She raised a hand from the wheel in greeting, then bent back to her work. Raven came in behind them and went to sit beside her.

"That's Linden," Hal whispered, and Erde agreed that

there was a special serenity in the room, a kind of living stillness that made you loath to break the spinner's concentration, that compelled you either to sit down and beg to be put to work, or to pass on through without disturbance.

Hal led her across the room, out onto a narrow covered walkway that framed the four sides of an open, stone-paved court. The roof of the walkway was the overhang of a second story, the first real indication of the building's size. Above a final, pitched slate roof, the maple grove loomed and swayed, so that light dropped into the court like sun through water, shifting and diffuse. In some more shadowy corner, a fountain played delicate music to a birdsong accompaniment. Erde was reminded of the peaceful cloister at the little convent in the valley below Tor Alte, where she had accompanied the baroness each Christmas with food and gifts for the nuns.

Out of this tranquil bird-sung dimness, a spot of color glowed. In the steadiest shaft of sunlight, a woman dressed in a warm riot of color sat reading at a stone table. Erde could not tell her shape or the shape of her garment, only that it seemed comprised of many layers, each one a different shade of red or orange or lavender or brown.

Hal stopped at the edge of the walkway, smoothing back his hair and beard, straightening his worn red jerkin. Silently, he waited.

The woman kept reading. One hand traced her careful progress through the text. The other toyed with an assortment of small stone tiles lying on the table. Finally she raised her head, without urgency, as if she'd heard a faint noise or wondered what time it was. She glanced their way but her eyes seemed to stare past them into the distance. For a moment, Erde thought the woman was blind.

Then her gaze focused, and she smiled. "Ah, Heinrich. There you are."

The slight pressure of his hand bade Erde wait. Hal stepped into the court, crossed the mossy flagstones with measured strides, and dropped to one knee as if the woman sat on a golden throne instead of an old three-legged stool. She gave him her hand, and he held it reverently to his lips. Then he rose, leaned over, and kissed her lingeringly on the mouth.

Waiting in the shadows, Erde blushed. Hal's familiarities with Raven now seemed merely playful by comparison.

She'd seen the soldiers stealing lusty kisses from the pantry maids, but true earnest tenderness such as this ought to be kept private. It made her feel funny inside.

Hal leaned against the stone table, his arms to either side of the woman's shoulders, and gazed down into her eyes. "Rose. I've missed you."

Her voice was low and so resonant that Erde felt it sing through her own body like lute music. "Then you should find your way to us more often."

"If only I could."

The woman raised a reproving finger. "And you could even come when there isn't something you want from us."

Hal's soft laugh honored this old debate between them, but refused the challenge. Erde recalled how ardently he'd spoken of her grandmother that first night by the campfire, of lovers separated by duty and distance. Was it always to be so for this loyal King's Knight?

"Meanwhile," said Hal, "there is something, and here it is." He straightened away from Rose and gestured Erde into the light. She approached shyly. Seated, the woman appeared to be of trim, middling stature. Her curly auburn hair was shot with gray and, to Erde's delight, cut short as a boy's. She had thick brows over bright blue eyes and a strong jaw, a compelling face. Though she was not as old, perhaps closer to Hal's age, something about her reminded Erde of Alla, something that made her want to kneel at the woman's feet as Hal had done.

"Rose of Deep Moor," Hal announced, "Erde von Alte."

Erde noticed he'd left off her title for the first time and wondered why, not that such things mattered to her. When the woman stood, beads and little bells chimed faintly in her long loose sleeves and in the deep folds of her skirt.

"And if that weren't remarkable enough," supplied Rose, "she comes with a dragon."

"Yes."

She smiled without looking at him. "How wonderful for you, Heinrich. After all these years."

"Yes."

Rose grasped Erde's hands, looking her over. They were not quite matched in height. The commanding blue eyes gazed up at her and still Erde felt diminished by her presence.

"So this is the witch-child." Rose turned to level that same deep stare on Hal. "And her Paladin."

Hal snorted. "What? Me?"

Rose nodded.

"Oh, hardly, Rose. Not me."

"Oh, yes, my dear. Did you think you'd escape Fra Guill so easily, simply by backing out of his view? I hate it when he's right, don't you?"

"Rose, I'm not exactly the ravening image of Dark Power he conjures up for his witch-child's champion."

Rose drew Erde left, then right, as if showing her off. "Nor is she his nightmare vision of a witch."

He smiled. "But then, who is?"

Rose dipped her head. "Yet here she is, and here you are. Besides, I said her Paladin, not her Champion. But we'll speak of that later. Meanwhile . . ."

"Rose, there's no way Guillemo could have known."

"Heinrich, Heinrich."

"All right, so he got lucky."

Rose shook her head warningly. "You let your hatred blind you to the man's real power. He's a hound on a scent. If a pattern exists, he'll sniff it out. It's a true prophetic gift, tragically turned to evil ends."

"You haven't seen him in action. I have. He's a lunatic, Rose."

"Yes, and his madness springs from being unable to control what he sees so clearly."

This exchange and the long dark glance that passed between them filled Erde with unaccountable dread. She missed the dragon's comforting presence and hoped he'd finish with his hunting soon.

Hal sucked his teeth and turned aside abruptly. "Then we can't stay here." He paced away, then came back and drew Rose into his arms. "Forgive me. I've endangered you thoughtlessly."

Rose smoothed the stained red leather hugging his chest. "Not thoughtlessly. A still-sleeping dragon and a dream-reader who's lost her voice? Where else could you go for the sort of help you need?"

Erde waited for Rose to mention how she'd come by all this information, but she did not, and Hal seemed to require no explanation.

"Now, food and rest and a good hot bath for both of you.

Of course you'll stay, long enough to see what help we can actually provide." Rose looked up and touched a finger to Hal's jaw. "And long enough to remind this old woman what a man looks like."

He hugged her to him, laughing. "Why, Rose, you'll embarrass the young lady."

Chapter Twenty-Two

The denizens of Deep Moor gathered for the evening meal in the communal dining area at one end of a huge kitchen. Brick ovens and grills and spits lined the opposite wall. Windows let in amber dusk light along both sides. Two rows of sturdy worktables dominated the center, and the smoke-darkened beams were a hanging forest of herbs and onions in braided lengths and garlic and dried peppers and delicate nets bulging with winter squashes and potatoes.

Erde had napped and then been introduced to the pleasures of a hot bath. She'd always hated bathing, except sometimes in the summer. Now she realized that the water had never been warm enough, or smelled so fragrant with herbs and the softening oils that Raven poured on so liberally. In some obscure way, it felt sinful. She spelled this out for Raven, primly, shyly, in the dew gathering on the red floor tiles, but Raven only laughed and tossed her a square of fine knitted wool to rub the oils into her skin. She came down to the kitchen feeling reborn, wearing a clean linen shirt from the household stores and one of Raven's block-printed shifts with the divided skirts. Hal, who was lounging with his feet up on a table and a mug of ale in one hand, sat up in surprise.

"Milady, you look radiant!" He put down his ale and stood, handing her into a seat beside him with courtly formality while Erde blushed and stared at her feet.

Earth had still not returned from his hunt, so while Hal explained about the dragon and his unknown quest, and told the tale of her escape and their journey so far, Erde watched the dinner preparations. She wished Hal had not been so intentionally uninformative about the circumstances at Deep Moor, about who these people were and why Rose knew what she knew. But she could not ask him now, so she settled in to be patient and to observe. It did not occur to her to try to make herself useful until Doritt plunked down a basket of apples and a knife on the table in front of her.

"Well, I'm sure this dragon's Purpose isn't to stay and eat up my herd. Here, slice these up. I'll find a bowl to put them in."

She sailed off to the far end of the kitchen. Erde stared at the gleaming red fruit. She had never sliced apples in her life, though her grandmother had taught her the proper way for a lady to section a small apple for eating. This knife was much too large for delicacy, but she gave it a game try. Doritt returned, watched her struggles for a moment, then grabbed a stool and drew it alongside.

"Tell you what: I'll peel and quarter, then you just cut 'em up any old which way, all right?"

Erde observed carefully, admiring Doritt's deft skill with the knife, and learned the preparation of apples for pie. Meanwhile, she counted: five, ten, twelve women drifting in and out of the kitchen, bringing fresh milk, washing vegetables, slicing bread, stirring the pots. A pair of lithe redhaired twins in their late teens did a lot of the heavy hauling. A chunky laughing woman was clearly the chief cook. Two elderly women wandered in rather vaguely. They were fussed over and treated with great deference by the others, but did not sit by idly. They went right to work slicing up whatever was set in front of them with concentration and efficiency. Erde heard Lily and Margit mentioned often, as one woman or another stepped in to do a task usually assigned to one of the absentees. She sensed in this a fond sort of ritual, as if the frequent naming of the missing women would keep them safer and bring them back sooner. She had also been waiting all afternoon to learn where the men and the servants were. Now she discovered there weren't any. There were no young children either.

A community made up entirely of women, which wasn't fortified or walled in any way, and wasn't a nunnery. Erde had never heard of such a thing. And no help but themselves. In a way, it reminded her of Tor Alte while her grandmother was alive. Of course, there were plenty of men at Tor Alte, but the women had felt easier about themselves under the baroness' rule. And though they were not at all similar physically, Rose did have the baroness' same sure authority.

Yet at dinner, she watched Raven tease Hal as she laid steaming platters on the table, flirting with him outrageously, and all the while Rose smiled benignly, nestled into the curve of his arm. Her grandmother would never have stood for that. Erde asked herself again how these woman protected themselves. She surmised that there was a lot going on here she did not understand.

The long refectory-style table was as well-worn and shining as the floor. The food was fresh, plentiful, and delicious. There was clear springwater to drink and a pale, dry ale that made Erde feel refreshed rather than light-headed. The conversation was not quite boisterous, but it was lively and certainly informative.

"The honey is from our hives, of course," Linden was explaining in the mild precise way that seemed to characterize her. "And the candles as well. Raven makes the most beautiful candles, don't you think?"

Erde nodded. The many candles burning on the table were amazingly tall and thin, and even more astonishingly, they were pink, the blushed color of a wild rose. She thought to ask how one made a colored candle, and readied quill, ink, and the little pile of paper that Raven had supplied her with, rejects from the Deep Moor paper press. But Linden was busy being very serious about the bees and how sensitive they were to mistreatment or neglect. Erde wiped her quill and laid it aside.

Linden, whom she had seen at the spinning wheel earlier, was as pale and dry as the ale, but with its same hidden sweetness. Pale jaw-length hair, pale gray eyes, pale flawless skin, with flush-spots on her cheekbones so distinct they might have been painted there by a rather wobbly hand. Her color bloomed whenever she spoke, especially when she was speaking to Hal, as if the very act itself put her in mortal danger of exposure or embarrassment. It took Erde some time to learn that Linden was Deep Moor's healer, for she would never boast of such a thing herself. But she had spent the late afternoon examining the she-goat and now, as Raven and a slim older woman named Esther cleared the dishes to make room for the sweets, Rose asked for her report.

Linden placed both hands before her to grip the edge of the table and cleared her throat. "She is fully healed."

"Healed," repeated Rose, and Erde wondered how you could pack so much mystery and meaning into a single word.

"So I didn't imagine all that blood and gore," said Hal.

Linden focused carefully on the smooth plank in front of her. "There is clear evidence of serious injury, long tears and deep claw punctures. But this must have been at least three weeks ago, from the amount of healing already completed."

"Last night," said Hal. "It was just last night, was it not, my lady?"

Erde nodded.

"I don't see how that's ..." began Linden.

"Well, it is. It happened." With a grin, Hal leaned forward and replenished his mug of ale from an earthenware pitcher. "We have a magic goat." He eyed Doritt mischievously. "I'll bet you don't have one."

Linden frowned at the tabletop, shaking her head ever so slightly.

"What else occurred," asked Rose, "between the attack and when you noticed her healed?"

Hal shrugged, then decided to stop pretending that he wasn't taking this seriously. "We made camp, we ate, we slept. The goat slept very deeply."

"All right. Yes." Linden bobbed her head, staring at her thumbs. "Animals do often go into a kind of trance state when they're badly injured. But that's usually to ease their dying."

"What else?" Rose prodded. "Any other detail?"

Erde reviewed the previous evening moment by moment: the cat screeching and the attack, Earth struggling to turn around within the walls of rock, then the goat streaking in over his back and the dark blood on Hal's hands. Then what? Then ...

She grabbed for her quill and paper, and wrote carefully: EARTH WASHED HER.

She was amazed that the ink did not sink deeply into the thin pliant sheet and bleed her letters out of recognition. Apparently, Raven made very fine paper as well as candles.

Linden peered at her message, then read it aloud. The women murmured thoughtfully. The two elderly women at the far end of the table put their heads together in lively muttered discussion.

Then Hal swore softly and slapped his head. "Of course!

Where is my mind? It's very common in the lore to claim that a dragon's tongue has healing properties!"

The two old women nodded approvingly, though one of them frowned when Doritt said, "I thought their jaws dripped acid and stuff."

"No, no, that's just fairy tales ... or if you listen to what the Church says. The *lore* says ... ah, why didn't I think of it sooner?"

"It will be just so lovely to have a real dragon to study," ventured one of the old ladies. Her voice reminded Erde of butterfly wings.

Hal bent his head to her. "I plan many hours in your excellent library, Helena, while you're off dragon-watching." He offered Erde a crooked apologetic smile. "Won't he be relieved to know there's something else he can do."

"That's a fine way to talk about a dragon," Doritt snorted.

Gentle laughter rippled around the table.

"But isn't it typical?" chided. Rose. "A man finds what he's been searching for all his life, and right away he's complaining that it doesn't fulfill his expectations."

"Well, he doesn't," Hal retorted. "Does he yours?"

"I've not yet met him," replied Rose sweetly.

"Don't worry, he won't. Maybe someday, but now ..."

"I think he's a very nice sort of dragon," said Raven.

"Nice?" Hal was peevish. "He's not meant to be *nice*."

"Why not?"

"He's meant to be powerful, magnificent, omnipotent, and ..."

Rose smiled. "Perhaps he could be all those, and nice, too."

"What a concept," remarked Doritt.

HE IS STILL LEARNING, Erde wrote, in a broad admonitory hand. Briskly, Linden passed the paper to Hal.

"True," he conceded. "I only hope he can discover himself in time."

"In time for what?" asked Rose.

Hal drained his mug and pushed his plate away with a definitive gesture. "In time to save us from the apocalypse according to Guillemo Gotti. I can't imagine what else he would have been sent for. Have you heard the priest is raising an army?"

"Oh, yes. To cleanse the world of the likes of us. That's why we sent Lily and Margit to Erfurt, to find out all they could." Leaning into his shoulder, Rose turned the thin wooden stem of her goblet between two fingers. "But what if Fra Guill is not the dragon's purpose?"

"Not? What do you mean?" He sat up straighter in order to gaze down at her sternly. "Are you saying it isn't? Do you know what his Purpose is?"

"Without talking to him? Of course not. What am I, a fortune-teller?"

Brighter laughter drifted around the table. Raven snapped her fingers rhythmically and hissed, "Gypsies!" Erde wondered what was so amusing.

Hal caught her eye over his shoulder. "This is my punishment, you see. Rank mockery, because I don't show up to pay homage often enough."

This drew hoots and catcalls, echoing about the warm candlelit room. Erde had never heard such raucous laughter from women.

"Oh. Homage, is it?" laughed Raven.

"Well?" he challenged. "That is what you want. Isn't that what you all want?"

"We want a lot more than that." She ran her finger around Hal's ear and pinched his earlobe. Hal brushed her hand away, glancing self-consciously at Erde.

Across the table, Linden was giggling, and blushing furiously. The older woman Esther paused behind her with an armload of empty platters, her grin expectant. Rose tickled Hal's arm. "Don't get them started, my dear. You know you'll only be sorry."

Raven leaned in, her lips soft against his temple. "Sorry? Oh, I don't think so. I don't remember you ever being sorry." Hal's breath caught as her tongue snaked out and licked his ear.

"Raven," Doritt murmured. "We have a guest."

"Oh, pooh," said Raven, but she eased away from Hal to gather up a final stack of dishes.

A guest. Erde had heard the singular and knew it meant her. Heinrich Engle was no guest here, that much was clear. But neither was he a member of the household. Erde was confused. She did not understand these women's behavior. She knew her grandmother would have had a name for it, and it would not have been flattering. And yet, Erde could see nothing overtly wrong with it . . . only if you thought about what you'd been *told* was right and proper.

Hal cleared his throat, then went on as if nothing had happened. "But why do you question the dragon's Purpose?"

"Not that he has one," Rose replied, equally unfazed. "Only that it might be other than what you expect."

"Some Larger Purpose, you mean. Beyond my ken."

The knight's deeply humble expression made Rose smile. "Not necessarily *beyond*, my dear. Just different."

"Well, Gerrasch said the Purpose was 'to fix what's broken.' A bit cryptic, I thought."

"No more than you'd expect."

"From a badger," muttered Doritt.

Rose smothered a grin. "But what I was referring to is that another candidate has arisen for the job you have in mind."

"What?" Hal came bolt upright. He looked almost frightened. "Another dragon?"

Raven laughed loudly from the sink. "Well, that got to him!"

"Of course not another dragon!" said Rose.

"Hal, Hal, where have you been?" Doritt leaned forward on her elbows. "Haven't you heard about the Friend?"

"Whose friend?"

"That's what people call him."

"Just ... the Friend?" He glanced at Rose. "Interesting coincidence. What about him?"

Doritt noted Erde's puzzlement. "Loyalist code," she explained. Then Erde recalled Griff's response to the word.

"Delicious rumors." Raven waltzed back to her seat beside Hal. She twirled one finger in his bristly hair. "You know how women are."

Hal scowled and batted her hand away, causing another trill of general laughter.

"They come in from the west," Linden put in kindly, without looking at him. "The rumors. If you've come from the east, they may not have reached you yet."

"From widespread parts of the west," Raven added more seriously. "Even as far as Köln. Some claim that's where he's from."

"City boy," noted Doritt.

"No, that can't be right."

"Why not?" asked Linden.

Raven smiled and shrugged. "He just doesn't sound like a city boy to me."

Doritt frowned. "What does it matter? You don't believe in him anyway!"

Erde recalled her grandmother talking of Köln. Köln was a true city. It was said to contain at least twenty thousand people. She had no image of it except that it must be very crowded, but then, she had no image of any city at all besides her fantasy one.

Hal asked, "So why do they call him the Friend, if not. . . ?"

"Supposedly, it's because he does all kinds of reckless acts of goodness."

"Reckless and random," added Raven. "So they say."

"Remember that random is in the eye of the beholder," murmured Linden. "I mean, random is simply whatever you weren't expecting."

Raven wagged a playful finger at her. "Oh-oh, Linnie, you'd like to meet this Friend, wouldn't you?"

"Leave her alone." Esther came back from depositing her pile of platters in a corner washtub. "It's me bringing these tales in, mostly. I hear them when I go Outside to the markets."

"Ah." Hal sat back. Erde thought he seemed relieved. "The idle gossip of farmwives."

Esther raised a sharply pointed brow. "And farm men as well, and traveling merchants and big, bully convoy men. The best I had was from a troupe of actors. Their leader said he liked the tale so much and heard it so often, he was working up a play about it."

"Lily and Margit were to look into it," said Rose. "Perhaps even try to contact him if such a thing seemed possible."

Hal grunted, crossed his arms. "But who, if he even exists, is this so-called Friend supposed to be?"

Raven giggled and nuzzled his shoulder. "Poor Heinrich. You'd really prefer to save the world single-handedly, wouldn't you?"

Hal ignored her, leaning forward to hear Esther's tale.

"Well." Esther shoved back her sleeves. She found room on the bench between Linden and Erde, and prepared herself self-consciously, much like the actor she had just spoken of. "The stories tell of a mysterious young man—he is always young and always nameless . . ."

"Because they don't know his name, or he won't tell it?"

"Sometimes one, sometimes the other. But nameless anyhow, and thus always referred to as the Friend or simply "he," and in the markets these days, they know who you're talking about." Esther's long slender hands illustrated her words as gracefully as a dancer's. "Sometimes he's a poor farm lad, sometimes, yes, a city boy. Sometimes he's even a prince. Last week, he was a *foreign* prince!"

"A *gypsy* prince!" crowed Raven, getting up to fill her mug.

"It's been suggested. Or Frankish, if he's really from the west. He's said to be well spoken and handsome, of course. Not dark, not light. Everything about him seems to be the middle road."

"Where's his shining armor, and his golden helm that he never takes off?" Hal scoffed. "Clearly we're dealing with fantasy here."

Esther stared him down. "Perhaps. Anyway, an anonymous young knight of indeterminate breeding who travels about the countryside warning the farm folk against the evils of Fra Guill."

Now Hal looked interested. "Hunh."

Rose nodded. "He's brave, if nothing else."

"A rabble-rouser!" exclaimed Doritt appreciatively.

"A handsome gypsy rabble-rouser!" Raven twirled and stomped, her arms entwined to support a pitcher of ale above her head. "Better and better!"

Rose held out her goblet to be refilled. "They say Fra Guill flies into a mad rage at anyone who takes the Friend seriously because he has no place in the Prophecy. That's enough to make him very interesting, as far as I'm concerned."

"If he exists," said Hal.

Esther planted both long palms on the tabletop. "Do I get to tell this story or not?"

Raven slunk back to her seat, gripping her mug to her chest in mock-contrition.

"Tell it, then!" Doritt whooped.

"Well, you haven't left me much." She continued over a chorus of sighs and groans. "Only that he's supposedly gathering followers as he goes along, and that although his route is rambling and slow, in general he seems to be headed east, toward Erfurt."

"And toward us," Hal noted. "With his own little army behind him."

"Around him, actually. And if they're armed, it's only with knives and pitchforks." Esther folded her hands pensively beneath her chin, suddenly reminding Erde of the elderly monk who had taught her reading and writing much against his own better judgment. "This is where it gets interesting. There appears to be some confusion about the exact nature of this gathering. They're not spoken of as an army."

"Then they're a mob."

"Those who don't like the idea call it a mob. Either way, the Friend apparently refuses the usual privileges of leadership. He sleeps among his followers—some even call them disciples, but for most this comes too close to blasphemy. He marches among them and defers to their counsel. He dresses as they do and shares their food, which is happily supplied from the countryside, the same food that people out east are hiding away from Fra Guill at great risk to their lives."

"And he's particularly outspoken against Fra Guill's witch-hunting," noted Rose quietly. Erde decided that each time she spoke, it was like a phrase of a song being dropped into the conversation.

"Well, no wonder you're all so in love with this chimera," Hal declared. "But have you thought this out? What if it's some new kind of peasant rebellion? 'Friend' or not, the last thing His Majesty needs is a new enemy."

"If you'd just let me finish." Esther caught his eye and held it. "The name may not be coincidental. Those who claim to have seen him say he carries the King's Banner."

"The King's Banner? Openly?"

Esther nodded. "And beside it, the emblem of a dragon."

For the first time since the meal began, silence prevailed. Then Rose said, "I hadn't heard that part."

"New, as of yesterday." Esther preened, pleased by the stir she'd created.

Hal blew out a long breath between his teeth. "King and dragon together. The people actually favor that connection?"

"There's a lot of debate, but mostly, they do."

"Hmmm. And the barons?"

"As you'd expect. They're denying he exists."

"And he's heading toward Erfurt." Hal looked down at Rose. "What truth to it all, do you think?"

"I don't get Out. I'd only be going on hearsay. Esther?"

Esther's shrug was that of a skeptic still willing to be convinced. "We'll know more when Lily and Margit get back, but in the markets, tales of the Friend are accepted as news, that is, as true as any word that comes from so far away."

"So what are they really saying?" mused Hal.

"It could be the country folks' way of expressing their dislike of Fra Guill, by inventing a hopefully invincible enemy for him."

Raven sighed. "Or that the people dream of a hero to rescue them from bad harvests and early winters and rumors of war. Who can blame them? It feels like the end of the world."

"But what if there really is some man on his way east with an army?" proposed Doritt reasonably.

"Indeed. What if? And carrying the King's Banner ..." Hal was slumped in thought. "I wonder ... could it ...?" He sat up slowly. "What if it's *him*, Rose? What if it's Ludolf? It could be, you know ...?"

Rose gazed into her goblet as if she wished he wouldn't get started on this matter. "There's been no word, Heinrich."

Raven rolled her eyes. "And you call us romantics!"

"But it could be. Why not?" Brightening, he faced Erde across the table. "This is going to sound like another tall tale, but it's true, I was there at the beginning of it. The king had another son, Ludolf, two years younger than Prince Carl."

Erde nodded. Everyone knew Prince Ludolf had died when just a boy. The king had produced no other children since then.

"I know what you're thinking, but that's just the story we gave out. Because His Majesty's relations with the barons were becoming treacherous, the lad was fostered out in secret for his own protection, so secretly in fact that his whereabouts are unknown, even to the king."

Hal had been right. It did sound like a tall tale, but Erde thought it very romantic indeed.

"Most of us assume he really did die," Esther put in sadly. "Both of them in some accident or killed by brigands on the road or in some betrayal we never got wind of."

"Only this one ..." Doritt jerked her thumb at Hal. "... persists in the folly of believing the boy's still alive."

"A boy no longer. A young man now, nearly twenty. And I'm not alone in this so-called folly. The king himself agrees with me."

"Of course. A father would," said Esther.

"A leap of faith," said Rose.

"Admittedly."

Esther laughed. "Dear Hal. Your endless capacity for belief is one of your most endearing qualities. May you never lose your faith."

"If I can maintain my faith while I'm in this household, nothing can shake it." Hal leaned forward onto the table as if over a map, suddenly businesslike. "Now. How big is it supposed to be, this unarmed army?"

Esther flicked her hands pointedly, a comment either on her sources of information or on Hal's shift of subject. "One story will say fifty, another will say a thousand. It depends on the teller."

"No surprise in that. I fear he will get them all killed and himself hung in the bargain . . . if he exists." Hal sucked his teeth, his characteristic gesture of doubt. "Come on, surely you have some feelings about this, Rosie."

But Rose had noticed Erde's abstracted gaze. "What is it, child?"

Slowly, Erde wrote: IS THE FRIEND EVER A KNIGHT?

Esther laughed. "Not this particular Friend."

"Why, dear?" asked Rose.

EARTH DREAMED A KNIGHT. Erde passed her scrawl to Rose.

Hal read over Rose's shoulder. "He did? You didn't tell me that. It wasn't . . . who was it?"

Erde met his eye sympathetically. She hadn't mentioned it, to save his feelings. He'd want it to be him, and she knew it wasn't.

HE WORE A CROWN.

At this, even Raven gave a small gasp of surprise.

Rose arched her brows. "What did the knight do in his dream?"

NOTHING. HE WAS THERE AND THEN HE FADED AWAY.

"When was this?" asked Hal.

Erde erased and scribbled. THE NIGHT OF THE EARTHQUAKE.

The candles were burning low on the table. Raven snubbed two of them. Linden held Erde's scrap of paper up to the nearest guttering flare and read it aloud. The women exchanged glances.

"Earthquake?" Rose asked. "Where?"

"That's something you read about in the Bible," scoffed Doritt.

"No," said Esther, "I think they've actually happened. There are stories."

"Well, they don't happen around here."

"One did," said Hal. "Two nights ago, only a day's travel north of here."

EARTH DREAMED THE EARTHQUAKE, Erde wrote.

"Right. I forgot to mention that." Hal scratched his beard uncomfortably. "Apparently, the Dragon dreamed that the earth moved, and it did. Woke us up out of a sound sleep."

"*Earth*quakes!" Raven snatched up Erde's paper and waved it triumphantly in front of Hal's nose. "How can you be disappointed in this dragon?"

Rose nodded thoughtfully. "I've never heard of a dragon making earthquakes. That is a very rare and ancient skill. Of course there is the undeniable coincidence of his name." She turned an approving eye on Erde. "And yours. Well. Earthquakes. An unknown knight. An undisclosed purpose. Is it time for us to take a Look?" She glanced around the table, inviting consensus.

Hal relaxed back into his chair, arms loosely folded but eyes watchful. One hand drummed a faint staccato on his elbow.

Linden nudged Erde. "This is what he's come for, you see. But we must all agree to it, 'cause there's always danger in a Seeing, especially to Rose." She lowered her voice to the barest whisper. "And he knows some of us do not respond well to being pressured."

Erde thought to ask who, but had already noted Esther's jaw tightening and Doritt's dubiously pursed lips. But Linden was hiding a girlish grin behind her hand.

"We'd do it anyway, for your sake, but it doesn't do to let him know that."

Covertly, Erde wrote: WHY?

Linden's giggle was as soft as water over moss. " 'Cause no matter how much you'd like to, you can't give them everything they want just right off. They're too spoiled with getting already."

THEY? scrawled Erde.

Linden nudged her again, her cheeks crimson. "Men, of course."

Erde nodded sagely. This was an interesting notion. Certainly all the women she'd known, except maybe Alla and her grandmother, spent their lives waiting for things to come to them—a meal, a new gown, a husband back from the hunt or from the wars—and by waiting, often did not get what they waited for. Men, however, just went out and took what they wanted. Like Fra Guill. Or her father. She remembered Alla complaining about how spoiled the baron was. Yet he had called his daughter spoiled for wanting something so simple as to walk in the woods by herself. She recalled his sudden dark scowl, his peremptory tone. Of course the alone part had bothered him. But not because he feared she was meeting some boy. He'd never let her meet any boys. What he really couldn't stand was the idea of her managing on her own outside of the walls, outside his protective embrace. She decided that those unladylike walks were preparation for her escape, and was grateful for them. They'd kept her first act of real rebellion from becoming a total disaster.

She looked at Hal, an impatient man waiting with all the patience he could muster. She had no problem conjuring the tantrum her father would have thrown in such a situation, and she loved this good and earnest knight the more for not being so spoiled after all, no matter what the women of Deep Moor might think.

"Any discussion?" asked Rose. "Dissenting views?"

The women shook their heads, even Esther, and Doritt, last of all but emphatically, as if it had simply taken her that long to clear her mind of any lingering doubt.

"Then we're agreed." Rose brought her palms together soundlessly in front of her, then pushed them apart. The stilled table erupted into activity.

Chapter Twenty-Three

The meal was cleared and the dishes washed and stacked with dizzying speed. Erde sat with the old women to dry the plates and bowls. Even Hal was pressed into labor, hauling brimming buckets from well to kettle, then kettle to basin. The sight of a red-leathered King's Knight, a baron at that, tipping a steaming kettle over the big tin washbasin was a memory Erde would treasure. Whatever this Seeing was, Hal wanted it very much indeed.

When the kitchen was tidied and all the candles snuffed but one, Raven took up the single flame and led them through the dim lamp-lit rooms of the farmhouse, out into the fresh and temperate night. The women grabbed lanterns from the stone porch, lighting them one by one from Raven's candle. The young twins pulled a low, brightly painted dogcart out from under the branches beside the steps. They helped the two elderly ladies in, settled them comfortably, and stepped into the traces themselves.

"Treasures, those old ones," murmured Hal in Erde's ear. "Keepers of the knowledge, scholars, librarians. They collect the books and write down all the spoken traditions. I've spent many fruitful hours consulting them. They're sure to have a useful notion or two about our dragon's Purpose."

Watching the lore ladies and the gentle attention the twins lavished on them, Erde mourned once more for Alla. Tor Alte had not shown that wise old woman the respect she'd deserved, not ever.

Then, lanterns in hand, the whole party set off along the meandering roadway through the farm, looping past the murmuring darkness of the sties and barns, raising the occasional sleeping duck or dog from the path. Several of the dogs decided to come along. Doritt's flock of black geese discovered her and fell in behind, mere shadows bobbing through the grass, uncharacteristically mute. The cart rattled along and the twins began to sing softly to the rhythm of their stride. The other women laughed and chattered as if off to some midnight festivity. Their joy and energy was contagious. Erde felt it expand inside her chest, like the soap bubbles Alla had taught her to blow within the loop of her fingers, luminous and big and so fragile that it hurt her heart to think of not being with these women forever, on balmy moonlit nights like this, filled to bursting with laughter and singing and belonging.

The path forked beside the apple orchard. Raven led them over the stone bridge that crossed the narrowest waist of the stream, then up the hill among the fruit trees. Doritt and Linden joined the twins in the traces to draw the cart up the steeper incline.

Near the top of the hill, the trees thinned, leaving a grassy rounded crest exposed to the night like the dome of a man's head left without a hat. The women gathered at the very apex of the curve, eased the two old women onto the grass, then joined them without ceremony in a circle that took the highest point of the hill as its center. Rose pressed Erde's hand and sat her down between Linden and Esther. She seated Hal next to herself on the opposite side, so that Erde faced her directly across the crest of the hill. The black geese nested into the grass at Doritt's back with a minimum of fuss, and over Hal's rather self-consciously hunched shoulders, the moonlight drew a familiar silhouette, the mule with his head down to graze but his long ears flicking about, alert to the night. A rustling behind Erde announced the arrival of the she-goat and a spotted dog she'd taken up with. Their coats and coloring were so similar that Erde wondered if one knew the other was a goat, or a dog. Or perhaps it didn't matter on such a night, when the very air vibrated with fellowship. Erde shivered deliciously. Only in the forests had she ever felt like this. Surely this was what the presence of magic felt like. She had heard no incantations and seen no casting of spells, and this was only a bunch of women and animals on top of a hill together. Even so, every nerve in her body thrilled with expectation.

Perhaps it was only the stillness that settled over the circle, waiting yet content. The women set their lanterns on the ground in front of them. Erde noticed that the grass inside the circle was cropped short, as if grazed down to a velvet brush by very careful sheep. She thought suddenly of the Mage City. Wouldn't it have lawns this soft and manicured? She became convinced that if anyone could tell her how to get there, it would be these women.

Rose rested her elbows on her knees, her hands making a nest for her chin. She spoke to the circle at large and formally, but her voice strummed inside Erde's chest. Listening to her was like breathing in sound.

"Our sister Erde comes to us haunted with dragon dreams. If she will share them with us, perhaps we can offer some insight as to their meaning."

Erde glanced at Hal for a clue to what to do next. She'd left behind her pen and paper. Besides, you couldn't read out here in the darkness anyway. But Hal's smile only encouraged. He was eager, nervous, like a young boy finally allowed to stay up late with the adults. He tipped his head toward Rose.

"We'll need no words," said Rose. "But understand, my child. I can only See what is, and of that, only what is open to me, and my sisters here like a lens provide the focus, with the hope that Seeing will bring enlightenment, about what is to be, about how to act. So now, gather up these dreams in your mind as if you were picking flowers. Hold them there until your memory is secure. Then think of offering them to us, to all of us, generously, as you would give a gift."

It was not going to be like speaking with the dragon. With the dragon, he was just *there,* in her mind. This would apparently take some effort. Erde hadn't given many gifts in her life. She was more used to receiving them. But she thought and then remembered a small silk pillow she had embroidered when she was six or seven, for her grandmother's birthday. She'd always lacked patience for the fussy detail work of sewing, but this one task she worked at night after chilly night, head and hands gathered close in the candle's dim light, long after Fricca had fallen asleep by the cooling hearth. And not just because it was a gift for her grandmother. For once, she'd been allowed to choose the design she was to embroider, and she'd rejected the usual ladylike basket of fruit or floral bouquet. Over Fricca's protests, she had sewn a dragon for the baroness.

Erde hadn't thought about that pillow for a very long time, but now its image flashed into her mind, as clear as a painted miniature, minute silken stitches all green and gold and brown against soft beige linen. She recalled her grandmother's delight when the gift was revealed within its brocaded birthday wrappings, how her long forefinger, heavy with the baronial ring, had lovingly traced the dragon's tiny shape.

"A fat little dragon," she'd exclaimed with satisfaction. Then she'd caught Erde's eye. "But he looks a bit shy. Why is that?"

Erde couldn't remember her reply, only that she hadn't intended the dragon to look shy. The stitches had just come out that way. She knew she hadn't told her grandmother that. It might sound like she hadn't worked on it hard enough.

And then the baroness had said, "And he has no wings. How interesting."

Erde reeled in a moment of vertigo.

Beside her, Linden gasped softly and caught her elbow. "Are you all right?"

"Why, that's lovely," murmured Rose. "Is that what he looks like?"

Erde stared across the circle, but she was hardly seeing Rose at all. Instead she saw Earth's thick arching neck, his short muscular lizard-body, his stubby pointed tail and curving ivory horns. And especially his humble demeanor. It was all there. She had embroidered him exactly, seven or was it eight years ago?

"What is it?" Hal whispered urgently, glancing from Rose to Erde and back again.

"A carnelian jewel . . ."

"Yes! Meriah's brooch!"

Rose's gaze on Erde was distant. "Does it warm to your touch?"

Erde nodded. No one but Hal knew that, not even the dragon.

"What about it, Rose? What do you See?"

Raven nudged Hal reprovingly but Rose nodded, as if his impatience was only to be expected. "Destiny," she replied.

"Whose? Hers? The Dragon's?"

"They are intertwined. I see lines of force, not where they will lead. I can confirm, Heinrich. I cannot predict."

I should not be surprised, thought Erde. But she was. And frightened. No one had ever read her mind before. Oh, there'd been those winter parlor games with walnut shells and playing cards, where coincidence and body language occasionally conspired to produce a delicious whiff of the uncanny. But this was so direct and unambiguous. It was like the Mage-Queen would have done, in her fantasies. But the Mage-Queen was haughty and magical, and always wore white. Rose was so . . . normal.

"Perhaps his Purpose can be Read from his dreams," murmured Rose. "Tell us a little of them."

But the little embroidered Earth would not leave Erde's mind. The image and its implications crowded her consciousness. She recalled what Hal had said about the carnelian brooch and its "ageless history," and was suddenly overcome by the responsibility. All those ages of history devolving down to her, and she hadn't the slightest idea what she was supposed to do about it.

Rose's deep voice vibrated through her paralysis. "Think of taking hold of something and setting it carefully aside."

This offered a distraction, and with some effort, Erde complied. The little dragon image faded and, dutifully, she turned her mind to Earth's most recent dream. At first it was easy to conjure up, like looking at a mural on a wall, the hard gleaming surfaces and sharp planes of the nightmare landscape, with its constant overlay of cacophony and stench. She pictured the knight fading away in the corridor and heard again the ringing call of the Summoner. But she couldn't hold onto the image. The details quickly went soft, as if the artist's elbow had smeared the still-wet paint. Some other din distracted her. Erde concentrated harder, but the clash of steel was drowning out all thought.

"Ah, yes. Now I see them," said Rose. "The two swordsmen."

The blurred painting fell away like an evaporating fog and Erde saw the source of the noise: her father, in pitched battle with a much younger man. The young man was tall and slim, more agile than the baron. His face, handsome even while distorted by fear and rage, was familiar to her, but she could not recall his name or who he was to her. For some reason, this filled her with despair. She remembered a sword, but not a name, could not conjure it to fit his image, no matter how desperately she tried. She would have wept but for the comfort of Rose's steady voice filling her ears.

"There, there, child, not all can be Known at once . . ."

But I did *know it once,* Erde told herself. *I know I did.* Perhaps she really was damaged after all.

"What? What is it?" Hal begged. "Rosie, please."

"I see Josef von Alte," Rose reported. "Overmatched, fighting his final battle." Then, to Erde, she said, "As for this other, his truth is still hidden from you. When you can name him, you will be free of him."

Erde shook her head. Was Earth dreaming her father's murderer?

"Try to speak his name," Rose urged.

Hal made a sound of protest. Rose laid a staying hand on his knee. To Erde, she urged, "Speak it. You can, you know."

But she couldn't speak and didn't know the name, and if that's what speaking it would mean, she was glad. She didn't want to be free of this young man, whoever he was.

"Well, perhaps it's not time to face that truth yet," said Rose. "But these are not dragon dreams?"

Erde frowned. Indeed. How would the dragon know her father? Her own dreams, then, mixing with Earth's, getting in the way. For the first time, she considered the source of dreams. Where did a dream come from, and how did you tell one to go away?

"Your dreaming is not like the dragon's," said Rose. "He hears the voices of Power. Yours come from within. Human dreams are our inner voices begging to be heard."

Erde vowed to silence these importunate voices. She must allow the dragon to be heard.

"But you must listen to your own dreams as well," said Rose. "Self-sacrifice is rarely the answer."

"Some sacrifice is inevitable," Hal put in sharply.

"She is a child. A child must have her dreams in order to grow."

"She is the Dragon Guide."

Rose glared at him. "And you are the Paladin, who will keep her always to her mark."

He took a breath, then set his jaw. "If I must. If that is my destiny."

"Your destiny. *Your* destiny!" Rose stood abruptly and walked away through the long grass to the edge of the lantern light, raking her hands through her cropped graying hair. "Your destiny!"

"Rose . . ."

The other women relaxed. The tightly drawn circle eased into a ragged arc of casual arms and legs, listening.

"Rose, you saw it yourself. She is the Dragon Guide. If I walked away from this today, she'd still have no choice."

"No. You are assuring that she'll have no choice."

"The Dragon assures that."

Rose paced away from Hal's reasonable tone. Erde did not understand this sudden irritable concern. Surely if Rose could read minds, she knew no other choice was wanted. Erde would always choose for the dragon, and willingly.

"Rose, you said it yourself," Hal repeated. "You said you saw Destiny."

From the edge of the shadows, Rose replied, "I saw it, but I don't have to like it."

"You shouldn't judge the . . ."

"Don't tell me what I can and cannot do!"

"Rose!" Hal threw up his hands. "I mean, is this useful? Does this offer us a single bloody clue about what to do next?"

"You take what you get with a Seeing, you know that! You can't control it like one of your household servants!" Rose stalked off into the darkness.

Hal leaped up to shout after her, "I don't have any servants! I don't even have a household!"

Esther leaned over to murmur in Erde's ear, "He would have, if the two of them could get along for longer than an evening's meal."

"They have, they do," protested Linden softly. "It's just that he's always leaving, from the moment he gets here."

Raven wrapped an arm around Hal's legs, hushing him. "Sit down. Let her come to it her own way."

Hal sat. His long back curled over his crossed knees, he massaged his forehead. "Sorry," he mumbled.

Raven patted his arm.

Erde was disturbed by being a cause for disagreement, but thought that if Rose and Hal really loved each other, they wouldn't fight so often. She was sure that when she fell in love, she'd never disagree with her beloved. She remembered the handsome young man in her dream and wondered again who he might be.

Hal straightened with a sigh. "Rose, please come back. The child needs your help."

And Rose returned out of the darkness and sat down beside him as if all was forgiven. The women resettled themselves alertly. Hal sighed again, his face shuttered with relief.

Rose gazed across at Erde without apology. "There is also a white city in your dreams. At the end of a long white road."

Erde nodded, her heart suddenly in her throat. The white towers swam in brilliant light before her eyes. Was this the moment she found out her true destination?

Carefully, Hal murmured, "Gerrasch did mention a city . . ."

Rose ignored him. The lanterns gathered their deepest shadows beneath her brow but threw off a reflected glimmer within. "That white road is longer than you can presently conceive of."

"What the hell does that mean?" Hal growled.

Raven elbowed him, sharply this time. "If she knew, she would say so."

"But what city is it? Can you see where it is?"

"Please!" Rose shaded her eyes with her palm, as if blinded by some bright sun. "I don't . . . it's odd. I can't tell. The image is so very clear, yet I have no sense of where." She paused for a moment, then added slowly, "Not even of *when*."

"The when must be now, Rose," Raven reminded her. "You only See the now."

"Yes, but . . ." Rose frowned at Erde distractedly. "You think that it isn't, but it is."

"Is what, isn't what?" Hal fumed.

But Erde thought she knew what Rose meant. The city was *real*. But how could it be?

Rose met her puzzled gaze. "I don't understand it either."

"Is this city our destination?" asked Hal.

"Yes." Rose bowed her head, as if there were something else she found even harder to believe.

"How can I take them there if we don't know where it is?"

"I don't know." She spoke with sudden gentleness, though still without looking at him. "You will take them to the gates."

"To the . . ." Hal blinked at her, absorbing her meaning. Erde had never seen a man's hopes collapse visibly before. She had to restrain herself from scrambling up to comfort him. Finally Hal licked his lips, cleared his throat. "Only to the gates."

"You will be needed outside."

"Outside what? I don't want to be outside! Because I don't share his dreams, I have to be left outside?"

Erde stared at her knees. Hal's dragon-envy was a swift and treacherous current flowing within him. Occasionally, it surged free and flooded them both with its tides of guilt and longing.

Rose raised her head as if surfacing from a deep pool. The shadows had faded from her eyes and moved into the hollows of her cheeks. She looked exhausted. "You ask to know Destiny, Heinrich, but what you really want is to be able to choose the one you prefer."

"Wouldn't any man?"

"This is not given to mortals, man or woman. Not even to dragons is it given."

A breeze sprang up, setting the lanterns aflicker. For a moment, their light dimmed and the night flowed into the circle like dark water into a pit. Erde shivered. She had taken it for granted that the knight would be there to protect her for the full length of her journey, wherever it was leading, which appeared to be into some place of her own dreaming. She could not imagine how to get to such a place, but how else might she understand Rose's Seeing?

At length, Hal answered softly, with bleak humility, "I know. And therefore, so be it."

And the breeze died, the lamps flared, and the pain and tension was drawn away out of the circle, along with the darkness.

"The Seeing is over," said Rose.

"Now let us offer our love and silence to the night," Esther intoned ritualistically.

The women sat quietly, and Erde thought to fill the time appropriately by chanting various little benedictions she'd learned from the nuns. But she was too distracted for prayer. Sometime soon, she had to admit to Earth that the Mage City was only a fantasy she'd let run out of control to soothe him, to offer him—no, both of them—a goal, a hope when there'd been so little. Now that the aura of power was gone from the circle, Erde was sure Rose must have misunderstood her Seeing, to suggest that they could actually go to such a place. She vowed never to lie to the dragon again.

As she sat, restless and uncertain, a certain stillness came to her after a while, alive with the night breeze and the scents it carried of grass and earth and ripening fruit, and the sounds of insects and owls and the noisy brook at the bottom of the hill. She felt so welcome among these women and content, and as it had on the road out, this sense of well-being filled her chest like a great intake of breath. She felt her ribs expand with it, and her back straighten. It grew until it was so big she knew she could not contain it. She felt she might burst, and began to think of letting a little of it go, letting it flow out of her into the night like warm water, like milk, releasing the pressure of joy inside her.

Around her, the women sighed and smiled. Rose smiled also, but glanced at Hal to see if he had sensed this invasion of warmth. She was answered when he leaned over and kissed her quickly, sweetly, then grinned like a boy who'd just gotten away with something.

"When this child finds her voice," Rose murmured, "she will be dangerously charismatic."

Poised for another kiss, Hal raised a brow. "When? Then you know she will?"

"Oh, yes. This much is certain."

"I thought maybe Linden could . . ."

"No healer can cure this. She must find it herself."

Erde heard, yet didn't hear. The joy in her was drawing together into a presence. Finally she understood it was the dragon returning from his hunt. It disturbed her that she hadn't recognized him immediately. There was something different about him, something . . . bigger. She sensed his same plodding gait as he toiled up the hill, the same distracted curious air, nosing her out yet knowing exactly where to go. But there was an aura of bigness, a new sense of resolve. He had come in search of her and he had something on his mind. Clearly, the dragon had eaten well.

Across the circle, the mule leaned in to nudge Hal's shoulder. The dogs stirred and the she-goat stood up and shook herself. Erde thought Earth's image at Rose as hard as she could, but only caught the edges of her attention. Rose frowned vaguely and glanced her way as if she'd mumbled something incomprehensible.

But by that time, the dragon's approach was audible, the rhythmic swish of his bulk pushing through the tall grass, the sigh of his breath, so like the sighing of the wind in the berry bushes. All around the circle, the women drew up into postures of expectation. Those with their backs to him turned in place but the arc remained unbroken, a circle of lamps inside a circle of women. The solitary man leaned back on one arm and tried to look casual, but his waiting was as poignant as the rest.

Earth gained the top of the hill and halted when he saw the lantern light. He had expected to find Erde, but not the rest. He paused a moment in confusion, puffing slightly, then regained his dignity. Erde noted with a shock that he did seem bigger, even brighter. Another trick of the light? She would swear the dragon had grown substantially since noon-time, when she'd sent him off to hunt. Even his color was bigger, more luminous. The moss greens and dirt browns were brighter and shone with highlights of bronze and gold. Admiring murmurs ran around the circle, and the dragon stretched and preened.

Erde was overjoyed to see him, and felt his own welcome rush through her like a fever. She gathered herself to leap up, but he sent her an image of waiting. So she held back, while Earth came forward to offer his formal greeting, a deep bow to the circle with ivory horns presented, gleaming like arcs of light in the reflected lamp glow.

But once he'd completed what he considered to be the necessary formalities, he was all over the inside of her head like a puppy dog. Images raced past too fast for Erde to grasp.

—Earth! Slow down!

She was stunned to see Rose clap her hands to her ears as if she'd shouted out loud. She offered a look of apology, hoping Rose would understand that sometimes she just had to yell at the dragon, or he wouldn't listen. But Rose continued to hold her head, curling over her knees as if in real pain.

Hal leaned in. "Rose? Rosie? What is it?"

"It's ... him!" Rose gasped.

"What's happening?" Hal turned to Erde. "What's he doing?"

Frightened, she shook her head.

"Whatever it is, tell him to stop!"

She tried to get the dragon's attention, but he was too caught up in what he wanted to tell her. Pictures flashed in and out of her head like the colors on a spinning top, all blending into incoherency. Erde considered more drastic measures. She built a detailed image of an open door, held it in her mind and with all her strength, slammed it shut.

The dragon started and blinked. His torrent of images stopped dead in astonishment.

—You were hurting this woman here.

Earth dismissed the possibility. He'd been nowhere near her.

—She can hear you. Sometimes when you think too fast, it's like . . . like that waterfall we nearly went over.

The mention of the waterfall seemed to impress him. He went very quiet for a while.

Rose uncurled, massaging her temples in relief. "Is he always like that? How do you listen without burning your brain out?"

"You can hear him? You can hear the dragon? You can hear what he . . .?" Hal foundered midway between pride and hopeless envy.

"Not very well." Rose shook her head as if clearing it. "Not very well at all. Mostly his enormous power. It was how I imagine a god would speak." She regarded Erde with new respect. "Child, you have a remarkable gift."

"She is the Dragon Guide," Hal reminded her simply.

"Will you introduce me?" Rose asked Erde. "Perhaps we can learn a way to talk together in a less painful fashion."

The new deference in Rose's rich and wonderful voice made Erde self-conscious. She wasn't sure she deserved it. After all, it was the dragon who was remarkable, not she. But it was interesting to think about what it meant to be able to do something other people couldn't do. There was a kind of power in that, especially if it was something other people wanted to be able to do.

—Dragon, this is Rose of Deep Moor. She has a great hearing gift. I think if you think very small and quietly, she might be able to understand you. This might be useful right now, since she has a working voice, and could translate for you.

Earth blinked again and turned his huge eyes on Rose in a deeply speculative gaze. Erde saw faint flickers in her mind, little whispers of image, but Rose smiled and sighed as if she'd been given the most wonderful treasure.

"Can you hear him?" Hal demanded. "What does he say?"

"He doesn't exactly *say* . . . anything."

Hal nodded sagely, fighting to keep his envy in check. "No words. That's what she told me."

"He greets me, and you, the women of the circle. He's very polite. But there is something he's eager to tell us . . ."

New images ghosted into Erde's mind, appearing slowly like the sun through a mist. The scale was small, the colors were bland, but she recognized the Mage City, a pale echo of itself.

Rose inhaled sharply. "It's the city, the one you showed me! He says he knows where it is!"

The women exclaimed softly. Doritt let out a small cheer. Then Esther said, "Listen!"

On the night wind came an insistent clanging, from the direction of the farmstead.

"The alarm bell!" breathed Doritt.

"It must be Lily and Margit come home," said Raven, "wondering where we are."

Rose raised her face to the breeze like a wary animal. "Oh, this is the darkness I've felt all day. It's Lily, and she brings us bad news."

The circle broke instantly. Raven and Doritt scrambled up and took off down the dark hill at a run. The twins made quick arrangements for the return of the dogcart, and sped after them.

"Margit is the twins' birth-mother," Linden told Erde nervously as she helped the old lore-keepers into the cart. Hal had promised to pull them home so the others could hurry ahead. Rose thanked him gravely, then moved into his arms for the offered embrace.

His lips brushed her forehead. "All will be well, Rosie."

"No, my love, it won't. Not any more." Rose pressed her face briefly into his chest. "Deep Moor's grace time is over, I feel it. The world has come to our doorstep. I only hope we've not waited too long to act."

Chapter Twenty-Four

Earth spent the whole trip down the hill babbling to Erde about his discovery. It wasn't exactly true that he knew where the Mage City was—Rose had misunderstood some of the finer details. But lying out in the meadow enjoying himself after a satisfying meal, he had heard the Summoner's voice for the first time while he was awake, in his head, not like a real sound, but the voice was now directional. It drew him like a lodestone. He was sure he could follow it to its source which, of course, was the city.

Erde told him what Rose had said about the city. He took this as further proof, which she would have been inclined to do also, were the Mage City not her own invention. She felt too deeply mired in her "righteous lie" to see a way out of it. Besides, she did have to wonder about what Rose had seen. Perhaps she had not made it up. Perhaps the image of the Mage City had come into her mind from somewhere else, from some*one* else. Once again, she decided to say nothing of this to the dragon. Even a fantasy destination was better than no destination at all.

The yard in front of the house was deserted when Hal and Erde reached the farmstead. The lanterns burned in scattered groups on the porch where they'd been hastily abandoned. The lore-keepers looked grim.

"All inside, I suspect," said one. The other hung a lantern to either side of the door, then blew the rest out and replaced them neatly in their rack. Erde left the dragon pacing impatiently in the yard. She followed Hal into the house.

Inside, oil lamps flared around the stone hearth, where the women were gathered. A young woman lay bleeding in Raven's arms, struggling to speak while Linden sponged her wounds. Her clothing was torn and mud-spattered. Rose knelt alongside, holding the woman's limp hand and bending close to hear her broken whisper.

Doritt caught Hal's arm as he came up beside her. Her big dark eyes glimmered with unshed tears. "Margit's been taken!"

"What! Where?"

"Erfurt," she hissed. "Lily's run back all the way alone."

"How's she doing?"

"She'll be all right."

"Who got Margit?"

"Adolphus of Köthen."

"Of ... Köthen? *Köthen?*"

Doritt nodded. "I'm sorry, Hal."

"Köthen in Erfurt?"

"He's leading the barons' army."

Hal seemed to wish he hadn't heard her right. "What about the king?"

"The king has fled."

His only response was a soft moan.

"Toward Nürnburg, with a few of his household. Prince Carl stayed with Köthen."

"Willingly?"

"Willingly."

Erde watched the knight's entire body reel under this last piece of news. In their month together, she had never seen his manner go so hard and cold, and yet somehow so sad. "Köthen always did have an abnormal influence over the boy. Is Margit alive?"

Doritt's mouth tightened. "So far. We don't have a lot of details yet, but Lily's afraid that Baron Köthen will use Margit to prove his loyalty when Fra Guill arrives next week to give his blessing to the barons' coup."

"The hell-priest in Erfurt, too? Oh, too close, Doritt, too close for comfort. I hope Lily covered her trail."

Doritt looked offended. "Lily's our most gifted Seeker. Of course she covered her trail."

"Erfurt taken. The king's own seat." Hal glanced about furtively as if he were being held against his will. "I must get to Nürnburg. I must get to His Majesty."

"What about Margit? You know he'll burn her, Hal."

"She knew the risk, as we all do. My duty is with the king."

Doritt looked away, frowning, then nodded. "And Margit would surely agree. Will you leave the girl and her creature with us?"

His nod was businesslike. "They're safer here than anywhere."

Erde grabbed his sleeve and shook her head.

"Milady, please understand. Speed is essential now."

She was sure from his posture that he was about to explain how this was men's work ahead of him. She searched about, found a scrap of Raven's paper in her pocket. EARTH WILL NOT STAY. HE IS CALLED.

"Ah, yes," agreed Doritt. "He's on his own quest, after all. They'll just go off on their own without you."

"And Fra Guill will have them in a blink of an eye. Ah, sweet Mother, help me. What do I do?" Hal paced away and back. "King or Dragon? Must I choose?"

Erde wrote: WE'LL ALL GO TO NÜRNBURG.

"Milady, our little walk in the woods has just become infinitely more dangerous."

She nodded, once and briskly.

"Rose's Seeing proves you've still a ways to go together," Doritt pointed out.

"He moves too slowly! He's like a snail!"

HE'LL MOVE FASTER, Erde promised.

Because the knight did not refuse her outright, she knew that the session up on the hill had changed something fundamental in his thinking about her and the dragon, a change she sensed in her own thinking as well. New sensations of confidence and potential were spreading through her like slow warmth, a growing need to act, to stand against the evil tide of events rather than be swept along by it. She had fallen in with this loose network of royalists by accident, if there was any such thing as accident (which she was beginning to doubt), but they were her natural allies. Her enemies were their enemies. Most importantly, she had a notion that the dragon was also readying himself to act. She had no idea what form his action might take, but as Dragon Guide, she might well influence his choice.

She had a strange moment of self-awareness, as if she were standing across the room looking back. She saw a tall young woman with a ruddy boyish face and determined jaw, strong and lean from travel and the knight's training exercises, clothed in a man's pragmatic garb. The sallow long-haired child in slippers and velvet dresses was a fading memory. Her mouth twisted with reflective irony. She'd become what she'd always pretended to be in her fantasies, what her father had always feared and despised. Interesting that it had required the sacrifice of her entire life as she'd known it to accomplish the transformation.

Possessed by this new self as if by some benign but reckless demon, Erde grinned at Hal and scrawled: WE'LL SAVE THE KING TOGETHER.

Hal squeezed his eyes shut once, then nodded helplessly.

PART FOUR

EARTH

The Meeting with Destiny

Chapter Twenty-Five

She promised him haste, and he got it. With twelve women bending their efforts to it, the provisioning was quickly accomplished. Food, a skin of wine, a new linen shirt for Erde and her old one clean. Presents, too, casually produced and packed away as if they'd been hers all along. There were warm gloves and new stockings from the fine wool of Doritt's sheep. Rose gave her a thin rectangle of slate pierced by a thong, and a soft pointed stick that made bright letters on the gray stone. This gift Erde hung gratefully around her neck, but not before scrawling THANK YOU on it in large letters.

Hal hunted up a leather breastplate and greaves that he'd left behind on some past visit. He stowed them in the mule packs along with a borrowed supply of extra woolens. Erde touched his arm in question as he was stuffing them into an already full pouch.

"Rose says we'll need these." He closed the pack briskly and tied the thongs. Then he went to draw Rose aside from the women crowding around the loaded mule. He said his good-byes and Erde said hers. They were on the road before the moon had set.

Raven and Doritt came out with them as far as the oak grove. They walked arm in arm beside Hal, their mood somber. The dragon did not share their foreboding. He was as eager as if the Summoner awaited him right outside the valley. He forged off like a happy hunting dog through the tall grasses to the right and left of the track, vanishing into the darkness and then returning to report to Erde on the beauty of the night and the interesting smells to be had out in the meadow.

Meanwhile, under the steady pressure of Raven's persuasion, Hal reconsidered his itinerary.

"Nürnburg is a week's hard ride," he grumbled, "Never mind what it will take with this group. The king on the road, exposed and vulnerable . . . what if Köthen's sent men in pursuit?"

"But Erfurt's on the way," she reminded him. "A swing up there won't add more than a day."

"If all goes well." Hal sighed as if bullied and overmatched. "Well, let's say we do it. Four or five days to Erfurt, then I slip in quickly by night. We must still have a loyal source or two who could help me find Margit. All right. If I'm not too late, I'll do what I can."

"It wouldn't be the first time."

"No," he admitted gloomily. "It wouldn't."

Raven put her arm around his waist and leaned into him gratefully. Doritt's brisk, serious nod said she didn't hold out too much hope, but she was relieved that he would try.

"I hope they won't have taken her crucifix," murmured Raven. Doritt muttered sympathetic agreement but Hal shook his head.

"Pray she'll not endanger her soul with that."

"Don't be so disapproving," Raven chided. "You know the same Church that makes such prohibitions is the Church that's burning innocent women. Would you begrudge our Margit a quick and comfortable passing?"

"Pray there'll be no need," Hal repeated primly.

Raven released her arm and stood away from him. "Heinrich, are you really a man to whom the law means more than human life?"

"Not man's law. I'd deliver the grace stroke myself, were murder the only way to save her the agony of the stake. But we're talking here of God's Law." He shrugged delicately, as if embarrassed by his own obstinance. "I do truly believe it's a sin to take one's own life."

"It's men who've decided what God's Law is," Raven returned. "What if they were about to burn you?"

Erde, who'd been listening mystified, saw it all in a bright and sickening rush: some fast-acting poison from Linden's stores of herbs and elixirs, a tiny lethal reservoir inside the crucifix. She'd heard of such things in the bard tales. It was a once remote and romantic notion that now seemed pragmatic and humane. Surely it was not a sin to save yourself from suffering a prolonged torture? She wished the witch-woman in Tubin had had such an option. She was surprised that Hal could be dogmatic about suffering, especially when he had seen so much of it.

But on the other hand, Raven's reply did amount to out-right heresy. Every good Christian knew that God had decided God's Laws.

The birds were just stirring in the oak trees as they reached the grove. Their early songs hung crystalline in the still air. The heady sweet scents of fern and wet leaves were like fairy voices begging Erde to stay. She knew she would, were it not for the dragon. She was probably mad, having found such a wonderful place, to be leaving it so quickly.

Hal squinted through the branches toward the lightening sky. "We'll travel till dawn, then rest until dark. I want to get well clear of this valley in case we're noticed."

Raven took the late rose she'd worn in her hair and laid it on the stone cairn by the pool in the middle of the grove. "For your safety this day and those to come," she intoned. She took Hal's hands. "Find our Margit." Then she kissed him and embraced Erde, turning away briskly with tears in her eyes. Erde found her own suddenly wet.

"Come, Doritt. Let them be on their way."

"Yes, yes, soon enough." Doritt shook hands around, finishing with a firm pat on Erde's shoulder. "We've not seen the last of you, girl. Don't fret."

Raven was already lost in the shadows. "Is that a true notion, Doritt?" she called.

The tall woman nodded. "You can count on it."

"Well, that's encouraging," remarked Hal as they approached the steep switchbacks leading out of the valley. "Doritt's notions are her gift. She gets them about how things will turn out. Not like Rose's Seeing what *is,* much vaguer and long-term. She doesn't get them very often and she can't call them up—they just arrive, or they don't. But Deep Moor swears by her."

They found the dragon at the foot of the cliff, stock-still, staring upward. When Erde asked him what he was looking at, she received his blank-mind state, the same as she did when he was being invisible. Several times, he glanced at the base of the trail, then back at the top of the cliff, a good half-mile above.

Erde pulled out her new writing slate. HE WON'T TALK TO ME.

Hal laughed. "You know how he hates to climb. He's wishing he had wings, like a proper dragon."

As they stood watching the dragon stare intently upward, the first pink of dawn flushed the mountain range to the west. Hal sent the mule and the she-goat up the trail.

"We must be moving. If you go ahead, he'll follow."

Which he did, but with a puzzled, distracted air. Erde sent him a wistful image of himself with sleek reptilian wings, soaring toward the cliff top. His response was the closest thing to a chuckle she'd heard out of him yet: a vision of himself with his tongue lolling ridiculously. It was her first clue that he knew what humor was.

—You thought I was making a joke?

He returned assent and a new image: himself decked out with giant bird wings, flapping and panting, but unable to lift his massive body off the ground. Then he showed her how wings large enough to lift his weight would be too cumbersome to carry around on the ground. Erde thought this was unimaginative thinking for a mythic creature such as a dragon. She wrote out the conversation laboriously for Hal on her slate.

"Dragons," he offered seriously, "er . . . *winged* dragons are said to have hollow bones made of magical substances that cause them to weigh nothing at all."

Erde made a face. NOT THIS DRAGON.

"No," the knight mourned. "Apparently not."

Earth had more to say on the subject of travel. He'd been thinking about it a lot, but the results were hard to express in visual images. He'd become convinced that knowledge of an easier way lurked just beyond the edges of his memory. Because she knew how miserable and inadequate he felt when his memory failed him, Erde concentrated on soothing his frustration, simply to keep him going up the hill. She asked about the Summoner. Earth told her the voice came and went. It was not as constant in his waking existence as it was in the dream, but he was confident he would hear it soon again, and know which way to go. Erde hoped it would be in the direction of Erfurt and Nürnburg.

The air cooled noticeably as they climbed. Erde recalled the torn but heavy layers of clothing that Lily had arrived in, and the woolens that Rose had made Hal bring along. She thought of the mud and chill of her journey from Tor Alte, and stole many backward yearning glances at the receding valley. She'd hoped to stay a while, to sleep in a warm soft bed again and wake rested to the sound of birdsong and the comfortable chatter of women.

When they gained the top of the cliff after an hour's hard climbing, it was like walking out of a warm house into winter. A stiff cold wind rushed down off the mountains, as lung-searing as a torrent of ice water. Just past dawn and the sky already glowered with dark and shifting layers of cloud. Panting from his climb, Earth perched on the edge, his snout raised to the gusts as if the wind itself might bring a message.

Hal had not looked back once since starting the ascent, but now he settled on a rock to catch his breath and faced the valley, his red-leathered back to the gale. "Rose swears it's a coincidence of geography that keeps Deep Moor so temperate when the rest of the world's halfway to winter. It's like a place set apart, where the usual rules just don't apply, where the society is humane, and nature's always in balance. A religious man would say it's God's grace. A superstitious one would call it sorcery. I don't know what I believe. But of all the places I go, Deep Moor is the only place I ever really *want* to be. I just ... my life ... well ..." He shrugged, gave up, and rose from his rock. "We'll unpack those woolens now. Put 'em on soon as the sweat dries. Damn unseasonable weather."

They retraced their steps up through the gray army of standing stones, where the she-goat had nearly met her end, and back across the barren ridges that hid the valley from the world of men. The wind stayed gusty and biting. The summer foliage was black and slimy with frost. Along the way, Hal covered their tracks obsessively, searching for any sign that Lily might have left in her panicked homeward flight. Finally he had to admit how astonishingly careful she'd been for an injured fugitive at the very end of her strength.

"Somehow, they always keep it hidden. You ask around at the nearest market town? People never know where Esther comes from. It's as if they never think to ask. Yet there she is, with vegetables twice the size of theirs, and crockery and weaving that bring the farmwives from all around. Remarkable, these Deep Moor women. Remarkable, every one of them."

Witches, thought Erde, *real ones,* and knew it to be true.

They camped at noon deep in the woods on the downward slope. The animals lay down as soon as Hal called a halt. Even the dragon, despite his eagerness to be following his Voice, recognized limits to a day's travel that the knight seemed to have forgotten. Hal's impatience made him restive. He talked of the king as they set up camp, told stories of their better days together. He insisted on a rigorous sword practice before their meal and bed.

"Twice a day now. You're strong enough. Just at the point where you can start actually learning something. Here." He tossed her the practice stick. Erde snatched it out of the air with one hand and did not fumble it. "See? Now, present your weapon."

Erde took her stance, gripped her stick, and held it out in front of her. Hal turned to face her, his own stick laid across hers for the first time. Erde felt a twinge of nervousness, but it was performance anxiety, not fear. She had been looking forward to the moment of actual engagement, to see if all this effort would amount to any real skill.

"Now, watch. This third move we've been practicing becomes a right cross-parry. Try it. It's a standard parry for swordsmen who can't count on superior strength. Good. Now use it when I come at you like this. One and two and . . ."

He came at her slowly, in the speed and rhythm of their usual practice routine. Erde cocked her wrists, straightened the appropriate arm, and his stick slid neatly off hers toward the ground. She knew he had relaxed into the parry, but the move still felt right and it gave her a most unwholesome sort of satisfaction. She grinned wickedly. Hal grinned back, winked, and sobered. "Now, again! Faster! One and two and . . ."

They rested, and awoke at dusk to move along again. The terrain became rocky and broken beneath stands of young trees thick with thorny undergrowth. The going was slow. Even the goat and the surefooted mule found it treacherous.

"I know I'll be breaking my own rules of safety," Hal said on the second night out, "but a little north of here, we'll come up on the road west toward Erfurt. I'd like to chance it for a while, till we get free of these hills." He daubed at the raw scrapes and scratches on Erde's palms with a salve Linden had sent along. "We've made maybe eight to ten miles a day this way. It's too slow. On the road, we could make twelve to fifteen, and turn five or six days to Erfurt into four. What do you think?"

Erde sent back a tired grin. Surely he wasn't actually asking her advice?

"What would you do if you were out here alone?" he pursued.

He wanted an answer. Erde considered, then wrote on her slate: MOVE MORE SLOWLY.

He laughed. "What if you had to move faster?"

I WOULDN'T. HE CAN'T.

"Ah. But what if you were without the dragon?"

THE ROAD.

He nodded. "Good. Then that's what we'll do."

Had he only wanted her agreement, or was he insisting that she begin to take part in the decision-making? Now they knew Hal would not always be there to guide her. Their paths had nearly divided in Deep Moor. Erde had an inkling of some new aspect being added to her training, and vowed to pay more attention to such things. She had no sense of how fast or how far they'd traveled. Hal had told Rose that she and the dragon had covered some two hundred miles in the month since she'd left Tor Alte. Two hundred miles seemed an enormous distance, yet she was not halfway across the east-west stretch of the kingdom, Tor Alte being on its extreme eastern border. She was beginning to understand why a kingdom was so hard to rule and keep together, why it could be so easily split apart by the machinations of a few dissident vassal lords.

"It'll be risky, but a lot easier on him." Hal jerked his head at the dragon, who was nursing a deep gouge in his flank from a broken limb he'd tumbled into. All his injuries healed with miraculous speed, but the forest had become so dense he often could not squeeze between the trunks. He'd have to cut a wide arc around to find a way back to them. "To say nothing of easier on us," Hal added ruefully. "And it might improve our chances of getting to Margit in time."

He got no argument, so the next dusk found them hunkered down in the trees above a rough track cut through the forest, wide enough for four men to ride abreast without their helms and standards being snagged in the overhanging branches. Earth eyed the open roadway with approval. Hal studied the muddied wheel ruts.

"Well, it's in use all right, and by more than just a few local farmers. Horses carrying men and armor. Mostly heading west. West . . ." Hal blew air through his teeth. "Ah, would I could fly like a bird. Would I were with His Majesty."

He didn't say, would this dragon had wings. Erde laid a sympathetic hand on his arm.

"Right. Here's what we'll do. Pack up the Mule more farm-style, hide the swords, but keep them handy. Tether the goat, if she's willing to be led. You'll be the idiot goat-boy, should anyone come along. Earth will have to be invisible, which in the dark, shouldn't tax him too much."

They climbed down to the road as a peasant widower and his unfortunate son journeying to visit relatives outside of Erfurt. Hal embellished the tale as they strode along, both to tighten their cover in case they had to use it and to keep his mind off his concern for the king's welfare. The road was deep in mud and standing puddles of icy water, but it was easier going than the woods.

"Another good night like this and we'll be within striking distance of Erfurt," Hal remarked as they bedded down for the day high in the pine woods above the road. He would not allow a fire. Some traveler on the road might scent the smoke. But before they went to bed, he roused Erde for practice. This time, he untied the pack bundle that held the real swords, and freed them from their wrappings. His own was sheathed and he buckled it on with evident satisfaction, as if he'd missed the weight of it, companionable against his hip. The other, naked blade he passed to Erde hilt-first.

She took it confidently, then felt suddenly thrown off balance. It wasn't the weight. She could lift it well enough. But she'd taken it in hand assuming it was his, a spare he carried. Then holding it, she'd realized it somehow belonged to her. What was she doing with a sword? There was resistance as she tried to remember, as if that information was locked away in a shadowy place where her brain didn't want her to look. With great effort she recalled finding the sword under her bed at Tor Alte. But no straining would tell her how it came to be there. Another blank spot, another lapse. She thought of the dragon's dilemma and wondered if she was losing her memory as he regained his.

Hal read her stricken look and sudden paralysis as novice's nerves. "Oh, now. Just take a good grip on it, go ahead, like you would your stick. It's no different, really."

Being given a task to focus on broke Erde's daze. She did as he said, and found the hilt fitted well into her palm. She flexed her fingers around it, frowning. Perhaps it was hers after all.

"Good hands," approved Hal. "Strong hands."

She'd always been self-conscious about her hands. Too big and rangy for a girl, not frail and soft and white. Fricca had once advised her to sit on them in public. She gripped the hilt and found it warm as if from someone else's hand, though Hal had held it only by its linen wrappings and by the incised base of the blade. The uncanny warmth sparked a flare of memory that fled almost before she was aware it had been there—a face, a smile, then gone, leaving only an ache inside. Fending off this unidentifiable pain, Erde raised the sword with both hands out in front of her. Automatically, her body corrected for the weight. Her stance widened, her back uncurled, her hips tucked. She felt a transition into balance, into harmony with the shining length of steel. She twisted the blade back and forth, letting it catch the dapplings of dawn falling through the trees. The flash of light was powerful, mesmerizing.

Hal laughed softly. "See? You can lift it easily now. Don't look so thunderstruck. I told you I was a good teacher. Now let's run the whole routine. Face forward, blade down. Ready? And one, and two . . ."

It rained during the day, drenching them in their sleep, then it cleared and became cold and dry. But the next night, the road was ankle-deep in stiff black ooze, iced over in the shallows. It had narrowed considerably to wind through a steep-sided glen lined with dense stands of birches, as slim and white in the moonlight as old bones and set as close as prison bars. A grown man could scarcely pass between them to scale the darker slopes.

Hal was in a black complaining mood from loss of sleep and damp clothing and not being with the king, where his duty lay. He was so intent on hurrying his party along that he didn't hear the men approaching until they were nearly around the bend. He stopped dead in the middle of a complaint. "Christ Almighty!" he breathed. "Listen!"

Ahead, the creak of harness and the quiet splash of many hooves through the mud.

Hal shoved Erde toward one side of the road, the mule toward the other. "Scatter!"

Erde had reached the thicket of birch trunks and was scrambling up the slope when the horsemen came into view. They were moving slowly, cautiously, wary of the forest night. Helmets and lance tips gleamed in the moonlight. Erde dropped to her belly. The she-goat was a flicker of motion freezing into silence farther up the hill. Erde guessed that Hal had split to the other side with the mule, and the dragon was . . .

Still visible in the middle of the road. The close-packed birches might as well have been a stout palisade to him, and the road was too narrow for the horsemen to pass him by without touching. Invisibility would not conceal him. Earth was trapped, with a dozen armed and armored men coming straight for him, still unaware that they were about to run into anything unusual. The dragon, who could have done serious damage to them before they'd have time to strike a blow, was terrified. His fear clanged deafening alarms in Erde's head as he charged the trees like a battering ram, rolling all his weight against the trunks. The smallest gave way and cracked rendingly, the thickest swayed and held. He backed up and rushed them again, creating a barrier of splintered wood rather than a passageway. The armed men were closing in. The leader raised a hand and called a halt, peering down the darkened road. He was jumpy, unsure. He gestured to two of his men to investigate the strange racket. Glancing at each other nervously, they set their lances and eased their horses forward.

Earth saw the steel-tipped shafts moving toward him through patches of shadow and moonlight. He panicked. He threw himself again and again against a tangle of broken branches scarcely less sharp than the lances themselves. Sure that he'd impale himself, Erde leaped up out of hiding and tumbled back down the slope to stop him. One of the lancers spied her. He shouted a warning, the shrill cry of a man frightened of what might be lurking deep in a forest at night.

A sudden curve of flame arced through the darkness and

into the mud at the lancers' feet. Another followed. Their horses neighed and backed. The riders fought for control, their lances colliding, nearly unseating them. The rest of the party spurred forward at the leader's sharp command. Another burning arrow thunked into the mud, then another. A bright line of flame separated the lancers from their unknown quarry. The leader shouted. The horses shied and would not cross.

Erde reached the panicked dragon, her mind yelling at him with all her strength to be still. He saw her dancing around him, felt her too close, ducking his flailing limbs, risking the crush of his plunging bulk. He froze. She laid her palms on his neck and climbed up on his foreleg to grip his head with both hands and stare into his eyes. Desperate to calm him, to get him still and invisible, she sent him the safest, most soothing image she could conjure. His mind leaped at it and clung to it eagerly. He knew that place, knew it well. He wanted to be there, longed to be there, not in a muddy dark forest pursued by sharp points and cold steel. Not here but . . .

Erde felt her stomach turn over. Her mind went suddenly numb. She squeezed her eyes shut. He was falling or she was going to faint, from fear or . . .

The dizziness passed. The dragon relaxed beneath her, and she risked a breath, a deep breath of warm, moist air smelling of grass and flowers. *Familiar* smells. The shrilling of Earth's inner alarm bells ceased. In its place, an astonished but gratified sense of satisfaction. Still clinging to him, Erde opened her eyes.

They were back in the meadows of Deep Moor. Not even attempting an explanation, she let go of the dragon and climbed down into the tall, sweet-smelling grass. She walked around a bit, dampening her hands with night dew. It was not a dream. She stared around the moonlit valley, then back at the dragon.

—*You did this. How?*

He sent her an image of a shrug, a notion she had taught him and now wished she hadn't. It only encouraged his childishness.

—*Think how it happened! You must!*

His smugness unappreciated, he put his mind to remembering. It had actually been very simple. She had made him think of Deep Moor and he'd wanted to go there desperately, to the valley where he'd be safe, right here on this spot that he recalled so clearly, and so he just *was*.

—And me. You brought me with you.

Assent. Earth did not see anything particularly remarkable about that. She had been there in his mind, after all. What he marveled at was being safe again.

—But it's a miracle! Can you do it again?

Assent. He reminded her that the only good thing about this snail-paced process of regaining his memory was that once he remembered part of a thing, he remembered all of it, like unlocking a door gave access to everything behind it. This was the better way to travel that he'd been struggling to recall. If he could image a place accurately enough, he could quite simply *be* there.

Erde laughed in soundless delight, then stopped short with a gasp as she remembered Hal, alone, bearing the brunt and the mystery of their sudden disappearance. The flaming arrows were a stroke of genius, but they would have given his position away.

—We have to go back!

?????

She imaged Hal defending himself single-handedly against a dozen armed warriors. Earth countered with visions of lances and steel.

—We must go back! We can't desert him! He'd fight to the death to protect you.

The dragon moved away from her, pacing and circling anxiously, sending up rich aromas of dirt and crushed grass.

—Earth, please! We have to help him! What about the Mule and the goat?

He sent back horrific images of her being sliced and dismembered, of himself having to kill soldiers in order to save her. It was wrong to take a life without permission. He didn't want to do that.

—You won't have to. We can go back, grab Hal and the others, and bring them back here. You can do that, can't you?

Earth considered. He could go back, he knew that, and he could retrieve anyone or anything he could picture well enough to hold in his mind as a separate entity. Finally, he could not find an honest reason, besides his own fear, to deny her.

—Then we'll do it. Umm, how do we do it?

He pictured her drawing close to him, helping him remember the place they had come from, though his image of it was far more vividly recalled than hers could ever have been. Hers was night-dark and vague, distorted by the emotional state she'd been in, but he remembered everything because he noticed everything, despite his fear, in all the sensual dimensions, sight, sound, touch, and especially smell. What she could help him with was the motivation to take himself and her to a place he had no wish to return to, and since wanting a place, desiring to *be* there, was crucial to his new method of transport, she had to convince him. She urged and encouraged, she shamed him and pleaded with him and finally, she reminded him that he had accepted an oath of fealty which brought certain responsibilities in return.

Responsibility turned out to be the key. She felt him sigh and gather himself, then go very still. Then the same sudden dizziness and blankness of mind assaulted her, and she was back on the cold muddy road in the forest. Sound exploded around her like a bomb, the cries of men and horses, the clash of steel. Earth had returned them a neat hundred paces down the road from where they'd left. His accuracy astonished her. Ahead, the men and horses were caught in a melee. The arrows still burned in the mud. Someone was trying to light a torch. It looked like the men were fighting each other.

—*How will we find him in this mess?*

Earth imaged himself signaling the mule and the she-goat. His low bugled cry was barely audible over the neighing of the frightened horses. The torch finally burst into flame, illuminating a man dancing in and out among the others, whacking a horse here or a man there with his fist or the flat of his sword. The sudden light revealed him to the men as a stranger, and to Erde as Hal. The lancers howled their rage and humiliation, and turned on him as one. Hal ducked away from the horsemen to find himself confronting a man on foot with a sword raised to strike. Slewing his own blade around to parry, Hal lost his footing in the mud. He staggered, then dropped and rolled sideways as the other's sword sliced downward into the black ooze. The man was young and fast and recovered quickly for another chop while Hal struggled to regain his balance. Just before his downstroke, the man cried out and erupted forward, back arched and eyes wide.

His sword went flying, nearly decapitating the man racing to help him finish the stranger off. Hal stared for a split second, uncomprehending, then scrambled to his feet as the she-goat rocketed past. She saw him, skidded to a halt, and raced back again, butting and nudging him away from the fray. He swatted at her in astonishment, readying his sword again and turning, but then the mule was there with her, much more persuasive with a hank of the knight's sleeve between his big teeth and his broad chest pressed hard against Hal's ribs.

The lancers were recovering. A few more torches had been lit. A foot soldier spotted the stranger being dragged off into the dark by two animals that had appeared out of nowhere. The man muttered, crossed himself, then squeaked out a warning. His fellows stared. Some hesitated, a few retreated. Several of the bravest shouted a victory cry and charged, torches flaring. Hal shook the mule off and began to run.

And there, looming up before him, huge and menacing in the flickering torchlight, was every reason that the soldiers had feared going into the forest at night. They stopped dead to take in the horned head and reptilian neck, the raking claws and burning eyes of the creature that the priest had warned them about.

A dragon.

Frantically conjuring Deep Moor in her mind, Erde saw terror and dread drain all expression from the lancers' faces. Stock-still, bathed in torchlight, they watched the stranger-warlock sprint to meet his dragon steed, his animal familiars racing by his side. At the edge of the darkness, the demons slowed, gathered, and disappeared.

Chapter Twenty-Six

"**Y**ou mean he could do that all along? All those miles on foot when we could have been traveling like that? We could be in Erfurt now. We could be in Nürnburg!" Hal was a tall shadow stalking around the dragon and waving his arms, simultaneously apoplectic and elated. "Can he take us to Erfurt? How many can he take? Could he take a whole army?"

"Heinrich," said Rose patiently. "You don't have an army."

Erde sat cross-legged on the velvet grass of the clearing in front of the farmhouse, leaning back against Raven's shoulder, busy with her writing slate. Beside her, a lantern gave off soft, comfortable light.

HE NEEDS TO KNOW WHO HE'S TAKING, she scrawled.

She could hear the she-goat and the mule grazing serenely in the darkness along the edge of the trees. The breeze was soft and Erde was warm again. She was overjoyed to be back in this magical place, and wished she could stay this time.

Raven read her message aloud.

"He needs to know them personally?" Hal demanded.

"I understand, I think," Rose supplied. "He needs to feel them in his mind. Each person separately. It's like a conversation."

Beside Erde, Doritt muttered, "I knew they'd be back, but I didn't figure it'd be this soon . . ." She'd been talking with Raven on the porch when the dragon materialized in the clearing. She said it had sounded like music coming out of the air. At the very same moment, Rose had woken up out of a sound sleep. She'd heard a bell ringing, one clear ethereal tone, and knew they had returned.

"Well, then we'll just appear in the market square and snatch Margit from the stake, right out from under Fra Guill's pointy little nose!" Hal faced Rose, hands on hips, giddy with the potential of the dragon's latest gift. "We could do that." He turned to Erde. "Couldn't we?"

Rose tilted her head in disbelief. "And reveal Earth's presence to all his worst enemies?"

"But he can escape them now. Just picture it!" Hal did a boyish clenched-fist dance of anticipation. "It'll scare the piss out of that priest!"

"No, it'll only give him satisfaction to see his prophecies proven true. It will add to his power."

"It will save a life." Hal folded his arms. "The girl offered his help—now I'm calling on it."

"Rose, if it'll save Margit . . ." Raven murmured. "How else can we do it?"

Erde didn't want to seem recalcitrant. She understood the knight was challenging her to make good on her reckless promise, or be left behind for sure this time—with the rest of the women. But she had to make sure the circumstances favored success. She held her slate into the light of the lantern for Raven to read.

"She says he's never been to Erfurt."

"So? Does he have to have been someplace already to be able to go there? That could be awkward."

HE NEEDS TO KNOW WHERE HE'S GOING.

Hal stared back with one eyebrow raised. Raven giggled and he glared at her.

Erde tried again, writing very small to fit it all on the slate.

HE NEEDS AN IMAGE IN HIS MIND.

"Ah." Hal turned away, deflated.

"Can he take an image from someone else's mind?" asked Rose.

Erde smiled at her, then erased and scribbled briefly.

"She says, ask him," Raven supplied.

Erde did not feel possessive about the dragon. It was actually a relief to have someone else who could talk to him for a while. She reminded him to speak to Rose very gently, and while he was at it, to get a sense of Margit from her, to fix in his mind.

Earth was willing to try, now that the danger to his friends' friend had been explained to him. He was nowhere near as phobic about fire as he was about water, but the idea of burning to death horrified him.

"If I can put an image into his head," Rose reported, "he will know if it's good enough."

Hal cleared his throat. "I have no army, Rose, and you haven't been to Erfurt in thirty years."

"No, it confuses my Sight to go out into the world. But Esther has, and Lily, and I can read both of them fairly well."

"Lily's in no shape to do anything," said Raven.

"Linden says Lily's fine," Doritt countered. "She's just bruised and tired out.

"And terrified and grief-stricken and . . ."

"Oh, well, yes. I thought you meant . . ."

Rose raised both palms in a warding gesture, and the younger women fell silent. The lamp glare caught in Rose's short hair to make a fiery halo around her shadowed face. Out of the light came her voice, that voice that could not be disobeyed. "We'll let Lily sleep, as Linden has prescribed and as she deserves. Raven, would you go wake Esther?"

"Lily would want to be here if she thought she could do anything to help Margit," Doritt mumbled, a parting shot as Raven hastened toward the house.

"We'll see how we do with Esther," said Rose.

"You see, Esther's our tale-teller," Doritt told Erde. "She has the real eye for detail."

Erde could feel the dragon basking in all their approval, and was glad for him. He was so proud of having done something right.

"Who was it on the road?" asked Rose.

"A party of Köthen's men, coming out from Erfurt to hunt down royalists, no doubt." Hal spat into the grass. "He's so unashamed of his treason, his henchmen wear his colors openly. Rose, is there any chance Köthen's holding the prince against his will?"

"You know far better than I, Heinrich, to what depths Köthen will stoop."

"Thought I did," Hal muttered. "Guess I don't."

"Well, there's one piece of news Lily brought that might cheer you." Rose waited until he'd stopped pacing to listen. "The Friend is secretly arming his followers."

"What?"

She nodded. "And the forges in the villages are hot day and night, though there's not a weapon to be seen when the soldiers come around."

"Lily *saw* the Friend?"

"No, but she spoke to people who had. His existence is no longer in doubt. He was three days west of Erfurt when Köthen's coup took place. The Friend halted his progress, which Köthen took as a sign either of acquiescence or cowardice. Apparently he doesn't take the Friend or his notions any more seriously than you do."

"Or he's afraid if he does, Fra Guill will get after him," remarked Doritt.

"I took the idea of him seriously. I just wasn't sure I believed it."

"Now you must. Lily's source claims he's got three thousand men out there and the number's growing now that Köthen's made his move." Rose mimicked Hal's stance, hands on hips, and her small straight body seemed more than a match for him. "Heinrich, the Friend has your army, waiting within striking distance of Erfurt and Nürnburg."

The knight let out a snort of dismissal. "Peasants armed with sharpened rakes and plowshares."

"But three thousand of them."

"Three hundred, more likely, and every one an idealist who'll turn tail the moment he's faced with a trained fighting man."

"You don't know that." Rose cocked her head at him. "Are you afraid of actually being able to take action, Heinrich? Do you prefer hopeless causes?"

Hal winced and scowled. "Of course not!"

"Besides, what if he is the lost prince you still believe in? Don't you want to find out?"

"Of course I do!"

"Well?"

Erde scrawled on her slate, then got up and handed it to him.

Hal turned it toward the lantern, squinting. "Hmm, well, I guess I did, didn't I."

"Did what?" asked Rose.

Hal's grin was sour. "Milady reminds me I told her I could make a soldier out of anybody." He kicked at the grass irritably, paced around a bit, and stopped at Earth's snout to grasp his horns as if for moral support. "If he really has taken the Dragon as his sigil ... why would he do that?"

"Oh, one more coincidence, I'm sure," teased Rose.

"It is significant," Hal agreed, as if he'd thought of it all himself in the first place. "I'll search him out, at least. See what he's really about."

Raven hurried quietly from the house with Esther stumbling in tow. "I put tea on. Doritt, would you ... ?"

Doritt nodded, got up, and padded into the house.

Esther rubbed her long face with both palms. "Hello, Hal. Pardon my nightdress. I thought you'd left." She smiled at Earth sleepily. "Hello, Dragon."

Rose was brisk. "Sorry to get you up. Are you awake? We need your help with something."

"So Raven told me. Erfurt. I don't know. Think it'll work, Rose?"

Rose took her hands. "Remember the time I needed to know what a certain person looked like who you'd seen only once?"

"I remember you had to get me very drunk before I could relax enough to be useful to you."

"But it worked."

Esther laughed. "I thought you were making it up. Or I was."

Hal untied the plump wineskin from the mule packs and held it out with a serious grin. "Well? Let's get down to business."

Chapter Twenty-Seven

Esther recalled the location perfectly. Rose translated, and the dragon took them there. Erde was amazed at how easy it was.

The place was the back courtyard of a brick maker's, on the edge of town. Hal knew it also. It was a royalist contact site. They had settled on it, after some discussion, as a relatively safe destination, likely to be deserted in the early hours of the morning, and large enough for the dragon to shelter comfortably while the others were reconnoitering.

The courtyard was cold and dark when they arrived, with the tall cones of the brick kilns along one side and hard packed ground underfoot. After so long in the open, Erde felt immediately penned in by the brick and stone of a town. The air smelled like smoke and snow. Frigid gusts of wind tore the grit off the brick piles and flung it in her face. Hal found a straw-filled corner of a storage barn for the dragon to wait out the hours behind the brick stacks, until his skills were needed. They stowed their packs in an empty feed bin and covered them with old hay. Hal left the mule outside the door. He said when the brick makers arrived at dawn, they'd recognize him and avoid the barn without questions.

They slipped into the unlit streets with the she-goat in tow, the peasant laborer and his goat-boy once more. The town was not entirely asleep. Erde guessed that a town this big, nearly a city, probably never was. It was big enough that she could imagine getting lost in its narrow twisting streets. She wished Earth could be along to see it. Instead, she stored up images to bring back to him. Erfurt was the king's seat, the Royal City, she reminded herself, though she didn't think it very grand at the moment. It looked closed up and in retreat, the aftermath of Baron Köthen's coup. But now and then, a loaded cart passed by, and behind glazed windows, the bakers were already hard at work. And down some narrow alley or at the end of a darkened court, lamps burned and voices murmured around the thin warmth of dying embers. Men sat hunched over mugs of ale and argued. Hal left Erde crouched at the door of a few of these establishments, mostly the ones with no fancy painted sign overhead. Men came and went, quietly, paying no heed to the boy dozing with his arm slung across his goat's withers while his father got drunk inside. A few times, despite the cold, she did actually fall asleep, and then she'd feel Hal's hand on her shoulder, rousing her to move on.

"Not so many faces I recognize any more," he complained finally. "Or who'll admit they recognize me. About half the population either fled with the king or have sneaked away to the Friend's encampment. No further details about him, since none who made it out have come back to report. They could be alive or dead, for all I know. Only the barest bones of the underground are still in place." He shook his head irritably. "Come on. Let's see what all the noise is."

They followed the sound of sawing and hammering to Erfurt's huge market square. Erde halted in astonishment as they cleared the corner and faced the giant twin-towered cathedral and the ranks of fine houses to either side. Hal pushed her onward. "Don't stare. Supposedly you see this square every day." But he did let them pause to watch the joiners work by torchlight. His face was grim.

"My sources say Köthen's got the town surrounded, extra men at every gate, checking everyone who goes in or out. Noon today is the appointed hour, and no one can tell me where they're keeping her. In the church, is my guess. Köthen's declared a general holiday to welcome Fra Guill and your father, who are camped two miles out of town with an army of five hundred fighting men that the townsfolk are calling, at his own suggestion, the Scourge of God. Guillemo always did have a neat turn of phrase."

Her father and Fra Guill, at this very moment, merely two miles away. Erde shivered and pulled her cloak up around her nose. She hadn't realized how much comfort she'd derived from putting all that distance between herself and those two men.

She followed Hal along the long side of the square, past the shuttered four-story houses of merchants and guildsmen, away from the bustle of men and fresh-sawed wood in front of the cathedral, and away from the three or four white-robes who stalked among the workmen, barking orders and keeping up the pace.

"A very fancy affair Köthen has planned," Hal growled. "The stake raised on a scaffold, altarlike. That ought to appeal to Fra Guill. A viewing stand on the cathedral steps for the privileged guests. I wonder if he'll be serving refreshments? The last dregs of the town's larders." His face twisted. "Isn't it a lovely burning? Do you like the quality of the screams? Louder? You want louder? Can I offer you some wine and cheese?"

Erde slipped her hand into his and squeezed it tightly. He put an arm around her shoulder and held her close.

"Well, we'll do what we can." He sighed, letting his glance trail slowly around the big square, searching the doorways and balconies of the tall expensive houses where the king's court had so recently lived. "We need a place to wait, a launching point as it were, where we can see but not be seen."

Erde found herself searching the rooftops, recalling how the dragon had eyed the height of the cliff. But most were sharply peaked to shed rain and the weight of winter snow. One particularly tall one, however, seemed to have partly burned or collapsed, exposing the attic floor beneath. Builder's canvas hung from the skeletal rafters, billowing and snapping in the chill wind.

Hal followed her line of sight. "That was a beauty. Old Baron Schwarzchilde's house. One of the best wine cellars on the square. He would have stayed loyal. I hope he made it out alive."

Impatient with his nostalgia, Erde pointed to themselves and then at the roof.

He understood quickly. "Ah! Good idea. If it's a holiday, the repairmen won't come to work. Besides, all the joiners in town are working on Fra Guill's little celebration. We'll have the roof all to ourselves. Study it carefully, milady. Memorize each and every detail. You'll have to bring the dragon up there and then right to the base of the scaffold if we're to have a chance at getting away with this." He grinned nastily. "And ah, if we do, I don't care what Rose says, I hope the hell-priest is standing next to me when we land, so I can spit in his face!"

At dawn, they returned to the brickyard. A few workers sat yawning around a smoldering firepit in the yard, sharing a jug and a loaf of bread, and rubbing their hands briskly over the fire's dim heat. They nodded as Hal passed. The oldest looked him straight in the eye and touched his cap respectfully, then made as if he was only adjusting the fit.

Hal left Erde in the barn and returned to the streets, saying there was something he'd sensed, something stirring that even his few sources wouldn't talk about. He promised to be back soon with more news and breakfast. The dragon welcomed her gladly, complaining of particularly vivid nightmares. When she lay down with him to rest, the voice of the Summoner was immediately ringing in her ears.

She woke at mid-morning to the sound of Hal sharpening his sword. When he heard her stir, he laid his weapon down and went out, returning with fresh bread and a small bowl of soup still hot from the brick makers' fire. "It's all they could spare—there wasn't much to go around, but at least it'll warm your stomach." He'd stripped down to his red jerkin and buckled over it the leather breastplate he'd brought from Deep Moor. Beads of moisture dotted his shoulders. "Dress warmly, milady. It's snowing out there."

She blinked at him, but actually, the mad weather had ceased to surprise her. It had come to seem an appropriate metaphor for the state of the world. The broth was watery and its contents well past their prime but she wolfed it down appreciatively, meanwhile rehearsing her memory of the broken rooftop and the market square.

"Not much other news to be had, bad or good, though I swear there's something going on that they're not telling me." Hal went back to work on his sword, his tense aura of anticipation touched with dry amusement. "I'm glad you're not one of those anxious types who can't eat before a battle."

A battle. She hadn't thought about it that way, but then, it was not for nothing that the knight was honing the edge of his already well-sharpened blade. They were about to drop into the middle of a town square full of white-robes and soldiers, and snatch away the reason for the gathering. Erde decided to get nervous.

The first leg of the journey went well, though Erde worried for the strength of the joists as the dragon's full weight settled onto the attic floor. The roof was deserted, dusted with a fine layer of wet snow. Earth stilled immediately and vanished. Hal and Erde ducked behind the charred front facade and peered over the edge of the stone parapet.

Their view of the square and the scaffold was unobstructed.

"You'd think it was May Festival," grumbled Hal disgustedly. "Pennants and banners, silk drapings on the viewing stand, everyone decked out in their most colorful best. But then there's this snow." He glanced at the lowering sky. Huge black clouds were bundling on the western horizon. "Or maybe something worse."

The square was full—men, women, and children, thickly wrapped against the sudden cold—but strangely hushed for so great a number crowded into one space. Even at a distance, Erde could see their faces were pale and tired, their mouths tight, their eyes narrow and anxious. A few stragglers were still arriving, escorted by small parties of footsoldiers.

"A command performance," Hal noted bitterly. "Every able body left in town." He canvased the crowd, chewing his lip. "Not a lot of swords out there, though. A few of Köthen's personal guard on foot, the rest holding the gates. I guess he's feeling confident. Fine. So much the better for us. Though if I were him, I wouldn't bring Fra Guill into my town without the men to stand against him. I wonder if he's actually yet met the man face-to-face. He might not be so eager to . . . Ah, here we go!" He pointed diagonally across the square. "Speak of the Devil, and lo . . ."

Brother Guillemo made his entrance from the side of the square opposite the cathedral, a long stately progress on foot through the crowd with his phalanx of hooded white-robes in lock-step behind him. The throng drew away from him as he approached, like the Red Sea parting. As he drew near the scaffold, he glanced up at the sky, and Erde saw him brush snow from his robe. In his wake came a small party of armed horsemen wearing the black and gold of Tor Alte. To see her family crest and colors again was like a shock of ice water thrown full in her face. Erde ducked behind the parapet as she recognized the rider in the lead, her father decked out in his baronial finest.

My father! My father is here in Erfurt! She didn't want him there, didn't want to see him. Seeing him made her feel like a child again, yet she had to stare at him, his broad velvet-swathed chest, his ruddy face and prematurely silver hair. Perhaps seeing him would repair the gaps in her memory of those last days at Tor Alte. But there came no lightning bolt or revelation. It was only him, her father as she remembered him, though seeming a bit thinner, less robust. But perhaps that was only the effect of distance, diminishing him in her eyes. She was sure that no one else in the square could see beneath his show and swagger to the anxiety beneath. Josef von Alte. Her father. She had thought she would never see him again, yet here he was in Erfurt, her past and present lives commingling for the first time. Her old self-image, the one he'd helped form with his rage and his constant challenge, bubbled to the surface like air out of melting ice. Her newfound confidence drained away. She cringed against Hal's side, shaking uncontrollably.

"Easy, girl," Hal murmured. "They're only men. As mortal as any of us."

Erde wished she could snap back at him: *But one of them is my father!*

"Can't let them rattle you." The knight had put his nerves aside. The nearer it was to the moment of truth, the cooler he became. Erde drank up his calm like a draught of wine and let it soothe her. Then she felt his body tighten. "Here now, girl. Get up and pay attention. Here comes Margit."

The witch-cart came from the opposite corner, drawn by four foot-soldiers blazoned in blue and yellow. They followed a single rider, a stocky bearded man, blond and bareheaded but wearing darkly glimmering mail beneath his tunic. He wore no other ornament but his own blue and yellow crest. His sheathed sword hung on the pommel of his cloth-draped saddle. He carried his feathered helm in the crook of his arm, clasped in his mailed fist.

Hal pointed. "That's Köthen in the lead, looking the fine figure of a man as usual and doing his humble act."

She thought Hal stared at Köthen with a particular intensity, perhaps giving him special study as the one clearly in charge. And this in itself was interesting, because Baron Köthen was much younger than she'd expected, barely into his thirties, making him at least ten years her father's junior, which she knew must be particularly annoying to Josef von Alte. Plus, Köthen was impressive, even handsome in a coarse, worldly sort of way. Square-jawed and serious, he *looked* like a leader. Erde decided that for all his youth, Köthen could easily eat her father alive. She worried for Josef, despite all he'd done to her. And despite the way he stared so obviously at the woman in the witch-cart. Köthen hardly gave her a glance, though she wore the usual clinging white shift, sure to arouse the lust and envy of the men, and the pity and envy of the women. Erde recognized the twins' red hair and slim, muscular build. She wondered if these witch-hunting men ever considered it worthwhile to burn a woman who wasn't beautiful.

Köthen and Brother Guillemo met in the middle of the square, in front of the scaffold. Josef von Alte reined in some yards away. Both riders dismounted and bowed to the white-robed priest, then submitted to having their hands joined by him with great ceremony. Köthen stood back as soon as his hand was released.

"Ah, good." Hal's grin was feral. "They hate each other. That may prove useful. Now. We should get her while they're taking her up the steps, which could be any minute now. Are you ready?"

Erde nodded, though there seemed to be a lot of men and horses in the way. Plus her father, so close . . .

"Alert the Dragon, then."

She tore her eyes away from the square to concentrate on the dragon, but Earth was already prepared. He'd found a hiding place that provided a view of the scaffold. One corner of it was obscured by a charred rafter slung with canvas, but Erde could offer detail where it was lacking. And this time, she did not have to provide motivation. For the moment, not a thought was in his mind about the Summoner or his own particular quest. A subtle outrage was brewing in the dragon's depths. His sense of justice was awakening.

"Köthen's signaled his men to take her out of the cart." Hal drew his sword and reached for Erde's hand. "Listen carefully, girl, and do exactly as I say. Stay close to the Dragon. If they get me, don't worry about Margit. You get out of there. You have more important things to do, you and him. Go back to Deep Moor. They'll understand." His grip tightened, then released. "All right. Ready?"

Erde gathered the image in her mind and joined forces with the dragon. Poised together, they awaited Hal's signal.

"And . . . WAIT! Wait. Don't do anything yet."

There was a commotion in the square. Shouts and the

sharp ringing of hooves on the paving stones. Erde heard voices crying Köthen's name. She whirled back to the parapet. Hal had risen to his feet and she hauled him back down again. He shook her free but stayed low, peering over the edge, shivering oddly. Erde worried until she realized he was laughing. "I think . . . yes! It's our friends from the forest! Come hightailing back to report there's a dragon on the loose! You've got to see this!"

Erde looked. Baron Köthen was surrounded by frantic horsemen, all talking at once and jabbing their fingers in the direction from which they'd come. Brother Guillemo listened from the bottom step of the scaffold. His expression, even from fifty yards away, was a visible contest between terror and unholy glee.

Köthen bellowed for silence. The horsemen shut up immediately, but for one tardy one, whose last words floated like an echo into the hush that fell over the square.

". . . dragon, my lord!"

The crowd leaned forward as if pulled by a string.

The men dismounted and made a try at being orderly. Josef von Alte stalked over to Köthen to hear the details, but Brother Guillemo whirled and raced to the top of the scaffold.

"A sign!" he shouted. "A sign, oh my people! These men have brought us a true sign!"

Half in, half out of the witch-cart, Margit also listened. She stood nearly forgotten, watched by one guard and bound only by the cord that tied her hands in front of her. The throng was riveted on Guillemo as he pounded back and forth across the platform, warming to his tirade. The pale noon light dimmed as the dark clouds bunching at the horizon broke loose and sped closer. Guillemo took his cue.

"See how the heavens darken! The sun itself, God's given holy light, will be swallowed up! This is no natural occurrence! The forces of evil are gathering, oh my people, gathering around us now!"

"Now would really be the time to do it," muttered Hal.

And then the priest, who possessed a panoramic view over the heads of the crowd, stopped dead in the middle of a shouted sentence and stared, his face gone slack and pale.

Hal elbowed Erde hard and pointed. "Look! Over there!"

A new horseman had entered the square, a lone armored knight on a huge golden horse. His helm and breastplate gleamed with gold chasing. A closed visor concealed his face. The crowd gasped and murmured and opened a wide path for him as if expecting some new report of sorcery, perhaps even the sorcerer himself. And he did look magical, Erde thought. As he bore down on the center of the square, his sword raised above his head, she saw that his pure white tunic was blazoned in brilliant red, in the sign of a dragon.

"It's him!" Hal exclaimed. "I'll bet it's him! Who else could it be? He's decided to make the challenge official, the reckless sonofabitch! Got a real taste for theatrics! Esther didn't say her Friend was lunatic as well as idealistic!"

Erde stared as the golden knight galloped across the square, scattering what little resistance stood in his way. She was remembering the visored, shining knight in Earth's dream on the night of the earthquake. Could the dragon have dreamed of the Friend?

On the scaffold, the priest screamed "No! No! No!" and waved his arms as if he could make this sudden and inconvenient apparition disappear.

Hal gripped Erde's shoulder. "Wait, Jesus, he's coming for Margit! The man's insane. How did he get in, with Köthen blocking the gates?" He paused for breath, considering. "And how the hell is he going to get out?"

Before the men at the scaffold knew what was happening, the horseman had thundered into their midst. The soldiers were dumbstruck. Cursing, Baron Köthen dove at the man nearest him to grab his sword and shove him aside. Josef van Alte ran for his horse, shouting at his men to attack. Above, the apoplectic priest finally found words other than his helpless repeated denial of what was clearly a reality. He called for a sword. He raced about on the platform but did not venture down the stairs. The white-robes racing to respond and protect him blocked both von Alte's path and Köthen's. The two barons bellowed in frustration as the golden knight pulled up at the witch-cart, sliced the ropes binding Margit's ready, outstretched wrists, sheathed his sword, and scooped her up and onto the back of his saddle in a single unbroken motion.

"Bravo, lad!" whispered Hal. "Done before Köthen had a weapon to hand! I like this madman!"

The knight spurred his horse forward with a victorious whoop. The crowd's roar was ambiguous, but they cleared an escape route straight out of the square, then closed behind him, a few of them seeming to give chase.

"Bar the gates!" Köthen's shout echoed like drumbeats around the square, though he already had men posted everywhere. "Not a soul in or out!"

Still alone on the scaffold, Brother Guillemo ceased his screeching and fell to his knees, his arms outstretched in an apparent trance of prayer. The white-robes finally reaching him stood back in chagrin, then formed a circle around him, their swords at ready.

Hal leaped to his feet, not caring who spotted him. "There he goes, out of the square! And the crowd's blocking the pursuit! But can they get him past the gates?" He snatched at Erde's arm, already on the move. "Quick! Back to the barn! He may need our help!"

Help? The streets would be crawling with Köthen's men, and her father's. Erde had no idea what help Hal thought they could be, or how he even planned to find Margit's miraculous rescuer. Maybe he didn't need their help. If dragons could exist, why not magical knights? But she was eager enough to be away from their vulnerable position on the rooftop. She alerted the dragon and helped him image the brickyard.

The dragon was precise. He materialized within the same square footage in the barn from which he had left. The she-goat emerged from hiding in the straw and did her grave little dance of welcome. Erde made sure to praise the dragon effusively. Praise so improved his mood and his confidence, especially now that he was hinting at being hungry again, after all this work. She told him a meal was a hopeless notion for a while, and the best thing to do was to take a nap and not think about it. He agreed, but not happily.

Hal sped off into the courtyard the moment his head cleared. The wind gusted through the open doors, delivering little flurries of snow. Shivering, Erde went to close the doors, then peered through the center crack. Hal was slumped at the firepit with the old man who'd shown him such respect, warming his hands over the dying embers. Their conversation was slow, unanimated, like two habituated cronies. She thought how casual it would look to the idle passerby, if there was such a person left in Erfurt. The old man had a dusting of snow on his cap and shoulders.

She wondered why he hadn't retreated indoors or, more curious still, why he wasn't with the crowd in the market square. But watching him with Hal, she understood he'd been keeping an unofficial eye on the barn. Soon Hal rose, nodding, from his crouch and headed her way. He slowed as the sound of horsemen approached. From the barn, Erde could not see the passage under a second story that allowed access to the courtyard from the street, but she heard the clatter pass by in a hurry and breathed a sigh of relief. Hal sprinted for the doors.

"It's as I suspected," he whispered hastily as he shut the doors behind him. "The partisans got him in, and they plan to get him out . . . with Margit. I told old Ralf they didn't stand a chance with all that combined force after them, but that I did." He paced over to the sleeping dragon and regarded him with avid satisfaction. "I said if they'd bring the pair of them to me, I could get them out." He came back and sat down beside her. "I don't know if he believed me, or why he even should, but he said he'd carry the message. Of course I didn't want to tell him exactly *how* I could get them out, so we'll see. It depends on how desperate they get." He looked down, pushing straw around with the toe of his boot. "And on how much faith these diminishing royalists still have in an old King's Knight."

They waited, and no message came. Out in the street, horsemen came and went. Hal sharpened his sword some more, halting abruptly to listen each time the mule made an unusual sound outside the door. He replayed the events in the market square over and over, musing on the identity of the mysterious knight.

"He has the king's own stature, I'll say that much," he muttered at one point.

Erde didn't know how he could tell what the man looked like, under all that concealing armor. But he knew the king, and she didn't. Plus she supposed that men of war understood such things.

Growing restive after a while, Hal went out again to talk to the old man he'd called Ralf. He came back dispiritedly. "He says he passed the word along. He also says Köthen's men are searching the town door by door, and that we ought to look to our own safety, as they'll no doubt be here before long." Hal slapped his hand irritably against his thigh. "I didn't want to leave without her."

Outside, the mule came alert with a snort and a single loud kick against the wall of the barn. Hal sped to the door and barred it as the sudden racket of men and horses invaded the courtyard. Erde woke the dragon from his nap.

"Five, six, eight, damn!" Hal counted, squinting through the crack between the doors. "Two searching the sheds, two heading this way, three at the fire questioning Ralf . . . no!" He spun around, reaching for his sword. "Cowards! Beating a defenseless old man!"

Erde ran for him, snatched at his arm. Outside, the soldiers slapped the mule away from the doors and threw their weight against the bar. Quickly, the blade of a sword was shoved through the crack to pry the bar loose. Erde pulled Hal toward the dragon. In a dizzying split-second, they were back on the rooftop overlooking the square. Hal looked momentarily dazed and frustrated, then got his bearings and clapped Erde on the back manfully. "Good thinking!"

Ducking, he sheathed the sword still naked in his hand and scrambled toward the parapet. Erde stayed to praise the dragon for his quick response and share his palpable excitement. To him, this spiriting around town was like a game of hide and seek. His confidence bloomed with each successful trip, and with it, his pride. It didn't matter that he was clumsy on the ground. He was no longer a useless, wingless burden. He was the secret weapon.

But there was also a nagging worry. After the first time, escaping from the soldiers in the forest, he'd noticed that he was hungry, but he'd been recently so well fed that it hardly mattered. But after the second and third, he found himself growing steadily ravenous. This most recent trip had left him famished and weak, so much that he was unsure if he had the strength to transport anyone anywhere without refueling. Finally, hiding out on the burned-out rooftop, he laid out his predicament with irrefutable clarity.

—But can you get us out of here?

Earth thought he could, but as his weakness increased, so did his concern. Being able to think of nothing but his hunger was distracting. He worried about maintaining the concentration necessary to transport accurately.

Erde's own mind was crowding already with the dragon's thoughts of food. Now that he'd begun to awaken to his true power, she found it increasingly difficult to keep his images from dominating her brain, difficult even to separate her own thoughts from his. She didn't really know whose idea it had been to return to the rooftop. Earth did not consider this a problem. To him, *our* thought was a perfectly acceptable alternative to *yours* or *mine*. Perhaps even a superior one. Erde was not sure.

"It isn't a sight fit for a lady," hissed Hal from the parapet, "but you ought to take a look at this anyway."

Erde joined him at the edge. Brother Guillemo's white-robes, with their short thick swords now in full view, had blocked off all the streets leading out of the square. The townsfolk had been herded against the grandstand on the cathedral steps, and Josef von Alte's horsemen stood guard over them as if they were criminals. The wailing of children was blown upward by a biting wind thickening with huge wet flakes of snow. Men stamped and hugged their arms, having given their cloaks to the women to wrap themselves and the babies in. Hal touched Erde's arm and nodded toward the western end of the square, where the barrier of white-robes had parted to admit a stumbling group of elderly citizens, driven faster than they could walk by several of Baron Köthen's horsemen.

"Now it's the sick and the infirm!" Hal exclaimed. "Not enough he's hauled the poor nursing mothers away from their hearths in this churlish weather! This is Fra Guill's order, not Köthen's, surely. That priest'll have the whole town dead of ague before he's satisfied." Now he pointed toward the empty scaffold, crowned by its tall stake and unlit pyre. Beside the steps, so freshly built that the wood still leaked its sap, Josef von Alte stood barking questions at a young man pinned roughly against the stair by two von Alte foot-soldiers. The sight of him sent a surge of memory coursing through Erde's head, too quick and elusive to hold on to. Something about her father and the priest and . . . what? She wanted to look away and could not. On the scaffold, Brother Guillemo was now prostrate, flat on his face in prayer, watched over by a stout quartet of his brethren.

Köthen sat to one side, receiving the reports of the search from a velvet cushioned chair. A brazier burned nearby. His men came and went briskly. Köthen listened carefully, rubbed his hands in the heat of the flame, and every now and then, glanced at the sky, palming snowflakes from his brow.

"There's the only sensible man among them," observed Hal. "But he's at a loss, for once. He's thinking it can't get any damn darker for just after noon. He's thinking maybe the priest is right after all, something devilish is going on, and here he'd signed on just to take advantage of a power grab."

Erde wondered why Hal thought he could speak so assuredly of what was in Baron Köthen's mind. She pulled her slate out from under her jerkin. LIKE MY FATHER?

"Surely. Except Köthen's smarter and abler than your father, if you'll pardon my saying so, milady." He grinned at her crookedly. "D'you think intelligence is like twins ... it skips a generation?"

She showed him her slate again. EARTH NEEDS TO EAT.

"What, again?"

Painstakingly, she explained how the transporting process was draining the dragon's strength.

"How much more can he manage without eating?"

HE DOESN'T KNOW.

Hal chewed his lip. "Suddenly I don't feel so glib about this anymore.

Erde nodded a tense agreement.

"Can he get us back to the barn?"

HE THINKS SO.

"Then he'd better do it now. Köthen's men should be done turning the place inside out. Then you'll wait there in case Margit and the wonder lad show up, and I'll go search up something for himself to eat. There must be some hog or lamb left about that the soldiers haven't yet confiscated." He glanced over his shoulder. "Hello, what now?"

A dead hush had settled upon the square again, as heavy and soft as the snow that was blanketing the paving stones. Stirring at last from his prayer trance on the scaffold, Brother Guillemo rose to his feet with his arms still outstretched, as if drawn up by an invisible wire. Strange sounds spewed from his gaping mouth, deep animal growls and yelps that coalesced finally into harsh but human syllables and then into words. His astonished brothers deserted their guard duty to gather at the foot of the scaffold and kneel in awe. Guillemo's words became exotic names, names that Erde recalled from her Bible studies.

"Oh Hamaliel and Auriel! Ah! Ah! Raphael! Come, Asmodel and Zedekiel!"

Hal listened with alert suspicion. "He's calling on the angels, and not all of them from the official Word. That's a little close to the edge for a man of the Church."

"Ah, Gabriel! Come, Khamael! Come with your swords of light and your flaming brows! Descend and protect us from what is nigh! See how the sky darkens and the sun is taken from us! Come, Melchidael! Descend to us now! Save us from the coming of dragons! Oh great archangel Michael, hear our cries! Take pity on us as you would on little children!"

"How dare he ask for pity," growled Hal. "He who's never shown any in his life!"

"Come, holy ones, holiest of holies! Dragons befoul the land and today, this very day, we have seen Satan himself take human form to appear among us and snatch his handmaiden from our righteous grasp!"

The priest's ranting was familiar, playing through the full range of vocal possibilities. But beneath the pyrotechnics, Erde heard something new, some hint of genuine terror, some faint loss of control.

Hal heard it, too. "It's really gotten to him, having Margit stolen out from under his nose so spectacularly. He hadn't planned on that, and he doesn't like one bit what it implies about his precious prophecies. If ever he gets his hands on her again, he'll exact the worst revenge he can think of. Though what could be worse than being burned alive, I can't imagine."

BUT HE CAN, Erde scrawled.

Hal's mouth tightened. "You're right. Enough of this poison. Let's see if our steed has the strength to bring us home again."

Chapter Twenty-Eight

The trip back to the brickyard was momentarily terrifying. For Erde, it was a nightmare of drowning, a struggle in darkness with limbs too heavy, a desperate longing for the surface and for breath. Then for the split-second that she was conscious enough to think about it, she was suspended in a void without hope of escape. The arrival was like being flung down from a height. Erde gasped for air and wondered if she'd broken a rib.

Hal staggered to his feet, his chest heaving. "Christ Almighty! Don't want to do that again until he's eaten!"

The big double doors of the barn had been pushed open. The beam that had barred them lay askew on the floor. Past the dark rectangle of the opening, the snow-covered yard was scarred with muddy footprints and the signs of a fight. A man lay by the firepit, the thick white flakes dusting him like ash. From around the corner of the barn came the squeals of the mule and the bleating of the goat.

Hal made sure Erde was standing. "Check for our packs!" He prodded her toward the feed bin, then drew his sword and bolted for the yard. Erde ran to the bin and found their possessions still intact. She let the heavy lid drop and raced after Hal.

The searchers were gone from the courtyard but had left one of their own behind to confiscate the animals. He had tied the she-goat to a post and was fighting for control of the mule. The hapless man was thin and young, and the mule was lashing out with teeth and hooves, showing him little mercy. Hal showed him even less. He sprinted up behind the man, slashing the rope that held the goat as he passed. He wrapped his arm around the man's throat and yanked him back hard. The man flailed and went limp. Hal dropped him

like a stone. Without a second glance, he ran over to the
fallen man at the firepit and eased him over onto his back.

Erde met him there, her eyes full of what she had just
seen him do. The man on the ground was old Ralf, unconscious and bleeding from a gash across his cheek and from
others as well, judging from the amount of red staining the
snow. The knight glared about the yard. He seemed to Erde
a dangerous stranger, not at all the kindly elder gentleman
she had been traveling with. His movements were hard and
clean and fast, and he'd disposed of the would-be mule thief
with such unthinking despatch that it left her breathless. She
knew she should feel safer in his company, but mostly it un-
nerved her to see him transformed so suddenly and so entirely. She kept her distance, eyeing him warily.

But he was gentleness itself as he drew the old man's
head and shoulders into his lap. "Still breathing, but he's
lost a lot of blood. Ah. Here it is. Stab wound in the back.
Cowards! Bring the wineskin, milady, from the pack."

Erde ran back to the feed bin and struggled the heavy
packs out onto the floor. By the time she'd freed the wineskin, Hal was at the door with the old man in his arms, looking for a soft spot to lay him down. The mule and the
she-goat followed close behind. Erde hurriedly gathered up
loose straw to make a bed. Seeing the she-goat so nimble on
her feet reminded her of what the dragon had done the night
of the cat attack. She grabbed her slate.

EARTH CAN HEAL HIM.

Hal's scowl eased. "Right you are, girl! Quickly, close the
doors!"

The dragon was curled up at the back of the barn, in the
very darkest corner. Hal carried the old man over and settled
him on his side in front of the great horned head. He looked
to Erde. "You'll ask him?"

She did. Earth's response was sluggish. Erde hoped an attempt at healing would not exhaust him further. Yet he must
try. He opened one slow eye, then tilted his head ponder-
ously to sniff at the old man's injuries. Three long swipes of
his huge tongue cleaned the stab wound and staunched the
flow of blood. Earth sighed and went back to sleep.

Hal sat back on his heels. "Amazing." Gently, he hauled
the old man's unconscious weight to the hay mound Erde
had gathered. He swabbed blood from the gashed cheek with
a snow-dampened rag. "Good, this one's shallow. The rest,

mostly bruises. He was knocked fairly senseless, but look! He's coming around already!" He raised the old man's head and put the spout of the wineskin to his lips. "Never knew you to refuse a sip, Ralf. Can you take a little now?"

Ralf coughed and sputtered, but managed a gulp.

"Good man." Hal patted his shoulder and propped his head up for another swallow. He was careful to place his own body between the old man and the dragon. "How do you feel?"

"Dizzy," the old man muttered.

"Well, this was my fault and I'm sorry for it, but grateful just the same."

"Glad to see you . . . in one piece, my lord. They were . . . Köthen's men were . . ." Ralf paused to cough again, and take another sip of wine. ". . . very surprised to find the barn empty."

"But you were right to try to prevent them, Ralf."

Ralf's grin was crooked, as if from an old injury. Erde thought it made him look sly but could see that Hal trusted him implicitly. "If they'd known it was you, they'd have sure feared for sorcery."

"Still that old canard? I swear, a false reputation's the hardest kind to lose."

Again, the sly grin. "I never thought you did much to discourage it, my lord. Never hurts to put that extra fear into them, eh?"

Hal scratched his beard. "Well, thing is, Ralf, sometimes a man stumbles on magic without even trying. Do you believe that?"

Ralf shrugged but his eyes narrowed a bit. He tried to sit up. Hal caught him and eased him up against a stack of bricks.

"What I mean is, I guess, are you feeling strong enough to meet what you were protecting?"

Erde tried to stop him. She was sure he shouldn't be so free about revealing Earth's existence. But she'd purposely moved away when Ralf awoke, and couldn't get to him in time. She had to watch helplessly as the knight stood and removed himself from the line of sight between the old man and the dragon. Old Ralf's head may have been spinning but his eyes were sharp. He let out a sharp yowl and tried to crab sideways toward the door on his hands and feet.

Hal knelt at his side, his hands soothing. "Easy, old man, easy. Don't be afraid."

"But my lord baron . . . !"

"You're safe, I promise you."

Ralf quieted, but it was more like obedience than true calm. He stared hard into the shadows, his jaw dropping open like a door on a rusted hinge. He blinked several times, then shook his head and crossed himself hastily. "Was it the blow to my brain?"

"No, you're seeing truly."

"But is it . . . no . . . is it . . . a dragon?"

"A dragon it is indeed," replied Hal gladly.

"Angels defend us!" Ralf cringed behind Hal in a new surge of terror.

"There's no cause for fear. He's been working hard and he's tired. Right now, he's asleep. Besides, this dragon saved your life."

"How's that?"

"You'd a bad wound in your back. His healing gift kept you from bleeding to death. I promise you, my friend—this is none of Fra Guill's devil's spawn. This is a King's Dragon."

But the King's Dragon was not just tired. He was unwell. Erde realized that her head had been strangely vacant since the rough return from the rooftop. She sent him images of concern and got no answer. She cursed herself for letting mere events distract her, and ran to him. He lay inert. His hide was dull again, faded to the same color of windblown dust that it had been when she'd first met him, ravenous from his long sleep. There was no handy bear now for him to devour. The rise and fall of his breath was so slow and shallow as to be imperceptible. Appalled, Erde dropped to her knees and laid her head against his neck.

"What is it?" Hal called from the front of the barn.

Erde rocked back and forth in panic.

The knight left Ralf to recover from his shock, and joined her at the dragon's side. "Is he all right?"

Erde shook her head helplessly.

Hal dropped beside her, his face ashen. "What's wrong with him?"

NEEDS FOOD. FUEL. She underlined the last word several times.

"Then he shall have it." Hal placed a palm gravely on the

dragon's snout. "Your pardon, my lord. I didn't understand that this weakness could threaten you so suddenly."

IT'S THE EFFORT OF THE TRAVEL, Erde reminded him. AND THEN THE HEALING.

"Yes, yes, I understand. I'll go immediately." He rose, and found the old man on his knees, still gawking and shaky but willing to crawl a few brave inches nearer.

"Saved my life, did he?" He touched the livid bruise on his face as though it was his real cause for concern.

"Yes."

"Awful quiet. Don't a dragon snore when he sleeps?"

"He's ... unwell. Usually he's very sociable."

Ralf gazed slowly from dragon to knight and back again. "If you say so, my lord. But now he's sick?"

"Starving. Needs a meal very badly."

Still on his knees, the old man backed up a step. "You'll find naught left in Erfurt to feed a dragon. The soldiers have seen to that."

"Oh, come now, Ralf. You have an eye for these things. No one you can think of likely to have one or two stashed away somewhere?"

Ralf peered back at him oddly. Erde thought he suddenly did not look so respectful. "I hardly think, milord, that you should ask a man to give up his children, King's Dragon or no."

"His *children?* Sweet Jesus, man, what is it you think he eats?"

"He, is it? Ah." Ralf watched as the she-goat approached the dragon and lay down deliberately between ivory claws the length and breadth of a strong man's arm. "Well, milord, isn't it young virgins a dragons makes his meal on?"

In other circumstances, Hal might have laughed off this time-honored misperception and launched into a lecture about the feeding habits of dragons. But Earth was in trouble, so the knight was not amused. "Not this dragon!" he snapped. He waved an abrupt hand. "See there? A goat and a boy within easy reach and he makes nary a move, though he's fainting with hunger."

"Maybe he prefers an older meal ..."

Hal was outraged. "He saved your life, man! Would he do that if he was going to eat you?"

Ralf raised a defensive palm. "Well, they say, my lord ..."

"Well, they're wrong!"

Erde tossed a glare Hal's way. This was no time to argue the interpretation of lore. Earth was not entirely inert after all. He was engaged in some kind of discussion with the she-goat that he would not let her be privy to. She went to work trying to convince him otherwise. She told him she could not be his guide if he was going to keep secrets from her.

Hal blunted the edge on his voice. He helped Ralf rise shakily to his feet. "Forgive me, old man. I've had much longer to get used to him. Of course you were scared, of course you made the wrong assumptions. How is anyone to know, if they haven't met a real dragon? Believe me, all he needs are a few fat sheep, or even a few scrawny ones. Or maybe you know of someone with an old milch cow hidden away?"

Ralf tested his balance, then shook his head. "Everything on four legs was rounded up days ago, by Baron Köthen's order."

"Is there no food anywhere in Erfurt?"

The old man shrugged. "An army travels on its stomach."

"Then I'll take what I need from Köthen!" the knight declared angrily. "Where's he keeping it all?"

"The king's stronghold, milord." Eyeing Hal's worn red leather jerkin, Ralf awaited the expected response.

Predictably, Hal started to pace. "The king's . . . how dare he! That pup! That treasonous cur! Wait till I get my hands on him! Does he wear the king's crown as well?"

Ralf's bruised mouth twisted. "Not yet, milord. Though I imagine he tries it on now and then before he goes to bed nights." He peered again at the dragon, limping around to the side to study him, careful to keep a healthy distance. "A dragon, it is indeed. I never thought to have the privilege."

Hal calmed and joined the old man so that the two of them gazed at the dragon side by side. "Nor did I."

"Not and walk away from it, I mean. Pardon my asking, milord, but . . . well, a big thing like that . . . How did you ever get it in here?"

Hal caught his eye and held it solemnly. "Magic. Dragon magic, and if we find him something to eat, you can see that magic for yourself. This dragon can take us safely out of here, out of Erfurt entirely, along with the woman I spoke of and the stranger-knight."

"All of us?"

"All of us, safe and sound. If he can eat, and if you can bring them to me."

Ralf nodded, then turned away. "I'll go, then."

"You? You can hardly walk, and the streets are crawling with Köthen's swordsmen. Tell me where and I'll go for them."

Ralf cracked a real smile for the first time, showing pink and empty gums. "Each of us has our secrets to keep, milord."

Hal dipped his head. "Of course. Your discretion does you credit."

"Only way I know of to get to be as old as we are."

Hal chuckled. "Indeed. Go then, and Ralf . . ."

The old man stopped, glanced back.

"Remember me to His Majesty if you see him before I do."

Ralf laughed soundlessly, and slipped around the door. Almost immediately, he was back. "You might want to remove the evidence, milord, before they come looking for him."

"Ah. Right. I'd quite forgot."

Erde made sure the old man had gone before she showed Hal her slate. IS HE DEAD, THE MAN OUTSIDE?

"Oh, yes. Very."

A NECESSARY SACRIFICE?

"Um, well . . . yes."

She knew and he knew it had not been truly necessary, but she nodded, erased, and wrote again. THE GOAT HAS GIVEN PERMISSION.

He didn't understand at first, and then he did. "What? No! He can't do that!"

Erde underlined the whole sentence brusquely and held it up in front of his face.

"But she's his friend!"

She'd known he'd react like this. She recalled his argument with Raven about Margit's suicide device. But how could he be so self-righteous about a willing sacrifice when he was ready to die at any moment in the service of his king, or when he'd just killed a man he didn't even know because it was—there was that word again—expedient. She rubbed the slate briskly against her sleeve.

SHE KNOWS HE'LL DIE OTHERWISE.

"Die? No, I think he'll only go back to sleep. Dragons are immortal, milady."

She glared at him. MY ANCESTORS SLEW DRAGONS.

"Of course. Mine, too, the fools. A dragon can be destroyed with a weapon or a spell. But they don't just up and die on you."

HE WON'T TALK TO ME!

"He's hungry and tired."

HE SAID HE WAS DYING!

Erde didn't care what Hal's lore told him. Earth had told her he was dying. It was the only thing he'd had the strength to say to her, and now she felt him receding from her mind like an ebb tide. She would miss the goat, but she knew she could not live without the dragon. She erased the slate, scrawled DYING! in the largest letters that would fit, then grabbed Hal's arm and propelled him toward the door. Finally, to calm her, he gave in and let himself be led outside, granting the she-goat and the dragon the privacy appropriate to the gravity of their task. Just outside the door, Erde turned back. She ran to the goat and kissed her on the head. Then she followed Hal out into the snow.

Chapter Twenty-Nine

Outside, the wind had dropped. The snowfall was finer and steadier. Though the yard was a stretch of solid white, Erde saw no trace of Ralf's path of retreat. She wondered how he'd managed to cross without leaving any prints. The dead soldier was a long white lump beside the brick kilns. Erde regarded the body uneasily.

Hal had not expected to be scolded for doing what he considered to be his duty, especially when he'd accomplished it so cleanly and efficiently. "Leave him there a little longer, he'll look like just another dirt pile," he remarked sourly. Erde frowned and he shook his head. "I suppose you want me to give him last rites and bury him."

She kept her eyes steady on him, the way she remembered her grandmother looking when she'd done something wrong.

"Are you to be my conscience now? You don't think my own is active enough already?" He got very still, his jaw tight. "I thought you understood, milady, when you insisted on coming along, that this is war." He gestured sharply toward the yard. "That man was my enemy. He'd have killed me without a thought. You, too, though if what Ralf says is true and he'd seen you're a woman, he'd have had another use for you first!" He turned and stalked away to retrieve the soldier's body, brushing the snow off his red jerkin as it fell, as if loath to let it gather for even a moment.

He might as well have slapped her, and finally, Erde decided she deserved it. She had insulted him deeply with her naive disapproval of a skill he'd spent a lifetime perfecting. But she wasn't sure she wanted to be anything else but naive, if being worldly required an acceptance of murder as a common expedient. She wondered if it had anything to do with being a woman. Was this why women retreated into convents, or why Rose and her companions had withdrawn to the seclusion of Deep Moor, despite their self-sufficiency and their obvious relish for the more sensual aspects of life?

She turned her musings to the dragon in the barn. There he was, devouring—though with the greatest possible grace and mercy—a fellow creature he'd spent the last month traveling with. He was probably in the midst of it now, for as she reached out to him, his mind was shut to her. And in his case, it really was an issue of survival. Hal could have shown the soldier mercy, but the only mercy the dragon could afford right now was to do it quickly. Erde sank into a huddle in the snow against the wall of the barn. She felt as confused and alone as she ever had since the night of her flight from Tor Alte. Brushing tears from her eyes, she watched Hal grasp the dead soldier by the armpits and drag him toward the nearest of the brick kilns.

She owed him at least a gesture of apology. She'd started across the yard to help him when she heard the horsemen on the street. The snowfall had muffled their approach and they were clattering through the archway into the yard before either Hal or Erde had time to react.

Hal did not even try for his sword. He backed against the kiln, gesturing Erde to him. "Get behind me, lad!"

As she ran, she called to the dragon. He was still not answering. Across the yard, the mule shuffled into a less conspicuous position and began working his way around the perimeter.

There were six of them. The first three men were off their horses with their swords drawn before the others had pulled up inside the yard. They formed a quick semicircle around Hal, then looked to the fourth, a pudgy young man who remained astride his stout gray. He was not wearing Baron Köthen's yellow and blue, but some more garish colors of his own. A younger son of some minor lord, Erde decided, gone into service with Köthen for lack of any more promising future. Reading the insecurity in him, she had a moment of pity. She had known someone in service once . . . or so she thought. But the faint wisp of memory faded before she could identify it.

The last two men dismounted to see to the body. "Dead, my lord."

The lordling regarded Hal worriedly. His small, defensive eyes took in Hal's venerable red leathers and the well-used soldier's sword swinging easily at his hip. Hal drew himself to his full height and faced the young man calmly, as if he had every right in the world to be where he was, hauling around the corpse of their comrade.

"Your name, sir!" barked the younger son, playing at confidence but not taking the risk of forsaking his manners.

"That honor is for your superiors," Hal returned, not so politely. "Who are you?"

The other men murmured and made gestures with their swords that suggested they didn't care a whit about manners.

"I must ask you to surrender your weapon," said the lordling.

"Am I taken prisoner? If so, what is my offense? I demand the privilege of rank."

"You are not on the battlefield, sir knight." He pointed at the body. "That is your offense, just to begin with."

"Him?" Hal shrugged at the corpse as if it had just appeared in front of him. "Poor man, he was all stiff with the cold. I was helping him to a bit of shelter. Devilish weather, isn't it?"

The lordling scowled belligerently. "He's dead. You killed him. Are you claiming you did not?"

Hal shrugged again, a calculated annoyance. Would he have lied, Erde wondered, if he felt himself in any real danger?

"Your sword, sir, or I will have it taken from you."

Hal gave up his sword, as if it hardly mattered to him.

The lordling beckoned one of his men over and whispered briefly. The man swung up on his horse and cantered out of the yard. Then the lordling crossed his wrists on the pommel of his saddle and leaned in with a trace of bravado. "So tell me. What is a King's Knight doing in this town?"

Hal let his eyes widen. "Are we not in Erfurt? Am I mistaken? I thought the king ruled in Erfurt."

"Very funny."

"It was not intended as a joke." Hal grinned at him.

"Your king is the only joke."

Hal's grin died. "What would you know about such things?" He looked away and very deliberately, spat into the snow.

The lordling reached blindly to regain the advantage. "For all I know, it might have been you who snatched the witch-woman. I wouldn't have thought a man your age would be capable. Did she magic you?"

"Speak in comprehensible sentences, lad. What are you talking about?"

Erde was grateful for the anonymity of servants. She huddled behind Hal, observing the details of his performance. Meanwhile, she isolated careful images of the events for the dragon and sent them off into the ether, not knowing whether he received them or not. She worried that the she-goat alone might not be enough of a meal to restore his strength. She begged him for a sign.

The lordling brushed snow from the fringe of blond hair cutting straight across his brow. "Yes, I think it must have been you. Where is she? Where have you hidden her?"

Hal spread his arms. "There are no women here about, my boy, much to my regret. Is she good-looking, your witchy-woman? If so, send her my way, I do implore you." He threw a fraternal glance at the men surrounding him. "I've been a long time out in the East, you see, where cold as it is, the women have no need of clothing, so thick is the pelt on them."

One man suppressed a smile, another snorted. All three relaxed their sword arms a trifle.

"In fact, you wouldn't believe. One time I . . ." Hal continued, and the soldiers leaned in to listen.

"Quiet! This is not a tavern!" The men smirked and the lordling stiffened his jaw. "The barn. She's probably in the barn. You and you, search that barn!"

The two idle men took off at a trot. They found a recalcitrant mule between them and the doors.

Hal relaxed back against the brick kiln, looking unconcerned. "Is he any better yet?" he murmured to Erde. "I'll give him every second I can manage."

Imperceptibly, she shrugged, shook her head.

He bent to dig snow out of his boot. "Perhaps he should reconsider his prohibition against eating human flesh. Like right now."

The mule squealed and lashed out, striking the sword from one of the soldier's hands. The man swore in pain and hugged his wrist.

Hal straightened, suddenly smiling and helpful. "Oh, he's a real killer, that one. My boy here can't even handle him. I don't know why I keep him. Here, I'll do what I can." He

went toward the mule, dragging Erde with him. He made a
lengthy show of being unable to calm the spooked and violent animal while Erde stood in the snow silently pleading
with the dragon to listen, to respond, to give her just one
sign that he was alive and well and aware of what was happening.

But the lordling soon lost patience. "Quiet him down or
he's a dead animal, never mind the baron's order!" He signaled his men. "Get those doors open!"

The mule allowed himself to be driven off to one side, but
would let no one touch him. The soldiers hauled open the
heavy doors and rushed inside. Erde heard them thrashing
about, slamming bin lids and rustling through the straw. She
heard no exclamations of horror or surprise. She exchanged
a quick glance with Hal and as soon as both could casually
do so, they peered around the edge of the doorway. The soldiers stood at a loss in the middle of an apparently deserted
barn. One of them was searching the mule packs. All he
came up with that interested him was a second sword
wrapped in linen. He tore off the bindings, examined it possessively, then set it aside. Alla's little carved box he opened
and tossed back in the pack when he found it contained only
a strip of paper. Erde was glad she wore the dragon brooch
pinned to the inside of her shirt. She sent praise to Earth,
even though he never responded when he was being invisible. At least he'd found the strength to do that.

The lordling rode his horse into the barn and looked
around. "You've hidden her well, sir knight."

"I've hidden no one," Hal replied truthfully.

"Perhaps she's hidden herself. A vanishing spell. A witch
can do such things."

Erde shuddered to think how close to reality he'd stumbled.

Hal rolled his eyes as if the young man were raving. "So
I'm told. But then, why would she hide out in a barn? She
could simply vanish and walk right out of town."

The lordling drew himself up in his saddle. "She wouldn't
get past. The holy brother has an acolyte at every gate to
sniff out any unholy witchcraft."

"Is that so?" replied Hal, as one might to soothe a lunatic.

"Besides, you are her loyal minion who saved her from
the stake. She will come back for you, and we will be waiting. You there! Bind his hands!"

One man scurried for rope. Another yanked Hal's arms around his back and held them ready as his companion tied them tightly.

Hal looked up at the man on the horse. "Are you sure you're ready to face the Powers of Darkness all by yourself?" When the young man blanched, he returned an avuncular chuckle. "Really, lad, there is no 'she.' I've got no woman hidden. I'm hungry, you're probably thirsty, we're all of us freezing our asses off, and what you should really do is take me to Baron Köthen right away. I'm sure his hospitality will prove superior to this drafty old barn."

"Superior, no doubt, and a lot more secure," said a dry voice behind them.

The lordling slid quickly off his horse.

"Ah. At last." Hal turned easily. "Still so light on your feet, Dolph."

Baron Köthen stood in the doorway, snow melting on his bared blond head. His arms folded and his stance hip-slung, he looked both edgy and satisfied. "Well . . . I learned from the best."

"Just searching about town on your own, eh?"

"Oh, please, I came as soon as I heard. How many King's Knights are there left running about loose, after all?" Behind him, a large party of soldiers swooped into the yard amidst the multiple clinkings of harness and armor. Köthen moved in from the doorway, casually but in full enjoyment of his authority. His clothing was plain but well-cut, with just the right amount of swagger. His beard was neatly trimmed. His eyes, Erde noted, were dark, belying his lighter coloring. He spotted Hal's peculiarly stiff posture, bent to glance behind him, then turned on the lordling in a rage. "What? You've bound him? Fool, where are your manners? Release him immediately!"

The lordling himself jumped to untie the ropes. Hal rubbed his wrists ceremonially. "So. You come to me, Dolph? I'm honored."

"With all the respect possible, my knight, under the circumstances."

Something like pain shadowed Hal's eyes momentarily. The two men stared at each other, then Köthen took a step forward and held out his hand. Hal moved at the same instant to meet him. They clasped hands eagerly, with visible affection. The lordling stood by, astonished.

"You're looking well, Dolph."

"And you, considering. What brings you to Erfurt?"

Hal regarded the younger man steadily. "I came to visit a friend, but I gather he's left town."

Köthen laughed softly. The smile turned his rugged face briefly boyish. He reached out to pinch the red leather of Hal's jerkin between two fingers. "I hope you'll tell me, my knight, that you wear this still because the impoverished circumstances of your life deny you the luxury of a new wardrobe."

Hal looked down, spreading his arms to survey himself better. "What? You don't like the cut? Or perhaps it's the color. Yes, the color, no doubt. But I rather think it flatters me. I always hoped you'd grow to favor it yourself."

"There are more fashionable colors now in Erfurt."

"Ah, yes." Hal sucked his teeth noisily. "The blue and yellow, perhaps? But you know me better, Dolph. Never one to change my color at the whim of fashion."

When Köthen made as if to turn away, Hal grasped his wrist and pulled him nearer. Swords rattled all around the barn but Köthen held up a hand and waved them away. "Give us some privacy here, for Christ's sake!"

The soldiers backed out of the barn. The lordling remained in the doorway, feeling suddenly irrelevant.

"So, Dolph. What is this you're up to?" Hal demanded quietly. "Conniving with your fellow peers is one thing. It's what a baron does. But to take up your sword against His Majesty? Didn't I teach you better than *treason?*"

Köthen's head dipped. Erde saw his eyes squeeze shut briefly. He took a breath and when he spoke, she could barely hear him. "You taught me everything I know that's worth anything, but your most vivid lesson was one you never intended, and that was about the futility of devoting your life and loyalty to a weakling monarch." He looked up at Hal intently. "We live in woeful times, Heinrich, listen to me. I will be a better master to our people. I will keep them safe. I will hold the barons in control. I will make the kingdom prosper again."

"You could do all that, Dolph—and I don't doubt you could—and still do it in the service of your king. Come wear the Red with me. Make it honorable again. Are you so hungry for a crown?"

Köthen shook him off with a snort of anguish. "You'll force me to make an enemy of you."

"Your deeds here have done that for you already. Though it doesn't mean I love you any less."

Köthen's laugh was harsh this time. "Well, I'd rather you hated me!"

"If I were to hate you, I'd have to give up hope of changing your mind."

"Hate me, then. Show me some human foible, Heinrich! Cut yourself down to life size in my eyes, so I can bear the pain of disappointing you."

"Ah, Dolph, I'm a foolish old man still unfashionably loyal to his king. Is that not disappointing enough?"

"You're not that old, and you're certainly not foolish." Köthen stared at him resignedly. "Which means you're still dangerous, and my unwilling guest no matter what." He turned away to walk farther into the barn, stretching. The fine dark links of his mail jingled musically along his arms. "Well, I'll try to keep you alive as long as I can, though with this mad priest, there's no telling ..." He searched about vaguely as if at a loss for further conversation, then rounded again on the lordling. "Here! A seat for Baron Weissstrasse! For me, too, if you can find more than one." He noticed Erde finally and seized on her as possibly neutral subject matter. "So, is this your latest? Starting them awfully young now, Heinrich. Looks hardly old enough to lift a blade."

"As old as you were, when you came to me."

Köthen's shoulders hunched, then he shook off the memory. "What's your name, boy? Speak up! What household are you from?"

"He can't, Dolph, and he's not from any household. What lord would give their sons to me to train nowadays? He's a mute orphan lad I saved from starvation, and he serves me well enough."

"Well, I'm sure he's a worthy lad and I'll try to keep him alive as well. Though you don't make it easy for me, my knight."

Hal eyed him satirically. "If I gave up my principles at my age, what would I have left?"

Köthen turned back to grip Hal with both hands and shake him gently. "A comfortable rest of your life in my service, as my most valued counselor. Heinrich, I beg you, listen to reason."

"What is comfort without honor?" returned Hal recklessly, but his eyes over his grin were serious.

"What is honor without power?" Köthen replied.

"Ha. I should know never to debate the fine points with you. My sword was superior, but you were always the better politician."

"As events have proven."

"Perhaps. Though we haven't seen the end of this yet. What of the prince? Have you left him alive?"

Köthen flushed. "Of course! Did you think . . . ?"

"I think you won't actually claim a throne while it has a living heir."

"Carl is safe!" Köthen returned hotly. "Fool that he is."

Hal looked glum. "I won't disagree with you there."

"I'll rule as regent."

"The king still reigns."

"Where? You tell me where!" Köthen jabbed a finger at Hal like an angry schoolmaster. "You find me one corner of this land still loyal to that weak old man and I'll go there and clean it out with my own hands! My own bare hands, Heinrich. I swear! This kingdom is dying and it needs a leader, a *real* leader, to make it whole again!"

Into the chill silence that fell between them then came new sounds, from out on the street. Men's deep voices booming out a liturgical chant. Listening a moment longer, Erde knew her worst fears had been realized.

"Damn!" Köthen muttered, grinding the heels of his hands into his eyes.

"My lord baron," began the lordling from the door. "It's . . ."

"I know who it is, idiot! Why now? Maybe it's coincidence. Maybe he'll just pass by."

Fighting a panic so visceral that it nearly froze her to the spot, Erde glanced wildly around the barn for some sign of where the dragon was hiding himself. She found nothing, and began to doubt if he was there at all. She clutched at the dragon brooch inside her shirt for comfort. It provided her none. The smooth stone was icy to her touch, as frigid as the wind outside, as chilled as her doubting heart. What if Earth had gone off without them? What if the she-goat had provided just enough strength to take him to Deep Moor, and he'd gone back to feed? He'd have no way of knowing he'd be leaving her to the grotesque mercies of the white-robed priest. The chanting grew louder as it neared.

"They're singing an exorcism," noted Hal. Erde watched suspicion bloom across his face.

"Are they really," Köthen replied without a shred of interest. "Only you would know such a thing."

The singers rounded the corner and passed under the arch into the brickyard. Erde pulled her hood up and her cap down, and edged backward toward the darkest recesses of the barn. She knew it was hopeless. If the priest came in, he would sniff her out somehow. He had that gift.

Köthen sighed and started for the door. "If only he'd keep his mind on his own business!"

Hastily, Hal put himself in the way. "Dolph, don't let him in here. Keep him away from me."

"I'd as soon keep him away from all of us."

Hal lowered his voice. "No joke, Dolph. I mean it. You don't know what you're into here. Keep him out. You won't like what will come of it, even you."

"*Even* me. Ha. Spare me your contempt, Heinrich."

"Dolph, I'm warning you. He'll have me on the stake."

Erde knew who the knight was really worried about, and she was grateful. But she doubted that his offering himself up as a distraction would fool the priest for very long.

Köthen of course could not understand as she did. He laughed. "Is that old reputation still dogging you? Come now, my knight. What is this unmanly terror of a mere cleric?"

"You already know better than that."

"Well, all right, yes, I do. It doesn't take very long, it's true. But relax, he only burns witches and warlocks."

Hal nodded. "Precisely."

Köthen paused, eyes narrowing. "Heinrich, no one who knows you takes any of that old sorcery stuff seriously. You may die on the block, like a man, but at the stake? Not while I'm in charge."

"If you let him in here, you may not have the choice."

"I see." Köthen eased back onto his heels, studying him. "You tell me, then, my knight: just what am I into that I don't know about?"

As Hal quickly weighed how much was safe to tell him, too soon there was someone at the door. The lordling stood aside with a bow. Erde shrank further into the shadows, burrowing into the straw and screaming in her mind for the dragon to come and save her. But the man who entered was not Brother Guillemo. It was Josef von Alte. Köthen stiffened, then moved a long step away from Hal. Von Alte blinked, his eyes adjusting to the relative darkness of the barn. His silver hair brought in an icy glint from outside. He saw Köthen, then Hal. He squinted, then frowned.

"Weissstrasse? Is that you? What the hell are you doing here?"

Hal bowed deeply. "Your servant as always, my lord of Alte."

Köthen snickered. "Don't pick on him, Heinrich. He's had a hard day, too. No, come to think of it, pick on him all you like. Save me the trouble."

Erde wished that, like the dragon, she could become invisible. But for the moment, these three rival barons were too busy jockeying for position to notice a mere prentice boy. She watched her father covertly, breathless at being thrust into his presence like this, without warning. From the rooftop, he'd looked all right. She remembered how he used to fill doorways. She thought his slimmer shape suited him. But close up, his eyes were pouchy and his skin sallow. It wasn't just age. Hal was probably twenty years older and looked far more fit. She saw her father was ill at ease. At Tor Alte, she'd thought him a model of the worldly, modern courtier, even when she didn't agree with him. But here, shown up against the likes of Köthen and Hal Engle, he seemed provincial, a bit pretentious, and painfully aware of it. It wasn't his clothing or his accent, but his lack of confidence, as if somewhere in the journey between Tor Alte and Erfurt, his will had been shattered. (How ironic, that during the very same journey, her own had been forged.) Only cunning and bravado kept Baron Josef from complete collapse. Erde blamed it on the priest and his promises of glory. If her father had stayed at home to mind his own lands, like his mother the baroness had insisted on doing, Erde thought he could have learned to rule properly. Now he was working very hard to be bully and likable, which was not really in his nature, especially when faced with Köthen's unconcealed disdain. There was also the disadvantage of not understanding why these two men before him now, who ought to have been blood enemies, met him with an unidentifiable solidarity and identical expressions. A sharp rise in the volume of the chanting saved him from having to respond to Köthen's gibe.

"What is he doing out there?" Köthen was irritable, as if von Alte was responsible for the existence of the priest as an obstacle in his life. Which in a way, he was.

Baron Josef looked faintly embarrassed. "Performing an exorcism."

"Told you," murmured Hal.

"But why is he *here?*"

"My lord Köthen, he came on the word of your messenger."

"I sent him no messenger."

"Then one who claimed to be your messenger. An old man with a limp. Looked like he'd just been in a fight."

"Say again?" Hal came up beside him. "An old man? With a limp? Did he have a fresh gash on his cheek right here?"

"You describe him exactly. Perhaps he was your messenger, Weisstrasse?"

"Hardly."

"But you know the man? He didn't mention you."

"Well, that's something at least."

Von Alte frowned at him suspiciously.

"I mean, I was mistaken. I only thought I knew him." Hal turned away with a stunned and sickly look. "Alas for the world. Treason is everywhere." He wandered over to the nail keg that the lordling had pulled up for him moments ago. He sat down on it heavily and buried his head in his hands. Erde understood his anguish. You save someone's life, or teach them everything they know, and still they betray you.

Köthen stared after Hal curiously, then returned his attention to von Alte. "What did this messenger say to bring Guillemo so quickly and so . . . noisily?"

"The usual. I only heard part of it. Something about the witch-woman and a dragon." Josef chose this first opportunity of being alone with Köthen to make a play for his sympathy. "He's obsessed, you know. You saw his reaction to your men's dragon scare. He sees them under every rock. But there's never any truth to it. My whole time with him has been one long chase after specters and will-o-the-wisps."

"Then why do you stay with him if he's such a burden?"

"Why do you welcome him into your town? My lord Köthen, our reasons are the same."

"Why do either of you have anything to do with the man?" cried Hal from his nail keg. "He's not just inconvenient, he's unclean. Unclean! Filth spews from his mind and blasphemy from his mouth! He corrupts everything he touches!"

"Of course, Heinrich," soothed Köthen reasonably. "We all know he's mad, but the people believe in him. The man who brought you the message, von Alte, was he in earnest?"

"Oh, quite. The man was obviously terrified."

"You see, my knight? The people want to be saved—from hunger, from disorder, and especially from dragons. You don't understand this because if you see a disorder, you try to fix it yourself, and if you ever met a dragon, you'd welcome it into your library for closer study. But not everyone is so equal to the world. They want to be taken care of."

Erde was sure Köthen was right. Though Old Ralf had been told that Earth had saved his life, he'd only pretended to accept the idea of him for as long as he considered himself at risk in the dragon's presence. Once he was safely out of range, the old fear and superstition went back to work on him. Either that, or he'd been a spy for the king's enemies all along, but she thought the fact that he'd reported the dragon and not the King's Knight proved it was abiding terror that had driven him to it. Of course, the result was the same in the long run.

Outside, the chanting ceased.

Her moment of grace had ended, her brief idyll while time stopped for politics and manly posturing among three men whose decency had been sorely tried, but who still retained their basic humanity. Outside, the real evil lurked, and it was coming in to join them. With Hal no longer standing between her and her father, Erde's last illusion of safety evaporated. She burrowed deeper into the hay, hoping to back imperceptibly behind the feed bin.

When he appeared in the doorway, Erde recognized instantly that Brother Guillemo was no longer sane. Despite the biting cold, he wore his rough robe open to his waist, where the belt was cinched in so tightly that it left long red chafe marks on his belly. Snowflakes caught in the thick black hair matting his chest. His feet were also bare. The hard and blackened look of them suggested that he'd gone shoeless for quite a while. His hood was thrown back, revealing his bald head which, before, he had taken such trouble to conceal when not in one of his transports of prayer. But all this could have been detail for one more role, assumed like the others to fit his current purpose, except for the terror deep within his eyes. He looked like a man standing naked in a gale.

Erde wondered why it should be that she could read this man so truly, this one man whom she hated and feared above all others. She'd been able to from the moment she set eyes on him—even before, when in Tor Alte's great-hall she'd seen through the lie of the white-robe claiming to be Guillemo Gotti. She felt connected to him in some awful, inexplicable way, and recalled Rose's insistence with Hal about the priest's real gift for prophecy. She wished she'd had more time to discuss it and its relationship to her own future, before she had to face him again.

But here he was, waiting just within the door frame, rocking slightly, as if getting his bearings, the one thing she knew he would never quite have again. Köthen and von Alte moved instinctively to triangulate the priest, making Hal the third corner, unarmed though he was and with his head still buried in his hands. No one said a word. The lordling reached behind him for his horse's reins and backed out of the barn, grateful to leave Guillemo to his superiors.

In the silence, Guillemo's wild expression calmed a bit and became crafty. He glanced from von Alte to Köthen and back again. "Where is it? Is it here? Is it gone? Did it leave any sign?"

Köthen cleared his throat. "Do join us, Brother. What were you expecting to find?"

Guillemo squinted at him. "Ah. Then it's gone. Again, I'm too late."

"What is gone?"

"The witch's minion. The Devil-beast your messenger spoke of."

"Not my messenger, good Brother."

"Not?" Guillemo frowned and looked to Josef von Alte, who shrugged defensively. The priest's hands clenched, then brushed the air as if shooing flies. "Ah, I see it now. Some demon mocks me. I am being tested . . . no!" His restless movements stilled. He sniffed carefully and peered around into the shadows. "No, the dark clouds roil and gather. He was here. He's gone now, but he will return for her. No. He's here. I feel him near." He paced in a small circle, taking in all corners of the barn. "I *feel* him."

"He? Who?"

"The dragon, my lord baron."

Köthen rolled his eyes, but Erde shivered. Was it possible? Could he actually sense the dragon's presence, even when she couldn't? She wouldn't put it past him.

Guillemo walked his rapid little circle and halted in front of Hal. "Who's this?" He grabbed the short-cropped nap at Hal's temples and jerked his head back to see his face. Hal did not resist. He stared up at the priest with a vengeful death's head grin. Guillemo stared back for a breathless second, then let go and sprang backward with a bone-chilling screech. His continued wails brought three of his brothers crowding to the door.

"Out!" Köthen snapped. "You, out! All of you! This is a gentlemen's discussion, Guillemo. I want them out of here!"

Guillemo got hold of himself enough to cease his shrieking, but continued to stare and point, his whole arm outstretched as if reaching to touch the knight while keeping as far away from him as possible. "How did you get here? You're not supposed to be here!"

"What's the matter, Guillemo? Did you hope I'd died or something?" Hal rose from the nail keg and walked to the door to glance purposefully up at the glowering sky. The three white-robes backed away into the snow.

The priest balled his fist and dropped it to his side like a hammer. "I should have known it would be you!"

"I see you two are acquainted," noted Köthen dryly.

Hal turned smoldering eyes on him.

Köthen spread his hands. "What, what?"

"Christ Almighty, Dolph. If you're going to come charging in to steal a crown, you ought to at least take time to find out what goes on in the kingdom." The extremity of Hal's anger gave him strength to hold it in check. "Surely you're the only man left in God's Creation who doesn't know it's this so-called priest who made me a homeless wanderer!"

"Him? Thought it was your sons."

"He put the weapon in their hands."

Under the heat of Köthen's glare, Guillemo glanced aside but raised his chin. "He is the Anti-Christ."

"Who is?"

Guillemo jutted his chin in Hal's direction. "Him. Him."

"Hal Engle is the Anti-Christ? You've got to be kidding."

"He has converse with dragons."

"Ah, yes. Dragons." Köthen eyed Hal sympathetically. "You see what comes from too much study? It's that old reputation, getting you in trouble again."

"Mock, mock, my lord, on peril of your soul!" The priest was pointing again. "He brings the ice in summer! He brings dragons to lie in wait!"

Hal smirked at Köthen with sour satisfaction. "And you said nobody took it seriously."

Guillemo saw his advantage slipping away. He collected himself with effort. He tightened his robe a bit and smoothed its folds across his chest. "You may well mock, my lord baron, but do you consider it mere coincidence that finds us all here together at this moment?"

"What should I consider it?"

"Destiny, my lord of Köthen."

Erde absorbed the loaded word with a shudder and wished with every nerve in her body that she was back in Deep Moor. She'd used the distraction of Guillemo's screeching to gain the cover of the feed bin, but she still felt completely visible to him, sure that it was only a question of when he would choose to notice her.

"Destiny." Hal made a rude sound.

"Yes! The forces of Destiny have drawn us together! He should not be here now, and yet he is, with all that he can summon from the cold depths of Hell! It is not on the battlefield but in this humble unmarked place that the true contest will be won or lost!"

Köthen had no answer for that. He shrugged. "A battle of the spirit, then, good Brother, which I as a mere soldier can leave to your superior knowledge and experience. Heinrich, gather your kit and your boy. I'm afraid you'll have to leave your dragons behind. Let's find someplace warm and get some food in our bellies. Damned unseasonable weather, isn't it?"

Erde knew it would not be that easy.

"You leave at the peril of your immortal soul, Baron Köthen." The priest's voice was suddenly flat and sane, more like the Guillemo that she remembered.

"Ah, but I stay at the peril of my health and my stomach," Köthen returned with scant civility. "What a dilemma."

Erde's father watched this exchange avidly, as if to see if Köthen had any better luck mastering the priest than he'd had.

"You do not fear God or the Devil?" Guillemo gathered himself a little more. It was like watching a man rein himself in on a leash. "Then perhaps a threat to your newly acquired scepter will concern you more."

Köthen hesitated, and Josef von Alte smiled knowingly.

"Not acquired yet," Hal threw in uselessly.

"What is it, priest? Can't you ever just say what you mean?" Köthen crossed his arms. He knew he'd been snared and wasn't happy about it.

"I have, my lord. I am. I always do." Guillemo took up his diffident advocate's stance, though it remained a bit stiff and artificial, his brain demanding a posture his mad heart could no longer support. But his insinuating tone of voice sent another hot surge of memory through Erde's skull, a face again and blood, a young man's body flying through the air, then nothing. But now she knew it was only in hiding. She felt it lurking, just out of reach, the entire memory, awaiting its cue. Guillemo took up a slow back and forth pacing, and Erde heard the slap of sandals on stone, even though the floor was dirt and the priest was barefoot. "Perhaps the meaning is sometimes obscure to you, my lord Köthen, but I say it nonetheless, without concealment. And what I am saying now is that your soul is in danger and your power is threatened. I will leave it to you to decide which peril concerns you more, but how much clearer do you need me to be?" He turned to face Köthen with elaborate politesse.

"Go on," said Köthen.

"There is a conspiracy at work here, my lord, and it is both treasonous and unholy. My own heaven-sent visions are explained and proven out by the information I had from a man who I thought was your messenger but who now I see had fled to me in righteous terror to bare his soul of what he'd witnessed."

Guillemo turned to point at Hal again, a bit too fast, a bit too avidly, and jerked himself back into a more reasonable stance. "I'd thought, my lord, that I had prevented this, months ago, but alas, the Fiend has found a way around me to do his foul work. Tonight, the poor man told me, this devil's minion will tryst with the escaped witch and her rescuer, whom some call the Friend. But he is no friend to the godly. You will notice, my lord, how the name becomes 'fiend' with the subtraction of a mere letter. So then, when they are all met, this one here will summon his dragon familiar and spirit them away to the un-Friend's encampment so that the accursed witch can do her black magic with his godless mob. This I have seen in my visions over and over, though I did not at first comprehend it. The witch will render the mob into an invincible army, which will march on Erfurt in the name of the deposed king." Guillemo paused, lowered his pointing arm. "Does that stir your interest at all, my lord Köthen?"

"Do we know it was the Friend who rescued her?"

"I say it was."

The younger man stared thoughtfully at the floor, toed some broken straw around with his boot, then sighed and looked at Hal.

Hal chuckled. "I'd do it if I could, you know that."

"Except for the dragon part, my knight, it all sounds too plausible to be ignored."

"Ah, but the dragon part seems fairly essential. How am I to spirit them away otherwise?"

"How about the dragon part as a metaphor for the royalist underground? I know the town's riddled with ... 'friends.' This place in particular." Köthen nodded toward the shadowed corners of the barn. "I've had my eye on it for weeks. Haven't been able to catch anyone in the act ... before now."

"An unlikely spot for secret meetings." Hal waved a dubious hand around the room. "Too public. Look how just anyone can drop on by."

"Exactly. Who would suspect the odd coming and going? How else could a King's Knight be standing here before me within my own closely guarded walls? How else could Guillemo's witch and her rescuer have already evaded me for several hours? The royalists may have gotten them out by now, for all I know." He watched Hal closely for a betraying sign.

"I'd much prefer a real dragon," said Hal.

Köthen tried and failed to suppress a laugh.

"No, it's not true! They're not gone!" barked Guillemo, a little too loudly. He jabbed an agitated finger at the straw-dusted floor. "The specific persons may be obscured in my visions, but the force lines definitely meet here. They will be joined. It must be! There is . . . there is . . . here. It must be here!"

The priest began to pace his tight circle again, faster and faster. The three barons looked on with varying degrees of incredulity, concern, and contempt. Cringing behind the feed bin, flattened against its splintery slats, Erde knew not a whisper of contempt. She took in the priest's circling as the mouse blindly senses the hawk above and freezes in primal, animal terror. She called again to the dragon, a final attempt, a desperate yearning fling of her mind into the void that was still, unbelievably, dragonless.

And the priest, circling, also froze, and listened. "It . . . ? Or she . . . ? She. *She!* She is here! Here! Now I understand it! Now I see it all!" He lunged back into motion, circling still but even wider, brushing unseeing past the men who watched dumbfounded, shoving Hal aside as the knight stepped deliberately into his path.

"Really, Dolph, can't you do something with the man?"

Josef von Alte moved aside warily.

Köthen said, "Guillemo . . ." and reached for him.

"No!" The priest swerved, batting his arm away. "She. You. Didn't believe me. I knew. Here now. Right . . ." He circled toward the feed bin. Hal moved to intercept him, but Köthen stopped him short with a broad arm across his chest.

"It's the lad. He'll . . ."

"Easy. He'll come to no harm."

"Dolph, you don't know . . ."

"You keep saying that."

"Here!" shrieked Guillemo like a malicious child in a game of tag. He reached behind the bin, grabbed Erde by the back of her jerkin and hauled her into view. He snatched off her prentice cap and shoved her roughly forward so that she stumbled and went sprawling facedown on the dirty straw. The mud-stained boots she saw a short yard from her nose were not Baron Köthen's, but her father's.

"Behold the witch-child!" Guillemo bellowed in triumph. "Ha, Josef! I told you she lived still!"

Chapter Thirty

Erde pressed her face into the straw and prayed for dragons.

Josef von Alte stared. He glanced at Brother Guillemo uncertainly, then back at the person sprawled at his feet. "Witch-child? I thought . . ."

"You thought! You're a fool, Josef! You listened to rumor and the words of inferiors! But I told you what the truth was!" The priest jabbed both arms toward Erde, his hands as stiff as blades. "Now you will have faith! Now you will believe me!"

Von Alte did not move. Erde wished and did not wish that she could see his face. Would it be rage or joy that she'd find there? Slowly, she drew in her limbs beneath her, until she was curled in a turtlelike posture of retreat and submission. She wished she'd tried to learn the dragon's skill of invisibility. She was sure she could make herself still enough to vanish. She heard Baron Köthen murmur to Hal, but did not catch the older man's reply. Soon Hal stepped forward with a sigh and a rustle of straw, and bent down to grasp her arm and ease her ceremoniously to her feet.

"The granddaughter of Meriah von Alte need bow to no one." He brushed dry wisps from her cloak and hair, then backed away to Köthen's side.

Erde understood his unspoken message. She made herself stand tall and proud, the focus of all attention. It was easy to pretend to ignore the priest. Raising her eyes to meet her father's was the thing she could not manage.

"A woman?" Köthen marveled.

"A girl," amended Hal.

"His daughter? The one who was kidnapped?"

"No! Bewitched!" yelped Guillemo, beginning an agitated dance. "Corrupted! Suborned by the agents of Satan!"

"A child fleeing for her life," Hal countered. "The only evil she knows is the one she escaped." He looked to the priest. "Him."

"Liar!" Guillemo shrieked. He danced toward Hal but skittered sideways when Köthen did not move from his path. "Ha! I know! I see it now! It was you, wasn't it, all along? The signs were there but I . . . I misread them! I should have seen, when my visions perplexed me, that it was you, the knight in my dreams. The Devil's Paladin!"

The knight in his dreams. Erde shivered. Too much coincidence with Guillemo. But she knew that the knight in her own dream, the dragon's dream, was not Hal Engle.

"It was you who thwarted me at Tor Alte! It was your spells that broke the locks and put the weapons in their hands! You . . ."

"I wasn't even in the neighborhood," Hal said sourly.

"What proof is that? The Eye of Darkness sees farther than . . ."

Köthen's patience ran dry at last. "Brother Guillemo, stop your ranting! You disgrace your holy office!" To Erde's surprise, the priest subsided, though he continued to mutter and wave his arms. Köthen shook his head. "Well, you're right, Heinrich. This complication I would not have guessed. Von Alte's lost daughter. Where did you find her?"

"Starving in the forest. But my usefulness is ended now. You must give her your protection, Dolph."

"I? It's her father should do that, not me."

"He didn't the first time. Please, Dolph, she's too young for politics. Take her in. Does a young girl flee into the wilderness unless she's truly desperate?"

"Or very brave," mused Köthen. "Or both. Well, what about it, von Alte? Does the father say nothing?"

When her father did not reply, Erde could finally muster the courage to meet his tongue-tied stare. The eyes she looked into were distant and horrified. They rebounded from hers as if she had struck him a blow. They flew to the priest, then back again like frightened birds to look her up and down, taking in the details of her shorn hair and her travel-stained man's garb. At last they slid upward to meet hers furtively as if, Erde thought, he was peering at her from behind a shutter, or through a veil.

He's scared, she realized. *He sees someone he recognizes but does not know. It frightens him how much I've changed.* She watched her father run his tongue along dry lips and gather himself to speak.

"Is this truly my daughter Erde?"

She didn't believe that he could really doubt it. Without thinking, she opened her mouth to answer him. Her breathy wordless rasp made him recoil and glance away, first at the priest—who had ceased his dancing and circling to watch this exchange with his predator's eye—and then at the open doorway, where the grim gray light of day was already waning.

"See!" hissed Guillemo. "Beware, Josef, for your soul's sake. What was your daughter is no longer."

"He knows nothing of souls—don't listen to him," Hal warned. "She's your own flesh, von Alte. Meriah's dear blood."

"Ah!" murmured Köthen beside him. "Now it comes clear. I'd quite forgotten."

Baron Josef shifted his weight a few times, regarding the snow-drifted doorsill with elaborate interest. At length, he wagged his head slowly back and forth, without looking at anybody. "No, this cannot be her. This is not my daughter."

Erde started toward him instinctively, hands outstretched to deny his denial. Only then did he meet her straight and square, his eyes warning her off with a stare that said, *I know you and I reject what you are, what you have become.*

Erde felt a binding loosen within her, a constriction she'd hardly known was there. Though his denial could mean death for her, she breathed more easily. Her spine straightened of its own accord, as if its burden had lifted. She thought: *But I'm proud of what I am.* In her mind's eye, she saw a great gray sea from which Tor Alte stood up as a lonely island, and herself drifting away from a diminished and diminishing father who stood at the gate as if it were a dock. She was a boat cast off from its mooring, drawn swiftly away by the tide that was Life. Then the current eddied, leaving her without momentum, without identity. If she was not von Alte's daughter, who was she?

Yet despite her confusion, the moment had a certain inevitability to it. She'd chosen a new mooring, more like a sea anchor, that stabilized without denying movement and change. Her new identity would be forged with the dragon.

Erde did not permit herself to wonder if Earth's silence was permanent. She wished her father would act on his doorward impulse and simply walk away, thus ennobling this family rupture with a clean and dignified break.

But Josef von Alte was plagued with the weak man's need to justify. He took a step back, gesturing dismissively. "Not her. You're right, Guillemo. My Erde is a lady and an innocent, not some broken-down knight's whore and camp follower."

Hal growled deep in his throat and lunged. Köthen caught him, pulled the older man back again. "If your concern is for her virtue, von Alte, you've never known this particular knight very well." His dry chuckle held little humor, only scorn. "Might have been better for you if you had."

Hal eased himself free and brushed at his sleeves needlessly. "If she wouldn't marry me, she'd hardly have asked me to foster her son."

Köthen shrugged. "That's two bad decisions."

Brother Guillemo grew restless with being a mere audience to confrontation. He clapped both palms to his face and cried out, "Ah! I see! The vision clears! I should not fear the witch-woman's escape. It was trivial and temporary. It was a sign, to remind me of my true Mission! Oh, glory be to God who lends me such iotas of his omniscience!" He dropped his hands to his sides, palms outward in prayerful reverence, and beamed at the three uncomprehending barons. "Don't you see? It's so clear! It must be obvious, even to the likes of you!"

"And what 'like' is that, good Brother," asked Köthen darkly.

"The unenlightened, my lord baron, but it's no fault of yours. We cannot all be conduits of the Will of Heaven."

Hal spat loudly into the straw.

"Please enlighten us, good Brother."

"Oh my lord of Köthen, it's perfect! It's sublime! Our ceremony and great preparations were not wasted!" Guillemo began to circle again, as if he could not speak and be still at the same time. "It was all to make us ready for *this* moment, for *this* inevitability. But we were impatient. We were willing to be satisfied by a trivial burning. We tried to deny Destiny. So the Lord took us in hand and swept away our mistake, so that our holy pyre could await the true cleansing fire!" He halted suddenly and whirled to face Erde, his eyes glittering with lust and anticipation. "It will be the pinnacle of glory! God's Will be done at last! We will burn the witch-child! We will burn them all, and the Devil's Paladin, too!" He reached for Erde, his fingers like a claw fisting in the folds of her garment.

Quickly, Köthen stepped between them. He pulled the priest off her firmly but gently, as a chirurgeon would a leech. "Not so fast, good Brother. I think we must hear more of this before we put some innocent peeress to the torch."

"Innocent?" the priest yelped.

Köthen put him at arm's length and pushed him away. He turned Erde to face him and took a long moment to study her, long enough so that Erde tired of staring at her feet and raised her eyes to his out of mere curiosity. She tried to follow Hal's example: stand easy but strong. Köthen's gaze was frankly appraising. His dark eyes were surprisingly warm and she saw in them something that from a man, she had known only from Hal: respect.

"So, my lady ... Erde, is it? ... can you speak or no?"

Erde shook her head. She was trying to understand what it was about Adolphus of Köthen that made her feel so girlish and awkward.

"Ah. A pity. I should very much like to hear your side of this story."

Then Köthen smiled at her, a brief, almost intimate flash of complicity, and for a moment she couldn't breathe. Heat flushed her cheeks, every nerve focusing on the pressure of his hand on her arm. Erde dropped her eyes, grateful for the afternoon gloom already settling into the barn.

Köthen let her go, as if reluctantly, and turned back toward Hal. "Well, I'll do what I can for her."

"No, you shall not!" bellowed the priest. "She is mine! Mine! The prophecy must be fulfilled, and then we will be saved! The sun will return and the flocks will fatten in the fields—but only if the witch-child burns!"

A burly white-robe ducked in breathlessly at the doorway, his brows beetled with expectation. "Holy Brother, there's motion in the street."

Guillemo started, then collected himself visibly. He drew in his shoulders and his flailing arms. He stilled, became rodlike with purpose. "Go. Tell them to prepare as we agreed. The moment is now. The final coincidence of forces. Go." He turned to von Alte, then Köthen, formally in turn, pulling up to his tallest and putting on his deepest voice. "My lord barons, ready your men. What we thought lost to us returns. Destiny approaches."

Von Alte was relieved to be released into action. He strode to the doorway and signaled his men to hide their horses and take cover. Turning back, he drew his sword. "The witch-woman and her rescuer. Now we'll see, my lord of Köthen, won't we?"

"I guess we will." Dubious but never a man to be caught unready, Köthen unsheathed his own weapon. His own half-dozen soldiers had appeared in the doorway, awaiting orders. Hal caught Erde's eye, questioning. She shook her head. No, she had not yet heard from the dragon. She followed his straying glance toward the sword the searchers had discarded from their packs, still lying in the straw beside the feed bin. The dull hidden glint of its blade was like a last faint ray of hope.

Köthen directed two of his men to clear the yard of any sign betraying their presence. He told the others to prepare torches. "Or lanterns, if they can be found. It'll be dark soon. What should I expect here, Heinrich? What plot have you mastered this time?"

"You know as much as I, Dolph. Once I had the illusion of control, but these days, events just seem to happen to me."

"Try that on von Alte, my knight, but not on me."

"No plot, Dolph, I swear. The gifted plotter here is not me."

Köthen frowned, a quick flare of rage that lit his eyes with fire. "Careful, careful . . ." He turned away abruptly, flexing his sword arm. "Then we'll lie in wait as the good brother advises, and see for ourselves. Von Alte, take the left side, why don't you. And keep your lady daughter well out of sight."

Baron Josef wagged his head bearlike and slow. "Not mine, my lord. Let the priest manage the witch."

Two of the white-robes had returned to take up guard around Guillemo. He shoved them aside to come at her. Erde slewed her gaze around to fasten on Köthen, pleading. Again Köthen moved between them. He caught Erde in the arc of his sword arm. The sweep of his blade sliced the air at the priest's knees. Guillemo sprang backward with an outraged howl. Köthen drew Erde aside toward Hal. "Your responsibility still, Heinrich. Swear you'll make no sound to raise alarm and I won't have you bound."

"On my honor."

"Over here, then. We'll take the right."

"Is that divine or otherwise?" Hal quipped.

"Heinrich, I warned you . . ." Köthen split his remaining men to either side of the door. "Take straw. Brush the snow there. Too many footprints. Where are those torches? Quickly!"

Von Alte stared. "You'll trust a King's Knight, Köthen?"

"More than I would a fellow baron, my lord of Alte."

"On your head be it. He'll betray us all."

"He will!" raged the priest. "See how he works on you! Bind him! Gag him tight! Beware, Adolphus! He woos away your soul! You must stop his voice so he cannot lay his spells! He is the Anti-Christ!"

"To your place, Guillemo! Your voice alone will give us away."

Köthen set up a signal relay between his men outside and those inside the barn. He motioned to Hal and Erde to conceal themselves behind the high wooden partition of a stall. Erde could see the doorway clearly through the hand's width spacing between the slats. Across the barn, her father and the priest crouched behind the tallest stack of stored bricks, two white-robed bodyguards hovering at their backs.

Erde called again for the dragon. For the first time, real doubt assailed her. Perhaps he would not return. Perhaps her duty as Dragon Guide was past, just as Hal had remarked about his own usefulness to her. Perhaps Earth had already learned enough to be able to manage on his own. Perhaps he'd tired of following other people's quests and had decided to focus on his own. What would she do then? She did not think of the stake. She could not. Such thoughts were made too vivid by what she'd witnessed in Tubin. She did not want to panic and lose her newfound dignity. Instead, she thought about the Friend and felt badly for him, traveling all those miles from the West, giving hope to the people and gathering up so much support, accomplishing a daring and miraculous rescue—all this, only to die in a brickyard, betrayed by a false promise of escape. The promise had been Hal's and it had been rashly made, before the mechanics of the dragon's gift were fully comprehended. Still, Erde felt responsible. Another needless death on her conscience—

two, with Margit counted, and possibly Hal's as well, if Köthen could not save him. The only solace was that she would not have to live with this guilt, for if they died, she most certainly would die with them. She was not sure she minded very much, if the dragon was really gone from her life.

She stole a sidelong look at Köthen, so intent on the open empty doorway. There was a very sturdy feel to him. Her nose came to his shoulder. His profile was like the rock face of a mountain, though the skin over those crags was smooth and clear. His blond hair was thick and strong and tended to clump in bunches like the tines of a feather. Erde decided she liked looking at him. She was astonished and a bit ashamed to find herself thinking such thoughts when she should be preparing herself to die. She should be praying.

She glanced across the darkening barn. Between the rough-hewn support posts, she could see her father staring at her. When he saw he was discovered, he looked away.

As the light failed, Köthen kept his gaze tight to his man inside the left of the doorway, who in turn watched a man outside to the right. Hiding behind a brick kiln, Erde guessed.

After a few long moments of waiting, Hal leaned across her back to murmur, "They may have spooked already. You should have brought the old messenger man along to serve as bait."

Köthen would not shift his eyes from the door. "I would have, except you forget, my knight—this is the priest's game. I knew nothing of it. It was word of you that brought me here."

"Ah. Well."

"But I see you still feel the need to advise me."

"Old habits die hard."

"They needn't. You've still time to accept my offer."

"Dolph . . ."

The soldier at the door raised his hand. Hal and Köthen straightened and stilled, paired motions taken at a matched rate. If only they shared political alliances as they did so much else, Erde mourned. What a magnificent team they'd make. It should be them running the kingdom together. Then she realized this was exactly what Köthen was offering. She wondered just what would it take to convince Hal Engle to redefine such long-held loyalties. She almost wished he would. It'd be a sure way to wreak sweet revenge on Brother Guillemo.

But what of the king, and young Prince Carl? What of the hidden second son that rumor claimed? Erde put a stop to her treasonous train of thought, and turned her own attention to the waiting doorway, now a black rectangle framing lighter gray, the faintly luminous snowfield of the yard, and beyond, the darker brick of the enclosing walls. The silence was unnatural, missing even the mundane unremarked noises of a town. As if the whole world awaited this arrival. Erde prayed that the very abnormality might warn Margit and the Friend away. She prayed that it wasn't them coming at all, but someone else, some innocent citizen who could be justly enraged by rough handling at the hands of the barons' men.

For someone *was* coming, there was no doubt now. She could hear the moist crunch of their steps crossing the snowy yard, cautious but still in a bit of a hurry. As they approached the doorway, Köthen brought his sword around behind her and set its point to the small of Hal's back. Waiting, every muscle and sinew rigid, Erde swayed with sudden dizziness. She caught herself with one hand pressed hard against the slats, willing the sharp edge to prod her back to clarity. A soft ringing filled her ears. She gasped for the breath that she'd been holding back, but the ringing did not go away. She had no time to think about it. Köthen's arm slid up along her back as the tip of his sword rose toward Hal's neck. Someone was in the doorway.

At first it was only a silhouette against the gray, a tall man dressed in the loose, layered clothing of a laborer. He hesitated in the opening, listening, and once again Erde stopped breathing. There was something familiar in the tilt of his chin and his square, broad shoulders. Before she could absorb this mystery, a second silhouette joined him, a woman. When Hal's hand tightened on her shoulder, she was sure the woman was Margit.

They stood side by side in the doorway, uncertain, then moved into the dimness of the barn. The ringing in Erde's ears swelled to a buzzing inside her head. The dragon brooch was a point of hot light against her skin. What was it saying to her now? The man entering pulled up abruptly as his boot stuck something in the straw, something that clanged like metal. He bent quickly to search in the near dark around his feet. Erde heard his soft grunt of satisfaction as he rose slowly with the object in his hand. Hal's grip signaled again, and she understood. The stranger had stumbled across the discarded sword, the sword she'd carried all the way from Tor Alte without ever really knowing why. Now she was glad she had, if only for this single moment, to offer one last chance to an enemy of Fra Guill.

The man grasped the sword and tested its weight. He swung it a couple of times, back and forth with little pauses between, as if something about it perplexed him. Erde was struck again by the familiarity of his stance. She wished for a bit more light, to see him better, and then Baron Köthen answered her wish.

"Now!" he barked. His blade was inches from Hal's jugular.

The barn doors swung out and around and slammed shut heavily. The new arrivals were caught like deer in a flare as torches bloomed in the near corners of the barn. Erde herself was momentarily blinded, then she could see that the woman was indeed Margit, her red hair hidden beneath a soft-brimmed farmer's hat. The man had whirled away toward the door at Köthen's cry. His back was to her, but Erde's body responded before her brain was able to process the notion that there could be two such backs in God's universe. She bolted. Her head was full of noise and her lungs washed with heat. She tried to climb the stall partition. Hal grabbed her around the waist and hauled her backward. She fastened herself to the slats with hands like grappling hooks and fought him wildly.

"Keep her back!" Köthen warned, arcing his sword up over their heads to meet the tall stranger rounding toward the sound of his voice.

He was young and scared and ready. Erde froze as recognition jolted through her, palpable anguish, a torrent of fire racing upward from her heels. The face she knew, the bronze-gold hair, shorn though it was to near invisibility. The name she could not yet grasp, but she could feel it surging through her with the fire, searing her soul, rising to her lips with the memory, all the memories, of a young man she'd loved and thought was dead.

She didn't stop to ask how he could be dead, yet still alive. Out of the corner of her eye, she saw the priest leap up from his hidden crouch to grab the short-sword of the white-robe behind him. The young man was intent on

Köthen's leveled blade, with Margit close behind him, a small dagger in her hand. Guillemo sprinted forward, his snatched weapon raised to strike. Erde shook Hal off in a sudden ferocious seizure of strength and threw herself up the chest-high barricade. Hal caught her legs. Her chest slammed against the top slat. She would not reach him in time. Her jaw worked soundlessly, like a fish gasping in the open air, and then—

"RAINER!!! Behind you!"

The young man started, openmouthed, but glanced behind, in time to bring the sword he held around to meet Guillemo's charge. The priest, though bulkier, was no match for him. The short-sword clattered to the floor. Guillemo sprang back, his wrists pressed against his chest, then dove for the sword again.

But suddenly the earth roared and bucked and tossed him aside. He flung his hands over his head and rolled. The barn shook. The rafters groaned. Soldiers and weapons went flying and skittering across the heaving floor like leaves caught in a gale.

Erde tumbled backward into Hal's arms. He grabbed her and leaned hard into the corner of the wall, fighting for balance like a sailor on the plunging deck of a ship. Her brain was full of the same shrieking and roaring. She could not clear it, and yet she must, for what was coming. She felt it coming. She felt—

His return.

At last! Ah, the joy of it, the wholeness once again. She had not really realized how incomplete she'd felt without him until he was there again.

—Dragon! Is it you? Are you doing this?

Pride at his accomplishment, his first intentional earthquake.

—Where have you been?

He showed her the green meadows of Deep Moor.

—You've eaten?

Assent. The she-goat had lent her strength to get him there.

—You're nearly too late! I thought we were lost!

Great need. Nothing in his head but the call of the Summoner.

—I know, but I need first, and others of your friends. Once more, and then it will be only you, I promise.

The call is unceasing now. He feels only the need to follow.

—Dragon, I beg you, take us out of here!

She formed the constellation of identities in her mind: Hal, Margit, and herself he had a fix on already. The fourth she gave him from her memory and hoped it would do. She wondered briefly if it would be clever and strategic to kidnap Köthen, but decided that it would not be wise to offer such a man, however interesting he might be, the secret of Deep Moor.

—These four, Dragon, and then no more. Will you do it?

Assent. Reluctant but . . . *Yes.*

She heard him then in her mind, speaking. The voice was deep but querulous, the voice of an overgrown child.

In honor of the she-goat. Besides, Rose said I must.

—Language, Dragon! Words and sentences!

Pride again. ***So am I learning.***

—You've been teasing me! Let's go!

Yes.

The ground stilled. In the seconds after, the silence was broken only by the moaning of terrified soldiers. Köthen was the first to recover, then Josef von Alte. Both scrambled to their feet and snatched up their swords to bully their men back into action, ordering them to take Rainer and Margit, who'd managed to remain standing and were now back to back, Margit with her dagger at ready, Rainer with the sword, his sword, Erde remembered, his very own. She wondered if he recognized it, then watching him, was sure he did. The priest crawled about in the straw, raving about the wrath of God. His white-robes hovered around him, helpless and frightened. Köthen moved into the fray, his blond beard burnished to flickering gold by torchlight. Erde filled her eyes with him, with his strength and his intriguing otherness, stored him away inside her and let him go. She stirred in Hal's grasp.

"Milady? Are you well?"

"He's here," she croaked. "Get ready."

His grin was transfiguring. "And I'd thought I was hearing things . . ."

Erde gave Earth an internal nod. In the torchlit barn, where the shadows leaped about them like a legion of demons, the soldiers were terrified to find themselves suddenly grasping at air.

Chapter Thirty-One

Their arrival was as smooth as silk, dead center in the farmhouse clearing. A circle of women awaited them.

Margit blinked, saw where she was, and then the dragon in front of her. "Oh wonderful!" she cried. Then her knees buckled. She sank to the ground in exhaustion and relief, and began to weep the tears she had not been able to all the time she'd been expecting to die. The twins raced to her side and the three of them rocked and wept, while the other women gathered around them.

Rose pulled away first. She hugged Erde quickly, then pressed herself into Hal's arms. "When he turned up alone, I thought . . . I was sure . . . I couldn't SEE you anywhere!"

Hal stroked her hair, kissed her temples. "There, there, Rosie. There, there."

Separated from Erde by Earth's stubby tail, Rainer pulled himself slowly to his feet and gazed about him with the alert but jaded air of a man who's seen too much in his short life already to be astonished by anything. He'd carried the sword with him but dropped it on arrival, upon finding himself so suddenly translated. Erde restrained the impulse to throw herself at him, weeping her own tears of relief and joy. Her father's harsh rejection had made her self-conscious about her altered appearance. She considered ducking quickly into the farmhouse. Surely Raven or Linden could lend her a proper dress to wear. But by then it was too late. He'd spotted her standing at the dragon's side, and was staring at her guardedly. So she approached him with all the self-possession she could muster, picking up the fallen sword from the grass as she passed. Where to start? There was so much to tell, so many lessons learned and crises passed. She wanted him to hear it all, to know everything at once. And so she said nothing. The wonder of her voice returning seemed petty and uninteresting compared to the miracle of seeing him alive again. When they were face-to-face, she handed the sword to him, hilt-first.

For a moment, he just looked at her. Then he ran his tongue quickly across his lips. "I hadn't heard that name in a long while."

She smiled ruefully. "It's not been so long, really."

"What happened to your hair?"

"Oh, I . . . cut it."

"You look really different."

"So do you." Less of a boy, more of a man. She hadn't really thought of him as a boy before, though now she could see that he had been. Not anymore.

Gingerly, he took the sword. "How did it get here?"

He sounded merely curious, as if there was nothing much more important to talk about. Probably he didn't know where to start either. She decided to let him set the pace. She matched his casual tone. "I thought I might need a weapon when I left Tor Alte, and there it was . . ."

"You left with . . ." Now his jaw tightened. ". . . your father?"

"Not exactly. I ran away."

"Ah." He gazed past her into an immense distance, then gestured at the dragon. "He's yours, isn't he."

"It's more like I'm his. His name is Earth."

"Earth. Hmmm. Where did you find him?"

"He found me, in the caves above the castle." She felt the need to boast. "He made the earthquake that saved us. He brought us here."

Rainer nodded, impressed as she had wanted him to be. "So Alla was right, little sister. She told me you were destined for something strange and wonderful."

Little sister. He had never called her that, even when they were children together. Erde heard the distance in his voice and took a half-step backward as if he'd pushed her. No warmer welcome? Not even a hug for her? How could so much change so fast? She vowed not to pressure him. It was her impulsive gesture that had gotten them in trouble to begin with, those few months ago that seemed like years. "How did you escape from the priest and my father?"

"Alla. Didn't she tell you?"

"Alla's dead. She didn't have time to tell me anything."

"Dead? How?" For the first time, he looked shaken.

"Took her own life, before they could put her to the stake."

"Oh, no. Poor old woman. Well, you know she'd be proud of you. She had the Power in her, too."

The Power? Was that what he saw, looking at her from so far away? "I thought . . . I couldn't speak. I thought you'd been killed."

"You did? Well, I'm sorry, I . . ." He shook his head without looking at her. "I wouldn't have wanted you to worry."

What did you think I'd do? she nearly screamed at him. Impassive. That's what he was, as if he'd felt too much and gone numb from it. Erde remembered what that was like. "My father said you were dead."

"Your father!" Now a shadow of rage bloomed in Rainer's eyes. "He would, if only to save his face. Lucky for me, he even convinced the priest. If Fra Guill had known who the Friend really was, he'd have reached out and squashed me like a bug!"

Erde doubted that. She was losing faith in the priest's supernormal powers. Except his predictions. But she didn't want to talk about Fra Guill, and she didn't want to talk about her father. She wanted her moment of joyous reunion. She thought she deserved it, after all she'd been through. She thought they both deserved it. Perhaps Rainer was just waiting for permission. Erde remembered the shyness that had come upon him as she'd begun to mature. She reached to touch his arm, to bridge the gap, and then having gone that far, felt her own restraints slipping. If changes had happened, it was time to admit to them. She was a grown woman, and not answerable to her father anymore. She threw caution to the winds and hurled herself into Rainer's arms. "I thought you were dead and you're alive, you're alive! It's such a miracle!"

He caught her awkwardly. She could tell he was working hard not to recoil. Willfully, she misunderstood and hugged him harder. He reached behind and grabbed her wrists, bringing her arms around between them, pushing them apart.

"Oh, it's all right!" she giggled. "We're in Deep Moor! Nobody here is going to mind at all!"

"Well. Even so." He eased her away from him and stepped back. "You know, I . . . it's been a while, you know? A lot has happened. I never meant to . . ."

Indeed. Finally she began to understand how it was.

She felt a calm settle over her, like a protective veil. She recalled the very moment of hearing that he'd been killed, how the ice had formed in her heart and the grief had lodged in her throat. How she'd carried that grief and guilt with her into exile until she couldn't bear the burden of it any longer, and one day, had simply abandoned it along with all memory of the event, so that she could get along with her life. She could see now that Rainer would never understand any of this. The fateful kiss in the halls of her father's castle had been a lark to him, a curiosity, a dare. The great love she'd fantasized about and broken her heart over was exactly that: a tale spun of her own heated girlish imaginings. Somewhere deep within her was a sigh that was going to shake her very being when she got around to it. For now, it would have to wait. There was her promise to the dragon to consider. Surprising herself with her own poise, Erde turned away, beckoning to him over her shoulder. "Come, meet my new friends."

Hal met them coming, with Rose on his arm. He swooped up Erde's hand and kissed it victoriously. "A bit close for comfort, milady, but well done anyway!" He bowed to Rainer. "Heinrich von Engle."

Erde eyed him sideways. What happened to just plain Hal Engle? She felt politics closing in on her.

Rainer shook the hand offered him. "Rainer of Duchen. I'm honored, my lord baron. The name of Weisstrasse is spoken often among those loyal to the king."

Hal looked gratified. "We'll have a lot to talk about on that subject."

Rainer nodded. Erde saw how he aligned himself instantly with the knight. She pressed close to him. "Hal found me in the woods—Oh. Is it all right? May I call you Hal?"

"Milady, now that you've your voice again, you can call me anything you please."

"Hal saved my life, Rainer, and the dragon's, too. We were starving!" Erde thought her voice sounded disappointingly thin and childish, as if it hadn't yet caught up with her new self. Nothing had really changed. She was still just the little girl he grew up with. And now she could hear the dragon in her head, reminding her of her promise and his own impatience. "Rainer is my dear, dear friend. We grew up together."

"A Friend indeed, and a more than interesting coincidence." Hal had his own agenda. He eased his lady forward. "May I present Rose of Deep Moor."

Rainer bowed to Rose, who was studying his face as if there were paragraphs written there.

"What d'you think, Rosie?" asked Hal.

"Possible, Heinrich. Now that I see him, I'll have to say it's possible."

Rainer smiled in puzzled inquiry, and Erde decided what was most changed about him: on the surface, he retained all his former habits of interest and concern but there was no substance to them. Of who or what he had become, behind that pleasant manner, he gave no indication.

Hal was not so guarded. "We wish to ask you, lad, what you know of your parentage."

Rainer's chin lifted in surprise, his first real sign of discomfiture. "You've heard the rumors, then, even here."

"We have," said Rose. Her rich voice brought Rainer's attention around to her. "Are they true?"

"I don't know. I can't remember back that far."

Hal wanted a more definitive answer. "If your claim could be proved legitimate, with what you've already done for the people . . ."

"My lord baron, I make no such claim. The intent of my campaign was only to stop the priest's evil from destroying others as it nearly destroyed me."

"But if you did make a claim . . . if you could . . . the people would flock to you, and to your . . . to the king, if they could know his heir was no traitorous weak tool of the barons like Prince Carl. I knew the man who escorted young Prince Ludolf into hiding, a King's Knight like myself. He was from Duchen."

Rainer was silent a moment. He glanced at Rose, and when she smiled at him warmly, looked away. "Well. I can only say what the old woman told me just before I fled Tor Alte . . ."

"You mean Alla?" Erde gripped his elbow eagerly. She hadn't been able to talk about Alla since losing her, and needed to. "What did Alla tell you? Oh, don't you miss her, Rainer? I miss her so much!"

"Easy, lass, easy," Hal drew her back, jovial but firm, to Rainer's evident relief. "It's a joy your voice is back, but do let the man speak."

Rose intervened. "The man will speak, Heinrich, when he's had some rest and sustenance. All of you, in fact. Come inside first, and then we'll talk."

The other women were helping Margit into the house. Rose took Hal's elbow and urged him after them. Rainer followed a few paces, then stopped to glance over his shoulder. "Are you coming?"

Erde had not moved. "I'll just stay with Earth a while."

He either did not hear or avoided her invitation. "See you later, then."

"Yes. Later." But she knew already that she wouldn't.

She watched him walk away across the velvet grass, into the farmhouse where the lamps were being lit and pots were clanging in the kitchen, where animated conversation had already begun. They would talk long into the night about the king and the barons and their various armies and strengths and strategic positions. And Hal would start making plans for how to use the dragon to get the throne back into the hands of its rightful owner.

But the dragon had his own mission to fulfill, and therefore, so did she. Erde gazed at the empty darkening porch for a long long time, feeling that sigh still deep inside her, unable to be sighed. Then she turned to the dragon.

His great head rested on his claws, the very image of ageless patience. He could have been carved of stone, but for the fires of eternity burning in his golden eyes. He blinked at her gravely.

—*Thank you, Dragon, for saving my friends.*

You're welcome. Is it my time now?

—*It's your time. What do we do?*

Follow the Call.

There was no hesitation in him, no doubt. No talk of Mage Cities and Mage-Queens. Only pure hard purpose. She felt the dragon brooch warming beneath her shirt. Hal would be sorry to be left behind, but he had his own business to attend to.

—*We should go now, before they can stop us. Is it far? You know which way to go?*

I will take us there.

—*You mean, take us? It's someplace you've been before?*

Only in our dreams.

—*Our dreams? But ...*

I must! I am called! Are you ready?

Erde laid her hand on the hard curve of the dragon's snout and thought of Rainer's receding back. There went one dream that would never be fulfilled. "Yes. I am ready, " she replied aloud.

Well, she'd miss Hal and she'd certainly miss Deep Moor, but if she survived this quest, she'd head right back here. Oddly, the last image in her mind, as the reality of Deep Moor faded, as the sparkling whirling dizziness claimed her, was Adolphus of Köthen, smiling at her as if he knew something she didn't.

Chapter Thirty-Two

When consciousness returned, Erde took a deep breath to clear her head, and was seized by a terrible coughing fit. It was hot and dry and the wind was full of dust. It smelled of ... she wasn't sure. An acrid smell, thick and pervasive. Erde thought *There's something wrong with the air.* She opened her eyes.

She stood on a stretch of sand, pale and vast. The heat rose around her in visible waves, as if the sand itself was on fire, giving off transparent smoke. The sky was gray and lowering, tinged with yellow. To her right, the sand ended several stone's throws away in a wall of dirty green foliage. To her left, it fell in soft, debris-strewn mounds toward the widest horizon she had ever seen, a horizon of vivid turquoise that raced up to meet the sand in roaring, foaming curls. Water, in a torrent repeating itself, over and over and over.

—Dragon? Where are we?

I have no idea.

Earth did not bother with his usual curious survey of the new surroundings. He stared expectantly at the place where the sand met the foam.

There! She comes!

—Who?

The one who Calls me.

Erde squinted at the line of dirty froth, expecting to find someone walking along the shore. Then she spotted movement, a narrow head on a long neck lifted snakelike above the cresting waves.

Another dragon was rising from the water.

END OF VOLUME ONE